More . . .

TONIGHT I SAID GOODBYE

Michael Koryta

St. Martin's Paperbacks

Library of Congress Catalog Card Number: 2004046781

ISBN: 0-312-93209-X
EAN: 80312-93209-1

Printed in the United States of America

St. Martin's Press hardcover edition / September 2004
St. Martin's Paperbacks edition / November 2005

St. Martin's Paperbacks are published by St. Martin's Press, 175 Fifth Avenue, New York, NY 10010.

10 9 8 7 6 5 4 3 2 1

To Bob Hammel.

For his teaching, guidance, encouragement,
and friendship I am deeply indebted.

ACKNOWLEDGMENTS

My thanks, first and foremost, go to Peter Wolverton, Ruth Cavin, John Cunningham, and everyone else at St. Martin's Press who gave me a chance and made the process a wonderful experience, and to Bob Randisi and the Private Eye Writers of America, who, together with St. Martin's, give new writers an unmatched opportunity.

Grateful acknowledgment also goes to:

Bob Hammel, who made it happen.

Laura Lane, an excellent writer and editor and even better friend.

Don Johnson, a first-class investigator who gave me a chance of a different sort.

Michael Hefron, who held a door open as he was stepping out of it and always motivated.

Stewart Moon, who has the best hook shot of any graphic designer in the business.

Janice Rickert, Bob Zaltsberg, and everyone else at the *Herald-Times*.

David Hale Smith, who manages to be a good agent and a great guy simultaneously.

And to my family, who have always encouraged, supported, and tolerated, especially my parents, Jim and Cheryl Koryta, and my sister, Jennifer.

ONE

The last time John Weston saw his son alive, it was a frigid afternoon in the first week of March, and John's granddaughter was building a snowman as the two men stood in the driveway and talked. Before he left, John gave his son a fatherly pat on the shoulder and promised to see him again soon. He saw him soon—stretched out in a morgue less than forty-eight hours later, dead of a small-caliber gunshot wound to the head. John was saved the horror of viewing his granddaughter in a similar state, but the reason for that was a hollow consolation: Five-year-old Betsy Weston and her mother were missing.

John Weston told me this as we sat in his house in North Olmsted, a suburb on Cleveland's west side, five days later. Weston's living room was clean and well arranged but dark, with the window shades pulled, and smelled heavily of cigarette smoke. While he spoke, the old man stared at me with a scowl that betrayed no trace of grief but plenty of determination.

"Listen to me, Mr. Perry," he said, blowing a cloud of cigarette smoke in my direction, "I know my son. He did not kill himself, and he damn sure didn't hurt his family. Have you watched the news? You hear what those bastards are saying? They're saying my son killed his own wife and baby daughter, then killed himself." He slapped the coffee table with his hand hard enough to make some of my coffee splash over the rim of the mug. "I will not tolerate that. I want to know what happened, and I want you and your partner to help me."

Weston sat on an enormous leather couch across from me, and I was in a bizarre chair with a curved wooden frame and a large, rippled plastic cushion. When I leaned back in it I immediately slid down until my head was parallel to the armrests. Feeling pretty ridiculous in that position, I'd tried an assortment of others before, surrendering to gravity and the slick cushion, I leaned forward, sitting on the edge of the chair, my elbows resting on my knees. Now I looked more intense than I felt, but it beat the alternatives.

"I've heard the television reports," I said. "But the police haven't said the murder/suicide angle is a legitimate theory, Mr. Weston. That's just some talking head in a newsroom trying to hold an audience with sensationalism."

Weston kept the scowl. He was in his upper seventies but still a large man; when he was younger he must have been massive. His legs were skinny now and his belly soft, but his broad chest and shoulders were a testament to his former size. He still had nearly a full head of gray hair, a nose that seemed too small for his face, and calculating, edgy eyes that took everything in as if he were looking for an excuse to shout. The pinky finger of his right hand was missing, and the ring finger ended in a stump just past the middle knuckle. While I sipped my coffee, he turned and pointed at two framed paintings on the wall behind him.

"You see those paintings?" he said.

They appeared to be World War II military scenes, and they were well done. Nothing fancy, just a talented artist's precise rendition of what he had seen. My type of painting—something you could appreciate without a master's degree in art.

"A buddy of mine did those," he said, and then coughed

loudly, a wet, rasping hack like a shovel scraping snow off rough pavement. "Pretty good, aren't they?"

"Very nice." I finished my coffee and set the mug on the coffee table beside the business card I had given Weston. PERRY AND PRITCHARD INVESTIGATIONS it read. I was Lincoln Perry, and Joe Pritchard was my partner. We were just six months into the business now, but we'd already managed to accumulate a significant amount of debt. We tried not to boast about that accomplishment too often, though, especially to clients. Before going into private work, Joe and I had been partners in the Cleveland Police Department's narcotics division. I'd been forced into resignation, and he'd retired about a year later. Somehow, Joe had convinced me to meet with John Weston alone while he handled what would probably be a routine interview. I was regretting that arrangement now.

"What you see there in the paintings are a CG-4A glider and a tow plane," Weston said, looking back at the paintings again. "I flew the gliders."

"That was a one-of-a-kind experience, I imagine."

"You've got that right. There was never anything like it before, and there hasn't been since. By the time 'Nam rolled around they had helicopters to do that job. In my war, though, it was gliders."

I thought about it, the experience of drifting down onto a battlefield in silence with no motor to power you.

"What'd it feel like, flying the thing?"

He smiled. "Like sitting on the front porch and flying the house. I flew two combat missions and a handful of supply missions. Had a rough landing in the second combat mission and lost some fingers, but I still had to fight on the ground all that night. We had the same weapons training as the commando soldiers, and it was the job of us glider pilots to hold whatever territory we landed on. I fought Nazis all night without taking any medicine to help with the pain in my hand. But it was better than it could have been. A couple of the other gliders cracked up badly on landing, and a few were shot down. Hell, I had bullet holes through the canvas."

"Close call, eh?" I didn't know where he was going with this conversation, but I was content to ride it out.

"Close enough. The closest call I ever had was a mission I didn't fly, though. I was slated to fly into what was basically a German fortress in France, and the probability of survival was so low it was damn near a suicide mission. We were all set to fly out, saying our goodbyes to the world, you know, because we were pretty convinced this was a one-way trip. Just before we went up, they told us the mission had been canceled, because Patton took the Nazi fortress." He lit a cigarette with a steel Zippo and took a long drag. "People badmouth Patton all the time these days, but I'll tell you this—that son of a bitch is a friend of mine for as long as I live."

I've always been a bit of a Patton fan myself, at least in terms of respecting the man's battlefield genius and efficiency, but I guessed Weston would scorn such appreciation from a man who'd never served, so I kept quiet. He smoked the cigarette for a minute, staring over his shoulder at the paintings, lost in his memories. Then he turned back to me, and his eyes narrowed in a way that suggested focus and determination.

"I appreciate you meeting with me," he said. "After our first phone conversation, I thought you were turning me down."

"I'm here," I said, "but that doesn't mean I'm going to take the job, Mr. Weston. You've got some of the finest cops in the city working on this, and from what I hear, even the FBI is helping."

"Helping to dick around and waste time!" he roared.

"I don't think they're wasting any time, sir."

"No? Then where the hell are some results? Those damn cops come over here every damn day and tell me what they've produced. You know what they've produced? Jack shit, boy. In five days, they've done *nothing*." He stuck out his lower lip and exhaled a cloud of smoke forcefully over his face.

"It takes some time to make headway in an investigation of this magnitude, sir."

"Look," he said, trying to contain his anger, "this is my son we're talking about. My son and his family. I've got to do something, but I'm smart enough to realize I can't do it alone. I need someone working for *me*. Someone who can pursue this as aggressively as it needs to be pursued."

I sighed. John Weston was convinced his son had been murdered, although none of the police investigators seemed to agree. The prevailing media theory, courtesy of an "un-named police source," was that Wayne Weston had killed his family before offing himself. No bodies had been found, and there was little evidence to explain their disappearance. There had been no signs of violent intruders at the house; every-thing appeared normal except for Wayne Weston's corpse.

"Why us, Mr. Weston?" I asked. "Why do you think we need to be involved, when you have the police doing every-thing they can?"

"You knew my son."

I held up a cautioning hand. "I'd *met* your son."

"Whatever. You knew him, and he knew you and re-spected you. He told me he thought you and your partner were going to be very good when you started your business."

I'd met Wayne Weston at a private investigators' confer-ence in Dayton two months before. It was one of those two-day events featuring seminars on various business issues during the day and sessions of too much food, drink, and loud laughter in the hotel restaurant at night. Joe had decided we should go because it offered a chance to network with other local investigators, making contacts, and possibly at-tracting some business.

Wayne Weston had sat at the same table as me for dinner one night. He was a flashy guy, wearing expensive suits and driving a fancy car, but he was friendly and charismatic. And, from what I'd heard, a hell of an investigator. He'd been with the Pinkertons for a few years before returning to Cleveland to open his own firm, and he was apparently making good money at it. I hadn't talked to him individually for more than an exchange of names, and I was surprised to hear he'd said anything about Joe and me to his father.

"My son didn't kill himself or hurt his family," Weston said. "That's the most absurd and offensive bullshit I've ever heard. They came on the news talking about that yesterday, and I damn near drove down there and kicked some ass. I want to know what *did* happen to my daughter-in-law and granddaughter, so I can quit this damn worrying, and so those television people can shut their mouths."

His eyes flashed with anger as he spoke, and he tried to extinguish it with a tremendous drag on the cigarette. For a minute I thought he'd polish the whole thing off in that one ferocious inhalation.

"What exactly is it that you want Joe and me to do?" I asked. "Determine whether your son was murdered, or find his wife and daughter?"

"Both," he said, blowing out a cloud of smoke that made my eyes sting. "It seems to me one would be pretty well intertwined with the other."

That was a fair point. I still didn't like it, though. The cops would resent our presence, and I definitely didn't want to get caught up in the media frenzy.

"Look, I've got plenty of money," Weston said. "I've got a good retirement plan, I've got a savings account. I can afford to pay whatever it is you want."

"It's not about the money, Mr. Weston," I said.

"No? Then what the hell is it?"

"The police have a lot of investigators working on this case," I said. "They have resources and access that we don't, and they've also got a week's head start on it. I'd advise you to wait on the police, and see what they can do with it. If they haven't made any progress in a few weeks, give us a call again, and maybe we'll reconsider." I had no plans to reconsider, but I hoped the offer would placate the old man.

"You know why I showed you those paintings?" he asked. "Why I told you what happened to my hand?"

"No, sir."

He ground his cigarette out in an ashtray on the table and stared at me with contempt. Then he shook his head.

"Wayne was one of your own," he said. "Same city, same business, and that's a business without many people involved. That used to mean something to people. When I was in the war, we fought for the men with us. Before battle, during the preparation, it was all about patriotism and saving the world and protecting the freedom of our families back home. But you know what? When it came down to the firefight, that wasn't in your mind anymore. You were fighting for the boys next to you, fighting for your buddies, protecting your own." He looked at me sadly. "Maybe my generation was the last one that had that kind of loyalty, that kind of brotherhood."

It was a hell of a pitch. I didn't answer right away, but it resonated with me as he had hoped it would. I hadn't known Wayne Weston well, and we were in the same business, not in the same war, but somehow, sitting here in front of this man with his World War II paintings, gnarled hand, dead son, and missing family members, that line of reasoning seemed hollow.

"Why do you do it?" he asked. "Why are you even in this business? You want to get rich chasing cheating husbands? You think it impresses women to say you're a PI? Huh?"

I looked at the floor, trying not to snap at him. "Nope," I said evenly. "None of those, sir."

"Really? Then what the hell do you do it for?"

I didn't say anything.

"Well?" he said. "You gonna give me an answer, son?"

I raised my head and looked at him. "I do it," I said, "because I'm awfully damn good at it."

"You think you're awfully damn good at it, eh?"

"I don't think I am, sir. I am. And so is my partner."

He smiled without amusement or pleasure. "Then prove it."

I met his eyes and held his gaze for a while, then gave one, short nod.

"All right," I said. "We will."

TWO

"Well, that's the last time I let you meet a prospective client unattended," Joe Pritchard said. "I thought we'd agreed not to get involved in this mess."

We were sitting in the office the next morning. Joe had just finished a five-mile run, and he was still breathing heavily, soaked with sweat. I thought that was the best time to break the news to him, hoping he'd be too tired to care. No luck, though; it took a lot more than a five-mile run in the cold to fatigue Joe.

"Why not give it a shot, Joe? We're not making much money, so why turn down the offers we do get?"

"Because the cash isn't worth the hassle." He sighed and wiped his face with a towel. He was wearing running shoes, sweatpants, and a nylon jacket, and if you'd asked ten strangers to guess his age, all of them would have undershot it by a decade. "I just don't like the idea of having to tag along with CPD, Lincoln."

I understood that. Joe had retired only six months earlier, and I knew working on an active police investigation from the outside would feel strange to him. It was too late now; I'd made the agreement with Weston, and I had a two-thousand-dollar retainer check in my pocket to seal the deal.

"Oh, come on," I said. "You know the case interests you, and our plate isn't exactly full of other projects."

He grunted but didn't say anything, gazing around the office as if seeking support from the furniture. Our little office is on the city's west side, on the second floor of an old stone bank building. It has hardwood floors badly in need of a polish, two desks, a small bathroom and secondary office, and freshly painted walls that look frighteningly bright in the old building. My contribution to the office furniture sits across from our desks: a set of four wooden seats from the old Cleveland Stadium. The stadium had been torn down in the early nineties, and they'd auctioned off some of the memorabilia. I'd purchased the chairs and had them refinished, and I thought they looked pretty decent, if slightly out of place. Joe referred to the seats by various vulgar names and refused to sit in them. It was hard to believe he was an Indians fan. No sense of nostalgia.

"Well, I told Weston we're in it now," I said, "so let's not hassle over whether we should have taken the case. Let's figure out how we're going to get started."

"We could get started by grabbing a sandwich," Joe said. "I'm starving." Joe eats with a ravenous appetite, but he also drinks almost nothing but water and runs several miles each day, so he's still trim and fit even in his fifties.

"I haven't paid very close attention to the case," I said, ignoring him, "so we probably ought to review the newspaper articles before we make any calls down to CPD. Hate to look uninformed, you know."

"You're looking for an excuse to drag Lois Lane into it," he said with a sigh. "Just when I thought things couldn't get any worse."

I grinned. "I'm sure Amy will be happy to assist in any way possible."

"Fabulous," he said. "I'll tell you what: How about you track down the background information while I go get something to eat? Then, when I come back, you can give me a concise briefing and I'll be able to focus without being distracted by my growling stomach." He pushed away from the desk.

"That's fine," I said as he opened the door to leave. "I'm expecting to do most of the work around here. You old guys don't have the stamina to keep up."

Amy Ambrose agreed to come by on her lunch hour with all the relevant articles. Around noon she stepped through the door, wrinkling her nose.

"Your stairwell reeks. The winos taken to sleeping there again?"

"Hello to you, too."

"Yeah, yeah." She shrugged off her coat and flopped onto one of the stadium seats. She looked good, as she always did. Her hair was a little longer than it had been when we first met in the summer, but it was the same dark blond and had the same soft curl. Amy was a reporter for the Cleveland *Daily Journal* and in the summer she'd been assigned to cover a murder investigation. The murder victim had been a patron at my gym, and Amy showed up at my door looking for information. With my usual charm, I'd told her to go to hell. A day later she was back, with more information about the case and about me than most reporters could turn up overnight. She'd won my respect, my assistance, and, soon, my friendship. She was outspoken and brazen and cocky, but she was also completely her own person, and she was genuine. We were drawn together because of that—two self-reliant loners who trusted only our own judgment and ability when under pressure. Outside of Joe, she was my closest friend, and while I told people I thought of her as a sister, a small part of my mind recognized that my breath didn't catch in my chest when I saw my real sister the way it could when I saw Amy.

"So you and Pritchard think you can accomplish what dozens of cops and a few FBI agents haven't been able to, eh?" Amy said.

"We're not that cocky," I said. "I figure it may take us two, maybe three days."

She smiled. "Sure. Well, it looks like you've got your hands full. I read through most of this stuff before I came

over, and if the cops have any worthwhile leads they aren't
sharing them with the media, that's for sure."

"You're not working on the story?"

"No, they gave it to another reporter, a guy named Steve.
He's a good writer, but I don't know if he has much of a nose
for investigative work." She spotted a minute wrinkle on her
pants and frowned at it, then tried to smooth it with the palm
of her hand. It's the little things that bother Amy. She's indifferent to the striking resemblance the backseat of her car
holds to a landfill, but she can't stand wrinkles.

"Did you get me some background information?" I
asked.

"Here's everything Steve's written about the case," she
said, passing me a stack of printouts. "That's all I could get."

I read through them. Plenty of articles for just a five-day
span, but none of them said much more than I already knew.
Weston's body had been discovered Wednesday morning by
his cleaning lady. He'd died from a single gunshot wound to
the right temple, a wound determined to be self-inflicted.
The gun, a .38-caliber Smith & Wesson, was still in his right
hand when the body was discovered. It was registered in his
name. The police had been summoned, and they spent the
rest of the day trying unsuccessfully to locate Weston's wife
and daughter. By Wednesday evening, the police had put out
a missing persons report. There was no evidence to suggest
kidnapping, which would have made it an FBI case, but a
few agents from the Cleveland office were "assisting" CPD.
The article revealed some suspicion among neighbors and
acquaintances that the incident had something to do with a
case Weston had been working on, but the police hadn't supported that theory. It was likely nothing more than curiosity
and intrigue associated with the PI business. The police
searched Weston's office and home and were "actively pursuing leads," but the detective in charge of the case, Rick
Swanders, said they had no justifiable suspicion that
the wife and daughter had been targeted by anyone Weston
had investigated.

"Well," I said when I was finished, "I haven't cracked the case yet. I suppose I'll actually have to conduct an interview or two."

"I was expecting you to piece it out from the articles," Amy said with mock disappointment. "This is a real letdown."

"Any chance your buddy Steve knows details he isn't sharing with his readers?"

"There's a chance, but I wouldn't put much hope into it. You know how closemouthed cops are at the start of an investigation like this. Unless he's developed a great source, I doubt he's heard much more than you just read."

I nodded. It had been a while since I'd left the force, but not so long that I'd forgotten the well-founded distrust most cops held for the media.

"So where do you go from here?" Amy asked.

"When Joe gets back, we'll go over to see Weston's father. We'll interview him for details about his son and try to get a feel for what his life had been like in recent months. Then we'll talk to the police and see how much cooperation we can expect to get from them. Once that's been taken care of, I imagine we'll focus on his business, learn as much as possible about his recent cases, and determine if there's anyone he's really pissed off."

She nodded. "You think he was murdered?"

"From everything I've heard or read, no, I don't think he was murdered. I think he killed himself. But the father wants us to prove otherwise, so I'm going to have to go into the case thinking he didn't commit suicide. Besides, if his family's alive, then it's much more likely he was murdered. So until somebody can prove they're dead, I'll pretend the police are looking in the wrong direction."

"You don't sound too enthusiastic."

"I'm not. I've got a bad feeling we're going to take the father's money so we can stick our noses in this mess, and then the cops will hold a press conference a week or two from now and announce that they found the bodies of the wife and daughter where Weston dumped them. I hope that's not true, but it's hard not to think about it."

"So why take the case?"

"If someone wants me to investigate something as bad as this old man does," I said, "I'm damn well going to give it a try."

She ran the tip of her tongue across her lips and frowned. "I can't help wondering about it myself, just because of the line of work he's in. The nature of the business makes the whole thing seem a little more sordid, doesn't it?"

"A bit." I leaned back and put my feet up on the desk.

"So," she said, changing the subject, "how's *Angela*?"

"Why do you say her name like that?" I asked. "Like you're laughing at me?"

She raised her eyebrows and tried to look innocent. "Laughing at you? Not at all. Don't be so defensive. Now, what's the deal with you two?"

"Angela and I have gone our separate ways."

"Really? I'm sorry," she said, but I could tell she wasn't at all. "Might I ask why?"

"We were very different people," I mumbled. "She was, ah, a bit—"

"Of a ditz," Amy interjected.

I frowned. "I wasn't going to say that."

"Oops." She grinned. "My mistake."

"She wasn't a ditz," I said. "And you only met her once, so you're hardly one to judge."

"Once was enough, Lincoln."

"And how's your love life? Your sexy news-anchor boyfriend, Mr. Jacob Terry?" I said, dropping my voice to a deep baritone.

"We're fine."

I smiled. "What is it that most attracts you to him? The romantic musk of his cologne, or the gallon of hair oil he uses to shellac that striking mane into place for a windy live report?"

"Jealous," she said, "that's what you are."

"Almost uncontrollably," I said with a nod. "It's hard to sleep at night."

"Joke if you want to, Lincoln, but I know the real reason

you and Angela didn't work out. You can't stop thinking
about me."

I pointed at the door. "Hit the road, Ace. I've got work
to do."

She smiled and got to her feet. "So do I. But I expect a
phone call in the next few days to let me know what you've
found out."

"I'll call."

Joe returned half an hour later, and we left to visit John
Weston. While he drove I filled him in on what I'd learned
from the articles, which was basically nothing.

"I hope this old man's not as loud and fiery as you say,"
he told me. "I don't deal well with those types."

"You mean your peers?"

"Silence, boy."

Weston greeted us at the door in a cloud of cigarette
smoke. He shook Joe's hand when I introduced them.

"I sure as hell hope you don't drag your feet like your
partner," Weston said to him. Fond of me already.

"Neither of us will do any foot-dragging once we've
agreed to take the case," Joe said. "But he's the one who had
to talk me into it, sir. Not the other way around."

"I don't give a damn about that anymore. Just get
started."

He led us into the living room. I quickly headed for the
recliner on the far wall, leaving Joe to struggle with the tor-
ture chair.

Weston returned to his position on the couch and held up
a notebook. "I've been working on this since you left yesterday," he said, nodding at me. "I've written down as much information about Wayne as I could think of. I tried to keep it
focused on the recent stuff, of course, but I gave you some
background, too. I figured it might all be useful."

I looked at Joe, and I could tell he was seeing what I already knew. John Weston might be grieving, and he might be
temperamental, but his focus was on resolving this investigation. In many situations it's hard to get the victim's family

to put aside their emotions long enough to provide information. That wasn't going to be a problem here.

"Go on, take a look and see if there's anything I left out," Weston said, waving the notebook at me.

I took it, and I was impressed. He'd filled nearly twenty pages with neat, precise printing, all capital letters. Each category had a title, such as "Business History," "Acquaintances," and so on. He'd even taped photographs on some of the pages, complete with captions identifying those pictured. It was exactly the type of report Joe and I had been hoping to put together ourselves after this interview.

"It's very thorough," I said. "We appreciate this, Mr. Weston. This is the type of information we need to have available if we're going to get off to a fast start on the case."

He lit a fresh cigarette. "I figured that. The cops have already asked me about most of it, so I knew what you'd probably be looking for. I figured I'd save some time by putting it together for you."

I stopped turning pages when I saw a photograph of Wayne Weston in uniform.

"Your son was in the military?"

"That's right. Eight years in the Marines. He was Force Recon," Weston announced proudly. I knew the reason for that pride; Force Recon was the elite special operations unit of the Marine Corps, that branch's equivalent to the Army's Green Berets and the Navy's SEALs.

"How old was he when he mustered out of the Corps?"

"Twenty-eight. He left the Marines and came back here, then signed up with the Pinkerton outfit. He thought the investigation business sounded interesting, and they weren't going to turn down a Recon vet, that's for damn sure," Weston said. "He stayed with them for several years, and then he met Julie and got married. The Pinkertons had him doing a good bit of traveling, so he decided to cut out on his own."

"How long was he working independently?" I asked.

"Nine years," Weston said without pausing to think about it. "Making a hell of a good living at it, too. Beautiful house, fancy cars for both him and Julie, the works." Beyond the haze of cigarette smoke, Weston's brown eyes were somber.

"You told me you weren't aware of any sort of problem," I said. "No family quarrels, no financial problems, nothing of that nature."

"That's right. I talked to him at least once a week, and everything seemed to be fine. Well, almost fine. He'd seemed a little more serious in the past few months, you know, a little less quick with the jokes." He puffed on his cigarette and then shrugged. "It was probably just the winter getting him down, though. You know how these damned Cleveland winters can wear at you."

"Did he ever mention any business concerns?" Joe asked. "A tough case, tough client, anything like that?"

"Nope, not a thing." He said it uneasily—not like he was lying, but like it made him uncomfortable not to have something to blame.

"He worked alone?"

"Yes." Weston held up a finger and launched into a coughing fit that sounded like a sputtering diesel engine. He got it under control, swore, took a hearty pull on the cigarette, and returned to talking. "Early on he had a partner, but then that guy moved to Sandusky, and Wayne went back to being alone. I guess he had a—well, what would you call it—a research assistant, I suppose? Some graduate student he'd ask for help with research occasionally, when he was really swamped."

"Do you know his name?" Joe asked.

"Her name," Weston said. "Her name's April Sortigan. I put it in the notebook."

I stopped flipping through the notes and stared at the photographs Weston had included of his daughter-in-law, Julie, and his granddaughter, Elizabeth. I'd seen pictures of them on the news and in the papers, but those had been headshots, and John Weston had included snapshots of the two at various family activities. Julie Weston was beautiful, with dark, Italian features, the kind of body men dream about, and a smile so bright and genuine it made me want to look away from the picture.

Elizabeth Weston was a miniature copy of her mother. She had the same dark skin, hair, and eyes, and, if anything, the smile was more radiant. In one picture she was wearing a light blue dress and holding a bouquet of flowers, and she appeared to be laughing at something the photographer had said. John Weston's caption declared the picture to have been taken the past Easter. In another picture, Elizabeth was wearing a party hat and holding a hot dog, with a slight smear of ketchup beside that smile. John Weston had written "Fifth Birthday, August" beneath the photograph. I closed the notebook, wishing he had given us less-personal pictures, something closer to the cold, unsmiling mug shots cops are used to seeing.

We kept at him for a while, but it was too early in the case for precise questions, and the general background information awaited us in the notebook.

"We'll be in touch every few days," Joe promised as we left. "When we develop some leads, we'll probably call back with more questions, too."

"Fine," Weston said, standing at the door. "You do whatever it takes. I'm not worried about the money. I just want to prove my boy was murdered and find my granddaughter and her mother."

Joe worked his jaw back and forth slightly, looking away, out at the flagpole in the center of the lawn.

"Sir," he said, "we're going to do the best we can to get to the truth. But I want you to know, if after a little work it seems the truth is that your son committed suicide, we're not going to lead you on and play games with you. We'll tell you that appears to be the truth, and then we'll end our investigation."

Weston tightened his hand on the doorknob. "I appreciate a man who's not prone to bullshit," he said. "But I've been around for a lot of years, fella, and I'm no damn fool. If you two are any good, you'll find my boy was murdered. I'd stake my life on it."

Looking into his eyes then, I thought maybe he already had.

THREE

Joe leaned back, the old office chair creaking, and arced a paper wad up and over his feet, which were resting on the desk. The paper dropped into the wastebasket, adding to an already sizable pile.

"Best moment in baseball history," he said. "You first."

I fired a paper wad into the wastebasket and thought about it. "Bill Mazeroski hitting that home run in Game Seven of the World Series to beat the Yankees. For pure flair and showmanship, though, you can't top Ruth calling his shot and then hitting one out."

"Nah," Joe said. "Best moment *has* to be Kirk Gibson limping up to the plate and tagging that game-winner off Eckersley. And—for pure flair and showmanship, as you put it—it's Fisk waving the home run fair on his way to first."

"How's that showmanship? That's just childish enthusiasm. Not even close to Ruth calling his shot. And, Gibson, give me a break; that home run just won a game, not the Series."

"Whatever." He crumpled another piece of paper and fired it at the wastebasket. It hit the side of the can and bounced off. This was as productive as we had been for the past half hour. We considered it brainstorming.

I was about to quiz Joe on the best moments in basketball history when the office door opened and two men stepped inside.

"We really need to install a doorbell," I said. "People don't appear to remember how to knock anymore."

"Hello, Rick," Joe said to one of the visitors. Rick Swanders, the detective in charge of the Weston case, was a short, thick man with drooping jowls and a florid face. His partner was taller and thinner, with an obtrusive Adam's apple and sandy hair. He was wearing jeans and a Cleveland Indians parka. Swanders was in a rumpled winter-weight suit.

"Hi, Pritchard." Swanders looked at me. "Perry."

"Hi, Rick."

Swanders jerked his thumb at his companion. "This is Jim Kraus; he's with the Brecksville Police. We were told this morning that John Weston's hired you two, and we thought it'd be a good idea to drop by for a chat." He eyed the piles of paper wads in the wastebasket and on the floor. "I hope we're not interrupting anything too important."

"Have a seat," Joe said. Swanders pulled up one of the client chairs, but Kraus settled onto a stadium seat. I liked him immediately.

"So what exactly are you two planning to do?" Swanders asked. "Show up the old boys down at the department, make some headlines, ride off into the sunset?"

"Don't have to have the sunset," I said. I knew Swanders vaguely from my days on the force, but I'd never dealt with Kraus. Brecksville was a small, upscale suburb, and its police force wasn't equipped to handle a major case like this, so CPD had stepped in to help. Kraus didn't look like he thought he was in over his head, though; if anything he seemed cooler than Swanders.

Swanders stared at me and chewed on his lip. "You looking for the wife and daughter or trying to prove it wasn't a suicide?"

"We're trying to find out what happened," I said. "That encompasses both aspects, I think."

"Get paid whether you break this case or not, don't you?"

"Yeah. But so do you."

"True, but the victim's family ain't the one cutting me my check."

I started to say that wasn't entirely true, since John Weston was a taxpayer, but it was a petty, silly response, and I managed to shut myself up in time.

"You have a reason for coming down here other than griping, Rick?" Joe said. "We're not out to make you guys look bad, hassle you, breathe down your neck, or anything else. We're in the business of investigating things. John Weston wants us to investigate this thing, and that's what we'll do."

Joe was the person to convince them of our harmlessness, not me. My rapid promotions hadn't endeared to me to some of the older cops, but Joe's endorsement had helped me overcome that hostility. Joe was a cop's cop, a fourth-generation member of CPD. There had been Pritchards in uniform on the city's west side for as long as anyone could remember. Joe's father had been a homicide detective, and his uncle had been killed in the line of duty. There wasn't a cop on the force who didn't know of the Pritchard family, and in the family itself, it was seemingly unthinkable that a male do anything else. Joe represented the last of his line; when he was thirty he'd married a woman nearly twenty years his senior, limiting the likelihood of a son to follow in his footsteps. It had been devastating for Joe's father, to whom the police legacy meant a great deal. Joe and Ruth had been happy, though, as happy as any married couple I'd ever seen. When she'd died a few years earlier, she'd taken a part of him with her. The work—always important to Joe—became everything for him, and rather than sit on his pension he'd decided to become a PI. There was nothing else that could satisfy him.

Swanders and Kraus exchanged a glance, not happy about it, but Swanders nodded, giving Joe the respect he'd earned in the last few decades.

"Fine, Pritchard. I wasn't thrilled to hear that you two are involved, because this case is messy enough as it is. But if you play it straight with us, we'll play it straight with you."

He sighed and scratched his chin, where a day's worth of stubble had developed. "With all the damn media attention this case is getting, it's no picnic. You better hope those reporters don't get on *your* ass, too."

"That bad, eh?" I asked.

"You got it." Swanders leaned forward, bracing his forearms on his knees. His sleeve pulled up when he did it, exposing a gold watch too small for his wrist, with folds of fat bulging out on either side. "So, since we're all going to be getting along together, how about you tell us what you've done so far."

Joe pointed at the piles of paper wads. "That."

Kraus grinned. "Stuck already, eh?"

"Hey," Joe said, "it's our first morning on the job."

"Just for the record," I said, "I want to point out that most of those paper balls on the floor are Joe's. Mine went in the basket."

"You guys think Weston was a suicide?" Joe asked.

"Yeah," Kraus said, and Swanders nodded. "The evidence at the scene makes it hard to call it anything else."

"What about the psychological profile?" I asked. "Any signs of a problem, some indication that Weston wasn't too stable?"

Kraus squinted and frowned, and Swanders nodded at him to speak.

"Yes and no," Kraus said. "Some acquaintances told us that he'd been tense, morose, whatever. But I never put much stock in those stories, because after the newspaper declares a guy was a suicide, everyone who knew him starts imagining these things, you know, trying to rationalize it in their own minds."

"But you couldn't come up with any reason for him to have offed himself, let alone the family?" I said. "The wife wasn't cheating on him, he wasn't an alcoholic or a cokehead, nothing like that?"

Kraus and Swanders exchanged another glance, silently consulting on what they should offer to us.

"He was a gambler," Kraus said eventually, after Swanders gave him some sort of osmosis approval. "Sounds like a pretty high roller, too. Frequent trips up to Windsor, and lots of betting on sports."

Windsor, just across the river from Detroit, was home to Canada's largest casino. I wasn't necessarily surprised by the statement; it fit my image of Weston just fine.

"Lots of people enjoy gambling," Joe said. "Doesn't mean they're suicidal. Just foolish."

"His bank accounts were cleared out," Swanders said. "We're expecting to find he was in some pretty serious debt."

"Any idea who he might have owed?"

He shook his head. "Not yet. That's what we're working on."

"If that's the truth, I'd think it would open up some other theories," Joe said. "I mean, I can see the gambling debts as a reason for suicide, but what about his family? Is it possible the people he was stiffing on the debts could have grabbed the wife and daughter, maybe even killed him?"

Swanders and Kraus shared a frown. "Possible," Swanders said. "But damn near anything is possible at this juncture. There's absolutely no physical evidence at that house to suggest a break-in or any sort of violence. The neighbors say both Mrs. Weston and the daughter were at the home Tuesday evening, but they never showed up anywhere Wednesday morning. Weston's time of death was somewhere between midnight and four in the morning Wednesday, according to the medical guys. That means whatever happened had to happen Tuesday night, and the neighbors didn't hear or see anything unusual. It makes an intruder scenario less likely, unless they were taken out by the damned Delta Force or something."

"What about the gunshot?" Joe asked.

"Nobody's claimed they heard one, but that's not surprising," Swanders said. "Three in the morning, one shot fired from a handgun? That's easier to sleep through than people would think. Besides, this is in Brecksville. People out there hear a handgun fired, they probably think it's a backfire on the gardener's leaf blower."

"Any chance we could take a look at the crime scene report?" Joe asked.

Swanders shrugged. "I'd say no just to be a bastard, but that report's not going to offer you much help anyhow, so what the hell. You got a fax machine?" he asked, looking around the office doubtfully, as if unsure we even had a phone.

"Yeah," Joe said, and gave him the number.

"All right." Swanders got to his feet. "We'll keep in touch with you boys, and I expect you'll do the same."

"We will," Joe said.

"Hey," I said as they were heading for the door, "did you talk to April Sortigan? Some student who worked with Weston, I think?"

Kraus waved his hand. "Yeah, she's nothing to bother with. Just some kid who met Weston through a class project, and he liked her and let her do some bullshit court records research now and then so she could add to the résumé. I talked to her on the phone, and it was a waste of time."

They left, and Joe and I sat and stared at the closed door. "Well," Joe said, "I suppose we ought to get to work."

"Probably."

"The gambling angle sounds interesting," he said. "Depending who he owed, or who he pissed off."

"I don't like it. Too cute and simple."

"Perfect," Joe said. "I'm cute and you're simple. Just the case for us."

"You know anyone in Windsor?"

"Not yet, but give me an hour or two on the phone and I'll have some friends."

"Sounds good. I've got to see this April girl in half an hour, so we can rendezvous later this afternoon, if you're still awake."

He faked a heavy yawn. "You're going to see her even though Kraus said it was a waste of time?"

"Two things about cops," I said. "One, they've been known to overlook leads before, and, two, they've been known to lie to pain-in-the-ass private operators like us. So, yeah, I'll go see her."

April Sortigan lived in a cluttered apartment about ten minutes from our building. She didn't have a roommate, but she did have seven cats. In the tiny living room, they seemed to be coming out of the walls. At first I assumed there had to be at least three dozen. Sortigan was a tall, slender girl with raven-colored hair, a slim, slightly hooked nose, and glasses with square black frames. Her body was willowy and firm, not unattractive, but nothing that would draw wolf whistles on the street. She sat with her legs crossed and drummed her fingers on the arm of the couch while we talked. After a few minutes of questioning, she'd assured me of her general ignorance of Weston's life and business. Maybe Kraus had been right. She looked like a dead end—and, unfortunately, a talkative dead end. That would have been all right, but the focus of her talkativeness was herself, not Weston. I tried to pay attention while counting the rings on her fingers. I was up to nine and still going when she fell silent.

"You met Wayne Weston during your undergraduate years?" I asked, trying to steer her back to the point before she began listing her personal references and extracurricular activities.

"That's right. I was working on a project about structural accidents, and I learned he'd investigated one in a liability lawsuit. I interviewed him, and the work interested me, so I kept in touch. He offered to give me some background in public records before I went on to law school."

A large tiger-striped cat sprinted into the center of the room and attacked a newspaper that was lying on the floor. Apparently, the cat believed the paper had been ready to make an aggressive move at any second. April Sortigan ignored it.

"How much work did you do for him?" I asked.

"Oh, not too much. He showed me around the process; you know, the clerk's office and auditor's office and all of that. I probably did a few checks for him each month. Just minor research."

"Anything recently?"

"Actually, yes. About two weeks ago he sent me a list of three names and asked for a basic check through some of the computer databases and the county clerk's office. He said he couldn't do it because he was going out of town, and asked me to fax a report to him."

"You know where he went?"

"Nope, but I still have the fax number."

"Can I see it?"

"Sure."

An obese gray cat waddled out from behind my chair and, with the great effort necessary to move such bulk, hoisted itself up on the couch beside Sortigan, meowing loudly. It wasn't really a meow, more like an air raid siren. Sortigan cooed softly to it and scratched under its chin.

I cleared my throat to regain her attention. "Do you still have those names?"

"Sure. In fact, I have all the information I gathered on them. Kinda shady guys, to be honest with you."

"The cops ask you about this?"

"Yes. But as I said, I have no idea what the significance of the case was. And it's not like many of the people we check out *don't* have criminal records, you know? It wasn't unusual."

"Sure. Could I take a look at those names and that fax number?"

"Definitely. Hang on, I'll go grab the folder." She dropped the fat cat to the ground. It uttered a squawk of protest and then collapsed on the floor, where it promptly decided that was as comfortable a place as any and went to sleep. Life as a cat.

A moment later Sortigan returned with a manila folder. Inside were three sets of printouts detailing the records she had found on three men. It was the type of routine background check Joe and I were doing on a regular basis now, and she seemed to have done a pretty thorough job on it. All of the gentlemen were Soviet nationals, and all of them had criminal records. Perhaps there had been some confusion over the customs and ordinances of their new country.

"Can I make copies of this?" I asked.

"You can keep the originals. It's not like I need them anymore. Dead bosses don't pay."

FOUR

"Vladimir Rakic, Ivan Malaknik, Alexei Krashakov," I read. "All in their mid-thirties, all born in the Soviet Union, all with criminal records. And all investigated by the deceased Wayne Weston in the weeks before his murder."

Joe raised an eyebrow. "Murder? We know that now?"

I shrugged. "It sounded more dramatic that way."

"What are the criminal charges?"

"Petty stuff, mostly. Several counts of battery, two of assault, one robbery charge involving all three that was dismissed, a few public intoxication charges, one charge of battery of a police officer, and one count of intimidation."

"Aw, shucks," Joe said. "They sound like good boys. Just misunderstood."

I nodded. "These barbaric Cleveland police officers clearly lack the appreciation for subtle differences in culture and values that our Soviet visitors expected to find in American authorities."

"Clearly," Joe agreed. "What do you plan to do with them?"

"Knock on the door and tell them I'm looking for a missing mother and daughter?"

"Perhaps that's a little too direct."

"Ah," I said. "Well, in that case, I'm out of ideas."

"No surprise there," Joe said. "Fortunately, I've been a good deal more productive than you. I made a few calls to Windsor, and I must confess I had little luck. But, ever undeterred, I shifted gears and called John Weston. I told him to get his attorney on the phone with his son's bank and bitch until they gave us some records. Which they did pretty quickly. Swanders and Kraus were right; Wayne Weston was basically cleared out. Two grand in checking and about five hundred bucks in savings. He'd cashed in bonds and mutual funds."

"Gives some credence to the gambling problem, maybe."

"Uh-huh. I also asked for the details about the recent checks cashed by Weston's agency account. Five checks in the past two months, from five businesses." He glanced at a notepad in front of him. "Two real estate agencies, two construction companies, and a law firm."

I frowned. "The law firm makes sense, but I wonder what he did for the real estate agencies and construction companies?"

"Maybe he ran some checks for wiretaps or installed electronic surveillance equipment," Joe offered. "There are some firms that do that type of thing."

"Maybe, but why would the real estate agency request it and not the homeowner? It seems strange to me."

He waved his hand indifferently. "Any individual and any business can hire a private investigator."

"Fine. We probably ought to look into the jobs, though, and see what we can learn. On the off chance Weston stirred something up with his work, it makes sense to check the most recent jobs first."

"I guess." Joe didn't sound enthused.

"You got a better idea?"

He shook his head. "Not really. Let's check on those jobs and check on the Russians."

"What are you thinking?"

"That this guy didn't kill himself," he said. "If it was just Wayne Weston, I'd say forget about it, this case isn't worth messing with. But the family bothers me. It takes one kind of guy to run up some gambling debts and eat a bullet for the easy way out. It takes a different kind of guy entirely to murder his own family. And if he murdered them, how'd he do it? When did he do it? Where are the bodies? Most murder-suicide cases I've heard about, both acts are usually done in fairly close proximity, you know?"

"Yeah."

"And," he said, gathering steam with his argument, "if he killed them, he obviously took great pains to hide the bodies, which doesn't fit the thinking of a guy who was planning on suicide. Why bother hiding the bodies if you're not going to be around to worry about it?"

"So you think we should operate on the assumption he was killed."

He gave me a tired grin. "I don't know. But regardless, I'm not so worried about Weston. He killed himself, or someone killed him. Fine. We've got the body lying there, you know? But what the hell happened to that woman and her little girl?"

"That's what we're supposed to find out, old man."

"I know." He waved a handful of papers at me. "Swanders kept his word and faxed the crime scene report over."

"And?"

"And the physical evidence makes it look like a suicide. They did a damn thorough job of checking the house, and they've also got no evidence of an intruder or any sort of struggle. Weston was killed with his own handgun, fired into his temple at point-blank range."

"No chance someone else could have shot him, wiped the gun for prints, left it in his hand?"

He shrugged. "Well, there wasn't any gunshot residue on his hand, no real convincing evidence he fired the shot himself. That doesn't always exist in a suicide, though. So your idea is possible but unlikely. I mean, the guy was a pro, right? A Force Recon vet and a professional investigator? It's hard to imagine a scenario where someone takes Weston's gun away from him and shoots him at point-blank range so easily, then deals with the family, all without causing enough noise to attract attention from the neighbors. You don't think the mother and little girl would get out even a scream?"

"Maybe the guy kills them first."

"While Weston sits around chewing on his fingernails? You kidding me?"

I sighed and scratched my head. "When were the mother and girl last seen?"

"Neighbors said they were in the backyard at seven that night."

"So they leave the house, meet with some kind of trouble, and then the guy or guys head back to the home and finish off Weston."

"Weston wasn't killed until after midnight. Probably closer to three or four than midnight. While his wife and kid are out missing that late, he sits around the house relaxing?"

"Maybe he was asleep, didn't realize they hadn't come home."

"Guy sleeps wearing a shirt and tie?"

I was running out of maybes. "I guess we're going to have to leave the office for this."

"Depressing, isn't it? We're not so good after all."

In the next hour, Joe and I agreed on a preliminary plan of action. He thought it would be more efficient if we worked separately on the early steps of the investigation, allowing us to tackle multiple angles as quickly as possible. He would look into Weston's most recent cases and pursue the possible gambling connections. I would check out the three Russians and talk to Weston's closest friends, whose names were in the notes provided by John Weston. I hoped that at least one of them would give me a better idea of Weston's gambling tendencies.

Amy called, wanting an update on the case. Patience was never her strong suit. I told her about our meeting with Swanders and Kraus, then explained the questions that were nagging at Joe. She didn't have any solutions.

"Anything I can do to help?" she asked.

"I'm not giving you a story, Ace."

"I don't want the story, Lincoln, I'm just asking if you could use any help."

"Okay," I said. "If you're so eager to be helpful, you can run the names of my three Russian friends through your archives and see what you find. My guess is there will be at least one story. The robbery charge probably warranted some sort of attention from you guys."

"Give me the names."

I did, and she promised to check them out and get back to me. That settled, I began to call some of Weston's closer acquaintances. John Weston had listed six names under the "Friends" category, along with the phone numbers he had for the five of them who lived in the state. The sixth was an old Marine buddy who lived in Florida. I'd try to find a number for him if I couldn't turn up anything productive from the others. I assumed the police would have talked to all the same individuals, but it was still the place to start.

Four hours later, I'd conducted five interviews. Three of the "friends" John Weston had listed told me they weren't really that close to Wayne Weston, just casual acquaintances who sometimes played golf with him. When asked about the gambling, they all claimed limited knowledge.

"He'd make bets on the golf course fairly often," one man told me. "Never big money, just betting ten or twenty bucks on a round, or maybe five or ten on a hole. It was just something he did to make it a little more fun, increase the competitiveness a bit."

The other two admitted being close with Weston, but both dismissed the idea that he might have had serious gambling debts, saying betting was nothing more than recreation to Weston, and not something he did recklessly. I stuck with them for a while, searching for other motives or sources of trouble, but found none. I finished the afternoon with no leads but with a growing list of questions about Wayne Weston. His father had provided names of the people he felt his son was closest to, yet none of those people seemed to know the man intimately. Even the self-proclaimed "close" friends had only casual relationships with Weston, and all of them described him as a private person, not given to a great deal of socializing or conversation about his personal affairs. It was not the response I had hoped to generate.

Joe left the office while I was doing the last of my interviews. It didn't sound like he had made much progress with the Windsor calls. By the time I hung up, it was growing dark out on the street. Amy, for all her burning desire to help, hadn't called back with any information about the Russians. I decided to call it a day and head to my gym for a mind-clearing workout, hoping to return the next morning with a fresh focus and some better ideas.

I own a gym called Sweat Alley just a few blocks from our office. After I was dismissed from the police department, I invested the meager inheritance left from my father's estate in the gym and attempted to make it as a small business owner. Since then, I'd turned the management over to Grace, my middle-aged and sharp-tongued employee, but you could find me there most evenings.

When I arrived, the parking lot was fairly crowded. I had to admit Grace had more of a knack for running the place than I did. She'd started cardiovascular classes and generated a good-sized turnout for them after she began targeting the senior citizens' centers in the area with advertising. The result was that the gym was making me more money than ever before, and I had an odd mix of burly power lifters and white-haired grandmothers.

It was after five, so Grace was gone and the office was closed. I used my keycard to enter, then did some light stretching and headed for the free weights. A black guy named Alan Belle was on the incline bench, pressing a pair of eighty-pound dumbbells, and we exchanged nods. Alan had been coming to the gym for a few months now, and we talked occasionally. As I started in on my own workout, I remembered that he'd served in the Marines.

"Hey, Alan," I said when he had finished his set.

"Yeah?" He turned to me, wiping sweat away from his eyes with a towel. There were lots of guys in the gym who were big, or in great shape, and then there was Alan Belle. He wasn't power-lifter thick but lean and cut, with an athlete's hard muscle. He was tall, at least six-four, and he'd been a star in both football and basketball at St. Ignatius, Cleveland's perennial high school powerhouse.

"You were in the Marines, right?"

"Six years, Marine Expeditionary Unit," he acknowledged.

"Same group my father was in," I said. "Guy I was named after was a Marine, too. Saved my dad's life in Vietnam. You know anything about Force Recon?"

"Recon." He grinned and rubbed his shaved head. "Yeah, I know Force Recon. Those boys are flat-out badasses, that's all there is to it. I was recruited for Recon, but I wasn't planning on making a career out of it and I liked my unit, so I passed."

"They go through pretty tough training?"

"*All* Marines go through tough training, Perry. Force Recon boys go through specialized training. They get taught all the dirty tricks, the special ops techniques. That's what they are: special operations. See, I was in an expeditionary unit. We were considered special operations *capable*. There's a difference. And as far as the training is concerned, yeah, they're pretty well taught. They've got to pass airborne training, combat diver training, escape and evasion training, close-quarters combat—all the fun stuff."

"I see."

"Why are you interested?" he asked.

"I met a guy who was with Force Recon, and I was curious," I said.

Belle laughed. "Sure, Perry. I just hope you're on this fella's good side. You don't want to be pissing off any Recon boys."

I returned my attention to my own workout, beginning with military presses, then moving on to shoulder shrugs and lateral raises. I concentrated on steady breathing and careful form, trying to make each repetition identical to the last in motion and power, like cylinders working in an engine. Sweat beaded on my forehead, and the muscles began to ache. It wasn't a bad pain, though, but one that promised better things ahead.

I finished my weight workout and then went outside and ran. The air was cold; it was only March, and in Cleveland March feels a lot more like the end of winter than it does the beginning of spring. There were still traces of snow in the parking lots, but the sidewalks were clear and the footing was safe. I ran regardless of the conditions, but it was nice not to have to worry about the slick patches of black ice that blended with the shadows.

I ran four miles, my body becoming hot under the sweat-shirt despite the cold, the sweat beginning to drip down my face. When I returned to the gym I remained on the sidewalk until my breathing was back to normal, and then I went up-stairs. I live in an apartment above the gym, and sometimes, late at night, I can hear the distant thuds of dropped weights and the clang of metal on metal from some night owl's workout.

I showered and changed clothes, then stood in front of the open refrigerator debating what to make for dinner. The phone rang while I was considering the limited options and thinking it was time for a trip to the grocery store. I picked up the receiver, expecting it was Joe and hoping it wasn't Angela calling again to question my judgment in ending our short-lived relationship.

"Hello?"

"Lincoln, I need you." It was Amy, and she wasn't happy.

"What's wrong?" I said. Silence. "Amy? What's wrong?"

"Just come over. I'll explain when you're here."

She hung up, and I sighed and let the refrigerator door swing shut. So much for dinner. I grabbed my keys and left.

I'd driven a Jeep until recently, when I'd traded it in and purchased a four-year-old Chevy Silverado pickup truck. I like big cars, and the two settings of four-wheel drive meant I could handle any weather the Cleveland winter chose to dish out, but both Amy and Joe ridiculed the truck con-stantly. On the other hand, when I wanted to drive fast in the big truck, as I did on the way to Amy's apartment, people tended to get out of my way.

The first thing I noticed when I pulled into a parking spot in front of Amy's apartment was her car. The Acura was parked in its customary place but that was where the normalcy ended. The side panels and trunk were covered with large dents, all four windows had been broken out, and the windshield was spiderwebbed with cracks.

I turned my truck off and climbed out, staring at the car in amazement. I was standing beside it, running my fingers over some of the larger dents, when Amy came out of her apartment.

"Pretty, isn't it?" she said. She was wearing jeans and a sweatshirt, holding her arms tightly around herself, seemingly more to offer comfort than warmth. Her eyes were dry and she was calm, but at the same time I sensed a quality of tension and fear that I had never seen in her before. As long as I had known Amy, she'd always presented an attitude of confidence and bravado. I was surprised to see her this rattled.

"What happened?" I said.

She smiled. "I got a little too eager to help."

"Excuse me?"

"When you gave me those names this afternoon, I ran them through the archives and didn't find much. There was a story about the robbery they were involved with, and that was about it. But I didn't want to report back with nothing, so I decided to do a little investigating on my own. I located addresses for two of them and drove out to talk to the neighbors." She forced a tight-lipped smile. "Apparently, that wasn't the wisest choice."

I stared at her. "They did this? The guys on the list I gave you?"

She nodded. "Yeah. The neighbors weren't real helpful, and they all seemed nervous. I left without learning anything, went back to work for another hour, and then came home. When I pulled into the lot, four men were waiting for me. Three of them had bats, and they started hitting my car, smashing the windows. I was screaming and trying to get my cell phone to call the police, and then the fourth one, this big blond guy, leaned down beside the driver's door and smiled at me." She gritted her teeth and frowned, angry. "People in the parking lot were screaming, someone was yelling about calling the police, and this guy, he's smiling. Completely nonchalant. He hands me my own business card through the broken window and says, 'I think it would be a good idea for you to forget all about us, ma'am.' And then they left. They just got inside this fancy SUV and drove away."

I looked at the car again, at the thousands of dollars of damage done so casually, and I took a few long, slow breaths, pushing down the rising anger.

"How are you so sure it was the guys on my list? Could it have been people from the trial you're covering, or some other story?"

She shook her head vehemently. "No, Lincoln, it couldn't have been anyone else. First of all, I'd been handing out my cards to all the neighbors, which is probably where that ass-hole got his. And he had a definite accent. His English was flawless, but it was spoken in this clipped, careful voice. It was obviously a second language for him, and I'd be willing to bet he was Russian."

"Did the police come?"

"Yes. They filled out a vandalism report, which should help me with the insurance company, but I told them I had no idea who the guys were. I don't think they believed me, but that's fine. I figured I'd talk to you first." She cocked her head and looked at me. "Who are these guys, Lincoln?"

"I don't know," I said, wondering the same thing. "I know they're criminals who were of interest to Wayne Weston shortly before his death. That's all I know, so far." I tapped on the side of her car. "I'm really sorry, Ace."

She waved me off. "Don't be, Lincoln, it wasn't your fault. All you wanted was a computer archives check. It was stupid for me to go around asking questions without knowing what I was getting into, but that's my job, so it was a pretty natural response."

"I suppose you could press charges, if it really was the

Russians," I said. "But I think it would be best if you let me look into things first."

"No way I'm pressing charges. I mean, I just asked some questions, and they did this." She gestured at the car. "It probably wouldn't be wise to do anything else to piss them off."

I looked away. Intimidation is a powerful and ugly tool. And an effective one. They'd intimidated Amy, and she'd never struck me as the type of person readily susceptible to such tactics.

Apparently, she was thinking similarly.

"I'm used to thugs," she said softly. "I deal with con men, murderers, thieves, and rapists. I write stories about them, I push their personal affairs into the public eye, and I upset them. And I've never really worried about it. But with these guys, it wasn't the same. They were totally indifferent, you know? The one who talked to me, he looked just . . . I don't know . . . empty. He looked like he could have raped me, killed me, or given me roses and felt exactly the same about all of it." She took a deep breath. "Who are these guys, Lincoln?" she asked again.

I was saved from reaffirming my ignorance by a white Lexus coupe that squealed to a stop beside my truck. Amy and I both turned, and she put her hands to her head.

"Jacob," she said. "I completely forgot he was coming over."

Jacob Terry stepped out of the Lexus and looked at us with a wide smile. He was a tall, good-looking guy, with perfect teeth, eyebrows, and nails, and a haircut that said "beauty salon" where mine said "barber shop." He's supposedly the most popular news anchor in the city, but I remember a time when Pee Wee Herman and Geraldo Rivera were successful television personalities, so that's not saying much.

"Hey, babe," he said to Amy. "And you're Lincoln Perry, correct?"

"Uh-huh."

He beamed at me and offered his hand, apparently thrilled with the pleasant surprise of my company. "Good to see you again, Mr. Perry."

"Likewise, Mr. Terry," I said, realizing for the first sickening time that our names rhymed. Maybe he could join me when Joe retired. Perry and Terry Investigations. Yikes.

Terry was still smiling, completely oblivious to the wreck that was Amy's car. "What brings you here?" he said.

"The smashed-up vehicle two feet in front of you," I answered, releasing his hand. "Geez, for a professional journalist, you're not the most observant guy in the world, are you, Jake?"

Amy fought to hide a smile while Terry fought to keep his in place.

"I guess not," he said, looking past me and seeing the car for the first time. "Amy, what in the hell happened? Were you in an accident?"

I glanced back at the car myself, studying the damage and trying to comprehend how anyone could think it came from an accident. Maybe he thought she had rear-ended a semi that spilled a load of Louisville Sluggers onto her car.

"No, not an accident," she said. "My car was vandalized."

"What? That's awful. Do you know who did it?"

She glanced at me and shook her head. "Nope. Probably just some kids, drunk and high and looking for a good time."

"I'm sorry, baby," he said, crossing over to her and kissing her, rubbing her back with his hands. I returned my attention to the dented Acura.

"It's fine," she said. "I'm fine."

"Are you still up for dinner?" he asked.

"Sure," she said. "Lincoln, would you like to join us?"

I looked at her and Terry, sorting through all the responses that came to mind and trying to select an option that wasn't a wise-ass remark. It took a while, but I finally came up with one: "No, thanks."

"Okay. Well, thanks for coming over. And, um, let me know what you find out, will you?"

"Sure thing." I nodded at Terry. "Nice seeing you again, Jake."

"Jacob," Amy said. "He hates being called Jake."

Terry seemed to blush, but he didn't deny it. I bowed in apology. "My mistake, Jacob. It won't happen again."

I climbed into my truck and drove away, glancing at the rearview mirror and noting that Terry's arms were still around Amy. It didn't bother me, though. Did it? No. Why should it? No reason. I turned the music up louder.

Back at the apartment, I called Joe and filled him in.

"Is Amy okay?" he asked when I was through.

"I think so. She was a little shaken up, but she's tough. Jacob Terry is there now to comfort her."

"Don't say it with such bitterness."

"I didn't."

"Sure. Well, I have some news of my own, LP. I checked out the real estate agencies, the construction companies, and the law firm. The law firm refused to talk to me, saying they could have an associate attorney call me back on Friday if I'd like. Helpful folks. Officials at each of the real estate agencies, as well as the construction companies, seemed truly confused by my questions. They all claimed I must have been misinformed, but when I insisted I had accurate information, they told me they had no idea what I was talking about and promised they weren't aware of anyone at the company hiring an investigator."

"They're lying."

"I don't think so," he said. "Initially, I did. But when they all were singing the same song, I sat down and thought about it and decided I should check out the companies a little more. Assuming the managers didn't cut Weston a check, then who else would be able to?"

"If it wasn't a company president or manager, then I'd say it could have been a company accountant."

"Or?"

"Or?" I thought about it. "Who else is there, Joe? Company officials, company accountant, and the owner. Those should be the only people with access to the checking accounts."

"There you go," he said. "The owner. Turns out both the real estate agencies and the construction companies have the same owner. And you'll never guess who that owner is."

"No," I agreed, "I won't. So just tell me."

"Jeremiah Hubbard."

"You're kidding."

"Nope."

Jeremiah Hubbard was one of the richest men in the city. He was a self-made multimillionaire who built his fortune in real estate—Cleveland's answer to Donald Trump. He was also, not surprisingly, one of the most influential private citizens in town, a man who supposedly held great sway with the city government.

"You think Weston was working for Hubbard."

"It's the only thing that makes sense so far," Joe said. "And, with a little bit of research, I confirmed that the law firm that paid Weston also represents Hubbard."

"Why did he pay him through the companies, though? Why not just cut him a personal check?"

"Maybe," Joe said, "he wanted to keep it a little more discreet."

I didn't say anything for a while, just sat and listened to Joe's even breathing and the faint sound of the television in the background.

"A dead detective, a missing family, Russian thugs, and one of the city's richest," I said eventually. "A compelling little mess, isn't it?"

Joe sighed. "Do you have the feeling that this case isn't just about gambling anymore?"

"Yes," I said. "I do, indeed."

FIVE

Bat-wielding thugs might be able to intimidate Amy, but even they couldn't keep her rattled for long. When I arrived at the office the next morning, the fax machine tray was filled with copies of the articles involving the Russians, along with a personal note from Amy: "When you find them, kick some ass for me."

I read them carefully before setting them aside with disappointment. Most of the charges had been petty stuff, basically ignored by the *Journal* reporting staff. The most serious charge was armed robbery, but that case had been dropped before it ever got to trial.

I was considering going to the county clerk's office in search of more details about that charge when Joe walked in. He shrugged out of his jacket, and I saw he was wearing a snubnose .357 in a holster beneath it. I looked at it and raised my eyebrows.

"You paranoid about something or just hoping to be the heir to Charlton Heston's throne?"

"Call me paranoid if you want," he said. "I don't like anything about the way this case is developing. And if we should happen to bump into those Russian assholes, I'd be happy to express my displeasure with the way they've treated our associates."

I smiled. "I knew you loved Amy."

"Uh-huh." He sat down at the desk beside me and nodded at the faxes. "What do you have there?"

I passed them over and sat while he read, wondering about the gun he was wearing. When I'd worked with Joe on the street, he'd always possessed an uncanny sixth sense for impending trouble. If he thought he should wear a gun, I probably should join him. Or take a vacation.

"Not a whole lot of help there," Joe said, handing the articles back to me. "I'm working on Hubbard. I called Aaron Kinkaid last night. He was Weston's partner for a few years, lives out in Sandusky now?"

"Yeah."

"He said he remembers Weston working a case involving Hubbard, but not for Hubbard."

"Say again?"

Joe shrugged. "I don't know. I asked for details, but he was on his way out the door and said he couldn't talk. He agreed to meet me this afternoon, though."

"In Sandusky?"

"Yeah."

"Long drive."

"Could be worth it."

"Take anything we can get at this stage."

He nodded. "You want to come along, tag-team the poor guy?"

I shrugged. "I will if you'd like, but maybe we can make more progress if we stick to our plan and pursue different angles on this, at least at first."

"That's why I wanted a partnership," he said. "Saves time, makes us more efficient, and allows us to kill off bad leads without losing a week on it."

"And it allows me to go chasing Russian thugs around the city while you drive out to Sandusky to interview some guy over a latte."

"I don't drink lattes."

"Oh," I said. "Well, that makes all the difference."

Joe left for the drive to Sandusky, and I grabbed a legal pad and pencil and headed downtown. I went to the county clerk's office, used the computer to look up the cause number for the robbery trial, and then requested the file. I reviewed it quickly. It didn't take long for me to find what I was looking for. A deputy prosecutor named James Sellers had handled the case. I wrote his name on my pad and returned to the office.

James Sellers was still a prosecutor. I was transferred to his extension without hassle, and I explained who I was.

"Is this about a current case?" he said. "I can't talk to you about cases. I'm prohibited from doing that by the prosecutorial code of ethics."

Prosecutorial code of ethics? Ethics, among attorneys? It was an interesting notion.

"It's not about a current case," I said. I told him quickly what case I was interested in, hoping he wouldn't blow me off before I'd even completed the request. It turned out to be a wasted concern.

"Hell, yes, I'll talk to you about those bastards," he said. "I've got plenty to say about them. What are they into now?"

I'd already decided I wanted to keep Weston's name out of it if possible. Gossip spreads quickly anywhere, and the prosecutor's office was certainly no exception. I told him I was working on a case in which the Russians had come up, but I didn't specify its nature.

"I'd been on staff for maybe six months when I got that case," he said. "The evidence was shit, though, just eyewitness testimony. Eyewitness testimony sounds great until you're in court with no forensic evidence and the defense attorney finds out your witness is a recovering heroin addict. Besides, those guys had Adam Benson representing them, and that meant big money. I was just a rookie, so I asked a couple of the veterans down at my office what they thought of my chances."

"And?"

"And they laughed at me. Told me there was no way I'd beat Benson with the evidence I had." He cleared his throat. "You ever heard of Dainius Belov?"

"Say it again?"

He did, and I shook my head. "No, I don't think so."

"I thought you might have, since you were a cop. Supposedly he's some sort of Russian mob kingpin. At least that's what I was told."

"These guys are affiliated with him?"

"One of our senior prosecutors—a woman named Winters, if you care—told me the FBI had tagged those three as low-level foot soldiers for Belov. And, to clinch the deal, guess who Belov's attorney of choice is?"

"Adam Benson."

"Circumstantial evidence might not hold you in court, but I find that's pretty convincing."

I knew a little about the Russian mobs, but not much. The Italian Mafia, while still being glorified in movies and shows like *The Sopranos,* has been severely crippled—not just in New York but across the country. The Cleveland families, reasonably powerful in the Pizza Connection days of the seventies and eighties, have pretty well disappeared. Since the fall of the Soviet Union, the Russian mobs have become a far more powerful force in American organized crime. I knew the local FBI had an organized crime task force that worked with some of the Cleveland police detectives, but I'd never been among them. If I'd ever heard the name Dainius Belov, it hadn't stuck with me.

"You know anything about these guys?" I asked. "When they came here, who they associate with, things like that?"

"Not really. The case was a while ago, and like I said, we dropped charges fast."

I hesitated then, wondering what else I could try to get from Sellers. I wanted to ask if he'd ever heard of a connection between Jeremiah Hubbard and Belov, but I didn't want to be responsible for sending that rumor ricocheting through the corridors of City Hall. If the Russians didn't kill me for it, Hubbard would probably suffocate me under a pile of hundred-dollar bills. I thanked Sellers for his time and hung up.

Joe and I had worked an insurance fraud case shortly before signing on with John Weston, and I spent the afternoon completing that report and sending it out along with a bill. I had the feeling we'd need to clear the deck as completely as possible for the Weston case. Joe got back late that evening, and he came by my apartment to talk. Apparently, the Sandusky trip hadn't been a total waste.

"Turns out Kinkaid didn't leave Weston by choice," Joe said, looking around my apartment and frowning as if the décor didn't please him. I knew that wasn't it, though. I'd moved some things around, and he sensed the change and was trying to place it. That's how Joe is—incredibly observant, and incredibly irritated by anything that doesn't match his expectations and memory. Once he notices something that doesn't fit, he won't let it out of his mind until he has determined the source of the irritation.

"Weston fired him?" I asked, trying to bring his focus back.

"I don't know if you can call one partner asking the other to leave a 'firing,' but, yeah, Weston bailed on him. After three years in the business together, Weston suddenly decided he wanted to run it solo. Kinkaid was pissed, because they'd built up a decent client base and were making money, but Weston bought him out and let him take all the clients he'd handled. Kinkaid isn't investigating anymore. He's more focused on security now, runs a guard company up in Sandusky. But he still has some hard feelings for Weston."

"He must not have put up much of a fight."

"Would you really want to stick with a partner who said he didn't want you?" His eyes were locked on a brass floor lamp with a round glass table that sat next to the couch.

"Good point."

"So I started out by asking him about Weston, you know, just basic things about their relationship and how long he was with him—" He cut himself off in mid-sentence and pointed at the lamp. "You moved that, didn't you?"

Since Joe's last visit, I'd rotated the lamp maybe two feet, moving it just enough to eliminate the glare it had placed on the television screen.

"Yeah, I moved it, maybe a year ago," I lied. "You're getting old, Joe. Memory's starting to fade."

He gave me a look that let me know he wasn't buying it, then continued. "So, anyhow, I kept it to the basics for a while, but then I decided to go ahead and ask him about the gambling and the Russians."

"He know anything?"

"He'd never heard of the Russians, and he said if the cops are really buying this gambling theory they've got their heads up their asses. According to him, Weston was anything but a serious gambler. Liked going up to Windsor for the shows and the atmosphere of the casino but never gambled much. Bet on sports just because he was a big fan, always thought he should have been a broadcaster or a sportswriter—you know, another armchair expert. Kinkaid said the guy actually was pretty good when it came to picking winners, but he never put up big money."

"Maybe he got carried away in the last few years."

Joe shook his head. "I threw the same question at Kinkaid, and he blew it off. He said Weston was too much of an accountant, too fussy about budgets. Said the guy used to check his bank accounts daily and review the company books every week. And he apparently was never *more* aware of his money than when he was gambling. Always allotted a certain amount of what he called 'mad money' for betting and vacations, that type of thing."

"I see." I put my feet up on my old coffee table and stared at my scuffed sneakers. It was time for a new pair, but that would require going to the shoe store and having some kid dressed like a referee try to coax me into buying the hot new style. Maybe I could get a few more months out of these. "Just because a guy had his gambling under control six years ago doesn't mean he did six months ago. Anybody who gambles regularly runs the risk of getting carried away with it."

"I suppose."

"Kinkaid have anything else to say?"

Joe nodded, smiling. "I asked him about Jeremiah Hubbard. Apparently Weston worked a case involving Hubbard just before he told Kinkaid he wanted to cut out on his own."

"Maybe Hubbard wanted him as his personal lackey but didn't want to have to pay Kinkaid as well," I suggested, thinking of the frequent checks to Weston from Hubbard.

"That would have been an odd turn of events," Joe said, "considering Hubbard had never been a client. He'd been a target."

"A target?"

"You got it. Wayne Weston's first association with Old Man Hubbard was working for Old Mother Hubbard."

"Speak English, Aesop."

"Aesop didn't write about Old Mother Hubbard. He wrote fables, not nursery rhymes."

I sighed. "Save it for *Jeopardy,* Joe. Just tell me what happened."

"Weston and Kinkaid worked for Mrs. Rita Hubbard, Jeremiah's beloved wife. She suspected he was having an affair and wanted to prove it. Weston and Kinkaid didn't like cheating-spouse cases, but with money like that involved, who could turn it down? So they took the case, with Weston doing the majority of the work on it. And they worked a hell of a case, apparently. Kinkaid told me they had taped interviews with hotel employees who saw Hubbard and his mistress; they had photographs, video, and even some audiotapes, which must have been a real treat. A beautiful, full-service job. They were paid handsomely by Mrs. Hubbard."

"The former Mrs. Hubbard, I assume?"

He shook his head. "Nope. She was apparently prepared to threaten divorce, but it never happened. I'm not real surprised about that. Jeremiah would probably agree to damn near anything as long as he didn't have to lose half of his fortune in a divorce settlement, and the wife probably wasn't real eager to give up her status. And you know how those big-money couples are; they hate the idea of a public scandal. Better to live in private misery than in public disarray."

"Any chance Weston was still working for her?"

"Doubtful. Here's the interesting part: Apparently Hubbard called Weston about a month after the case. Jeremiah Hubbard, I mean, not the wife."

"Pissed off, probably."

"You'd think so. Weston met with him, and all he told Kinkaid about it was that Hubbard told him he'd drive him out of business if he ever tampered with his life again. I guess the wife gave Hubbard Weston's name, or maybe he found out himself."

"That's bullshit."

"You think?"

"Has to be. Hubbard goes from threatening to drive Weston out of business to *giving* him business? No way. Either Hubbard's wife was still hiring Weston, or Weston lied to Kinkaid about that conversation."

"But why lie to his partner?"

I shrugged. "He didn't want to have a partner anymore, so why not? Probably he worked out some sort of high-paying job with Hubbard and wanted to take it alone."

Joe rubbed his temples gently with his thumb and index finger. "So Hubbard's so impressed by the work Weston did, he wants to hire him personally, even though the guy screwed up his marriage and likely ended his affair?"

"Why not? Hubbard didn't make millions by being petty; he made them by being smart as hell, and ruthless. If he needed an investigator and he liked what he saw of Weston's abilities, I think he might pursue him. Maybe he wanted to get him off the wife's team to keep future affairs quiet."

"That's possible. I definitely don't believe Weston continued to work for the wife. She's having her husband's attorneys write the guy checks? No way."

I got off the couch and went into the kitchen to make some coffee. I put a good Guatemalan blend in to brew and then returned to the living room with a glass of water for Joe.

"When was the last time you dusted in this dump?" he asked, tracing the edge of the coffee table with his fingertip. He lifted it up and showed the gray grime it had gathered.

"Take off your apron and leave it at the door when you come in my apartment," I said.

"You find out anything on the Russians?"

The coffee was percolating now, clicking and clacking coming from the kitchen, the rich scent drifting into the living room.

"Dainius Belov," I said. "That name mean anything to you?"

"Of course it does."

I frowned. "Am I the only person who hasn't heard of this guy?"

"You don't know Dainius? You've got to be kidding me, LP. How the hell did you do two years as my partner and stay this stupid?"

"Who is he?"

"Dainius is the closest thing to a don this city has. Of course, he's not a don, that's the Italian Mafia, but he's the Russians' answer to one. He's been here for fifteen years now, maybe more. Don't you even remember the Chester Avenue auto bust?"

"Nope."

He groaned and rolled his eyes to the ceiling as if searching the heavens for help in dealing with his moronic partner. "LP, I'm ashamed of you. The Chester Avenue bust was the biggest car-theft success the department had in the last decade."

"I didn't work on car thefts, I worked narcotics," I said.

"So did I, but I'm not completely clueless. They found an old warehouse out on the east side, off Chester Avenue, with about twenty stolen cars inside. Arrested two of Dainius's soldiers, but they couldn't touch him, because no one would testify against him. Still, it was a big find, headline news, made our detectives look good."

I vaguely remembered the recovery of quite a few stolen vehicles, but I certainly hadn't connected it to Belov. That had happened in my early years on the force, when I was working nights and didn't know many of the detectives.

"Is he still involved with car theft?"

"As far as I know he is, but he certainly isn't limited to it. He's got organized muscle and big money, I can tell you that." He drank some more of the water and stared at the bottom of the glass as if he didn't like what he saw there. "Are you telling me Dainius is connected to those jackasses who smashed up Ambrose's car?"

"That's what I was told." I explained my conversation with Sellers to him, then went back to the kitchen to pour my coffee. When I came back to the couch he looked grim.

"I don't like the way this thing smells," he said. "Jeremiah Hubbard and Dainius Belov? There's nothing good coming out of that combination."

"Figure they're linked?"

He nodded. "Oh, yeah. As far as I'm concerned, they're linked already."

"By?"

He looked at me. "By Wayne Weston's corpse."

I nodded. "Think the Russians could have the wife and daughter?"

"Possibly, although I can't think of any reason they'd have to keep them alive. Of course, right now, I can't think of any reason for any of it, because we don't know shit." He shook his head. "If I remember right—and I always do—several of Belov's boys used to be with Spetznatz. You know, the Soviet answer to our special forces and covert operations units."

"Sounds like a pretty dangerous bunch."

"Yeah." Joe grinned. "But at least we know what we're up against. They don't."

SIX

Wayne Weston's home in Brecksville had an air of modest elegance. The large brick ranch was impressive, and clearly expensive, but not overly extravagant. A blacktop driveway led past a row of spruce trees. Traces of snow remained in the shadows under the trees, where the sun hadn't been able to reach. There was a detached two-car garage set slightly behind the house. Everything about the home and yard gave an impression of serenity and safety. The police had searched every inch of the property, but Joe and I agreed that we wanted to see it, to try to absorb a little more of who Wayne Weston was, and how he and his family had lived. As the sun came up that morning and people with normal jobs made their commute to the office, Joe and I arrived at a dead man's house to soak in the ambience. It was a hell of a way to start the day.

John Weston's Buick was parked in front of the garage, and I pulled in beside it. Behind the house was a deck with a propane grill and a picnic table. We found John Weston sitting on the picnic table, staring at the remains of a snowman in the backyard.

"My granddaughter made it," Weston said, his voice

thick, as we joined him on the deck. "The day before she . . . before she went missing."

The snowman had melted slowly, and was hardly two feet high. The carrot nose had slipped as the snow melted and loosened, and now it sat in the grass. There was a pink ski cap perched on the snowman's head, and the two rock eyes were still in place, staring back at John Weston, seemingly taunting him. *I'm still here,* the snowman seemed to say, *but she's not.*

Weston took his eyes away from it with an effort and handed us a key. "That's for the front door. You go in, take all the time you need. Look at whatever you want, I don't care. But I can't go in that place."

That place. Like a small child afraid to go down the cellar steps. A child would be afraid of what he might find in the cellar, though. John Weston was afraid of what he knew he would not find in the house.

Joe took the key, and we left the deck and walked back to the front of the house and let ourselves in. The front door opened into an entryway with hardwood floors. A hallway led away to the left, and a small sitting room with a couch, a wooden rocking chair, and an antique sewing machine was on the right. There were a few pictures on the walls, and a small table with back issues of *Time,* but the room appeared to have been more for show than use. We went right.

Behind the sitting room was the kitchen. We rifled through the cupboards and drawers. The refrigerator was full of food; the freezer had two New York strip steaks and an unopened box of Popsicles. Everything was neat and well organized and gave the impression that the residents had every intention of returning home to their normal lives and routines.

Next to the kitchen was a dining room with an oak table that would probably seat twenty. Past the dining room was a sunken living room with comfortable, well-worn furniture and a high-end entertainment system. This was the room where Weston's body had been found, but you'd never be able to guess it now. We went over it carefully, turning the cushions upside down and opening the videotape boxes, but it was a formality. The police wouldn't have missed anything. It was the only way Joe and I knew to search a room, though, and it beat standing around and feeling the emptiness. We finished the living room, returned to our starting point, and went left, down the hall. We had not spoken since entering the house. The silence was a heavy thing. The house seemed to hold a sense of a family; it made you feel as if at any second the door might swing open and a mother's voice and a child's laughter would fill the home.

Four doors opened off the hall. The first was to a bathroom, the second to an office with a flat desk, a file cabinet, and two bookshelves. There was a large empty space on the desk, and several electrical cords lay coiled on the floor. Weston's computer had likely sat there until the police removed it. The bookshelves held some family pictures, a framed program from the '53 World Series, and some John Grisham and Dean Koontz novels. We started on the desk drawers and the file cabinet.

I took the file cabinet and found two of the drawers completely empty. Others held files containing warranty information on various household appliances, insurance records, old high school yearbooks, equipment catalogs, and numerous other items that bore no relation to Weston's work. The only file of interest I found held his military papers. His discharge sheet included the specialist's training he had received, and there was plenty to list. Weston had certification as a combat diver, airborne specialist, long-range reconnaissance specialist, and demolitions specialist. He was qualified as an expert in both handgun and rifle marksmanship. It was a hell of a résumé. My father had frequently boasted about his Marine Expeditionary Unit training, but it couldn't touch Weston's.

"Find anything?" Joe asked, looking over my shoulder.

"Just this." I handed him the file, and we went through it together. Weston had earned some service ribbons, but there were no details about the missions. That's how it goes with special operations soldiers. He'd received an honorable discharge.

"Pretty impressive," Joe said. "But it doesn't help us much. Nothing worthwhile in the desk, either, unless you need Scotch tape or pencils. This card was on the desk, though. Check out the initials."

He passed me a plain white envelope with Weston's address on it. The postmark was from early February, just a few weeks before Weston died. There was no return address. Inside was a simple but elegant piece of stationery with a gold border. Someone had written an inscription with a black fountain pen: "Many thanks on yet another job well done. It had the intended effect." There was no explanation of what the "it" was, nor what effect the "it" had created. The note was signed with the initials J.E.H.

"Hubbard?" I said.

Joe shrugged. "I have no idea what his middle initial is, but it's possible. Let's hang on to the note. Maybe we can check the handwriting out."

"And if it's Hubbard's writing?"

"Then it's still worthless, but at least we know who to blame."

We moved on to the next rooms. Joe took the master bedroom, and I went into Elizabeth Weston's bedroom. It was a bright room with pink walls and lots of stuffed animals. The bedspread had kittens on it. A large plastic dollhouse stood in the corner of the room. Everything about it was happy and innocent. The window looked out on the backyard, and I could see John Weston, still sitting on the picnic table staring at the snowman his granddaughter had made. The sun was out now, and the snowman was glistening as it continued to melt. Weston watched it, and I thought that he could at least have the satisfaction of watching it disappear slowly. To him, that probably meant something right now.

A piece of fishing line was tied to the curtain rod, and from it a small, heart-shaped crystal prism hung in the window, reflecting the sun and distorting the light, bathing the white curtains with rainbows. I took it in my hand and ran my thumb over the chiseled surface, then removed the fishing line from the curtain rod and put it in my pocket. It was a spontaneous decision, and I wasn't sure what had provoked it. I just wanted to be sure I never forgot this room and this little girl.

I went through the closets and the drawers, moving quickly, pushing past clothing, board games, and toys. I slammed the last drawer shut without finding anything and sat on the edge of the bed, exhaling heavily. I hadn't realized I'd been holding my breath. I didn't want to breathe in this little girl's room. Maybe, if I didn't breathe, I could walk back out and tell myself that I'd never been inside, it had never been real, a five-year-old was not missing, her father was not dead.

As I sat on the bed, feeling a weariness that came not from fatigue or stress but from the realization that I lived in a world where children could vanish from happy, innocent rooms like this, I reached out and began to sort through the stuffed animals. There were dozens of them on the floor, ranging from bears to rabbits, with a special emphasis on kittens.

I turned a few of them over, squeezed them, felt their softness, and looked into their unblinking plastic eyes as if they could tell me something. Several of the animals were wearing outfits; some made noises when you squeezed them; others had movable limbs. One scholarly bear was wearing glasses and had a plastic piece of chalk in one paw and a plastic chalkboard tucked under his arm. I pulled the bear closer and saw that the chalkboard was the cover for a small booklet that closed with a snap. I slid the booklet out from where it was tucked under the bear's paw, opened it, and discovered the little book was a diary. The first entry, in a woman's writing, read: "Merry Christmas, Betsy! Love, Mom and Dad."

I flipped through the rest of it. The pages were filled with a child's drawings and writing. There were quite a few stick figures, lots of hearts, and the name Betsy, all done with various colors of crayon. Every now and then she wrote a few crudely constructed sentences. "Mom made me soop and greeled cheese," read one entry. There were maybe five or six entries for each month. On every page she'd used, the girl had carefully written the date. Her spelling of "April" was perfect, but "February" had given her fits. I continued turning pages until I reached the last entry. It had been made on March fourth, the day before Weston's body was found and the search for Betsy Weston and her mother became the city's hottest news story.

Joe poked his head in the door. "The bedroom was a waste. You got anything worth looking at?"

I didn't turn around. "They're alive, Joe."

"Excuse me?"

"Betsy Weston wrote this in her diary the night she disappeared," I said.

Joe crossed the room and knelt beside me, then read the diary entry, written in a child's scrawl with a green crayon: *Tonite I said goodby.*

SEVEN

"Tonight I said goodbye." Joe read it aloud and then raised his eyes and looked at me. "What the hell does that mean?"

"It means she knew she was leaving," I said.

"That's a beautiful thought," he said. "But you don't have much evidence to base it on."

"She wrote something, or drew something, every day this year, Joe. On the night she and her mother disappear, she writes this, and you don't think it means anything?"

He looked at the entry again, then sighed, his eyes thoughtful. "I'm not saying it doesn't mean anything. I'm just wondering how she possibly could have known to write it. Said goodbye to what? Her house or her dad?"

"Or both," I said.

"Keep the book," Joe said. "But don't let the old man see it. The last thing we want is for him to be any more convinced they're alive."

We left the house and checked the garage. A Toyota sport utility vehicle and a Lexus remained, as well as a collection of tools and more toys. Julie Weston and her daughter hadn't left in one of the family cars. But that didn't mean they couldn't have left alive.

We returned to John Weston and gave him the key.

"Find anything helpful?" he asked.

Joe and I exchanged a glance, then Joe said, "Just seeing the home is helpful, Mr. Weston."

He looked at Joe blankly and didn't respond. We left, promising to be in touch. When I pulled out of the driveway he was still sitting on the table. I wondered if he'd be there all day.

"Well," Joe said as I drove, "that wasn't much help. You think they're alive now, because of one sentence written in a little girl's diary. And, while I respect that hunch, it still isn't any help in finding them."

"No," I admitted, "it isn't." I pulled onto Brecksville Road and headed north, back toward the city, following roughly the same path the Cuyahoga River takes as it winds its way toward the heart of downtown and into the Flats. The sun was out, and the digital thermometer on the rearview mirror said it was forty-seven degrees outside—not warm enough for me, but the warmest it had been in months. The winter was still clinging to us, refusing to give in to the spring. It had been a long, nasty one, with nearly a hundred inches of snowfall and consistently low temperatures that felt even colder with the frigid winds that whipped in off the lake. Around the first of March it had begun to wear at me. I was annoyed by the lingering traces of snow now, irate at each forecast of another storm, frustrated with the way the cold air squeezed my lungs on every run.

"Next move?" Joe said, interrupting my thoughts. I took my eyes off the van in front of me briefly and glanced at him, not understanding.

"You spacing out on me?" he said. "What do you think our next move should be?"

I returned my eyes to the road and shrugged. "I don't know. We've got some possibilities now, but no facts, nothing close to hard evidence. Seems to me we need to shake something up a little, see what we can stir up."

"That sounds about right," Joe said. "You've always favored the loose cannon approach in the past."

I smiled. "When in doubt, shoot it out."

"Brilliant slogan." He shook his head. "So, who are we going to shake up? You want to find the Russians, take a bat to their car?"

"Have to save something for tomorrow," I said. "I figured we'd start with Jeremiah Hubbard."

"Take a bat to his car?"

"Only if he refuses to see us."

Joe twisted in the seat, looking to see if I was serious. "You really want to talk to Hubbard today?"

"Why not? He—or his associates, if we want to be anal about it—were paying Weston to do something recently. That's about the only thing close to a fact we have. Might as well take it and run with it."

"You assume he'll be so awed by our deductive abilities that he'll confess ties to the Russian mob and let us make a citizen's arrest?"

"It's hard to say what his reaction will be," I said. "But it's even harder to imagine someone *not* being awed by our deductive abilities."

Joe ran his hand through his short gray hair and let it keep going until it was on the back of his neck. He sighed and kneaded the flesh as if trying to drive out a pain that had lodged there.

"Shit," he said. "It's not like I've got any better ideas. Besides, I've always wanted to meet Hubbard."

"You know where his office is?"

He nodded. "Right downtown. Has a wide window that looks out from the Terminal Tower, or something like that."

"Beautiful. I'm sure he'd be happy to show us the view."

"Man that rich? He's got nothing but free time."

A quick check in the phone book confirmed Joe's memory; Hubbard's offices were in the Terminal Tower downtown. It is unquestionably the city's most famous building. Once the tallest building in the city—and second tallest in the world—it is now dwarfed by the Key Building. The Terminal Tower has a presence the city's other skyscrapers lack, though, regardless of their size. Offices in the building went for exorbitant amounts, and I was sure Hubbard's suite would be among the priciest.

Once downtown, I pulled into the Tower City garage and maneuvered the truck into a parking space that had obviously been designed for something more like a Geo Metro or a Honda Civic. Then we headed into the building. We found a directory in the lobby and determined the offices of Jeremiah Hubbard Enterprises were located on the thirty-second floor of the fifty-two-story building.

"Gosh," Joe said, "I guess we should just run the stairs, huh?"

The elevator door opened with a chime, and I shrugged. "As long as the elevator's right here, we might as well take it."

We rode the elevator up, then walked down the corridor until we located Hubbard's suite. I opened the outer door, and we stepped into an office with plush carpets, dark walnut furniture, and ornate brass lamps. A few paintings hung on the walls, and a small stone fountain bubbled softly to my left. The furniture and décor alone probably cost about what Joe and I would pay in ten years of rent. And it was only the secretary's office.

An attractive, middle-aged blond woman looked up from her computer and smiled at us. She was wearing a phone headset, speaking to someone about appointments, and typing furiously but looked completely nonchalant. Multitasking at its finest. She lifted one hand from the keyboard and held up a finger to indicate she'd be with us in just a minute, then returned to her phone conversation and typing. Joe and I settled into a pair of burgundy leather armchairs that matched the walnut furniture nicely.

"This isn't bad," I said. "I mean, sure, there's not the nostalgia of our office with the stadium seats, but other than that it's pretty decent."

"Maybe we should consider relocating," Joe said.

"Maybe."

The secretary finished her conversation, hit a button on the phone to disconnect her headset, and looked up at us once again.

"I apologize for the wait," she said. "Do you gentlemen have an appointment?"

"No," Joe said. "We were hoping to make a quick drop-in. It shouldn't take long."

"I see. And whom do you wish to drop in on?"

"Jeremiah Hubbard," Joe said.

She gave us a gentle, polite smile. It was the kind of smile you might give a four-year-old if he said he wanted to fly an airplane. "I'm sorry," she said. "Mr. Hubbard does not accept any meetings without an appointment. He's an exceptionally busy man."

"Oh, come on," I said, "he must get tired of counting all that money. He'd probably love the diversion."

"Mr. Hubbard will only accept diversions if they make an appointment beforehand," the secretary said, keeping her smile. She had a great mouth—full but not overly prominent lips, and nice white teeth.

I laughed. "Well, could you at least ask him? I think he might be more inclined to talk to us than you'd guess. Tell him we're here to talk about Wayne Weston."

She raised her eyebrows slightly. Weston's story had been all over the news for days, and the use of his name was probably going to raise quite a few eyebrows. I supposed I'd have to get used to it.

"Wayne Weston," she said. "I see. One moment, please."

She hit a few more buttons on the phone and turned her head slightly, then spoke softly for a few seconds and disconnected again. "Mr. Hubbard will be happy to meet with you," she announced. "Follow me, please."

I looked at Joe, and now I raised *my* eyebrows. I hadn't expected it would be quite that easy. The secretary stepped out from behind the desk and led us down another corridor, and I watched the movement of her hips and legs under the pretty-but-professional blue dress she was wearing. She seemed to be putting a little extra motion into the hips. I attempted to kid myself into believing it was for my benefit.

We passed a few doors and then the hall ended in a set of double doors with no nameplate. This would be Hubbard's office. Only he would warrant double doors, and only he would be important enough not to require a nameplate. She pushed open one of the doors and stepped aside, ushering us through.

I walked past her and into an office that came closer to taking my breath away than any office should. It wasn't as spacious as I'd expected, but it was still large enough for a game of touch football. The furniture was more of the burgundy leather and dark walnut, and the room was tastefully decorated, but it was the window that occupied all my attention. A tall span of glass shaped like the top half of an oval looked out on the city below us, and the view was amazing. I could see the War Memorial fountain thirty-two floors below, the sun making it sparkle. I wanted to walk over to the window and look down, spend a few minutes admiring the sights, but then Jeremiah Hubbard rose from behind his massive walnut desk and it was clear we were no longer supposed to find the view the most impressive thing in the room.

"Gentlemen," he said, walking around the desk and offering his hand as the secretary shut the door softly behind us.

Hubbard stood tall in a navy blue suit, his spine rigid, his shoulders back, and his chin held up a bit, but I could tell that beneath the carefully tailored clothes his upper body was softer and pudgier than most people would guess. His hair was something else—a collection of gentle, perfectly contoured white curls that reminded me of a well-trimmed version of a colonial powdered wig. The skin of his face was pressed tight against the bone, his lips narrow and drawn, pulling back a bit at the corners as if his face were stretched just a little too tight. Plastic surgery, probably, designed to keep him from developing a double chin in his advancing years. He wasn't a strikingly handsome man, but his bearing of complete and total assurance—the confidence that showed in his eyes and in every movement—would set him apart in a crowd.

"Lincoln Perry," I said, shaking his hand. "It's nice to meet you, sir. My partner, Joe Pritchard."

He nodded without speaking and shook Joe's hand, then

pivoted smoothly on his heel and returned to his desk. He settled into the big executive's chair with a paternal sigh, and I had the feeling we were about to be chastised for daring to barge into his office and waste his precious time. Time, as they say, is money, and Jeremiah Hubbard loved his money.

"Well," he said, removing his glasses and setting them on the desk, "what's on your minds?"

Joe looked at me, and I nodded for him to go ahead with it. "We'd like to speak with you about Wayne Weston," he said.

Hubbard ran the tip of his tongue over his thin lips and frowned. "Would this be the same Weston who has dominated local news coverage recently?"

"The very one," Joe said.

Hubbard nodded slowly, then leaned back in his chair and stared at us. After about ten seconds of silence he raised his eyebrows and rolled his hand slightly, telling Joe to continue.

"Did you know Mr. Weston?" Joe asked.

"Why is that a matter of your concern?"

"We have reason to believe he was working for you, Mr. Hubbard," Joe said. "We were hoping you could tell us a little about that."

"Why do you think he was working for me?"

"Because he recently cashed five checks from companies affiliated with you, and executives at these companies claim to have no association with the man."

"Many companies are affiliated with me, Mr. Pritchard."

"I understand that, sir. What I'm asking you is whether you ever employed Wayne Weston," Joe said bluntly.

Hubbard laid his hands on the desk, laced his fingers together, and leaned forward. "If I had employed an individual like Mr. Weston, it would seem to be for a confidential and possibly sensitive matter, wouldn't it?"

"We have no intention of prying into your personal affairs. However, we have been asked to investigate the possibility that Mr. Weston was murdered, and to do that effectively we must look into his recent cases. Any information pertaining to you will be kept confidential," Joe told him. "We just need to know what he was working on."

"Who employed you for this?"

"Weston's father."

Hubbard's face changed slightly at that. It was an almost imperceptible relaxation—a slight lessening of his scowl, an easing of the creases in his face. The news seemed to reassure him, though. I wondered who he thought we might be working for, and why he preferred to hear it was Wayne Weston's father.

"Gentlemen," he said, "I'm afraid I simply can't be of any help to you."

Joe nodded. "We respect that decision, Mr. Hubbard. However, I do want to be sure you're aware that we're going to have to pursue this angle, regardless of your cooperation."

The scowl that had lessened when Joe told him we were working for John Weston returned now.

"How much will you make from this case?" he asked. "How much money will you earn for harassing me and my associates?"

Joe frowned. "We have no intention of harassing anyone, sir. But we've been hired to look into Wayne Weston's recent dealings, and if it appears those dealings involved you, then we'll have to look into them."

"How much money?" Hubbard repeated.

"I don't know," Joe said. "That depends how long we're on the case. Why does it matter?"

"Will it be more than twenty thousand?"

Joe glanced at me and smiled slightly. "No, it won't be more than that."

"I'll give you twenty thousand, then," Hubbard said. "Twenty thousand dollars just to stay the hell away from me and my business associates."

I stared at him. We'd been in the office for roughly two minutes, asked only a few questions, and he was willing to pay us *twenty thousand dollars* to leave him alone?

"With all due respect," Joe said, "I don't understand why you're making that offer, sir."

Hubbard waved his hand at Joe, dismissing the question. "I'm a very busy man with many more important considerations than dealing with you and your questions," he said. "I have enough sources of stress as it is. It's worth it to me to keep you away and out of my affairs. Twenty thousand to me is the same as ten dollars to you." He paused and looked at us contemptuously. "Well, maybe ten cents."

I laughed softly, and Joe shook his head. "No one's tried to buy us off a case before," he said, "but I'm afraid we're going to have to turn that down. We already have a client, and we promised to do the best job we can for him. To accept your offer would be to fail him, and I have no intention of doing that."

Hubbard's scowl deepened, but he made a show of shrugging, trying to appear as indifferent as possible, like he'd simply offered us coffee and we'd turned him down because we didn't want the caffeine.

Joe and I looked at each other, then back at Hubbard. "Mr. Hubbard," I said, "we're in the business of finding things out. If Weston worked for you, we're going to find that out. We're going to find out what he did, when he did it, and why he did it. You can save everyone the hassle and tell us now, or you can send us on our way. We really don't care. But don't think for even one minute that stonewalling us is going to stop anything. It's just going to delay it."

It was the first time I had spoken since we shook hands, and Hubbard turned to me with distaste and aggression. It was the type of look I'd seen exchanged between men in bars in the past, and it had generally been followed quickly by the snap of a pool cue or the jolt of a punch. It was the look of a brawler, and coming here, in Hubbard's elegant office, from a man who displayed such refined manners, it seemed starkly out of place.

"You people disgust me," he said, and his voice was lower now, gravelly and grinding, like a pencil sharpener too full of shavings. "You spend your lives in the dirt. You build a career out of it, searching out secrets, peeping through windows, rooting through personal and private affairs. You have no honor, because your career, the very means of your existence, demands that you forfeit your honor so you might tarnish another man's. And that's fine with you. You don't make much money, but that's fine with you, too, because you get such satisfaction from the work, such satisfaction from wreaking havoc in the lives of others, for knowing the best manner in which to pry, provoke, pester, and harass. You," Hubbard said, his voice shaking with fury, "make me sick."

I gave a low whistle, looked at Joe, and shook my head. "I knew we were low-class scum, but I didn't realize we were *that* bad."

"Get out of my office," Hubbard said.

"You ever hear of a guy named Dainius Belov?" I asked.

His head canted sharply, and then he took a breath and smoothed his tie, frowning as if he were surprised and disappointed by his reaction, like maybe my question had tugged on a part of his brain he'd been determined to leave unresponsive during this conversation.

"If you have any further questions, I will refer you to my attorney, Mr. Richard Douglass," he said in a monotone.

"Dicky D.," I said. "How's the old boy doing these days?"

"Leave," Hubbard said emphatically.

"Dicky D.?" Joe asked me.

"I was trying not to look too intimidated," I said in a theatrical whisper. "Did it work?"

"No."

We got to our feet, and Joe turned back to him. "I'm going to leave you our number," he said. "Just in case you change your mind."

"That won't happen," Hubbard said.

"Nevertheless," Joe said, "I'd feel better knowing that you have it. Do you have a piece of paper I can write it on?"

"I have our business card with me," I offered.

Joe shook his head and looked annoyed. "I want to leave Mr. Hubbard my home phone number. He's important."

"I asked you to leave," Hubbard said. "Must I call security?"

"Sir, if you just give me a piece of paper so I can write my number on it, we'll be on our way," Joe said, stepping over to the desk and helping himself to a blank sheet, which he folded and tore in half. He wrote his name and number down quickly, then handed it to Hubbard. "In case you reconsider."

"Get out," Hubbard commanded.

We left. As I stepped into the hall, Hubbard yelled at me to shut his door. I left it open and followed Joe into the lobby. The good-looking secretary smiled at us.

"That was pretty quick," she said.

"We've got important business matters to attend to," I said. "We really can't afford to let Hubbard waste more of our time."

I was halfway through the door when Joe stopped short, and I almost ran into his back. He turned back to the secretary.

"Excuse me," he said. "Do you know what Mr. Hubbard's middle name is?"

"Elisha," she answered.

"Jeremiah Elisha," he said, closing the door behind us. "Catchy."

When we were back in the elevator I said, "Shrewd question, detective. I'd say Hubbard wrote the thank-you note, eh?"

Joe handed me a half-scrap of paper. It was the remains of the piece he'd written his number on before tearing it in two. It was also a perfect match to the stationery we'd found in Weston's house.

"Nice," I said. "Good eyes."

"Would be nice if it meant anything. Too bad it doesn't. The note doesn't say shit, and we'd already assumed it was from Hubbard."

We were halfway to the truck before we spoke again. I think we'd both half expected Hubbard to send security guards to cuff us and drag us back upstairs so I would shut his door.

"Friendly guy," Joe said. "I was expecting him to be a little standoffish, what with all that money, you know? But he's quite down-to-earth."

"Down-to-earth," I agreed. "Of course, we're down in the dirt, reveling in our filthy work."

Joe laughed. "That was a nice spiel. All the stuff about how we disgust him, how we make him sick? Priceless."

"We appeared to generate a lot of passion from him. Seems strange for a man who's got nothing to hide to get so passionate about our conversation."

"Almost as strange as offering us twenty grand to back off."

"Twenty grand's a lot of money," I said, using the keyless entry device to unlock the truck door for Joe. "Probably foolish of us not to take it. As a matter of fact, I have to say I resent you making that call without even pausing to discuss it."

"Very rude of me," Joe said, dropping into his seat as I started the engine and began to back out. "I don't know where I get off making such decisions single-handedly. But, if it makes you feel any better, we probably run a much higher risk of getting shot if we keep pushing on this case."

"That does help," I said. "I mean, sure, twenty grand would be nice, but it can't match the adrenaline rush you get from gun battles with the Russian mob. Shall we look them up next?"

"We'll look *for* them. I don't think we need any dialogue exchange with them just yet."

"Sounds good, grandpa. Don't want to rush you."

I spent the next five minutes maneuvering the truck out of the parking space. It was a small space to begin with, and by the time we returned a van had parked behind me, making it even tighter. I'd back up about ten inches, cut the wheel, pull forward, cut the wheel again, and throw it in reverse to gain another ten inches. Joe groaned.

"We live in the city," he said. "You've always lived in the city. So why do you feel the need to have this monstrosity? You have some sort of cowboy identity crisis? You want I should buy you some boots and a hat, maybe some spurs? Start calling you 'podnuh'?"

"Joe," I said, "you drive a Taurus. So shut the hell up, stick your head out the window, and let me know if I've got a few inches to spare on that side."

EIGHT

Vladimir Rakic and Alexei Krashakov, it turned out, lived in what was basically my old neighborhood. I'd grown up on a narrow street off Clark Avenue, and Rakic and Krashakov shared a two-decker about twelve blocks south. I'd never known anyone who lived in that house, but I'd passed it almost daily as a kid. Somehow, knowing they now inhabited my childhood territory made me like them even less.

Joe and I cruised the block a few times before a parking spot offering a good vantage point opened up. The sun was still out, and we had to park facing into it, squinting against the light, but it was the best we could do. Joe had insisted we take his Taurus; he claimed my truck would stand out as unfamiliar to the neighbors. I tried to argue that no car screamed "undercover cop" quite like a Taurus, but he ignored me.

We parked and settled in for the wait. There hadn't been any cars in the driveway when we drove past, and none were parked at the curb in front of the home, so it appeared the Russians were out on the town. The two-decker was painted a light blue that was turning gray from weathering, but it was in better shape than most on the block. The house was the same style as many others in the neighborhood, and I recalled from past visits to such homes that on each level there were two bedrooms, a small kitchen, a dining room, one tiny bathroom, and a living room. There would probably also be a dank cellar and an attic with low ceilings.

Joe looked around sourly. "This neighborhood's gone to hell. When I was a rookie, this actually wasn't a bad street. Nobody cares about their own home anymore."

"I grew up around here," I said.

He stopped drumming his fingers on the steering wheel and pointed at me. "That's right. I'd forgotten that. You know any of the neighbors? Someone who could give us some good dirt on the Russians, maybe?"

I shook my head. "Not this far south."

We sat and waited. I was thankful the temperature had crawled a little higher than in recent days, because we had to keep the engine off to avoid attention, and that meant no heater. The street was quiet. Behind us, on Clark, the traffic was thick, but on the little side street only a few cars passed. Once a man in an old military parka with several days' worth of stubble on his face stumbled down the sidewalk and glanced in the car, saw us, muttered something, and crossed to the other side. He was carrying a paper bag in his left hand, and I saw him lift it to his lips as he neared the corner.

"Told you this car wasn't discreet," I said. "He thought we were cops."

"Guy like that? Probably thinks every third car on the street is a cop."

"What do you think was in the bag? Southern Comfort?"

"Old Grand-Dad," Joe said confidently. "No doubt about it."

An hour passed, and then the monotony was broken by the arrival of the mailman. He moved slowly from house to house, wincing as he took the steps, as if maybe the years and the weight of the mailbag had taken a toll on his back.

"Think we should check their mail?" Joe asked. "See if maybe there's a letter from Hubbard in the box?"

"Don't see what it would hurt."

"It'd hurt if one of them *is* in the house, or they drive in while you're up on the porch."

"I like how smoothly you do that."

"Do what?" Joe said, eyes wide, the picture of innocence.

"Make it so I'm the one who's going up on the porch."

He smiled and spread his hands. "Hey, you're the one who's so anxious for action with these guys. I'd hate to stand in your way."

I stepped out of the car and walked down the sidewalk, head down, hands in my pockets. Just another neighborhood guy out for a stroll. I needed the bottle wrapped in the paper bag, though, to blend in better.

The house was about two hundred feet from where we'd parked. No one seemed to notice me, and the only car that passed didn't slow down. I took the four steps up to the porch, the dried, flaking paint crackling beneath my shoes. The two windows facing the porch were dusty, and inside it was dark. A heavy-duty steel storm door protected the wooden front door. The old tin mailbox was fastened to the wall beside the door. I lifted the lid with my finger and slipped the contents out. Four envelopes; four pieces of junk mail. A wasted trip. I dropped them back into the box and pulled on the handle of the storm door. It was locked. I stepped up to the window, put my face close to the glass, and shielded my eyes with my hand, trying to make out the interior. Tires crunched on the street behind me, and I turned to see a black Lincoln Navigator pulling into the driveway.

Two men sat inside, and neither looked particularly friendly. They opened the doors and stepped out of the vehicle, watching me carefully. The driver was a few inches shorter than me but thick, with dark hair, pale skin, and a jutting jaw. He had a heavy blue jacket on, and as he walked around the Navigator he pulled the zipper down, allowing him to reach inside the coat if he wanted to. The passenger was taller, with very broad shoulders and blond hair. His nose was large and slightly hooked, and his cheekbones and jaw were clearly defined and solid, giving a quality of strength to his face.

I remained on the porch, a smile fixed on my face, but I didn't speak. They approached slowly, then walked up the steps and stood in front of me, spaced so they blocked the steps completely.

"Children are dying," I said.

They exchanged a glance. Confused. The shorter one said, "What do you talk about?" His accent was thick.

"AIDS," I said casually. "Children are dying, now, gentlemen. Not just adults. Children. Think about that. Then think about what you've done to help the problem." I watched them as they stared at me. "It's okay, gentlemen. Not many of us are doing our share to combat the disease. That doesn't mean it's too late to step in and do your part, though."

The taller, blond one spoke now. "You want money?" His accent wasn't nearly as heavy as his companion's, but he spoke in a clipped, careful voice that made it clear English was his second language.

I shook my head. "We don't want money. We want a cure."

He nodded. "What group are you for?"

I cleared my throat. "I, uh, represent EAT."

He frowned. "Eat?"

"That's right. E-A-T. It stands for Eliminate AIDS Today. That's what our goal is, gentlemen. Surely you agree that it's an important one."

He studied me, and his eyes narrowed. "You have some literature for your group? A brochure, perhaps?" His careful, stilted pronunciation reminded me of a computerized answering machine.

I shook my head. "I don't come to you with a sales pitch, I come to you with a cause. Are you unaware of AIDS, sir? Do you really need a paper filled with statistics to make the danger real?" I tried to make my tone somewhat hostile, to put him back on his heels and keep him from getting too inquisitive.

He looked at me with cold, calculating eyes, like a man

studying cuts of meat in a butcher shop. I met his stare, and as I did I was sure he didn't believe a word of my story.

"I'm harmless," I said.

"You want money?" he repeated.

I smiled. "If you'd be willing to give, we'd be willing to accept. Each dollar is a small step toward a cure. Each small step toward a cure is another life saved. Possibly another child's life."

He reached into the back pocket of his black slacks and withdrew a thick wad of bills held in place by a gold money clip. The clip bore a military insignia, but his hand kept me from seeing it clearly. He slipped a twenty from the roll of bills and handed it to me.

"Twenty small steps, then," he said, and the short man laughed.

"Thank you, sir," I said. "You couldn't do anything better with your money."

"Sure," he said, then moved out of the way to let me pass. I walked down the steps and back up the sidewalk, whistling and trying not to look back, trying not to appear aware of the way they stood on the porch and watched until I was out of sight.

Joe's Taurus was gone. I kept walking up the street, toward the corner. They were probably wondering why I wasn't approaching other homes. Maybe they were coming after me now to ask me about it. Or break my legs.

A car slowed behind me. Joe. I stepped off the sidewalk and pulled open the passenger door, then dropped into the seat and said, "Drive."

He turned onto Clark Avenue, and I looked in the rearview mirror. The Russians' house was out of sight now, but at least they weren't watching from the sidewalk.

"Great timing I've got," I said. "We sat in the car for, what, two hours and they didn't come home? Then I'm on the porch for twenty seconds and they pull in."

"I thought about using the horn, but I decided it was pointless," Joe said. "You wouldn't have had time to get out of sight anyhow, and it would've attracted attention to me."

He pulled into a gas station parking lot and stopped the car. "So, what happened?"

I told him, and when I was finished he was laughing so hard he was resting his red face on the steering wheel.

"You took twenty dollars from them," he said, struggling for breath. "That's amazing, LP. Children are dying? That's the first thing you can think of to say?"

I shrugged. "Hey, it worked."

"I guess."

"I don't think the big guy believed me, though." I thought about it, remembered those calculating, flat eyes, and shook my head. "I'm sure he didn't. He knew I was lying, but he didn't know why, so he let it go."

"Wasn't he the one that gave you the twenty?"

"Yeah, but I still don't think he was fooled."

Joe wiped at his eyes and took a deep breath. "What a stunt," he said. "I was afraid you'd confront them about Ambrose's car and I'd have to rescue your ass. Instead you give them a speech about dying children and fleece them for a twenty." He laughed again, then started the car and drove us back to the same street. "I've got something to show you," he said. "I wanted to hear your story first, and I thought it would probably be a good idea to get you out of sight, but you'll be interested in this."

He made a left onto the Russians' street and drove down it slowly. "Check out the green Oldsmobile on your side." He drove past it, and I kept my eyes straight ahead but got a good look at the car in the side-view mirror. Joe turned the corner and started to circle the block again.

"You see him?"

I nodded. "Guy sitting in the front, looked like he was watching the same house we've been watching."

"You got it. He came in with the Russians but was hanging back a little. He circled the block once and picked a parking spot with a good view of the house, just like we did. Apparently we're not their only secret admirers."

"You get a plate number?"

He gave me a sour look. "Did I get a plate number? Who

do you think you're talking to? I got the plate number, and I took about six photographs of the car itself, as well as the Navigator the Russians drove."

"My mistake."

"Uh-huh. Well, we've got two of the Russians, and one car for them. Who are we missing?"

"Malaknik, I think. Amy said he lives on the east side."

"Want to go have a look at him, or should we stay and watch these boys a little longer? Apparently, it's a better show than we thought, because we're not the only audience."

I looked at the clock and saw it was approaching five. "You said you got photographs of the Navigator?" He nodded. "Well, let's get back to the office, then. I want to e-mail that photograph to Amy and see if it's the same car she saw. Then we can run out to Brecksville and check with the neighbors. We'll worry about Malaknik tomorrow."

Back at the office Joe uploaded the photographs from his digital camera to the computer. They were pretty decent shots, showing a good angle of the cars as well as shots with a tight zoom on each license plate. The green Oldsmobile had a South Carolina plate.

"He's come a long way to watch the Russians," I said to Joe. "Must be about something important."

"The car's come a long way," Joe said. "Doesn't mean the driver came with it."

Once the photographs had been uploaded, I e-mailed them to Amy, and Joe printed out a few copies. Then we returned to Brecksville.

We spent half an hour combing houses. Everyone regarded us with suspicion, and everyone denied having seen the Navigator. After the fourth house, Joe began showing them photographs of the green Oldsmobile, too.

"Why not?" he told me. "As long as we've got the photographs, it doesn't hurt to ask."

It didn't hurt. Five houses later, a woman who lived opposite the Westons and a few houses down nodded her head as soon as she saw the Oldsmobile.

"Well, sure," she said. "He's a police officer."

"A police officer?" Joe said.

She smiled. "Yes. He came around yesterday, asking about the same type of questions as you. Wanted to know what cars we'd noticed, all that type of thing. We really didn't have anything to tell him, though." She looked at us sadly. "It's so tragic. The little girl was so sweet."

"This officer," I said, "did he give you his name?"

She squinted, trying to remember. "Davis, maybe? Davidson? Something like that. He had a badge, though. He showed it to me."

We thanked her and walked back down the driveway. Joe kicked at a few pebbles in the street, and we stood with our backs to the house.

"No Cleveland cops are driving little Oldsmobiles," he said. "It's an Alero, for crying out loud. That's not a department-issued car. No antennas on it, even."

"You know of any detective named Davis or Davidson?"

"Nope."

"Me neither. Looks like we've got a fake."

He nodded and gazed back across the street, at the Westons' house. "What we've got is an unknown third party," he said. "Could be significant."

We finished up the block and talked to two more neighbors who'd been visited by "Detective Davis" the previous day. They'd all seen a badge, but he hadn't been in uniform, and he hadn't been one of the cops they'd talked to in the early days of the investigation.

It was dark by the time we left. Joe wanted dinner, but I made him drive back to the office first. I wanted to call Amy and ask if she'd seen the photographs. It was late, but Amy typically went to work late in the morning and stayed until the early evening hours. I caught her at her desk.

"That's the SUV," she said immediately.

"You're sure?"

"Absolutely. Those fancy alloy wheels stand out." I could hear keys clicking on her keyboard as she typed furiously. "You have any idea what their tie to Weston is yet?"

"No, but I do have another favor to ask."

"I don't know, Lincoln. My car's still in the body shop from the last favor I did you."

"Okay," I said casually. "That's fine. I don't blame you. Well, I'd better be going, but thanks for checking the photographs."

"Wait, wait, wait," she said, and I grinned. "I was just giving you a hard time, Perry, don't freak out about it. What do you need me to do?"

"You know who Jeremiah Hubbard is?" I asked.

"Of course."

"Good. I want to know everything he's been up to in the last six months. He's in the paper pretty regularly, but I want to know why, when, and who he was involved with."

The typing on her end of the line stopped. "You think Hubbard's got something to do with Weston?"

"He might."

"Lincoln," she said, "you've *got* to give me this story."

I sighed. "Amy, we've been over this a thousand times. It would be very bad for business if I kept turning confidential cases over to you. I know you want a good story, but I can't do that."

"Bastard. Oh, well. As long as you keep me updated." The typing resumed again. "I'll check it out and get back to you."

As I hung up someone rapped loudly on the glass panel of the door with his knuckles, a sound like hail on a window. Joe and I looked at each other and frowned. We weren't used to receiving drop-in clients, and it was late in the day.

"Come in," Joe said. The door opened and Detectives Swanders and Kraus stepped inside, accompanied by a third man I didn't recognize. He was of average height, with a slim build and neat, carefully parted hair that looked like he spent a lot of time on it. His clothes were well tailored and unwrinkled. It was all I needed to see to know he wasn't a cop. The briefcase in his left hand confirmed it.

"Fellas," Swanders said, nodding at us. He was one of those rare guys who could say "fellas" as a greeting without making you wince.

"Swanders," Joe said, nodding back at him. "Kraus. How you boys doing?"

"Doing fine," Kraus said, dropping onto one of the stadium seats without waiting for an invitation to sit. Swanders joined him, but the stranger stayed on his feet, crossing the office with a purposeful stride that made me think he was used to being the dominant force in most rooms. He reached in his pocket as he neared the desk, withdrew a slim leather case, snapped it open, and held it out for us to see. There was a badge on the left side and an identification card encased in plastic on the right. Joe pushed himself up on his elbows to get a better look but kept his feet on the desk.

"FBI," he said. "Heavens. We're way out of our league now."

The stranger tilted the badge in my direction, and I looked at the name on the identification card. THADDEUS CODY, it read, SPECIAL AGENT, FEDERAL BUREAU OF INVESTIGATION.

"Thaddeus," I said. "No shit? I bet you resent the hell out of your parents, don't you?"

He gave a tight smile. "Call me Thad," he said. "Or Agent Cody."

He put the leather case back in his pocket and looked from Joe to me as if expecting further reaction. A look at our faces told him he wasn't going to get it, so he nodded and sat down.

"You gentlemen been in business long?" he asked, crossing his legs at the ankles after smoothing the crease in his slacks.

"Same office for nineteen years," Joe said.

Cody raised one eyebrow. "Really?"

"Uh-huh."

Cody glanced at Swanders and then said, "What's the point of lying to me, Mr. Pritchard? You're not exactly getting off to a great start."

Joe dropped his feet to the floor and pulled his chair up to the desk. "What's the point of asking questions you already know the answers to, Agent Cody? And I don't give much of a damn what kind of start we get off to, considering you weren't asked to come here. If you've got something to talk to us about, why don't you start talking? Otherwise, I'll be on my way to get some dinner. It's late, and I'm a grumpy old man who likes his food."

Swanders snorted and turned to Cody. "Told you."

"Told him what?" I asked.

"Told him you fellas might be difficult just because you feel like it."

I grinned at him. "That's the beauty of being self-employed."

Cody cleared his throat and gave us a pained expression, as if maybe he'd picked up a splinter from the stadium seat. "I apologize, gentlemen." He nodded at Joe. "There was no need for me to start off by asking questions I already know the answers to. And, yes, I've got something to talk to you about."

"Our rates are pretty reasonable," I said. "But if you're wanting us to crack a challenging case that has you FBI boys stumped, the retainer fee is going to be sizable. We run the risk of damaging our reputation by hanging out with Bureau boneheads."

Cody pointed his index finger at me and opened his mouth to snap off a quick retort but then stopped himself. He tucked the finger back into his fist and dropped his hand to his lap, then turned his head to the ceiling and exhaled heavily, like he was releasing tension and coming to peace with himself before assuming a yoga position. I thought for a minute he might roll right onto the floor, stand on his head, maybe, or strike a swan pose. He kept his eyes on the ceiling for a few seconds and then rolled his head back down, smiling now.

"I'll tell you what," he said. "How about we put a spotlight on you two, give you ten, maybe fifteen minutes for the comedy routines? You can take shots at my employer, my wife, my mother, whatever. When you've completed the first act, I'll applaud real politely, and then maybe we can get down to business."

Kraus laughed, and Joe shrugged. "Let's just get down to business, Cody."

He nodded, then leaned down and opened his briefcase. He withdrew a manila folder and took four eight-by-ten black-and-white photographs from it. He spread them on the desk, facing us. I immediately recognized two of the men in the pictures; they were Rakic and Krashakov, the Russians I'd spoken with earlier in the day. The other two I didn't know. One was a heavyset man with a thick mustache, fleshy chin, and small dark eyes. The other was younger, with dark hair, a goatee, and a nasty scar across his left temple.

"Recognize them?" Cody asked.

I nodded. "These two," I said, pointing at Rakic and Krashakov. "I don't know the others, though."

Cody leaned back in his chair and studied us. "How did you two connect those men to Wayne Weston?"

"Who says we did?" I said.

He sighed. "Gentlemen, I thought we were past this stage."

I looked at Joe, and he nodded, indicating that I was free to talk. We were being paid to bring the case to a conclusion, and the FBI had resources that could help us do that. There was no sense in stonewalling them or acting like we were competing with them.

"April Sortigan," I said, looking at Kraus. "She turned out not to be such a dead end after all. Sortigan told me Weston had asked her to do background checks on three men. She gave me the names, and we started to check them out ourselves. From what I've gathered so far, they're foot soldiers for the Russian mob."

"Who told you that?" Cody said.

"We're investigators," I answered. "We investigated. Now, do you want to tell us what this is all about?"

He nodded. "The Russian mafia in this city—and in the rest of the country—is growing," he said. "It's the most powerful organized crime syndicate in the world; nothing else even comes close. They have ties to eighty percent of the banks in Russia, so money laundering is no problem, and now they're spreading their claws across the globe. Cleveland is one of those new destinations."

He jabbed his finger at the man with the fleshy face and the mustache. "That is Dainius Belov. He's the don of the Russian mob in this city, and it doesn't pay to underestimate his power. He's got more weight than any of the Italian gangsters in this city ever dreamed of." He pointed at the photograph of Krashakov. "Alexei Krashakov is one of Belov's lieutenants. Rakic and Malaknik work closely with him. They're a little too wild for Belov's liking, so their power is limited, but they're busy boys. They've got ties to heroin, cocaine, insurance scams, prostitution, illegal weapons trafficking—you name it, they're involved." Cody's voice had taken on a haggard, weary tone, and I thought he'd probably spent too many hours poring over photographs of these guys, looking for a way to bring them down.

"We're particularly interested in the weapons trafficking," he said. "These guys are moving some serious contraband through the city, and we intend to stop it. Assault rifles, machine guns, and hell, even missiles. And they're very good at it. They're very good at all of it. Because they're pros. Half of Belov's boys were special forces soldiers in Afghanistan in the eighties. Some of them even have ties to the KGB. We've got a task force working on them, a joint effort between Bureau agents and CPD detectives." He sighed. "And, so far, I'll admit that we're not having much success."

"How's Wayne Weston involved?" Joe said.

Cody slid the photographs together and tapped them on the desk, straightening their edges before returning them to the manila folder.

"We've had wiretaps on these guys for months," he said. "Some of them we've had for years. A week before Wayne Weston was murdered, his name was heard in one of our taped conversations. The Russians speak guardedly on the phone, and the context of the remark was hard for us to distinguish. However, it appeared they found Weston to be a problem, or a nuisance, that's for sure. A few days later, he was dead, and his family was gone."

"And you think they're behind it," Joe said.

He nodded. "We're almost sure of it. We just need to prove it."

"Any idea how they're connected?" I asked.

Cody shook his head. "Not yet. We were prepared to open a preliminary investigation into Mr. Weston after his name came up on our wiretaps. Then he was killed, and it became a more urgent matter."

"Then he was killed," I echoed, and looked at Swanders and Kraus. "So you no longer believe Weston was a suicide?" They didn't respond, and I asked, "Did you *ever* believe he was a suicide?"

"Don't blame them," Cody said. "The initial investigation of the scene made it look like suicide was probable. Then we got wind of it and stepped in to, um, aid the investigation. The police were asked to stick with the suicide story for a while to keep the Russians relaxed."

I pointed at Swanders. "So the gambling angle was bullshit from the beginning, eh?"

He shrugged, and Kraus grinned. "Hope you didn't waste too much time with that," he said.

"Wasted just enough," Joe said dryly. "So why put us in the loop now? Because we're not quite as stupid as you'd hoped?"

Cody smiled. "I wouldn't have phrased it like that, but, basically, you're right. We were content to let you chase whatever leads you had as long as you didn't get in our way. But when you showed up on Rakic's front porch this afternoon, we realized we couldn't let this continue."

"You're watching the house?" I said. He nodded, and I said, "The green Oldsmobile, right? With the South Carolina plate?"

Cody raised his eyebrows and shook his head slowly. "We don't have anyone in vehicle surveillance."

"Oh, come on," I said.

"No, really," he answered. "I won't disclose the location of our surveillance team, but we don't have anyone in a car."

I looked at Joe. "That means they rented a house," I said. "These Russians are more important than we thought."

"What's this car you were talking about?" Swanders asked. "Someone else was watching the house?"

"And talking to the neighbors," I said. "Flashing a badge and saying he was a cop. Called himself Detective Davis."

"You kidding me?" Swanders sat up, not happy about this at all. "Some asshole is talking to those neighbors and pretending he's one of us? Who the hell is he?"

I shrugged. "If he's not FBI, and he's not a cop, it would probably be worth finding out."

"Did you get a good look at the car?" Cody asked.

Joe nodded. "I've got the plate number and some photographs. I assume your surveillance team will have him, too."

"I'll ask about it," Cody said. "Mind if I use your phone?"

Joe slid it across the desk to him, and Cody called someone and asked about the green car. He nodded grimly and hung up.

"They saw it," he said, "but they said it's gone now. They've got the plate number, and I told them to run a check on it. Apparently he was on the street for about an hour and then left. Never got out of the car." He chewed on his lip and stared at the phone. "I don't like this."

We didn't speak for a few seconds, and then he shook his head and grunted, tearing his thoughts away from the phony cop and bringing them back to us.

"Now, would you tell us what happened between you and Rakic and Krashakov today, Mr. Perry?"

I told them. When I finished the story, Cody looked at Swanders, a question in his eyes, like maybe he thought—or hoped—I might be making it up just to mess with him. Swanders shook his head and sighed.

"You pretended to be going door to door for charity?" Cody said.

"You took twenty dollars from them?" Swanders said.

"For AIDS research?" Kraus said.

"Yes," I said.

"I suppose," Cody said eventually, "it could be much worse." It was the type of statement you might hear from a man who'd just been told his cancer was fatal only in ninety percent of its occurrences. "I'm not happy with that interaction, but it could have been worse."

"It could have been avoided easily enough," I said. "If Swanders and Kraus had been straight with us in the beginning, we wouldn't be having this conversation."

"Hey," Kraus said, "the FBI's been calling the shots here. They told us to blow you off, so we blew you off. Nothing personal."

"It's nothing personal," Cody agreed. "But we needed this to be quiet. And now that you're involved, we can't allow you to jeopardize this investigation."

"So you plan to order us off the case?" Joe asked.

Cody frowned. "I'm not ordering you off the case. I'm just asking you to avoid engaging these men. We want them to be relaxed. The more relaxed they are, the more likely they are to make a mistake. And then we've got them."

"Not to be a wet blanket," Joe said, "but it doesn't sound like you've got shit."

The frown remained on Cody's face. "We don't have much," he said, "but we plan to change that. For now, we're concerned with Wayne Weston. Our investigators haven't been able to find any sign that the man was a legitimate private investigator. He was licensed with the state, of course, but there's no indication he ever accepted clients. We've found numerous stories of clients who went to other agencies in town after being turned down by Weston."

"You've got no idea who he was working for?" Joe asked.

"None. Do you?"

Joe's eyes flitted in my direction briefly, and then he nodded. "Jeremiah Hubbard."

"Jeremiah Hubbard?" Cody echoed in astonishment.

Joe explained what we knew, including the details of our visit with Hubbard, as well as the checks from various Hubbard-owned companies that Weston had cashed. Cody listened thoughtfully, and I could tell the idea that Hubbard was somehow connected to the Russians wasn't a pleasing one to him.

"We've got hundreds of names of people believed to be

Belov associates," he said when Joe was through. "Hubbard has never come up, nor any of his people."

"If he's associated with Belov, he'd definitely want to keep it under the radar," Joe said. "Hubbard's about as big a man as there is in this town."

"No kidding," Cody said. "He's the legitimate version of Dainius Belov."

We all sat in silence then, as the wind whipped around the building, making the old windowpanes rattle. Another cold front was sweeping in, driving out the small touch of spring that had settled during the day.

"How long have you had surveillance on Rakic and Krashakov?" I asked.

"Several months."

"The night Weston was killed?" I said, letting the rest of the question hang unspoken.

Cody shook his head. "They were home," he said. "That doesn't mean they didn't authorize the hit. It just means they didn't carry it out personally."

"What do you think happened to Weston's wife and daughter?" I asked.

Cody leaned forward, braced his forearms on his knees, and looked at the floor. "Several years ago," he said, "when the FBI was trying to bring down John Gotti in New York, their wiretap picked up a conversation in which one of Gotti's thugs was threatening an associate. He also warned this man about crossing the Russian mob, which was apparently involved somehow. He said, 'We Italians will kill you, but the Russians are crazy—they'll kill your whole family.'" He kept his eyes on the floor.

"So you think they're dead," Joe said.

"Yes," Cody said. "I think they're dead."

NINE

In the six months prior to Wayne Weston's murder, Jeremiah Hubbard had been a busy man. In late fall, he began to buy property in the river district downtown known as the Flats, and he announced his intention to build an "entertainment plaza" to rival anything found in New Orleans or any other river town. It would feature a five-star restaurant, two nightclubs that would host the nation's top performers, and a sports bar. The whole thing would be built along a beautifully landscaped river walk, and Hubbard promised it would become the hottest destination in the city. The Flats had already been transformed from an area of dingy warehouses and blue-collar bars into a popular nightlife district, but Hubbard's plan would take that to a new level. The only problem with this idea was that his vision was ten years late. Real estate prices in the Flats had soared as the area was rebuilt, and now it was going to cost Hubbard significantly more money.

In February, he took a great step toward his dream when he acquired three lots of prime property from a man named Dan Beckley, who owned a small restaurant, a gift shop, and a parking lot in the Flats. Beckley had initially balked at the idea of selling out to Hubbard, but he settled a few weeks later, apparently for much less than his initial asking price. Hubbard already owned some of the adjoining property, and he was now much closer to his goal. His next mission was to acquire property on either side of his current holdings. To the north, his property was bordered by a seafood restaurant that was pricey, well known, and always busy. It wouldn't be an easy deal for anyone to swing, even Hubbard. To the south, Hubbard's land met a strip bar called The River Wild: A Gentlemen's Club. It had been in existence for about six years, and the owner reportedly was making a good profit and had no interest in selling. The bar had received some unfavorable publicity a few years back, when an underage and intoxicated kid wandered away from his fraternity brothers, fell off the deck, and drowned in the river. It hadn't hurt the club's business, though. Nothing generates a steady cash flow quite like lap dances, apparently.

The newspaper reported February meetings between Hubbard and the owners of both the seafood restaurant and the strip bar, but negotiations hadn't gone well. Hubbard accused the owners of "outlandish" asking prices; the owners said if Hubbard didn't want to put up the cash, he was out of luck, because they were in no rush to sell. At the end of the month, it was still a stalemate.

Joe and I learned all this studying Amy's faxes early in the morning. Cody's visit the night before had effectively put an end to our surveillance of the Russians, but there was no reason to stop moving on Hubbard. We decided to begin by talking with Dan Beckley.

I made a few phone calls and learned that Beckley had purchased a laundry and dry-cleaning operation in Middleburg Heights after selling out to Hubbard. He apparently had an office in the back. We drove to Middleburg Heights.

Beckley's shop—E-Zee Kleen—was in a small strip mall on the west side of Pearl Road, just past the Bagley Road intersection. I pulled the truck into the lot and parked while Joe stared at the sign and sighed.

"What the hell is the matter with people?" he said.

"What?"

"E-Zee Kleen? Can you tell me what the point of that is? Is there a reason he can't spell it correctly?"

"It has more pizzazz that way," I said. "Catchier."

He gave me a withering look. "Spare me."

We went inside. Two women were loading laundry into the washing machines, and a short Chinese man was at the counter, talking in an agitated voice with the clerk, a bored-looking middle-aged woman. Joe and I stood behind him, waiting. He was ranting about a rip that had appeared in a suit he'd left to be dry-cleaned. The clerk was explaining that she couldn't help him if he didn't have a receipt and the supposed damage had occurred six months earlier, as he said. This was not the response he'd been seeking, and he let her know that for about five minutes while Joe and I grew increasingly impatient. Eventually, Joe cleared his throat and spoke over the man.

"We're here to see Dan Beckley. Is he around?"

The clerk nodded her head at the door behind her. "He's in the office, but he might be on the phone. Go on in, though."

The Chinese man turned to us and glared at Joe. "Excuse you for interrupting. I was talking."

Joe stared at him. "No," he said, "you were babbling." Then he walked around the counter and opened the door.

I looked at the outraged man and shrugged. "He's not a morning person," I said. "But, then again, not so much of an afternoon or evening person, either."

I followed Joe into the office. It was a small, square room, occupied by an old metal desk and one filing cabinet. A tiny television sat on the filing cabinet, tuned to a morning talk show. The room smelled of beer and body odor. A large, ruddy man with fat cheeks and small, sunken eyes sat behind the desk. He wore a plaid shirt, with the first few buttons undone, revealing a thin gold chain amid a cluster of gray chest hair.

"You here about the dryer?" he asked.

Joe shook his head. "No."

The man sighed. "Figures. Those sons of bitches have

been promising to come out here for days, and they still haven't showed. Meanwhile I got only four dryers that work. Sucks." Joe looked at him blankly and didn't say anything. The man said, "So what do you want?"

"You Dan Beckley?"

"That's right. Who wants to know?"

I looked at Joe. Who wants to know? There are some things that sound cool when said by Robert DeNiro that sound ridiculous when said by anyone else. Joe gave Beckley our business card, and he looked at it and then dropped it on his desk.

"I figured this day was going to suck," he said. "What's the problem?"

"No problem," Joe said. "We just wanted to talk to you."

"About?"

"About Jeremiah Hubbard."

Beckley screwed up his face like he'd tasted something foul. "I got nothing to say about Hubbard."

"You sold a fair amount of property to him not too long ago," I said. "Originally, you told him you weren't interested. Then you reconsidered, and from what we've heard, you didn't make out too well on the deal. What happened?"

"What happened? Nothing happened." He crossed his arms over his ample stomach. "I decided to sell, that's all."

I nodded. "I see. You ever hear of a guy named Wayne Weston?"

He frowned. "No."

"He's an associate of Hubbard's," I said. "An investigator, like us. He was murdered about a week ago."

Something changed in Beckley's face—not when I mentioned the murder, but a split second earlier when I told him Weston was an investigator.

"I don't watch the news shows much," he said. "I don't care to hear about murders and drug wars and the rest of that crap. And I never heard of this Weston guy, either." He tilted his chin up at us, defiant.

"Why'd you reconsider on the property deal?" Joe asked. "There has to be some reason. A guy like Hubbard has plenty of money. You probably could have taken him for a lot more than you did."

"I made out fine on that deal," he said. "Just fine, thank you. I got what I wanted to get, and I moved on. I don't see why it's any concern of yours."

Sometimes you just feel it. Call it a hunch, a gut reaction, intuition, an instinct—sometimes you can feel the truth in a way that's hard to explain, a deep, subconscious tug that tells you when something doesn't feel right. As I stood in Beckley's office and watched him glaring at us, with his arms folded over his stomach and his shoulders pulled back in a defensive posture, I had that tug.

"What'd Hubbard have on you?" I asked softly.

He jerked his head back as if I'd given him a jab on the chin. "What did you say?"

"What'd he have on you?" I repeated. It was his reaction to my description of Weston as an investigator that had given me the tug. Somehow, that had made something click in his mind; it had explained something he'd wondered about in the past.

"I don't know what you're talking about," he said.

Joe took a half step backward, an almost unnoticeable movement, but he was clearing out of the way, realizing that I was operating on a feeling he didn't share.

"Dan," I said, "do us both a favor and don't bullshit me."

"I'd like you to leave. Now." He pointed at the door.

"We're not leaving, Dan," I said, my voice still soft. "You didn't sell out so low to Hubbard just because you felt like it. You're too smart for that. You'd look at Hubbard, think about how deep his pockets are, and you'd bleed every cent you could out of him. Every last cent. Now why didn't you?"

"Go to hell."

I ignored him and leaned forward, placing my palms on his desk and lowering my face toward his.

"Listen to me, Dan. There are two ways of handling this. You can either tell me what Hubbard had on you, or you can let me find it out on my own. One way or the other, I'm going to get the information. And I don't like being lied to.

You're lying to me now, and until I find out what you're lying about, I'm going to make you my life's work. You're going to be my obsession, Dan. I'm not going away."

He looked up at me, and the defiant chin quivered slightly. He breathed heavily out of his nose and clenched his hands together. Angry. Then he pulled open one of the desk drawers, removed an envelope, and threw it at me. It hit me in the chest and fell to the floor.

"Go on," he said, his lip curling up in a snarl, spitting the words at me. "Go on and take a look."

I retrieved the envelope from the floor and opened it. There were photographs inside. I went through them slowly while Joe looked over my shoulder. In the first picture, Dan Beckley was in a car, talking to a woman on the sidewalk who wore stiletto heels and a short red skirt with black fishnet stockings. In the next, he was passing her money, and then she was in the car, her head buried in his lap. In the final photograph, she was out of the car again, walking away, while Beckley sat in the driver's seat.

I slipped the photographs back into the envelope. "So that's how it went," I said. "Hubbard sent you photographs of you with the hooker, and you made the deal?"

He shook his head. "Can't prove it was him. All I got were the photographs and a little Post-it note with the price he'd offered me written on it. The message was pretty clear, though." He looked down at the desk. "I got a wife and a son. I didn't want them seeing that shit."

"Did you call Hubbard on it," Joe asked, "or did you just agree to the deal?"

"I didn't call him out, but we both knew what was going on."

I dropped the envelope back on his desk. "Thanks for your time, Dan. And don't worry, this isn't going to leave the room."

He flipped me off and kept his eyes on the desk. Joe and I left. The Chinese man was still yammering at the clerk, who looked ready to strangle him. He shut up when Joe brushed against him, but he was back at it when we reached the door.

We sat in the truck, and I started the engine but didn't shift out of park.

"So that's what Weston was doing for him," I said. "No wonder the guy has such good luck with business deals."

"Explains why Weston didn't appear to be a legitimate investigator," Joe said. "He was just a well-paid extortionist. Hubbard probably gave him plenty of business."

"If Weston had been doing this for a while, it would add to the list of people who'd have liked to kill him."

"What about the Russians?" Joe said.

I drummed my fingers on the steering wheel. "Yes. What about the Russians?"

We sat there for a while, and then I said, "We could go back to Hubbard, confront him with it, and see what he gives us."

Joe shook his head. "I don't like that. Not yet, at least."

"All right. So what now?"

"Back to the office. Let's take another look at those faxes from Amy and see who else Hubbard might have been putting the squeeze on. Then we'll give Agent Cody a call."

I pulled out of the lot and started to drive, then realized Joe was looking at me.

"What?" I asked.

"Just thinking about you pushing Beckley back there," he said. "You've got some kind of instincts, LP."

"Lucky guess," I said.

Back at the office, the telephone message indicator was blinking. Joe checked the voice mail while I browsed through the faxes from Amy, writing down all the names she'd associated with Hubbard in recent months. I had a list of seven names by the time Joe hung up the phone. His face was thoughtful.

"Who was it?"

"Cody," he said. "He had his guys check the plate on that green Oldsmobile we saw yesterday."

"Yeah?"

"Plate's not registered to the car."

"It'd be too easy if it were. Maybe I should ask the Russians for the VIN number. They've been eager to help me so far."

He frowned. "I don't think this guy is with them. Why's he camped outside their house if they're associates? You ask me, he's working against them in some capacity. And he's definitely interested in Weston."

"Makes you wonder, doesn't it?"

"Uh-huh." He tapped a pencil on the desk and stared at the wall. "The plate was reported stolen from South Carolina, though. Two days ago, Cody said, in Myrtle Beach. That's a hell of a drive."

"If he drove. Could have stolen the plate beforehand, then flown up here, rented a car, and swapped the plates to cover himself."

"Now why's a guy from Myrtle Beach come to Cleveland with a phony badge to question Weston's neighbors? And how the hell does he know about the Russians? Even if he flew in, according to the license plate he couldn't have been here for more than two days. So we can assume he knew about the Russians beforehand."

"Knew what?"

He shrugged. "Something, anyhow. He's asking the neighbors about the night of Weston's death. Why?"

"Another investigator?"

"Who's he working for, then?"

I sighed and shook my head. I didn't have any answers. A dull ache had crept into my shoulders, and I rolled them slightly, trying to relieve the tension. I needed a good workout, or maybe a massage.

"What do you think of Agent Cody?" Joe asked.

"A Bureau boy, through and through," I said. "Smart, flashy, cocky. And probably full of shit."

He nodded. "That's what I think, too. I don't know if he lied to us last night, but I'm sure he didn't tell us everything he knew. He says the FBI took over this investigation just because Weston's name came up on a wiretap? Bullshit. There's got to be more than that involved."

"Do you think we should tell him about Dan Beckley?"

"I don't know. Our first duty is to John Weston. The FBI can make it awfully hard for us to get anywhere with this case if they don't like where we're going with it. I don't want that to happen."

"We can assume Weston was working for Hubbard, providing him blackmail material to use in his business negotiations," I said. "Hell, he's pretty active in city government, too. There's no telling how many secrets Weston gave him over the years."

"Enough to make some people mad enough to kill him."

"Sure. But where do the Russians fit in, then? I can see dozens of people willing to whack Weston for extortion if they caught him, but not many of them would involve his family. That sounds more like a mob tactic."

"And then we've got this guy in the green Olds," Joe said. "I'm thinking maybe he's FBI after all."

"Cody said he wasn't. And Swanders was pissed about it, when we told him the guy was flashing a badge and claiming to be CPD."

"Uh-huh," Joe said. "I believe Swanders is clueless, but I wouldn't put it past Cody. You know how the Bureau protects their agents, especially if they're undercover. If he didn't want to claim the guy as one of theirs, he wouldn't hesitate to lie about it. And it wasn't Swanders who left the message about the license plate being lifted in Myrtle Beach. It was Cody."

"You're saying he lied about that, too."

"I'm saying he could have."

We could have continued throwing questions and complaints about the case at one another for an hour or two, but it wasn't going to get us anywhere. Joe asked to look over the faxes from Amy again, so I passed those over, and, for lack of a better idea, I pulled out the small case file we had and began to look through it. The contents weren't particularly awe-inspiring: the notebook of recollections from John Weston, the folder of background on the Russians I'd taken from April Sortigan, and notes from my conversation with Deputy Prosecutor James Sellers. I read through it all again, searching for something I might have overlooked originally or for something that might have new meaning after our recent discoveries. I didn't find much. Sortigan's file wasn't especially helpful, just basic notes from her court research. There was nothing I hadn't already committed to memory, but I read through it anyhow.

My eye caught on a telephone number written on a yellow Post-it note and stuck to the outside of the folder. I tried to remember if it was related to the case or just a personal note she'd neglected to remove when she gave me the file. Then I remembered. Sortigan told me Weston had instructed her to fax information on the Russians to that number while he was out of town.

I turned on the computer and logged on to the Internet. There are a number of good databases for reverse lookups that take a phone number and match it with an address, or vice versa. I went to my favorite of them and typed in the number, then clicked the search button. A few seconds later the database reported there were no matches. I wasn't surprised. The databases are effective only for listed phone numbers, and most fax numbers aren't listed.

I stared at the monitor for a while, trying to think of another option. I could send a fax to the number on some pretext and hope someone responded. I couldn't think of a good pretext, though. Maybe I should just be honest, send a fax with our company letterhead and try for intimidating. When people are intimidated by investigators they generally clam up rather than provide information. I studied the fax number again and then went to a different database. If nothing else, I could find out what cities matched the area code. I entered the three digits into the search engine, and it fed me an immediate match. The area code belonged to a portion of South Carolina that included Myrtle Beach.

"Hey, Joseph," I said. He grunted in response. "When Weston told Sortigan to check out the Russians, he asked her to fax the information to him long distance. I can't find a match on the phone number, but I checked on the area code, and guess what city it includes?"

"Myrtle Beach."

I glared at him. "Do you have to be so damn clever? I was hoping to make a dramatic announcement."

He leaned over to look at the computer screen. "That's interesting, though. Maybe Cody didn't lie about the plate being stolen there after all."

"What would Weston have been doing in Myrtle Beach just a few days before he was killed?"

"Does he know anyone there?"

"Not that I'm aware of."

Joe looked at the monitor and rubbed his jaw idly. "Call John and ask him."

I picked up the phone and called John Weston. He answered on the second ring, and when I gave my name he said, "Yes, what is it?" with an expectant eagerness that made me want to sink lower in the chair. The days had seemed to go by quickly for Joe and me, but they were clearly passing with agonizing slowness for John Weston.

I explained that we were making some progress on the case, but I said we wouldn't discuss details until we'd corroborated theories with facts. He did some grumbling about that, but I held my ground. The last thing I wanted was to tell the poor man we thought his son had been an extortionist who'd pissed off the Russian mob. I had a bad feeling we'd have to tell him that sooner or later, but I wasn't about to rush into it until we were sure that was the case.

"We've turned up some connections to Myrtle Beach, South Carolina," I told him. "It looks like Wayne went down there shortly before his death. We were wondering if you knew of any friends or acquaintances he had there?"

"He went to South Carolina?" Weston said. "Well, he never said anything about that to me. Are you sure?"

"Did he have any friends or acquaintances there?" I repeated patiently. I doubted Wayne Weston had been sharing many things with his father, but apparently the idea came as a surprise to the old man.

"Well, sure," John Weston said. "Randy Hartwick. I told you about him already."

"You did?"

"It's all in the damned notebook," he snapped. "That's why I spent all that time writing everything down, so you'd have the information in front of you and you wouldn't have to waste time calling me with every damn question that came up."

I grabbed the notebook and flipped through it quickly. There was Randy Hartwick, listed under the "Friends" category. He was Wayne Weston's old Marine Corps buddy, but in the notebook it said he lived in Florida.

"I see his name here," I said, "but it says he lives in Florida."

"It's Myrtle Beach," Weston said irritably, probably more upset with his own mistake than with my comment. "All those damn beach-town tourist-trap shitholes are the same to me."

"Understandable. Have you heard anything from Mr. Hartwick recently?"

"No. I called and left a message with him about the funeral, because . . . well, because it just didn't seem right to put Wayne in the ground without Randy there. I never heard back from him, though." He said it carefully, like he was trying to keep any trace of bitterness from his voice, but he didn't completely succeed.

"I see. Did Mr. Hartwick and your son remain close after their Marine days?"

"Very close. Wayne went on fishing trips with him every year. Wayne told me that—outside of family, of course—the only man alive he trusted completely was Randy Hartwick. He said he'd trust his life to that son of a bitch in a heartbeat, no hesitation, no regrets. That's how it has to be in combat, you know. You have to have that loyalty."

"Yes, sir," I said, not anxious to hear another of John Weston's loyalty speeches. He should have stayed in the military. He'd have made a hell of a general. "In the notebook, you wrote that Mr. Hartwick worked for a resort hotel. Do you know what he did there?"

"He had the security contract for one of those big hotels.

You know, he installed alarms and cameras, provided guards, all that crap. It was one of those fancy resorts."

"Do you remember the name?"

"Shit." He grunted, and the line was silent for a while as he thought about it. "Golden Palms, maybe? No, that's not it. Not the Palms. Dammit. What the hell was the name of it? Golden Beaches, Golden Palms. Something like that."

"I'll check it out and see if I can find anything close," I said.

"Good."

"Well, that's all I had to ask you, sir. I'm going to try to track Mr. Hartwick down now. We'll be in touch soon."

"I hope so," he said, the words barely audible, the typical gruffness and command absent from his voice. "I hope so."

I hung up and looked at Joe. "I've got our Myrtle Beach connection."

"Who is it?"

"Randy Hartwick," I said. "He served in Wayne Weston's Force Recon battalion. Apparently, they were together from boot camp at Twenty-nine Palms all the way through Recon training and then went into the same unit. That's what it says in the notebook, at least. On the phone, John Weston told me Hartwick was the only man his son truly trusted. Said Wayne would have put his life in the man's hands without hesitation."

Joe listened with interest. "And Weston visited Hartwick just before he died," he said.

"Possibly. We don't know that for sure, but it's likely. John Weston said Hartwick was the head of security for a resort in Myrtle Beach. He hasn't heard anything from Hartwick, even though he called to tell him what had happened and to ask him to attend the funeral."

"You think the guy in the Oldsmobile was Hartwick?"

"Could be."

"So what's he doing up here pretending to be a cop?"

"According to John Weston, there was some pretty fierce loyalty between his son and Randy Hartwick. Maybe

Hartwick came up here to find out who killed his buddy, or maybe to find out what happened to the wife and daughter."

"He comes up here to investigate that, but he doesn't bother to contact John Weston while he's in town? He doesn't even show up for the funeral?"

I closed the notebook and tossed it onto the desk. "That bothered me, too."

"Look for the hotel," Joe said. "I want to move on this guy fast. If he's the man who has been talking to the neighbors and watching the Russians, he might have a whole lot of answers."

I returned my attention to the computer and did a few simple keyword searches for "Myrtle Beach," "hotel," and "Golden." It didn't take me more than five minutes to find a match. The Golden Breakers Resort in Myrtle Beach boasted a five-star rating, luxurious suites, a rooftop restaurant, hot tubs, pools, an exercise room, a sauna, and even a 422-foot "Lazy River" for children to float down. I located the phone number for the resort and called it.

"Hi," I said when a friendly clerk answered, "I was just about to fax something to you, but I lost the number. Could you give it to me?"

She happily obliged, and as she read the number off I compared it to the one Sortigan had been given. A match. I thanked the clerk, hung up, and looked at Joe.

"The Golden Breakers," I said. "Sortigan faxed the information to Weston at that number. I'm fairly certain we'll find the resort is also Randy Hartwick's employer."

"Call back and ask for Hartwick," Joe instructed.

I did so.

"I'm sorry, Mr. Hartwick is out of town," the clerk informed me after putting me on hold briefly.

"Out of town?" I repeated, and Joe looked over and gave me a thumbs-up sign. "Do you know where he went, or when he'll be back?"

"I'm afraid not."

"Damn," I said, feigning heavy disappointment. "I really

need to speak with him today. I'm afraid a very close friend of Randy's passed away, and I know he'll want to be notified as soon as possible. Is there any way you could help me get in touch with him?"

"Oh, that's awful," she said with sympathy that sounded so genuine I felt bad. "Mr. Hartwick has a cell phone. I don't know the number, but if you give me ten minutes I could probably find out."

"That would be great." I gave her the office number, and she promised to call back.

I had hung up and turned to Joe, ready to explain the phone call, when someone knocked on the door. We both looked at it, then nodded at each other, expecting to see Swanders and Kraus, or possibly Cody.

"Come in," Joe said.

The man who entered wasn't Swanders, Kraus, or Cody, but Joe seemed to recognize him. I'd never seen him before.

"What brings you here, Mr. Kinkaid?" Joe said, getting to his feet and offering his hand. "This is my partner, Lincoln Perry. Lincoln, this is Aaron Kinkaid. He used to work with Wayne Weston."

I shook hands with the visitor. Kinkaid was a tall guy, at least six-four, with a slender build and dark red hair. A few freckles spotted the bridge of his nose, drawing attention to the stark contrast of his red hair and green eyes. He had enormous hands, hands that could palm a basketball the way most people could hold a softball. His tall, rangy build, red hair, and freckles made me think of a farm boy, but he had to be nearing forty.

"Nice to meet you," he said. His voice had a slight drawl to it, a languid delivery that enhanced the farm-boy image. He sat down and clasped his big hands together, then frowned and stared at his shoes.

"I'm afraid I have something to say that you're probably not going to like, Mr. Pritchard," he said. Joe raised his eyebrows but didn't say anything. "You see," Kinkaid continued, "I wasn't completely honest with you when you came over to Sandusky to talk with me. But I'd like to make it up to both of you. What I mean is, well, if you'd be willing, I'd like to work with you."

"Work with us?" Joe said.

Kinkaid nodded. "Yes, sir. Work with you on the Weston case, I mean. I think I can help, and I want to help."

"Why?" I asked, and he looked up for the first time. "Why did you go from lying to Joe to wanting to help us on the case?"

He met my eyes for a moment and then looked back at his shoes. "Because," he said, "I'm in love with Wayne Weston's wife."

TEN

We all sat in silence for a minute after that, and then Aaron Kinkaid told us his story. He'd lied to Joe, he said, only when he'd explained the circumstances of his separation from Wayne Weston. He'd told Joe that Weston had been closemouthed and ended his partnership with Kinkaid for unknown reasons. In reality, Weston had an excellent reason to break off the partnership—Kinkaid had approached Julie Weston with feelings he said had been building for months.

"I know she had feelings for me, too," he told us. "She admitted that much to me. But there was her daughter to consider. Julie told me not to pursue it, and for a few weeks everything was calm. Then she became uncomfortable and talked to Wayne about it."

I glanced at Joe and noticed he was looking at Kinkaid with undisguised scorn, clearly unimpressed with anyone who would pursue his partner's wife. Joe's own wife, Ruth, had been dead for several years, and I think marriage seemed even more sacred to him now than before. He kept quiet, though.

Kinkaid told us an enraged Wayne Weston had confronted him about his advances toward Julie. Kinkaid hadn't denied his attraction to his partner's wife, and Weston demanded he leave the firm. Kinkaid resisted at first.

"Then I realized it was hopeless," he said. "We'd never have been able to work together again. Wayne couldn't trust me, and I understood that, and I didn't blame him for it. If you can't trust your partner, you need to move on. So we moved on." He ran one of his big, bony hands through his hair. "You need to understand that I really care about Julie, though. I see the way you're looking at me, and I know what you're thinking—that I'm a first-class prick, a guy who wants his partner's wife just because she's off-limits, or maybe just because of her beauty. That wasn't it, though. Julie's an amazing woman."

He looked at me, as if I might understand what Joe could not. "She's truly one of a kind. Yeah, she's gorgeous, but after a few months I was hardly even aware of her looks. She's unlike any other woman I've ever known. She has this depth, this quality of intelligence and compassion, man . . ." He shook his head. "It's like she figures you out, understands you better than you understand yourself. I tried not to think about her. I tried to stay away from her, even. It didn't help. Nothing could help. I know you look at me and all you can see is an asshole who tried to steal his partner's wife, but I tell you, I loved her like I've never loved anyone before. And I know I'll never love anyone like that again."

Joe and I didn't say a word. We're good at that, sometimes. If there's anything better than our tag-team wit, it's our tag-team stony silence.

"Listen," Kinkaid said eventually, "I heard about Wayne's death, and Julie and Betsy being missing, and I didn't want to have any part of it. I didn't want to allow myself to even think about it, because I knew if I did, I'd stop feeling sorry for my dead partner and start wishing I could see his wife again. You know what kind of a bastard that made me feel like? But I'm not worrying about it anymore. I've got to know where that woman is, and where that little girl is. That's all I care about. If I can learn what happened to them,

I'll walk away and be done with it. But I've got to know. I've *got* to know."

Joe cleared his throat. "That's great, Kinkaid. I respect your desire to help, but I'm afraid that's not how we work. Lincoln and I work alone. Exclusively. We don't posse up on anything, all right? You want to help so badly, I'll give you the number of the detectives in charge of the case. Maybe they'll appreciate the assistance more than we do."

"I understand that reaction," Kinkaid said, squeezing his big hands together and nodding his head. "But I remind you I'm not a stranger to this business. I know what I'm doing. In fact, I've got more experience working in the private sector than either of you. Yeah, you were cops, but it's a different world out there if you don't have a badge. I know how to work in that world, and I know how to do it quickly."

"We're stumbling along all right on our own, thanks," I said.

Joe nodded. "I have to hold his hand a lot of the time, but we've managed to get by so far. I think we'll continue to manage."

Kinkaid got to his feet, his broad frame towering over Joe's desk. "Fine," he said. "I'm not going to beg you. But it's your mistake. I know Wayne Weston better than anyone. I know his history, I know his mind, I know his habits. And I'm going to find out what the hell happened in that house. You can take that to the bank, gentlemen."

The phone rang. I ignored it at first, thinking I'd let it go to voice mail, but then I remembered the clerk at the Golden Breakers who was supposed to call back, and I reached over and answered it.

"Hello?"

"Hi, this is Rebecca with the Golden Breakers Resort in Myrtle Beach," a young female voice announced brightly. "I believe I spoke with you earlier about Randy Hartwick, our chief of security?"

"Yes."

"Well, I've located Mr. Hartwick's cell phone number." She read the number off while Kinkaid stood at the door, his hand on the knob. I thanked the clerk and hung up, wishing her voice hadn't been so loud. I hoped Kinkaid hadn't heard Hartwick's name.

He had.

"Randy Hartwick, eh?" he said, his back to us. I looked at Joe, and he shrugged, leaving the response up to me.

"What do you know about him?" I asked.

Kinkaid turned back to us, keeping his hand on the doorknob. "Randy Hartwick," he said, "is possibly the most dangerous man I've ever known." He hesitated, looking from Joe to me. "You'd be well advised to watch yourselves with him. It's too bad you don't posse up," he said, echoing Joe's phrase. "Because if you take a run at Hartwick, you'll need all the help you can get."

He opened the door and stepped halfway into the hall, then paused, giving us a last chance. Joe looked at me and then sighed.

"Get your ass back in here and sit down," he said.

Kinkaid grinned, shut the door, and returned to his seat. "All right," he said. "Now let's get to work."

Kinkaid's knowledge of Randy Hartwick dated to his early days with Wayne Weston. Hartwick had visited occasionally, and Weston introduced the two men.

"He's an old Marine buddy of Wayne's," Kinkaid said, "and Wayne stayed close to him since those Marine days, even though it was a bad idea."

"Why a bad idea?" I asked.

Kinkaid smiled tightly. "Those two were in Force Recon together. The baddest of the bad, right? They were the guys who fought the secret wars, did the dirty deeds, and kept their mouths shut about it. Covert operations were what they lived for, and Hartwick—well, he never really stopped living for them. He was addicted to the rush of it, the danger, and the adrenaline. Wayne had the bug, too, but it wasn't as bad. He used to talk about it with me after Randy would leave, and his eyes would kind of light up. He'd just float off in his own world for a minute. Then he'd look at a picture of Julie and his daughter and come back down to earth.

"Hartwick mustered out of the Corps two years after Wayne did. He tried to go into private security work, but it didn't hold his interest for long."

"It's what he's doing now," I said, and Kinkaid smiled at me like you might smile at someone who thought all his tax dollars were put to good use.

"It's a front," he said. "Where is he now? Doing a security guard detail for some country club? A private airport, maybe?" When I gave him a slight nod to indicate he was at least close to the truth, his smile widened. "Yeah, that's what I figured. It's a job he can manage easily without having to be on scene all the time. It leaves him plenty of free time to pursue his other interests."

"And what are those?"

"Weapons smuggling," he said. "And he's damn good at it."

I wanted to look at Joe, but I kept my eyes on Kinkaid, trying not to show any reaction. Cody had said the Russians were moving illegal weapons. Now Kinkaid said Weston's closest friend had been as well.

"Who's he moving them with?" Joe asked. "Or maybe I should ask, who's he moving them *for*?"

Kinkaid frowned. "I can't tell you that. Hartwick never exactly confided in me, you know, and Wayne, well, it's been years since Wayne and I talked about all this. I don't know any names, I just know that some Soviets were involved. Retired Spetznatz guys, the Soviet answer to Force Recon."

I *had* to look at Joe after that one. He gazed right back at me, and I knew what he was thinking: Maybe stopping Kinkaid at the door had been a good move after all.

Kinkaid followed my eyes. "What?" he said. When no one answered, he said, "Why'd you look at him like that? What have you heard?"

Joe shifted in his chair and leaned back, clasping his hands behind his head. "Weston was checking into some of Cleveland's very own Russian thugs shortly before his death. We started checking into them as well, and yesterday an FBI agent and some Cleveland cops stopped by to tell us not to."

"They give a reason?"

Joe nodded. "Said they think a group of Russians working under Dainius Belov killed Wayne Weston. Apparently, Weston's name came up in some conversation they pulled off a wiretap. They don't know what his involvement with them was—well, they *said* they don't know, at least. But they did mention the Russians are involved in weapons trafficking."

Kinkaid spread his long legs out in front of him and cocked his head to the side. "They didn't say anything about Hartwick?"

"Not a word."

He frowned. "So why are you interested in Hartwick today?"

Joe told him about the green Oldsmobile and the stolen South Carolina license plate and then explained how I had traced Hartwick to the Myrtle Beach hotel. Kinkaid listened with interest, his green eyes intense.

"When you came down to see me in Sandusky, you asked about Jeremiah Hubbard," he said. "Where does he fit into all this?"

"Good question," I said. "That's one we're hoping to answer." I told him about our conversation with Hubbard, as well as our visit to Dan Beckley earlier that morning. He nodded his head slightly as I talked, and he looked sad but not surprised.

"I figured as much," he said when I was done. "After Wayne and I went our separate ways, I still kept in touch with some of the people we'd worked with in the past. As the months went by, I heard rumors that he wasn't accepting new clients and that he was doing some extremely confidential, high-paying work and wouldn't talk to anyone about it. Hell, you've seen his house, you know he was making cash. But ask around the PI industry a little, and you'll hear a lot of rumors about him, almost none of which involve him being legitimate."

"It looks like he was supplying blackmail material for Hubbard," I said. "How'd he get involved with Belov, though? We don't have a clue yet. And now we've got this ex-Marine working the same streets we are. It adds up to a lot of questions and not nearly as many answers."

"You said Hartwick's going around the neighborhood posing as a cop?" he said. "I wonder what the hell that's about. If Wayne got involved with Belov's crew, it's a safe bet that Hartwick led him there. But what's Hartwick doing cruising the neighborhood and asking questions?"

"Could be trying to do exactly what we are," I suggested. "Maybe he's trying to determine what happened to Weston and his family."

Kinkaid made a face. "Possible, I guess. But with a guy like Hartwick, I'd be more inclined to believe there's money involved. And if there is, you can bet he's out to get it."

"You think the guy's stupid enough to try to rip off the Russian mob?"

Kinkaid smiled grimly. "Stupid enough to do it? Randy Hartwick would jump at the chance, Mr. Perry. It would offer a challenge he just couldn't refuse. Hartwick thinks he's the toughest, most dangerous guy there is. And he definitely believes he's the smartest."

"So what's he trying to do?"

"I don't know," Kinkaid said. "But you've got his phone number, don't you?"

"Yeah."

"Well, why don't we call and ask him?"

Joe looked at me and shrugged. "Why not?" he said. "If he doesn't answer, or if he hangs up on you, we'll go from there. But if he's willing to talk, it could save us a hell of a lot of effort."

"All right." I grabbed the phone and dialed the number the Golden Breakers clerk had given me. On the third ring, a male voice with a hard edge answered: "Hartwick."

"Mr. Hartwick," I said, "my name's Lincoln Perry."

"Yeah?"

"I'm an investigator working for John Weston. My partner and I were hoping to ask you a few questions about your relationship with John's son."

For a few seconds all I could hear was his breathing. "I'm afraid I can't help you," he said, and his voice had a measure of caution now.

"You still driving that green Olds?" I asked.

There was another brief silence. "You're the guys from the Taurus," he said.

"Uh-huh."

"You said you're working for John?" When I acknowledged that was true, he said, "All right, we can talk."

"Think you could stop by our office this afternoon? I can give you directions. It isn't hard to find."

"No way," he said. "Don't take this personally, but I'd kind of prefer to call the shots here until I know what I'm getting into." He paused, considering the options. "Where are you guys?"

I told him.

"All right, here's what we'll do," he said. "I'm going to take a little drive around, see if I can pick out a meeting place I'm comfortable with. When I find one, I'll call you back, and you can come meet me."

"That works," I said, thinking about Kinkaid's description of Hartwick as the most dangerous man he'd ever met. We could be walking into a trap, but at least we'd be somewhat prepared. I was glad Kinkaid had decided to make the trip to Cleveland. If he hadn't, Joe and I would have approached Hartwick with our usual caution—but with a man like that, the usual caution might not have been enough. I gave him the office phone number and hung up. Joe and Kinkaid looked at me expectantly.

"He'll meet with us, but only on his terms. He said he's going to pick out a meeting spot and call us back, then we'll go down to see him."

"Shit." Kinkaid frowned and shook his head emphatically. "I don't like that, man. That sounds like a setup to me. He's got too much control in that scenario."

I turned to Joe. He was expressionless, listening to Kinkaid's warning but not reacting.

"Well, grandpa?" I said.

"This Hartwick guy sounds like he could hold a lot of answers," Joe said. "If this is the only way he'll talk to us, then that's what we'll have to do. There's only one of him, and there's three of us. We should be all right."

"You're thinking we split up?" Kinkaid asked. "Keep someone out on the perimeter in case anything goes wrong?"

"I'm not expecting anything to go wrong," Joe answered, "but that's not such a bad idea. No matter what, I don't think you should be with us during the meeting."

"What? Oh, come on!" Kinkaid leaned forward and slapped the top of the desk with one hand. "That's bullshit, Pritchard. You want my help or not? I know this guy better than you do. I need to be there when you're asking him questions."

Joe shook his head. "No, you don't. I know you're more experienced with Hartwick, but that isn't necessarily a helpful thing. If he sees you, he might be more guarded than he would be with just Lincoln and me. He probably assumes you know some of his background, and that might hurt us more than it would help us. As it is now, you're the ace up our sleeve. Let's not throw you on the table just yet."

Kinkaid pursed his lips and exhaled heavily, his face forming an angry pout, like a child trying unsuccessfully to whistle.

"Joe's right," I said. "Right now Hartwick thinks we're clueless. And, while we don't know much, what we do know is thanks to you. The longer we can keep him off balance, keep him feeling smart and in control, the better chance we have of figuring out what he's doing here."

I almost believed what I was saying. In some aspects, it was true, but it wasn't the real reason I wanted Kinkaid kept out of the meeting. He'd been honest with us so far, and I had to give him credit for that, but I wasn't used to working with him. Joe and I had interviewed hundreds of people together, we knew how to work as a team, and I didn't want Kinkaid's presence disrupting that. And I had no idea how he'd perform under fire if something did go wrong. If Hartwick was setting us up, Kinkaid could be a liability.

"You mind if I smoke in your office?" Kinkaid asked about ten minutes later, breaking what had become a fairly long silence as we waited to hear from Hartwick again.

"Prefer you didn't," Joe said. "I can't stand the stench of stale smoke, and it's too cold to open the windows."

"No sweat. I'll step outside for a few minutes."

He left, and I turned to Joe, thankful for the opportunity to discuss things without Kinkaid in the room. "What do you think of him?"

"Kinkaid?" He shrugged. "He lied to me once, and he tried to hit it with his partner's wife. Makes him an asshole, right? But his desire to help us out now seems legitimate, and, love him or hate him, you have to admit he can be useful to us. He knows Weston, and he's already been helpful with Hartwick. I say we let him string along with us for a while. This case is heavy already, and there's no harm in having a little help with it."

"That's about how I feel," I said. "His track record seems a little suspect, but if he can help us, I don't give a damn who he wants to sleep with. If we can find Julie Weston, he can have her."

"You're sticking with the idea that she and the girl are alive."

"Got to stick with it. The other option is too depressing."

ELEVEN

After parting ways with Wayne Weston, Aaron Kinkaid had moved to Sandusky to work as the chief investigator for an established security company. A few years later he'd become part owner, and now he ran business operations alone, with a silent partner. He told us this as we sat in the office, waiting impatiently for Hartwick to call.

"How'd you end up in the business to begin with?" Joe asked. "You weren't a cop?"

"No, I was never a cop." Kinkaid gave a sheepish grin. "I know how pathetic this sounds, but, to be honest, I liked the way it looked in the movies. You know, Bogart as Sam Spade or Philip Marlowe? Or Nicholson in *Chinatown*? Man, I ate that stuff up when I was younger. I was in college, studying business marketing, anticipating a life of hyping paint thinner to hardware stores or some crap like that, but at night I'd go home and watch those old movies on TV and think about how much I'd like to have that job. The constant change intrigued me, the idea that a mysterious client could walk into your office any day and put you in the middle of something . . ." The words died off as Kinkaid stared at the wall, lost in his memories. He shook his head, bringing himself back into reality.

"Funny," he said, "I went into the business for the intrigue, and now I'm running a security company, dealing more with marketing ploys and bottom-line figures than I am with investigation. I basically ended up doing the same thing I set out to avoid."

"It works like that sometimes," I said, and Joe looked at me with an understanding Kinkaid couldn't share. After being forced to leave the department, I'd attempted to leave all the remains of my old life behind with the badge. I'd cut ties with almost everyone on the force, and I'd purchased the gym and plunged into work as a small business owner. It had been several months before Amy had convinced me to look into the murder of one of my gym patrons and pushed me back into the life I'd tried to abandon. Somewhere along the line, I'd realized what a mistake I'd made. I couldn't be happy in the business world. I fed off the investigative process, off the questions and the answers, the unknowns and the facts. I fed off the pursuit of truth. It was what made me complete, what gave my life purpose. I wouldn't try to leave it behind again.

"I remember Bogart as Spade," Joe said, breaking in on my thoughts. "I was a kid when I saw it, and I've got plenty of years on either of you. Hell of an old movie. Who wrote the book?"

"Dashiell Hammett," Kinkaid and I said in unison, and then all of us laughed.

"What was it about that story that grabbed people so much?" I wondered aloud. "I mean, yeah, the movie was well done, and Bogart was a phenomenal actor, but what about the story itself? How'd that one endure so well? Hell, the book's still in print after seventy years."

"It's all in the ending," Kinkaid said. "The idea that Spade's loyalty to his partner means more to him than money or love. He didn't like his partner much—he's even sleeping with the guy's wife—but he's still got that loyalty . . ."

He stopped talking abruptly, his mouth still half open, as we all realized what he was saying. Joe and I looked away, and for the first time since he'd entered the office, Kinkaid seemed unsure of himself. I knew why. Kinkaid wasn't in this case because of loyalty to his partner. He was in the case because he still loved Weston's wife. If anything, he viewed Weston's death as an opportunity.

"So," he said awkwardly, then laughed at himself. He was spared further comment by the ring of the phone. Joe picked it up.

"Pritchard and Perry. Yeah, this is Joe Pritchard. You talked to Lincoln before, he's my partner. You need to hear the comfort of his voice this time, or can we handle this? Uh-huh. Right."

Unlike the clerk at the Golden Breakers, this caller spoke in a soft voice, so Kinkaid and I could only hear one side of the conversation, but it clearly was Hartwick. We waited. Joe said a few more words, but nothing that suggested what was being discussed, and then hung up.

"He'll meet with us," he said. "But it's a hell of a place he picked out."

"Where is it?" I asked.

"Just down the avenue. You know the little cluster of picnic tables behind the take-out Chinese place?"

I took a moment to place the scene in my mind and then nodded. "I can picture it."

"That's where he wants to meet. Seems like a strange choice."

I shook my head. "Makes good sense, actually."

"How do you figure?"

"Think about it, Joe. If you're sitting at one of those picnic tables, you've got a clear view of everything in front of you and on either side, and the cemetery fence protects your back. There are three parking lots bordering that Chinese place. If he has his car up there, he could get out in a hurry, make a right turn onto the side street and head for Chatfield, pull out on the avenue and head in either direction, or even cut all the way through the Ford dealership parking lot."

"I've already figured that out," he said. "That's why it's a good choice for someone afraid of being set up. But I thought we were playing that role?"

It was a good point. I'd automatically considered the location from the perspective of someone looking to avoid danger. If I were looking to cause it, the location wasn't so good after all. There was too much open space, and visibility was too good.

"Well," I said, "we shouldn't be too disappointed at his selection, then. It indicates he's not planning to kill us."

"Yet," Kinkaid said.

Joe grimaced. "You're a real optimist, aren't you?"

He frowned. "In general, yeah, I am. But as I said before, I know Hartwick better than you. If he's involved in something dirty—and chances are he is—then he'll be looking to eliminate any threat. As far as I can tell, that's what you two are going to be to him."

"It was your idea to call him."

"I know. It wasn't my idea to be kept out of the meeting, though. And I'm not about to let you two wander over there alone."

"We've been over this," Joe began, but Kinkaid held his hand up and interrupted.

"I understand you don't want him to see me, and even though I don't like that, I'll go along with it. I'm just saying you're going to need some backup with this guy. Now, is there anyplace I can sit with a good look at the scene?"

"Nowhere close," Joe said. "That's why this was a good choice for him, if he's afraid of us. If you're nearby he's going to see you."

"It's getting pretty dark."

"Come on, Kinkaid. The guy was a special ops soldier. This is what he's trained for. I suppose you could hang out across the street, but even that's a gamble."

"The cemetery," I said. "That's where we can put him. Cemetery access isn't from the avenue, but once he gets inside he can work his way up to right behind us."

"That fence is six feet tall," Joe objected. "It will block his vision."

"It's a chain-link fence, so it won't be that much of a problem. But I wouldn't have him up close to it anyhow. We're not wanting him to be right on top of us, we're wanting him to have a clear line of sight to watch for an approaching threat, right?"

"Right."

"Okay. On the other side of the fence, the cemetery's built on a hill. It's a pretty gradual slope, but if he got up at the top of it he could see us clearly, as well as the rest of the parking lot."

Kinkaid's head was oscillating back and forth between Joe and me like a fan, listening to the debate. Joe considered it all, then gave me a nod.

"Top of the hill is the best option. He's going to be fairly far away, but he'll be able to see clearly, and that's the most important thing. And it will be easier for him to get up there undetected than it would be to keep him on the other side of the street or hidden in the parking lot."

"That's the nice thing about Hartwick being an out-of-towner," I said. "He's got to handle this on the fly. We already know the terrain."

"Right." Joe looked at his watch. "And we've got to be moving. He said he's down there now, and he expects to see us soon." He looked at Kinkaid. "You have a gun and a cell phone?"

"Yes."

"Good. If you see anything you don't like, call my phone, let it ring once, and hang up. If Lincoln and I hear that, we'll clear out fast. If anything starts to go down, call the cops."

Joe gave Kinkaid his cell phone number and told him how to get inside the cemetery. I opened my desk drawer and withdrew my Glock nine-millimeter. I checked the clip, then chambered a round so I'd be ready to fire instantly. I fastened my holster onto my belt, up against my spine, and then put the gun in it. My heartbeat had picked up a little, my senses heightening. I was ready to go.

Kinkaid left, and Joe and I waited a few minutes to give him time to get inside the cemetery. Outside the sky was darkening quickly, the shadows deepening along the window. Joe checked the Smith & Wesson he kept in his shoulder holster, then replaced it, leaving the buckle open.

"How do you feel?" he said.

"Couldn't be better. You?"

He was calm, but there was a new tension to his posture. "I don't know, LP. Something doesn't feel good about this guy."

"It's just Kinkaid," I said. "All that talk about how dangerous Hartwick is went to your head."

"Sure." He got to his feet and pulled his jacket on, leaving the zipper halfway down so he could reach for the gun easily. "Let's roll."

We took Joe's Taurus. The Chinese restaurant was only a half mile from the office. Amy and I occasionally picked up carryout there. Not bad food, but a little heavy on the garlic. Fabulous wonton soup, though. Traffic was still quite thick with the lingering hangover from rush hour. Joe drove while I rode with my eyes on the street. Just like we'd done it thousands of times before. Only now we didn't have the badges, and there was no dispatcher waiting to send us backup.

Joe pulled into the restaurant parking lot and stopped the car. A Dumpster stood in the corner of the lot alongside the cemetery fence. To the right was another wide expanse of parking lot, this stretch belonging to a drugstore. To the left was a Ford dealership with bright lighting and rows of shiny cars. There were five round picnic tables at the rear of the Chinese restaurant lot. In the summer there would be umbrellas over them, but now they were empty. A lone man sat at one of them, his back to the drugstore parking lot instead of to the cemetery fence as I'd expected. The green Oldsmobile was parked in front of his table, pointed toward the Ford dealership.

"That's him," I said. "With his back to the parking lot, no less. I guess he's more trusting than we thought."

Joe shook his head. "Nope. Just smarter than we thought. He's got that Olds parked so he can look straight ahead and still keep an eye on the lot behind him using the side-view mirrors. He figures the cemetery presents more of a threat because it's darker and less open, so he wants to be able to see it better than the parking lot."

We got out of the car and walked toward the picnic table. Hartwick had his head turned slightly, watching our approach. His hands were under the table, out of sight. I kept my own right hand on my hip, edging toward my back slightly. I didn't like not being able to see his hands.

We reached the table without incident, and I breathed a little easier. Hartwick nodded for us to sit. He was an average-size guy with a shaved head. His scalp was tan from the South Carolina sun, and the corded muscles of his neck told me that his body was well toned. He was like many of the Marines I'd known—not particularly large or intimidating but with a tightly muscled look that implied speed and power.

"Perry and Pritchard," he said with a hollow smile. "Have a seat, gentlemen. And, Perry, do me a favor?"

"What's that?"

"Keep your hand away from the gun at your back."

I took the hand away from my hip and placed both palms on the table as I sat. Hartwick was good, all right. He'd read my movements easily, and they hadn't been overt.

"Nice to meet you, boys," he said. "In case you're wondering how I picked you out, Perry, it wasn't too hard. Pritchard sounded older on the phone."

"He's pretty ancient," I said. "Not a tough guess to make."

"Uh-huh. You guys made a decent call yourselves, getting my name so quickly. I've got to give you credit for that. When you drove by the second time yesterday, I knew you'd noticed me, but I thought I'd bought a few days by putting the stolen plates on the rental car."

"That wasn't a bad trick," Joe said. "We're just too damn smart. Now, you want to tell us what you were doing there?"

"Watching the Russians," Hartwick said. "Same thing you were doing, only I didn't feel the need to talk to them in person." He cocked his head at me. "What was that all about?"

"That was just bad timing," I said.

His eyes left us momentarily and went to the cemetery, scanning the darkness, as if he'd heard or seen something he didn't like there. I hadn't heard a thing, but I knew Kinkaid should be up on the hill. Hartwick stared into the shadows for several seconds, then shifted position slightly and looked back at us.

"So you're working for John?"

"That's right." Joe leaned forward. "All we care about is giving that man some answers, Hartwick. We don't give a damn what you're doing here, but we want those answers."

Something seemed to flicker near Hartwick's shoulder. I squinted and looked closer, but it was gone. He was wearing a black sweatshirt, and his right arm was hidden in shadows. I kept my eyes on the spot where I'd seen the light, wondering if he had a gun or a knife tucked between his arm and the side of his body that had been caught momentarily in the glow of the streetlight.

"You want some answers," Hartwick said, and his lips parted in a small smile. "Well, maybe we can do some answer-sharing, Pritchard. That's something I think we can probably manage. But I've come here to settle a score, and I'm not going to let you two, or anyone else, prevent me from doing that."

The flicker returned, and this time I saw it clearly. It wasn't reflected light but a tiny red dot, the kind produced by a laser pointer or a—

"Get down," I shouted, rising out of my seat and reaching for my gun as I realized the dot belonged to a laser scope.

The red dot disappeared as quickly as it had come, and then there was a dull thumping noise, like an uppercut being landed on the soft part of the belly, and a dark hole punched through the center of Randy Hartwick's chest. Joe and I dived to the pavement as Hartwick fell forward onto the table and slid to the ground, dead, blood seeping from the gaping cavity near his heart.

I hit the ground hard and rolled onto my side, pushing my body partially under the bench of the picnic table while I drew my gun. I knew Joe was somewhere to my left, but I didn't bother to look at him. Hartwick's body lay just in front of me, his mouth half open, his eyes vacant. I stayed on the ground for a few seconds, waiting for another shot. None came. Behind me, Joe was yelling into his cell phone, giving the 911 dispatcher our location. I rolled back to my right and got into a crouch, then slipped the safety off the Glock and lifted my head above the table.

The parking lot to our right was empty, and to our left the brightly illuminated Ford dealership appeared harmless. No one was visible among the rows of cars. Behind us, on the street, traffic moved along as usual and the sidewalk was empty. The gunman had used a suppressor to silence the shot, and no one else even seemed aware of the incident. I dropped back to my knees and looked at Hartwick again. There was no point in wasting time with him. He'd been dead before he hit the ground.

I'd seen the red dot of the laser scope pass over his right shoulder before coming to bear on his chest. That made the cemetery a possible location for the shooter, but it was more likely the bullet had been fired from somewhere near the Ford dealership. I set off for the rows of cars at a jog.

"Lincoln, dammit, where are you going?" Joe yelled after me, but I ignored him and kept running, gun in hand. I circled the lot quickly and saw no one. There was a clear exit onto both the avenue and a side street, though. If the shooter had been inside a car, he would have been long gone by the time I got back to my feet. I returned to the picnic table.

"He's dead," Joe said when I came back. He was kneeling over Hartwick's body.

"No shit," I said.

"Shot probably came from the car lot."

"Already checked it. Nobody's there. It could have been fired from the cemetery, though. Bad angle, but it's possible."

Joe looked up from the body. "Where the hell is Kinkaid?"

We both looked at the cemetery fence and yelled for him. No one responded.

"This isn't good," Joe said, and I knew he was wondering if Kinkaid was still alive. I headed for the fence as sirens began to wail in the distance. Before I reached the fence, Kinkaid appeared in the darkness, his face pale and confused.

"What's going on?" he said, putting both hands on top of the fence and pulling himself up so he could jump over it. He took a few steps toward us before seeing the body.

"Oh, shit. What the hell happened?"

"Someone took Hartwick out," I told him. "Where have you been? You see anything in the cemetery?"

He shook his head, his wide eyes still locked on the body. "No. I just got *in* the cemetery a minute ago. You didn't tell me the gates would be locked. I had to leave my car outside, jump the fence, and run up here. It's a big cemetery, too."

"There was no one else inside?"

"Not that I saw." He'd slipped his own gun out now, a gigantic Colt Python that would probably bring a charging elephant to a halt. He looked around the parking lot nervously.

"Where did the shot come from?"

"Either the cemetery or someplace near the car dealership. I was hoping you would have seen someone."

"No." He crouched down and stared at the wound in Hartwick's chest. "That's a pretty long shot, from either location. Probably was a rifle."

"It definitely was a rifle," I said. "And it was silenced, too. They used a laser scope. I saw the dot a half second before Hartwick got aced."

A squad car pulled into the parking lot, lights flashing and siren wailing. The driver cut the siren when he stopped, but he left the lights on, bathing Hartwick's body in colorful flashes and making me squint. Two officers in uniform approached, guns drawn, and shouted at us to step away from the table and raise our hands. We did as they asked.

"We all have firearms," Joe said calmly. "Take them from us, but don't freak out about it."

The taller cop, who had a thin, pointed nose like a bird's

beak and a shrunken chest that left his uniform shirt hanging loosely, squinted at Joe.

"Holy shit," he said. "Is that Pritchard?"

"Yeah, it's Pritchard," his partner said. He was shorter and rounder, and I recognized him. His last name was Baggerly, but I couldn't remember his first name. They took our guns and then stepped back, studying the corpse at their feet.

"Ouch," the tall cop said. "Put one right through his heart. Who is this guy?" He looked at Joe.

"His name's Randy Hartwick," Joe said. "You're going to need to get someone from the detectives division out here as quickly as possible."

"Looks like that, don't it?" He looked at the three of us, then spoke in a whisper to Baggerly, who walked a few steps away and spoke into his microphone. After a minute he returned.

"Detectives are on the way," he said. "Until then, we'll sit tight. Medical examiner will be out shortly to deal with the body."

We sat tight. Another squad car arrived, and Baggerly instructed those officers to establish a perimeter and keep away the curious bystanders who had gathered, attracted by the police car. A few minutes later, the detectives arrived. I watched them get out of the car and stifled a groan. It was Janet Scott and her partner, Tim Eggers. Eggers was a decent guy, but Scott was a colossal bitch. We'd never gotten along in my days on the force, and I knew she wasn't Joe's favorite person, either.

Janet Scott was dressed in jeans and a leather jacket, and she had her badge hanging around her neck on a nylon cord. Her short blond hair was cut in jagged ends that I supposed were stylish. She'd probably paid fifty bucks for the haircut, but I could have given her the same look with a weed whacker. Scott was a small, trim woman, and I knew plenty of the male cops thought she was dead sexy. I'd never been able to see past the abrasive personality and poor judgment, though. The few times I'd had to work with her, she'd been a tremendous pain in the ass. Her investigative skill was limited, to say the least, but her confidence in her ability was not. It was a disastrous combination. Eggers had been her partner for a few years now, and, although his meek personality kept him in the background, it was no secret that he was the brains of the duo.

"Lincoln Perry and Joe Pritchard," Scott said as she strode toward us. "I'll be damned. I remember when you used to be with the good guys." She eyed the corpse. "Now it doesn't look that way, does it?"

"Unfortunately, we didn't kill him," Joe said.

"That's what all the murderers say." She dropped into a crouch beside the body as I had done and studied Hartwick carefully, shaking her head and making a soft clucking noise with her tongue, like a scolding mother. Eventually, she got back to her feet and looked at me.

"Long time, eh, Perry?"

"Too long," I said with mock sincerity. "I've missed you, Janet."

"I'll bet. Let's see, when was the last time I saw you?" She frowned and looked at the sky as if she were trying to recall something. "Oh, right, shortly before you beat up one of the city's most prominent lawyers and got axed for your stupidity." She smiled sweetly. "How could I have forgotten?"

"It's funny how easily things can slip your mind," I said. The lawyer had been involved with my fiancée, and I'd been drunk at the time, but basically she had the facts right.

"So what have you been doing since then, Perry?"

"Working as a massage therapist in Belgium. I just got back to the States today."

She gazed at me with unfriendly eyes. "Don't get too cute, Perry. I've got all night to deal with you. And, thanks to your pal on the pavement, it looks like it'll be a long time before you get to sleep."

She turned away then and went to consult with Eggers. The medical examiner had arrived now to deal with the corpse. I looked back down at Hartwick and swore softly.

He'd been ready to talk. Ready to do some answer-sharing, as he'd put it. Now he'd never share any answers with anyone. Someone had been awfully afraid of what Hartwick knew. It was up to us to find out what that had been.

TWELVE

It took Scott ten hours to turn us loose. She held us at the scene for a while, and then she had some of the uniforms take us to the station to wait for questioning. We were there the rest of the night. Scott pressed us for details about Hartwick, but we didn't have much to provide. Kinkaid told her he knew Hartwick only as Wayne Weston's friend, and he didn't mention Hartwick's involvement with weapons smuggling. Joe and I admitted we'd come across Hartwick while working on the Weston matter. Scott's eyes lit up at that news, and I knew she was dreaming of the headlines and prestige that would come with the case. I also knew she wasn't going to see any of it. The FBI was calling the shots on it now. Even though the Hartwick murder was under CPD jurisdiction, they'd keep Scott out of the loop and away from the Weston case, no matter how intertwined the two seemed.

For a while Scott tried to bluff as if we were suspects in the murder. Probably she thought she could scare us into giving up more details about Hartwick. It was a stupid ploy, considering Hartwick had been taken out at long range with a rifle. They questioned us separately and then brought us together for more rehashing. After that session, Kinkaid left to go to the restroom, and Scott left to make a phone call, leaving Joe and me alone with Eggers.

"Hey, Tim," I said, "you might want to check out Kinkaid."

He frowned. "You think he shot the guy?"

Joe looked at me, too, eyebrows raised. I shook my head. "I don't think he shot Hartwick, but I do think it would be worth taking a look at him. Kinkaid was in position for the shot, and we don't really know much about him yet. He lied to Joe originally, or he says he did, then showed up in our office offering to help. It was a nice gesture, but we haven't had time to check him out yet. For all we know, he could have been scared of what Hartwick was going to tell us. Maybe scared enough to kill him."

"Why does he care what Hartwick tells us?" Joe asked. "The guy hasn't worked with Weston in years. Hell, he hasn't even been in the city in years."

"I'm not saying it's likely, I'm just saying he deserves a careful look."

Eggers shook his head. "I'm sure we're going to find the dead guy was killed by a rifle bullet. Kinkaid's carrying a Colt Python revolver. It's a damn big gun, but it's not going to be the gun used in this killing."

"He's carrying a Colt Python," I said. "Doesn't mean he didn't have another gun with him."

"You're saying he might have used a rifle from the cemetery, dumped it back in his car, and then ran out to meet you?" He shrugged. "We're going to check all the cars, don't worry, but I doubt that's possible. It's a hell of a run across that cemetery."

Joe nodded. "Kinkaid didn't do it," he said. "To make that run and show up right after the shooting would have been impressive, and he wasn't even out of breath. Besides, if he dumped the rifle anywhere in the cemetery, they'll find it."

Kinkaid stepped back into the room, his face clouded with anger. "Thanks for the vote of confidence, Pritchard," he said, then pointed at me. "And, you, Perry, are an asshole."

I felt a flush creep into my neck and face. "I'm sorry, Kinkaid. I'm not saying I think you killed him, okay? But the fact is, we don't know much about you, and you were in a position to make the shot."

He shook his head at me, his lip curled up in distaste. "Whatever, Perry." He turned to Eggers. "Where's the men's room? I couldn't find it the first time. Good thing, too, or I might have missed out on that conversation."

They finally cut us loose around five in the morning. By then we were all exhausted, and we had to call a cab because the police had impounded Joe's Taurus and Kinkaid's car.

"Look, Aaron, I apologize," I said as we stood outside waiting on the cab. "It wasn't anything personal. It's just an old detective's reaction of trying to consider who might have been in position to do the crime."

He nodded without looking at me. "It's all right, Perry. I understand. I'm not going to lie and say I don't care, because it pissed me off, but I'm also not going to let it get in our way. I want to find Julie Weston, and we're going to need to work together to get that done."

"You're already booked into a hotel?" Joe asked.

"Yeah, I made reservations before I came in today. I was planning on staying in town for a few days."

"Go get some sleep, then. When you wake up, come down to the office, and we'll get started. Someone killed Hartwick because they didn't want him talking to us, and we need to find out who that person is."

"We'll hear from Cody tomorrow," I predicted. "He'll be full of questions when he finds out about this."

"I'd imagine," Joe said.

"We're stirring things up now. That's obvious. Someone's concerned by our investigation."

"So why didn't the shooter take you out, too?" Kinkaid said. "Or at least try?"

Joe shook his head. "I don't know. But let's not complain."

Kinkaid took the first cab that arrived, and Joe and I remained on the sidewalk, waiting for another. I watched the taillights of Kinkaid's cab disappear down the street and then turned away as they grew smaller. I'd seen enough glowing red dots for one day.

When I woke later that morning, the ache that had crept into my neck and shoulders the day before had intensified, and I groaned as soon as I moved. My back muscles felt like guitar strings after a Jimi Hendrix solo. A glance at the clock told me it was almost eleven, which meant I'd had four hours of sleep. I needed a long, hot shower, but I knew Joe would already be at the office, and I didn't want to delay. I got dressed, splashed some cold water on my face, brushed my teeth, combed my hair, and headed out.

Joe was at the office, of course. He was sitting behind the desk and talking on the phone, dressed in khakis and a shirt and tie, looking like a man who'd just returned to work after a week's vacation, refreshed and invigorated. I shook my head. Joe was amazing. When I'd worked with him as a narcotics detective, I'd learned just how long he could go without much sleep, or any sleep. And, somehow, he never seemed to lose his mental edge. His ability to avoid—or ignore—physical fatigue was incredible.

I dropped into my own chair beside him and eavesdropped on his conversation. It appeared he was talking to a cop about Hartwick. Eggers, maybe. Scott would still be in bed after pulling the all-nighter. Her work ethic was almost as well known as Joe's, but for an entirely different reason.

Joe hung up and smiled brightly at me. "Morning, LP. Have a pleasant evening?"

I glared at him. "I hate you and your damned energy."

"I'm almost twice your age, kid. Don't give me that crap."

I grunted and sipped the coffee I'd picked up at the doughnut shop on my way down. "Who were you talking to?"

"Eggers."

"I knew it. What'd he have to say?"

"He wouldn't say his partner's an idiot, although I tried to elicit agreement from him. He did say they found Hartwick's hotel room."

"Anything in it?"

"Not really. Nothing that helps explain what he was doing in Cleveland, at least. Eggers said they did find plenty of ammunition, though—along with two extra handguns, and even a grenade. Sounds like Hartwick was ready to go to war."

I raised my eyebrows. "A *grenade*? You kidding me?"

"That's what Eggers said. I'm just glad the guy left it at the hotel room, otherwise maybe it goes off by accident last night and blows up half the avenue, including you and me. Oh, yeah, we're going to have to go back down this afternoon and chat with Scott and Eggers some more."

"So they aren't getting anywhere, eh? If they were, they wouldn't have more time to waste on us."

"They're not getting anywhere. Personally, I assume the shooter was one of the Russians. Don't you?"

The coffee had cooled enough to drink now, and I took several long swallows before responding.

"I guess it's safe to say I *assume* it was one of them. Can't prove it, obviously, but it makes sense. We know some of them were special ops guys, and whoever made the shot was pretty familiar with a rifle. The scope was high-tech, too."

"Uh-huh. By the way, Cody's due down here any minute. I told him to give you until eleven. Kinkaid will be here soon, too."

"How long have *you* been here?"

He glanced at the clock. "Oh, maybe three hours."

"Did you sleep at all, Joe?"

"I'm fine."

I didn't push it. "So, here's a question for you."

"Yeah?"

"After all the chaos yesterday, our interview with Dan Beckley seems insignificant, but it established some pretty important points about Weston's professional relationship with Hubbard, I think. Should we pursue that or focus on Hartwick and the Russians?"

Joe pressed his fingertips together and lifted his hands to his chin. It looked like he was praying. "I don't know," he said. "I think they're both important, and I think they might be connected. One thing I *don't* want, though, is for us to tell Cody about that."

"About Dan Beckley?" I said, and he nodded. "Why not?" I asked. "We've already given him Hubbard."

"I know we have, but now that we've got a better idea of what was going on between Weston and Hubbard, I want to keep it quiet for a while. Hubbard's a hell of a powerful guy, LP, maybe the most powerful man in this city. And I don't completely trust Cody. He's fed us bad leads before, and I don't like that."

"You're saying Hubbard might be pulling strings with the FBI?" I said. "*Now* who's having trust issues, Joseph?"

Someone knocked at the door, and then it opened and Aaron Kinkaid poked his head inside. "Morning," he said. I was pleased to see that he looked even worse than I did. He came in and sat down.

"Long night," he said. "I'm exhausted."

"A guy named Thad Cody's going to be here soon," Joe said. "Probably with a couple of Cleveland cops in tow. Cody's with the FBI, and he's calling the shots on the Weston investigation. He's going to have quite a few questions for you."

As if on cue, the door opened again and Cody entered, with Swanders behind him. Kraus was missing this time. It was a good thing I'd woken up when I had, or I might have been roused from bed by a pissed-off FBI agent.

"Is this Kinkaid?" Cody said, pointing at our redheaded visitor.

"I'm Aaron Kinkaid."

"Good. Then we're all here." Cody pulled up a chair, but Swanders remained on his feet, leaning against the wall. Cody was wearing a suit today, and he had his briefcase with him again. He'd been a little overbearing in our first meeting, but that was nothing compared to the attitude he carried with him today. He was angry now.

"All right, gentlemen," he said. "Let's hear what you've got to say. And it better be true, and it better be detailed. Because if you've compromised my investigation, I'll spend the rest of my career making you regret it."

It was a hell of a way to get the ball rolling. We talked. Joe explained Kinkaid's arrival in our office the day before, as well as how we'd determined Randy Hartwick's identity. Kinkaid then jumped in to explain what he knew of Hartwick. This time, he didn't leave out the weapons smuggling. Cody frowned at that and leaned forward, intense.

"Who was he running guns for?"

"I don't know," Kinkaid said.

"No ideas? You never heard any names? Do you know what kind of weapons he was involved with? Anything?"

Kinkaid shook his head. "I don't. All I know is what Wayne Weston told me. He didn't offer any details, and I didn't ask."

"I see. So, what brought you here in the first place, Mr. Kinkaid?"

Kinkaid looked at his shoes again, as he had when he'd talked to Joe and me the day before. "I, uh, well, I care about Julie Weston," he said. "I was pretty close to her, you know? And, well, I'd like to do what I can to help."

We talked for more than an hour. Swanders jumped in occasionally with questions, but it was clear that Cody was in charge. No one offered an explanation of where Kraus was or why he was missing.

"I've got to hand it to you assholes," Cody said. "You really know how to make things more difficult. This Hartwick guy could have been just who we needed to break this case open. But do you call me, give me a heads-up? No, you don't. Instead you try to play the game your own way, and then you get burned. And, in the process, I get burned, because now a guy I need to talk to is dead." He shook his head with disgust. "I told you I wanted to work with you on this. But now you've made it clear you aren't willing to work with us."

I felt like a schoolboy being chastised by the principal— aware of the consequences of my actions, but at the same time somewhat amused with the whole scenario. Cody had never wanted to work with us. He'd made that clear when he had Swanders and Kraus feed us the bogus gambling tip. And he could have had the first crack at Hartwick if he'd been sharper. If he *had* found Hartwick first, I was sure he wouldn't have bothered to notify Joe and me. Now he was griping at us, but his own investigation seemed to have stagnated. He didn't want to work with us, but he saw we were making more progress than he was, and it was pissing him off.

"We've tried to work with you," Joe objected. "We told you to check out Hubbard. Have you done that?"

"Yeah, we're working on that, Pritchard. But it's going to take more than a day, all right?"

"We found Hartwick in one day," I said.

"And you got him killed in that same day, you jackass." Cody sighed and tugged at his tie. "I'm furious with you for the way that turned out, but there's no use crying about it now. He's dead, and he can't tell us anything. We need to find someone who *can* help us, though. You have any idea who might be associated with Hartwick?"

Joe and I shook our heads, and Cody looked at Kinkaid.

"I don't know," Kinkaid said. "Like I said, he was just a guy from out of state I met a few times. That's all. If you ask me, you're wasting time focusing on Jeremiah Hubbard, though. The Russians are clearly involved with this thing. What Weston was doing for Hubbard isn't necessarily re-lated. In fact, it's more likely his connection to them came from Hartwick, not Hubbard."

Cody seemed to like that suggestion. "You're right. Hub-bard's a businessman. Hartwick was a professional thug."

It seemed that Wayne Weston had been one, too. Or at least a professional extortionist. I looked at Joe, thinking about Dan Beckley, and he gave me an almost imperceptible shake of the head.

"Here's the deal," Cody said. "I'm going to see what we can find out about this Hartwick guy. In the meantime, you are going to sit on your hands, got me? I was content to let you stay on the case when I thought you'd cooperate, but, obviously, that's not how it worked. You jeopardize my investigation again, and I'll see that your licenses are revoked. Understand?"

"That's the deal?" I said. "Hell of a deal, Cody."

He smiled coldly. "Okay, it's not a deal. It's a command, Perry. An order. And you'd be wise not to test me on it." He got to his feet. "I'll be in touch."

After Cody and Swanders were gone, Kinkaid looked at us. "That's bullshit," he said. "You two run a legitimate business. He can't tell you what cases you can and can't take, not unless he's got something to charge you with."

"No, he can't," Joe said. "But he can make it damn difficult for us."

"Surely you're not telling me you're going to listen to him? Dammit, Pritchard, you can't quit on this."

Joe stared at him with surprise and distaste, as if Kinkaid had suggested Joe give up the PI trade and become a figure skater. "I'm not going to quit on this," he said condescendingly. "I'm just saying it will be more difficult now. We're going to have to keep something of a low profile."

"So, what now?" Kinkaid said. "How do we move forward?"

"The way I see it, we've got to do two things," Joe said. "We've got to find out much, much more about the Russians. We need to find out who they deal with, what type of scams they're running—absolutely anything that might connect them to Weston or Hartwick. Or Hubbard. And we've got to do the same thing with Hartwick. Basically, we've got to perform some thorough background investigations on everyone we've connected with this case."

"It's going to be hard to do that with Hartwick," I said. "He's based in South Carolina, not Cleveland. As far as we know, he was just a visitor here."

"Well, then," Joe said, "it seems to me one of us should go to South Carolina."

Kinkaid frowned. "Split up? I don't like that."

"You didn't like it last night, either, Kinkaid, but we ignored your advice then and we'll ignore it now," Joe said, making the remark lighthearted enough to avoid riling Kinkaid again. "If we all go trooping down to South Carolina, Cody will throw a fit. And we'll be losing time up here."

"Cody's going to shit a brick, regardless," I said, "If we all go down, or just one of us."

"I'm assuming a few days down there should be sufficient for you," Joe said. "Until then, I'll try to keep your absence from attracting Cody's attention. If he does find out, I'll tell him you're out of state on another case, something unrelated to Wayne Weston. He can't prevent us from working altogether, although he'd surely like to try."

"You're assuming a few days will be sufficient for *me?* I gather I've been nominated as our South Carolina man?"

Joe nodded. "Yeah, you have been. Scott and Eggers will more likely want to keep on eye on Kinkaid than on you or me, so I figure he and I should stay in the city and see what we can do with the Russians. Besides, the Russians present the greatest threat, so it would be best to keep two men here."

"Scott and Eggers," I said. "Shit, I forgot about them. They'll never let me leave the city a day after witnessing a murder."

"Gee," Joe deadpanned, his eyes wide and innocent, "maybe we shouldn't tell them you're leaving."

THIRTEEN

When I stepped off the plane in Myrtle Beach late the next morning, I closed my eyes and took a deep, contented breath. It was seventy degrees, and the sun was out. When I'd left Cleveland a few hours earlier, it had been in the upper thirties, with snow flurries spitting through a stiff wind off the lake. For the first time since I'd heard of him, I was thankful Randy Hartwick had lived in South Carolina.

I drove down the town's beach strip in a rented Ford Contour with the idea of scanning the hotels until I found the Golden Breakers. After a few blocks, I realized that was a bigger task than I'd anticipated. The hotels seemed to go on endlessly. I drove slowly down Ocean Avenue for fifteen minutes and saw nothing but hotels, hundreds of them. Most of the hotels on the beach side of the street were tall, elegant structures, while just across the street they tended to be tacky one- or two-story buildings that were a far cry from their impressive neighbors. Only fifty yards apart, and yet the difference in quality—and, no doubt, in room rates—was amazing. After passing dozens upon dozens of hotels and resorts without locating the Golden Breakers, I gave up and pulled off Ocean Avenue in search of a gas station. Running parallel to Ocean Avenue but a few hundred yards farther inland was Business Highway 17, the commercial strip. On this road hotels were scarce, but you couldn't spit out the window without hitting a T-shirt shop or a seafood restaurant. I pulled into the first gas station parking lot I found and went inside to ask for directions.

The clerk, a bored-looking girl who was twirling her blond hair with her fingers, told me I was eight blocks south of the resort and then said, "All the hotels have maps on their brochures and reservation mailings, you know." Smartass. I didn't have a brochure or a reservation.

I found the Golden Breakers eight blocks north, just as the gas station clerk had promised. It was a hell of a building, too. A single-story lobby was bordered on each side by a sixteen-story tower containing the rooms and suites. On top of the lobby was a sundeck with a pool. Nice. I parked in the entryway and went inside. The sign indicated there were vacancies, so I decided I might as well stay at the Golden Breakers. I asked for room rates; while the figure was higher than I wanted to pay, it was also much cheaper than it would be a few months down the road, when tourism season hit its peak. It would be on John Weston's tab, anyhow. I asked for a two-night stay and paid with my credit card, keeping an extra receipt for the expense account.

Once the bill was settled, I returned to the Contour and drove across the street to park in the hotel's garage. For the first time I was thankful to have the little car. The parking garage had the lowest ceiling of any garage I'd ever been in, and I wasn't sure my truck would have fit. Maybe everyone down here drove small sports cars. There would certainly be little need for four-wheel drive. I found a spot, took my suitcase from the trunk, and went back to the hotel. My room was on the second floor of the north tower. I took the elevator up, found the room, and went inside.

The hotel room was actually three rooms: a living room with a couch and television, a small but fully equipped kitchen, and a bedroom. Both the bedroom and the living room had sliding glass doors that opened onto a wide balcony overlooking the beach. I dropped my bag onto the couch and went out on the balcony.

The sun was shining, reflecting off the water and making the waves sparkle. Several people lay on blankets on the sand, working on their tans, and a group of kids were tossing a football back and forth near the water's edge. Too cold for them to be swimming yet. A single boat with a bright blue-and-yellow sail was cutting through the water a few hundred yards off the beach. I leaned over the rail and looked down. The beach wasn't very crowded, but that didn't surprise me. It was too early in the year for family vacations, and there was at least a week still to go before spring break would bring the college kids down. I left the balcony door open to let the warm breeze in and went back inside. It was a beautiful day and I had a beautiful hotel room, but I was here to work. I took off my long-sleeved shirt and pulled on a thin polo shirt, then slipped the Glock into its holster at the base of my spine. I wasn't expecting trouble, but Randy Hartwick had certainly attracted some in Cleveland, so I wasn't about to go in search of his associates unprepared. I slipped the keycard for the room into my pocket and rode the elevator back down to the lobby. The receptionist saw me coming and smiled.

"Is the room satisfactory?"

"It's amazing," I said, and her smile widened, as if I'd just made her day. "But I have another question."

"What's that?"

"I was hoping to speak to the owner. Do you know where I might find him?"

She hesitated. "Well, Mr. Burks isn't here. Is there something a manager could help you with? Can I ask why you want to speak to the owner?"

"Because I want to know who's responsible for this dump," I said, waving my hand at the gleaming lobby. Her smile disappeared, and I said, "I'm just kidding."

"Oh." Her smile was back in place now. Relieved.

"I need to talk to the owner about a mutual acquaintance," I said. "Someone who passed away, I'm afraid."

She put her hand to her chest. "Oh, no! Why, we're really having some bad luck lately. Just two days ago a man called to tell our security chief that one of his close friends had died."

This was the same woman I'd talked to on the phone. Possibly the nicest person in the world, and now I'd cast a shadow over her day twice in the same week. I was from Cleveland, though. She probably expected it.

"Hmm," I said. "Yes, that is depressing. Now, do you have any idea where I might find the owner? A Mr. Burks, is it?"

"Yes, Lamar Burks. As I said, he's not here today, and I don't think he will be, but I could take a message for him."

"Well, I was really hoping to find him today."

She frowned. "I think he's playing golf, but I don't know which course."

"I suppose I could call around and ask," I said, and she smiled at me and shook her head.

"You're in the wrong place for that. There are about one hundred golf courses within an hour of this hotel."

"Yikes." I drummed my fingers on the counter and thought about it. The receptionist was wearing a name tag that said REBECCA. Pretty name. Pretty face, too. Probably nice legs under that counter. What was I thinking about again? Oh, right, finding the owner.

"You said the hotel has golf packages available?" I asked. She nodded. "Yes."

"Well, maybe Burks plays those courses frequently. It seems like he'd be on pretty good terms with the management."

"Good idea," she said, sounding truly impressed, and I tried not to blush. Shucks. I'm full of great ideas, Rebecca. Having a few about you right now, in fact.

She crossed the room and pulled a brochure from the rack on the wall. I'd been right; she *had* been hiding some damn fine legs under that counter.

"It looks like we have packages with five different courses," she said. "That would be a place to start."

I took the brochure from her. "Mind if I use your phone?"

"I'm not supposed to let you use it, but I won't tell if you don't."

"Deal."

She put the phone on the counter, and I began calling and asking the pro shops if Lamar Burks was around. I said it casually, as if I fully expected he'd be there, trying not to make anyone uneasy with my calls. On the fourth call, I found him at the Sweetwater Bay Golf Course.

"Yeah, Lamar's around," the man who answered said. "Hell, he's been here all day. We've been trying to throw him out for hours." Someone laughed loudly in the background. Nothing like a little fun in the pro shop, smoking cigars and talking golf all day while everyone else is working for a living. "I don't see him right now, but he's got a tee time in an hour," the man told me. "He's probably down at the putting green, maybe out at the range."

"Thanks," I said, "I'll try to catch up with him."

I hung up and smiled. "Success, Rebecca. Thanks for your help."

She seemed to like my using her name. "You're welcome. Should you need anything else, I hope you won't hesitate to ask me."

"I'll probably have to hesitate," I said. "Sweet, elegant women like yourself shouldn't be corrupted by men like me."

She smiled and ran the tip of her tongue over her bottom lip. "A little corruption never hurt anyone."

Oh, man. I needed to leave, or Lamar Burks and Randy Hartwick were quickly going to become forgotten goals of the afternoon.

"I've got to go, Rebecca," I said. "But promise you'll miss me."

"I promise," she said, and laughed. I left the hotel. I was starting to like South Carolina just fine.

The Sweetwater Bay Golf Course was only a fifteen-minute drive from the hotel. There was a map on the brochure, and I found the course without trouble. The pro shop was a small, white clapboard building surrounded by palm trees. If you've just spent a winter in Cleveland, palm trees rank among the most welcome sights in the world. Signs pointed down golf cart paths toward the "Championship Course" and the "Executive Course." I parked and went inside. An overweight man in khaki shorts and a Nike polo shirt was seated behind the counter. I asked him if he'd seen Lamar Burks.

"You the guy who called earlier?" he said, not taking his eyes off the small television suspended from the ceiling. The Golf Channel was on, and someone was demonstrating the art of chipping. Fascinating stuff.

"Yeah, I called earlier. Is Lamar around?"

"Uh-huh." He waved his head toward the front of the building without looking at me. "He's on the range. He'll be going out on the executive course soon."

I looked out the window and saw the driving range at the far end of the parking lot. There were only six people there, and three of them were women. There were two young white men and a middle-aged black man.

"Can I get a bucket of balls?" I asked.

"Grab one from the rack," he said. "It's five dollars."

"Okay. Got any clubs I can use?"

He finally looked away from the screen, staring at me as if I'd asked to borrow his underwear. "You don't have any clubs?"

"I'm from out of state. Wasn't planning on playing."

He shook his head as if this were stunning news. "Well, there are some beaters on the stand against the wall. Grab whatever you'd like."

I paid him for the bucket and selected a seven-iron, pitching wedge, and driver from the stand of clubs on the wall. The "beaters" were nicer than any clubs I'd ever owned.

I went outside and walked up to the range. The white guys had left, leaving only the women and the black man. As I approached, one of the women said, "Nice shot, Lamar."

Lamar Burks was hitting off the grass. I emptied half of my bucket beside him, and he smiled and nodded at me. He was about forty, a short, powerfully built man, with shoulders like gigantic hams. He was wearing white shorts and a white shirt, and under the shorts his thighs and butt were massive. Not fat, either, just thick. It was the kind of backside that would have made for a hell of a post game in basketball.

I found a tee lying in the grass and placed one of the balls on it, then took the driver and got into position. I'd never been much of a golfer. The game was a little too slow for me, and certainly not athletic enough to compensate for a good workout or game of pickup basketball. I played occasionally but planned on saving most of my outings for my retirement, when my aging body would no longer take the basketball games and workouts but would certainly be up to golf. It had been nearly a year since I'd even swung a club. I took a few practice cuts, trying to get the feel of the driver, and then stepped up to the tee.

My first shot went about a hundred and fifty yards, but all of them came on the ground. I'd sent the ball whistling across the grass, bouncing occasionally but never rising more than a foot in the air. I put another ball on the tee and swung again. This time I got it in the air, but it sliced horribly. So did the second shot. And the third.

Beside me, Lamar Burks chuckled softly. "Boy," he said, "maybe I should move down a bit, keep out of the line of fire."

"No need for sarcasm, Lamar. I'm just shaking off the rust."

He raised his eyebrows. "Uh-oh. It knows my name."

I offered my hand. "Lincoln Perry," I said. "I was hoping to talk to you about one of your employees."

"Which one?" he said as we shook.

"Randy Hartwick."

His eyes narrowed. "And who exactly are you, Mr. Perry?"

I got out my wallet and showed him my license. He studied it carefully, then nodded. "Well, all right. We can talk. But you'd better believe I'm going to finish hitting my bucket first."

"Fair enough."

"Go ahead and hit your bucket, too, and I'll try not to

laugh. Won't be easy, though. That might be the ugliest swing this county's ever seen."

I set down the driver and picked up the seven-iron. "Tell you what, Lamar. I'll bet you fifty dollars I can hit this seven-iron farther than you can hit yours."

"You gotta be kidding me, son! Oh, yes, yes, yes. If there's anything I like more than a betting man, it's a betting fool," he said, and laughed loudly. "How many swings?"

"Your call."

"Three swings, then."

"Deal." I wasn't too concerned about losing my money. I'd seen Burks take several swings now, and, while he was a hell of an accurate golfer, he wasn't much for distance. His arms were short, and his swing was very controlled. He'd been hitting his five-wood when I arrived, and he'd hit that only about two hundred yards. He also had a driver with an enormous, oversized head, the kind that was so popular among golfers who struggled to hit a long drive. I couldn't hit woods well, but I was pretty decent with clubs that had more loft. I didn't have much of an aptitude for the game of golf, but my length and strength usually allowed me to hit very well for distance.

Burks took his seven-iron out of the bag and took a few practice cuts. I liked what I saw. He had a short swing.

"I'll go first," he said. He hit his first shot right down the middle, but only a hundred and forty yards. A pretty ball, but not a long one.

"Damn," he said. "I hit that like my grandmother. Next ball." He swung again, snapping the wrists through a little quicker this time, and got an extra fifteen yards out of it, although the ball tapered off to the right.

"One fifty-five," he announced happily. It was a pretty long shot for a seven-iron; most golfers would take it. He hit the third ball, but this time he was back at one forty again.

"You've got to beat one fifty-five," he said, stepping back. "And I know that ain't going to happen."

"We'll see." I used the club head to pull a ball into posi-

tion and then took my first swing. I pulled my chin up as I
made contact, and the ball sliced again, going about a hundred twenty yards, and almost an equal distance to the right.
Burks laughed loudly. I set another ball up and rolled my
shoulders, trying to relax. The smoother the swing, the better it would work for me. This time, I kept my head down
and swung through the ball smoothly. It was the closest
thing to a straight shot I'd hit yet, with just a slight slice, and
I put it almost to the one seventy-five marker. I turned to
Burks and smiled.

"Bullshit," he said. "You didn't just do that! Damn, and it
was on an ugly-ass swing, too. I mean an *ugly-ass* swing."
He shook his head.

I laughed. "The bet wasn't about swing quality, it was
about distance. You owe me fifty, but I'll probably let it slide
if you're cooperative."

"I'll tell you only what I think I *should* tell you," he said
seriously. "I'm an honest man, but I'm not the type of man
who encourages trouble. If you're looking to cause Randy
some sort of hassle, you'll need to look elsewhere."

"I won't be causing him a hassle," I said. "Nor will anyone else. Mr. Hartwick was murdered in Cleveland yesterday, Lamar."

He'd been taking practice swings with his pitching
wedge. Now he dropped the club and turned to me, surprised. "Is that the truth?"

"It is."

He stared across the course, and I could see true sadness
and compassion in his eyes. Lamar Burks had liked Randy
Hartwick. Eventually, he picked his club back up and put it
in the bag.

"Let's you and I go have a drink," he said.

We went up to the clubhouse and took seats on the patio
that looked out on the driving range and practice green.
Burks had a beer, and I had lemonade. All the good humor
that had filled the man during our golf bet was gone. I had a
way of spoiling people's days.

"You don't drink?" he asked.

I shook my head. "Not while I'm working. I had one bad night and lost my job because of it."

"What was your job?"

"I was a cop." I let it go at that, but he waited, obviously hoping for more details. I sipped some more lemonade and told him about it.

"I was engaged to a woman I cared about a lot. More than she cared about me. I found out she was sleeping with a big-shot attorney, and I went down to the police bar to drown my sorrows in booze. Somewhere between the tenth and eleventh beer, I decided it would be a good idea to find the guy and talk it over with him. His helpful secretary told me he was having dinner at his country club, so I poured my drunken ass into the car and drove out there. I found him in the parking lot, and it didn't go so well. He kept smiling as if the situation were funny, and he called me 'champ' a few times too many."

Burks was watching me with interest but not judgment. "I only hit him once," I said, "but it was a hell of a punch. When I left he was lying on his face in the parking lot with a broken nose. I drove away, and about ten minutes later a highway patrol officer pulled me over after being dispatched to look for my car. I was arrested for drunk driving and assault. Convicted on both counts and dismissed from the force. The chief told me I was an embarrassment to the department." I finished the lemonade and pushed it aside.

"At least you got the satisfaction of breaking the bastard's nose," Burks said.

"It wasn't nearly as satisfying as you'd think."

He nodded. "So Randy's dead?"

"Died two nights ago, I'm afraid. I was with him when it happened. Someone took him out with a rifle from long range."

"What was he involved with?"

I spread my hands. "That's what I'm trying to find out. He was killed before he could tell me anything. My partner and I are trying to find a missing woman and her daughter.

The woman's husband was a shady operator; he might even have been involved with Russian organized crime. Hartwick supposedly has ties to the same folks, and he showed up in Cleveland a few days ago."

"Randy Hartwick was involved with the Russian mob?" Burks said it as if he found this hard to believe.

"That's what we've heard."

He shook his head. "I suppose anything's possible, but I'm awfully surprised to hear that. He was a hell of a nice guy."

"How long had he worked for you?"

"About ten years. I bought the resort twelve years ago. I was hoping to upgrade the security, you know, to avoid liability issues and all, and I started asking around about security companies. One of the guys I talked to suggested Randy, said he was fresh out of the Marines and looking for a job. So I called him, and we worked it out. He's done a fine job for me, too."

"A guy in Cleveland suggested Hartwick was using the security job as a front while he ran weapons in and out of the country," I said. "Was he around much?"

"He took vacations now and then, but, yeah, he was around for the most part. I never had any complaints about him. We'd meet every few weeks to talk things over. He always seemed serious about the job."

"Who's this man who recommended Hartwick to you?"

"A guy named John Brewster. He manages another one of the hotels, and he's an ex-Marine like Randy. You know how those Marines are about helping each other out with jobs? It's almost like a fraternity thing, except the Marines aren't a bunch of rich, pansy white boys."

"You think he could tell me more about Hartwick?"

"More than I can, that's for sure."

We kept at it for another half hour. Burks couldn't tell me much about Hartwick's personal affairs; he knew him only as a reliable and trusted employee. He did offer to pull Hartwick's personnel file and let me have a look at it. That might give me some new resources, if nothing else. He also gave me a phone number for John Brewster.

"I'm sorry I couldn't help you more, son. And I'm sorry about what happened to Randy, too."

"It's all right," I said. "You've helped as much as you can, and I appreciate that. Besides, it was fun taking your money."

He laughed and shook his head. "Shit, son, it was worth a few dollars to see that ugly swing of yours in action."

I left the golf course and drove back toward the Golden Breakers. I called John Brewster from the room and received no answer. Burks had promised to get me the personnel file by the next morning, but I didn't have it now. I left the room and found two of the resort's security guards, but neither of them could tell me anything about Hartwick. Apparently, he was the sort of guy who kept to himself. At five, I gave up and went for dinner.

I ate at a calabash seafood restaurant that offered an all-you-could-eat buffet for a reasonable cost. I hadn't eaten any lunch, so I definitely took my money's worth. When I was full, I returned to the hotel and went for a walk along the strip, my stomach still too heavy for a run. The people on the sidewalks were mostly older couples—middle-aged women clutching bulging shopping bags while their husbands trailed behind, reliving the day's golf game in their minds. In the summer there would be families with young children, and college students looking to party, but now, in early March, the town was quiet. I had a feeling I'd like it less if I came in the summer.

I walked a few miles south before I turned and went back. This time I left the sidewalk, cut behind the hotels, and walked across the sand, staying just a few feet ahead of where the waves washed up. The tide was rising, and in the morning this stretch of the beach would be submerged. It was dark now, and a full moon had risen, casting a pale glow on the black water and giving the waves a golden shimmer as they crested.

Back in the hotel room, I flipped through the television channels just long enough to determine there was nothing worthwhile on and then tried calling Joe. I didn't get an answer at the office, and his cell phone went right to voice mail, which meant it was turned off. Perfect. I sat on the balcony and watched the water some more, then tried calling Joe again and had the same result.

At ten I changed into an old pair of gym shorts and went downstairs. I hadn't packed swim trunks, as I'd been planning for business and not pleasure, but as long as I was here I might as well enjoy the whirlpool.

It was a beautiful night. The air was warm and smelled of saltwater and hyacinths. I turned on the jets in the whirlpool and settled into the steaming water. A cool breeze was coming in off the ocean, and the contrast of its feel across my face and the hot water on my body was a strange and invigorating sensation. I tilted my head back and looked at the moon, then closed my eyes and listened to the gentle thumps of the waves hitting the beach. I wondered what Joe was doing back in Cleveland and whether he and Kinkaid had been able to make any progress with the Russians or Hubbard. I wondered if they'd be disappointed in the utter lack of progress I'd had so far today. Probably. I thought about John Weston, and Randy Hartwick, and then flashes of Betsy Weston's smiling face and her beautiful mother slipped through my mind. It was easy to forget about them as I sat in the whirlpool with a refreshing night breeze bathing my face and the sound of waves in my ears. I didn't want to think about them. It was too nice a night.

I'd been in the whirlpool for about twenty minutes when I heard the door to the hotel open and close. I opened one eye and saw a woman with dark hair standing in the shadows, unwrapping a towel from around her waist and placing it on a lounge chair. Even from the side and in the shadows, it was obvious she had an amazing body. For a moment she looked vaguely familiar, and I wondered briefly if it could be Rebecca, the desk receptionist. Then I realized the hair was too curly. I closed my eyes again, disappointed. Maybe Rebecca would be back behind the desk in the morning.

The wind picked up off the ocean, cooling my face and neck and sending a chill down my spine despite the steaming temperature of the whirlpool. In the distance, someone was playing soft jazz music on one of the balconies. It was a fitting and welcome addition to the night. I heard the water splash beside me as the woman stepped into the whirlpool, and I reopened my eyes and looked at her. She gave me a shy smile and then did as I had done, leaning her head back, glancing at the moon, and closing her eyes. I kept mine open this time, though. There had been something familiar about the woman, all right. She was Julie Weston.

FOURTEEN

The jazz music kept playing, the waves kept crashing, and the wind kept blowing. Julie Weston kept her eyes closed, and I kept staring. I don't know how long I sat. My brain had caught up to the realization that Julie Weston—a woman sought by police across the country, a woman most people thought was dead—was sitting within feet of me, but it hadn't figured out what to do with this information. Eventually, I took a deep breath and looked away, out at the sea. I closed my eyes, took a few more deep breaths, and opened them again. She was still there. So much for the mirage theory. Now I'd actually have to deal with her.

I sank lower in the water, the breeze more chilling than refreshing now. Julie Weston seemed content to remain in the whirlpool for a while, so there was no reason to rush into action. That was a relief, because I hadn't decided how to handle the situation yet. I was too caught up in trying to process the facts.

Julie Weston was in Myrtle Beach, staying at the hotel where Randy Hartwick had worked. Hartwick was in a morgue in Cleveland. He'd been alive and in Cleveland for a few days prior to being murdered. Where had Julie Weston been during that time? Here? Then why had Hartwick left?

And where was Betsy Weston? I'd tried to enter into the case
without preconceived ideas of what had transpired the night
of Wayne Weston's death, but deep down I'd always believed
he'd been murdered and the wife and daughter abducted or
killed. Betsy Weston's diary entry had given me more hope
they were alive, but I'd still anticipated finding them in a situation of danger or crisis. I'd certainly never expected to
find one of them *here,* lounging in a resort whirlpool. For the
first time, I wondered if Julie Weston had murdered her own
husband. But why? To run away with Hartwick, who then
ran away to Cleveland? And where the hell did the Russians
come into play? None of it made any sense. But none of it
ever had. Tonight, though, I sat across from a woman who
could finally make some sense of it for me.

As if detecting the intense focus of my thoughts upon her,
Julie Weston opened her eyes and looked directly into mine.
I would have expected it to be impossible to distract my
thoughts from the questions swirling through my mind, but
she did it with one shy smile in my direction. The woman
was breathtaking. Her fine-boned face was perfectly propor-
tioned; her dark eyes were enchanting sparkles against
smooth skin; her full red lips looked as if they could chase
all the troubles in the world away with one soft touch. Her
dark brown hair seemed almost black as it fell around her
bare shoulders in curls that were wet from the steam of the
whirlpool. The water hid her body, but I'd seen it once already, and that brief viewing had been enough to leave it
permanently etched into my memory.

"Nice night," she said. I didn't speak. She smiled again,
seeming slightly awkward now, and I realized belatedly it
was from my lack of response.

"Beautiful night," I said, and I tore my eyes from her with
an effort and looked up at the moon, which seemed to hang
almost within reach above the palm trees, as if maybe by
climbing to the top of the fronds and stretching to your
fullest you could pull it down. She followed my eyes and
sighed softly.

"The moon's gorgeous, isn't it? It seems so different here."

"So different from where?" I asked, and with that simple question the carefree attitude vanished from Julie Weston. Her eyes narrowed slightly, her shoulders tensed, and she shifted on the whirlpool bench.

"Chicago," she said, her voice clipped and cold. "I'm from Chicago."

She hadn't changed her appearance since she left Cleveland. Her hair wasn't cut in a different style or dyed to another shade. She'd made no effort to change her complexion with makeup. Maybe that was what surprised me more than anything. She'd vanished from Cleveland more than a week ago, and now she was here, apparently unharmed. If she wanted to hide, why had she not attempted to alter her appearance? Since she hadn't altered it, how had she avoided being spotted? Her face had been on national news stations. Someone should have recognized her by now.

"Chicago," I said, and she nodded. "Nice town," I told her. "I'm from a lake city, myself."

"Really?" Her bored voice implied a complete lack of interest, and she slid down into the whirlpool and leaned her head back again, closing her eyes. It was forced, though, an act designed to end any questioning.

"Uh-huh," I said, pretending to be oblivious to her signals. "Similar city but a different lake. I'm from Cleveland."

She sat so still in the water she seemed not even to breathe. I realized after a few seconds that she actually *was* holding her breath, whether she was aware of it or not. For a moment I considered joining her in the silence, leaving her with the Cleveland comment lingering in her mind while I thought of a better way to approach her. Then I gave up on that idea. There wasn't going to be an easy way to approach her. Screw it.

"What are you doing here, Julie?" I said softly.

Her eyelids snapped open like shades pulled down and then released too quickly, and there was terror in her eyes.

She pushed herself out of the water and lunged for the purse she'd brought to the edge of the whirlpool. I went after her, the weight of the water slowing my movements. She had her hand inside the purse now, and I dived toward her, aware she was probably reaching for a weapon. My outstretched left arm caught her around the waist as I fell back into the water, pulling her away from the edge and down with me. She had something in her right hand: a small, slim canister I recognized as pepper spray. I chopped at her wrist, harder than I wanted to, but hard enough to ensure she wasn't going to be able to use the pepper spray against me. She dropped it into the water and turned against me, trying to put her knee into my groin. The weight of the water killed her momentum, though, and the blow glanced harmlessly off my upper thigh. I grabbed her forearms and forced them behind her back, pinning her, as she tried to use the knee again. She opened her mouth to scream, but I got my left hand over her lips, muffling the yell as I held both of her slim wrists in one hand.

"Relax, dammit," I said, pulling her body against mine to limit her ability to use the knee jabs with success. "I'm not here to hurt you. I work for John Weston. I work for your husband's father."

She continued to struggle, but her eyes changed with the words, and she was no longer attempting to scream. She tried to bite my hand, so I removed it from her lips. She didn't use it as an opportunity to shout for help, though.

"Relax," I repeated. "If I'd come here to kill you, Mrs. Weston, you'd be dead already."

I released her and stepped into the center of the whirlpool, rubbing my foot across the tile floor in search of the pepper spray. I found it, bent at the knees, and picked it up, keeping my eyes on her. She backed to the edge of the whirlpool and stood with her arms wrapped around her torso, hugging herself like a small child. Her damp hair hung in her face, and she was breathing heavily, watching me with the wary eyes of an animal that was used to being the prey and not the predator.

"There are a few things you can do now," I said, returning

to the edge of the whirlpool and lifting my body out of the water to sit on the concrete. The moisture on my skin immediately chilled as the breeze caught it. "You can get out of the water and run like hell. But I'll be right behind you. Not because I want to hurt you, but because it's my job. You can start screaming like a banshee, and you'll attract some attention. But do you really want to attract more attention? You're the woman the world is looking for." It was a bit of an overstatement, but for a Cleveland resident who had seen Julie Weston on the news every night, it didn't feel like one. "Or," I continued, "you can trust me, Mrs. Weston. I'd recommend you take that third option."

She retreated to the opposite edge of the whirlpool and sat on the concrete as I had done. She was still hugging herself tightly, but I didn't think it was because of the cool wind. She looked like a woman who felt very vulnerable. A woman who had felt very vulnerable for a while, maybe. She rubbed her hands over her upper arms and stared at me.

"You said John hired you?"

"That's right."

"Tell me about him."

I frowned, but then I realized this was her way of testing me, of seeing if I was who I claimed to be. "He's a loud, opinionated old soldier," I said. "And many people probably find him intimidating. He's a lonely man, and he's lonelier now than ever." She winced when I said that.

"He loves his son, he loves his granddaughter, and he loves you," I continued. "He's opened his savings account to me and my partner, just in hopes of finding you, or at least finding out what happened to you. That is his reason for living right now. The last time I saw him, he was sitting on the deck behind your house staring at a snowman your daughter built as if it held everything that was left of his soul."

I hadn't meant to make her feel guilty or sad. I'd simply described John Weston with the first images that came to my mind. By the time I mentioned the snowman, though, Julie Weston was crying softly. She kept her hands clutched against her arms, and the tears slid along her nose and down her cheeks before falling in fat drops to her thighs. I sat across from her, motionless. I wanted to cross the whirlpool, put my arms around her, and tell her everything would be all right. But I knew she wouldn't want me to, and I didn't know if everything would be all right.

She cried for a few minutes, and I kept my mouth shut. If she was going to trust me, she'd have to do it on her own. If she didn't, I was going to have to call Cody and have him send a group of agents out to scoop her up and take her back to Cleveland. That was what I *should* do. My job had been to find her, and now I'd done that. It was time to turn it over to the feds now and let them have their fun with the rest of it. I didn't move, though. I wanted to hear what she had to say. Eventually, she stopped crying and took a long, shaky breath. Then she lifted her head and looked at me again, the shadows and her damp hair hiding most of her face. Her eyes were visible, though, and they caught me and held me, seeming to look right through me, as if she were searching my soul before determining how to deal with me. When she spoke, her voice was as soft as the rustle of the palm fronds in the breeze above us.

"I need help," she said.

I waited for more, but nothing else came. I nodded. "Then I guess it's a good thing I showed up."

She asked me to show her identification and my investigator's license. It was a pointless routine—IDs can easily be faked, and she'd already decided she had to trust me—but maybe the trivial precaution made her feel better. We went up to her hotel room, and she dried off and pulled a sweatshirt over her swimsuit while I stood in the living room and waited. It was a three-room suite, and the door to the second bedroom was closed. When she came out of the bathroom, she saw me looking at it.

"She's in there," she said, knowing who I was wondering about. She watched me hesitantly, then stepped past me and opened the door. I stayed where I was, but enough light from the bathroom filtered into the bedroom to display the little girl asleep under the covers, her dark hair spilling across the pillow. Betsy Weston. I stared at her for a few seconds.

"I'm glad she's safe," I said, and my voice sounded slightly hoarse.

Julie Weston stood in the doorway, out of the light enough so that I could see into the room, but in my way enough to block me if I tried to move past her. Protective. I turned away, and she closed the door quietly and led me onto the balcony.

"We should talk out here," she said. "I don't want to wake her." She leaned over the rail and looked down at the pool below us. "I should never have gone down," she said. "I was so scared to leave her here alone. But I needed to get out. I had to get away from this damned room. It's been like a prison."

I sat on one of the plastic deck chairs and watched her as she stood with her back to me, looking at the pool. The sweatshirt extended just beyond the bottom of her swimsuit, but the slim, graceful lines of her legs were visible in the shadows. She turned back to me but stayed on her feet, pressing her back against the railing. Then she told the story.

They'd been the perfect family, she said. Happy, healthy, and wealthy. She'd met Wayne while he was working for the Pinkertons. It had been a blind date arranged by one of her friends. They'd gone out once, and at first she thought he'd been a little too arrogant, a little too slick, a little too confident. But he was good-looking, and smart, and charming. So when he called again, asking for a second date, she'd found it hard to refuse. There'd been a second date, and a third, and eventually they'd spent a week in Switzerland, and he'd proposed to her in a beautiful chalet in the mountains. They'd married six months later, and Wayne had taken a risk, leaving behind the benefits of the Pinkertons to set out on his own.

And it had worked. Worked very well, as far as Julie Weston knew. Wayne originally had a partner named Aaron Kinkaid, she told me, but they'd decided to go their separate ways, and her husband had worked alone from then on. I watched her face carefully when she mentioned Kinkaid, but if there was any emotion or passion there, she hid it well.

So the happy marriage lasted, and the career thrived, and the family grew with the addition of their daughter. Wayne was making good money—great money, in fact—and he told her business was good, couldn't be better, there were new clients coming in every day. On their tenth anniversary, he surprised her with a brand-new Lexus. Good-looking, charming, and prone to extravagant gifts, Wayne Weston seemed like the perfect husband. He *was* the perfect husband, Julie Weston told me. Until one day in February. She smiled at the recollection, but it wasn't the product of emotions one typically associates with a smile. It was hard, cold, and bitter—a smile not at the memory but at her own foolishness, a mocking smile at her own faith that had turned out to be so undeserved.

"He came home early," she said, "and I knew right away something was wrong. Betsy always met him at the door, jumped on him, and hugged him, and he always responded playfully. That night, though, she just seemed to bounce right off him. He gave her an automatic hug and told her to go play in her room before dinner because he had a headache. She went to her room, but I looked at his face and knew right away it wasn't a headache that was bothering him." Her hands tightened on the rail, the knuckles pushing against the skin. "He told me he had a confession to make. And I was standing there in the kitchen, still holding the stupid meat tenderizer in my hand, just staring at him and thinking, 'Whatever it is, we can beat it. If he's having an affair, if he's got cancer, we can get past it.' And then he told me his confession. And it wasn't an affair, and it wasn't cancer. It was worse. He told me he'd been working for a businessman, helping him settle deals and get the best prices. And I said I didn't see what was wrong with that. So he explained it to me."

The cold smile came back again. "He'd been helping him by digging deep in people's private lives and then handing the information over. He shot videotapes of married men having sex with their mistresses, he dug up information on addictions and past psychological problems, on family secrets—anything and everything people were afraid of. And then he handed it over to his boss, and they went to work turning other people's fears into money. My husband," she said flatly, "was nothing more than a blackmailer. That was his profession. To ruin lives, or threaten to ruin lives, so another man could make more money on his business deals or have more pull with the city government."

I sat in silence. I didn't want to tell her that it was not an uncommon practice. I didn't want to tell her that secrets are money in the business world, that fear is leverage, that knowledge is power.

"I never pried about his job," she said. "I knew it was confidential, and the few times I asked questions, that was what he told me. But somehow I'd always imagined that he was nobler, that he was out there solving cases the police couldn't solve, or helping attorneys prepare for legitimate lawsuits. I knew the cheating-spouse cases would come and go, and there would be some unpleasant jobs, but . . . all he did was look for ways to hurt people. That's it. He went to work every day determined to find some dirty secret, some sensitive topic, so another greedy man could make a larger profit."

She sighed and shook her head, then took her hands off the railing and went back to rubbing her arms, even though she couldn't possibly have been cold in the sweatshirt.

"He'd been doing this for years. Working for this one man."

"Jeremiah Hubbard," I said, speaking for the first time since she'd begun her story. She looked at me and smiled.

"Very good," she said. "You obviously do your job well, Mr. Perry. Do the police know, too?"

I shrugged. "We've told them, but I don't know how seriously they took us."

"I see. Well, yes, it was Mr. Hubbard. And then one day, the whole beautiful arrangement fell apart. Wayne told me he'd been shooting video surveillance—using cameras that had been illegally installed, of course—and he'd videotaped a murder."

"A murder?" I said.

"Yes."

"Do you know who was killed? Or who killed him?"

"I don't know any names. Wayne didn't want me to know them."

"Okay," I said, not wanting to distract her from the story. "Go on."

She took a breath and paused, remembering where she had left off. "He'd videotaped a murder. He told me this, and I stared at him, and said, 'So what's the problem? Call the police.' But he said he couldn't. He said the people involved were too dangerous. He said they were professional criminals, part of a national Russian crime syndicate, and we'd have to go into witness protection if we turned the tape over. He said they'd come after all of us, him, me, even Betsy. I couldn't believe it. Witness protection. We'd have to throw our whole lives away." She shook her head vigorously, aggravated by just the memory of the night.

"I told him to call the FBI," she said. "That's what you do in a situation like that, right? If it's too serious for the police, then you call the FBI. And he told me he couldn't do that, because the cameras had been illegally installed. He said he'd committed a crime just to get the videotape. But that was absurd; obviously, the police wouldn't care about something so minor if it solved a murder for them. I told Wayne that, and he said he didn't trust the FBI or the police—the men involved in the murder were too smart, too powerful, too dangerous.

"And," she said, her voice tinged with anger and disgust, "he told me that Mr. Hubbard wouldn't like it." She raised her eyes to me. "Mr. Hubbard wouldn't like it. That's what he said to me. Can you believe that? My husband came home and told me that my daughter and I were now in danger because of his stupidity, because of his greed, and why couldn't we go to the police? Because the rich bastard who'd put him up to it wouldn't like it. He wouldn't *like* it." She spat the words out like they were something foul in her mouth.

"He told me that, and I just stood there and stared at him. I was still holding the damned meat tenderizer, just standing there at the counter, listening to my husband explain how our lives were falling apart. And, eventually, I asked him what we were going to do."

Her eyes seemed to grow distant as she looked at me. "I bet you're dying to hear that part, aren't you? I bet you'd love to know the master plan."

"I'd like to hear it."

"Great," she said. "I'd love to tell it. It's all worked out so perfectly, you know." The sarcasm in her voice rivaled anything uttered by Jerry Seinfeld or George Carlin. "He told me he was afraid the Russians already knew about the tape."

"How?"

"I have no idea. I asked him that, too, but he ignored me. He said we were in danger now, that we had to run. He said Hubbard was going to give him enough money to get away. And all of this is happening so fast. I mean, I'd just come home from the grocery store. I'd bought a week's worth of groceries, and now I was being told to run for my life."

"So you came here?"

She nodded. "It was supposed to be temporary, though. A stopover. Wayne said he wanted me to take Betsy and leave. He'd stay an extra day, work out the money arrangements with Hubbard, talk to his father, and fly down to join us. From here, we were supposed to go to South America. He had a job all worked out. He was going to be a scuba-diving instructor for some sort of resort. He told me it would be great, living in paradise, waking up each morning for walks on the beach." She shook her head sadly. "Paradise. That's where we were going to go."

"So he told you this, and you left the same night?"

"No. This was the day before we left. He thought we had

a little time. We had dinner and put Betsy to bed and then stayed up all night talking about it. As scared as I was, it sounded like the best option. If we stayed in the city, we were going to be killed. If we entered witness protection, we'd hand our lives over to the government. They'd tell us where to live; Wayne would be given a job at Wal-Mart or something like that. But if we did it Wayne's way and didn't go to the police, then Hubbard would pay for us to leave. He'd give us plenty of money to create a new life."

"What about your family?" I asked, thinking about John Weston and the agony he was suffering.

"I'm an only child, and so was Wayne," she said. "My parents are dead. I was going to be leaving some good friends behind, of course, but as far as family it was just Wayne's father and a few cousins. Wayne was going to tell his dad. But someone murdered him first." Her voice broke a little when she said that, and I could tell that despite all the shock and disappointment her husband had provided her, she still loved him.

"What happened that night?" I said. "The night Wayne was killed."

She rubbed her fingertips against her temples, trying to drive away the beginning of a headache, maybe, or perhaps the lingering of a memory.

"He came home nervous," she said. "He was real scared that afternoon. He came home and took me right into the bedroom. He told me he thought the Russians knew about him. He said I had to take Betsy and leave that night. He'd leave the house but stay in the city, and he'd talk to his father the next day and finalize the arrangements with Hubbard. He'd rented a car using false identification, and he piled us into it and told us to drive to Columbus. He didn't want us to use the Cleveland airport, so he'd arranged for a flight to Myrtle Beach from Columbus. He said Randy knew everything, and he'd take care of us. Randy was Wayne's closest friend. His most trusted friend." Her voice was a clipped monotone now, an obvious effort to hide all emotion while she told the story.

"We flew into town, and Randy picked us up at the airport," she said. "He told me not to worry, that he would take care of us until Wayne came down and we left. But the next afternoon we still hadn't heard from Wayne, and I was starting to get nervous. Then Randy came up to the room and told me Wayne had been murdered. He'd found a story about it on the Cleveland newspaper's Web site."

She stopped talking. I said, "And?"

"And?"

I raised my eyebrows. "And what the hell have you been doing since then? It's been days."

"I wanted to call the police right away. I figured I could tell them everything, and we wouldn't be in any danger. But Randy told me not to. He said the Russians were still going to be looking for us, because they knew we were alive, and they knew we could testify against them. And he didn't trust the police or the FBI for the same reasons Wayne hadn't— he thought Hubbard could pull strings. So we stayed here, waiting to see what the police would turn up. When it was obvious they weren't producing anything, Randy went to Cleveland to sort it out."

"Sort it out?" I said. "How?"

She frowned. "By killing the Russians, maybe? By killing Hubbard? By killing everyone involved? I don't know, but I'm sure that's what he had in mind. Randy is a very dangerous man in his own right, Mr. Perry. I've known him for years, and I'll admit he still scares me. I know he would never hurt Betsy or me, but I'm certainly not comfortable around him. After we found out Wayne had been killed, Randy made it clear he was in charge. I didn't argue. I was scared, and alone, and I had no one else to turn to. He told me he'd go to Cleveland and be back in a few days."

"So you let him go."

She pushed her hair away from her face and tucked it behind her ears. "What was I supposed to do? Stop him? Argue with him?" She shook her head. "You've obviously never met Randy Hartwick."

"I met him," I said. "For about ten seconds, until someone put a bullet through his chest."

She lifted her hand halfway to her lips and held it there, frozen, her mouth open and her eyes wide. "Randy's dead?"

"Randy's dead. That's what led me here. I wasn't expecting to find you; I was just trying to find out more about him."

She eased slowly into the plastic deck chair beside me, as if this last bit of news had extinguished the final flickering embers that had fueled her.

"So the Russians killed your husband?" I said, knowing she wasn't up to more questioning but still trying to sort out the details.

She swiveled her head and met my eyes, "No. The Russians did not kill my husband. Whoever killed him made it look like a suicide, Mr. Perry."

"Lincoln."

"Whoever killed him made it look like a suicide, Lincoln. The Russians would never have been able to get inside our home to do that. Wayne was too smart for that."

"So who do you think killed him?"

"Jeremiah Hubbard," she said flatly, as if there were no room for doubt in her mind.

I didn't know about that, but I didn't argue with her. It was easy to believe Hubbard might have been involved in Weston's death, but I had trouble imagining the aging real estate mogul doing his own gun handling.

"So you've stayed hidden in this hotel," I said, "because Hartwick told you not to go to the police?"

"That was my decision," she said firmly. "My life as I knew it is over. I understand that, and I have to accept it. My husband has angered the most dangerous group of men in the country. They will kill my daughter and me if they can find us. Jeremiah Hubbard will do the same. If we go to the police, we will be placed in witness protection and forced into whatever life they decide to give us. That is not how I will raise my daughter. But I also can't let the world believe Wayne killed Betsy and me like they've been saying on the news. And I can't let Jeremiah Hubbard get away with this."

"So what are you planning to do?" I asked.

She looked away. "I don't know. Randy told me to wait here, and that's what I was doing. But I know we're not safe here anymore. You proved that by finding us."

For a while we sat in silence. Then I said, "So that's the story? I know everything I should know now?"

"Yes," she said. "Well, almost. There is one other thing you should know."

"What's that?"

"Remember the videotape Wayne shot of the murder?" she said.

"Yes."

"I have it."

FIFTEEN

We stayed on the balcony for another hour, but I could tell she was fatigued, so around midnight I told her I would leave so she could sleep. She stopped me at the door, though, and asked me to sleep on the couch.

"I can stay," I said, surprised by the request but not unhappy. I'd had a slight fear I might wake up in the morning to find they'd checked out of the hotel and disappeared. Then I'd get the pleasure of calling Joe. *Yeah, good news, Pritchard. I found Julie and Betsy Weston. Where are they? Well, um, that's a good question. You see, they kind of slipped away while I was asleep.*

I told Julie I'd be right back, and then I went down to my own room. It was nice to have a moment alone. It had been only a few hours since I'd left, but it seemed as if it had been days. I closed the door to the balcony and then found my bag. The Glock was inside with a full clip and one spare. I checked the load in the gun and put it back in the bag. It was a Glock 26, known as a "Baby Glock" because of its short barrel, but still outfitted with a ten-shot clip. The gun was small enough to conceal easily in a spine holster and powerful enough to do some serious damage in a short amount of time. It was the first handgun I'd ever bought. An old friend now. I had no reason to believe I was going to need a weapon, but I still felt better knowing it was there. The last man who had tried to help Julie Weston was Randy Hartwick, and I'd watched him die in front of me. Before that, someone had killed her husband. I had no desire to repeat the pattern.

Before going back upstairs, I used my cell phone to call Joe again. This time, I called him at home, knowing he would be there, likely asleep. Joe didn't have an answering machine, and the phone rang eight times without being picked up. I let it keep going, though, trusting he'd be pissed off enough to get it eventually.

"Hello?" He finally answered, and he definitely sounded unhappy.

"Greetings from the beautiful beaches of South Carolina," I said. "Are we having an enjoyable evening, Mr. Pritchard?"

"What the hell do you want?" Testy.

"I found Julie and Betsy Weston. They're here in the hotel where Hartwick worked. I just spent the last two hours talking to Julie." I could hear him take in his breath sharply, but he didn't speak.

I summarized everything Julie had told me, but I didn't mention she had the murder tape. When he spoke again, he was wide awake and all the irritation was gone from his voice.

"When did he shoot the tape of the murder?"

"I don't know."

"Does she?"

"Maybe. I didn't ask."

"Ask."

"All right."

He exhaled loudly. "Nice work, Lincoln. I guess the case is closed, eh?"

"I guess so," I said slowly. "How do we handle it from here on out, though?"

"How does she want it to be handled?"

"She's not sure. She said Hartwick went to Cleveland to

'sort things out.' She doesn't know what this meant, but she thinks he was probably planning to leave some bodies behind. She said she can't let the media think Wayne killed her and the girl, but she's also afraid to enter witness protection."

"Afraid they won't keep her safe from the Russians? Why would the Russians bother coming after her if Weston is dead?"

"A couple of reasons," I said. "First of all, like Cody said, they're crazy. Second, they surely assume her husband told her things that could hurt them, and they know she'll be asked to testify. Third, they might suspect she has the tape of the murder."

"Why would they think that?"

"Because she does have it."

"You've got to be kidding."

"Nope."

"Have you seen it?"

"Not yet. I hope to tomorrow."

"So she produces the tape, testifies if she needs to, and they go to jail," he said. "End of story. Except that's not how it works with the mob. She testifies, they go to jail, and their buddies hunt her down and kill her just to make a statement." He sighed again. I'd really spoiled his night with this call.

"I guess it's not our problem," I said. I didn't want to hand Julie and Betsy Weston over to the FBI, but it seemed the logical way to handle the situation.

"You're thinking we turn them over to the police?"

"We have to," I said, "don't you think?"

"I'm a little hesitant to do that now, and here's why: While you were lounging poolside today, Kinkaid and I were doing some damn fine work. We spent the day wearing out shoe leather and interviewing anyone who might know anything about our Soviet acquaintances. Guess what we found out?"

"No idea."

"Turns out Dainius Belov is a silent partner in a number of local businesses. You know, fronts that he can use to launder cash. And one of these said 'businesses' is located in the Flats. It's a charming little establishment called The River Wild."

"You mean the strip club Hubbard's trying to buy out?"

"The very one."

I stared out at the dark ocean and thought about that. If Wayne Weston had been shooting film for extortion purposes and pissed off the Russians, it could likely have been at The River Wild. The timing was perfect, since Hubbard was actively pursuing the property.

"What are you thinking?" Joe said.

"Just that it makes sense. Heard of any murders at The River Wild lately?"

"No, but that doesn't mean anything. I'll check it out."

"Do that." I switched the phone to my left hand and leaned against the wall, watching the white crests of the waves glitter on top of the black water as the moonlight hit them. "A minute ago you said you were hesitant to hand the Westons over to the police. I'm not arguing with you, but I don't understand your reasoning."

"That's because I didn't get a chance to finish. Like I said, Kinkaid and I had a productive day. Finding out Belov owns a stake in The River Wild was just a small portion of that productivity. I also decided to check out our man Cody, since I never had a good feeling about him. I didn't like the way he had us misled initially, and I also didn't like the way he blew off our tip about Hubbard."

"Right."

"Well, we ran a pretty thorough background check on him. Turns out Mr. Cody is ten years out of law school."

"Okay." That didn't surprise me; many FBI agents are law school graduates. The best way to get into the Bureau without a police background is to have a degree in either law or accounting.

"While he was in law school, Cody held a summer internship in Cleveland. I'll bet you can't guess where he did his internship."

"Hubbard's real estate company?"

"Nope, but close. I'll give you a hint; you called him Dicky D."

My smart-ass comment in Hubbard's office when he'd referred us to his attorney.

"Cody worked for Richard Douglass?"

"Uh-huh. He worked three summers in a row for Mr. Douglass and his associates. Then, when he graduated from law school, he came back and worked another year and a half with the firm before he was accepted into the FBI Academy."

"Holy shit," I said. "You're saying Hubbard's pulling the strings in this investigation?"

"I'm not saying that yet," he said. "But knowing what we know about Hubbard and Weston, and knowing what we know about Cody, do you really want to call him and tell him where the wife and daughter are?"

"No."

"Exactly."

I ran my hand through my hair and squeezed my eyes shut. What had started out a relaxing evening was now anything but that. "What the hell should we do, then, Joe? We can't just pack them on a plane for Belize or wherever it is they were going and let everyone think they're dead. We owe John Weston more than that, if no one else."

"We'll work something out," Joe said. "For now, the most important thing is keeping them safe. That job's in your hands."

Great. I was the appointed guardian of a woman who attracted corpses almost as fast as she attracted stares from men.

"So I stay here? I just sit in the hotel with them, keep them safe? And then what? Eventually we've got to take some sort of action."

"I know that. Give me a day to sort things out."

Sort things out. That's what Julie had said Randy Hartwick intended to do. It hadn't worked out well for him.

"What are you planning on?" I asked.

"We need to know more about this murder. Once we have an idea of what went on with that, we can talk about our options. Tomorrow, you watch that tape. See what you can learn from it; see if any familiar faces are on it, whatever. In the meantime, Kinkaid and I will be doing the same thing on our end. Give me a call tomorrow afternoon and we'll see what we have."

"Okay."

"And LP?"

"Yeah?"

"Try to keep those two alive until then, all right?"

He hung up before I could answer. I set the phone down, pulled the drapes shut in front of the balcony door, picked up my bag, locked the room, and went back upstairs. Julie pulled the door open at my knock.

"That was a long time," she said. "I was starting to get scared." She was wearing an oversize T-shirt now, and her legs were bare and her breasts uninhibited by a bra. I tried not to stare. It was dark inside the room, but she was standing very close to me.

"Sorry," I said, "I called my partner."

She took a half step back, frowning. "Does he know where we are?"

"Julie," I said gently, "if you're trusting me, you're trusting my partner. We're a package deal, all right? And I promise you, there's no more reliable man in the world than Joe Pritchard. The last thing he said to me before he hung up was to be sure I kept the two of you safe."

She watched me thoughtfully and then nodded. "Okay," she said. "Okay. I guess you're right. Well, I'm going to go to sleep now."

"Goodnight," I said, setting my bag on the floor and stepping toward the couch.

"Goodnight," she said. She started into the bedroom, then hesitated and turned on her heel. She took three quick steps over to me and squeezed my forearm gently with her hand.

"I'm glad you're here," she whispered, and then she disappeared into the bedroom, shutting the door behind her.

As I stood staring at the closed door, my arm seeming to tingle and burn where her fingers had touched it, I was glad I was there, too. Maybe a little too glad.

SIXTEEN

An incredibly beautiful woman was standing just a few steps from me with a knife in her hand.

This was the first thing I saw when I opened my eyes the next morning. It took a few seconds for my conscious mind to shed the fog of sleep and dreams and recall how and why I'd found myself in this situation. The woman was Julie Weston, and in the hand that wasn't holding the knife was a plate of bagels. Julie looked down at me and gave me the same shy smile I'd seen the night before in the whirlpool.

"Good morning," she said. "I'm making breakfast."

"Great," I said. "Thank you."

I picked my watch up from where I had left it on the floor and looked at the time. Almost nine. Surprisingly, I'd slept well. I stretched and got to my feet, feeling the twinges and aches left from a night of sleeping on a short couch that had both my feet and my head at a higher elevation than the rest of my body. Julie turned away quickly and went to put the bagels in the toaster, and I remembered I wasn't wearing a shirt. I'd expected to wake up ahead of the rest of them. Oh, well, some women would be pleased to find a shirtless young man on the couch in the morning. No sense feeling guilty about it.

I went into the bathroom and turned on the shower. When the cold water turned warm I climbed in and let the spray hammer me in the face, driving away the last vestiges of sleep. My body still ached from the uncomfortable sleeping position, but at least I was awake. I got out of the shower, dried off, and dressed. When I stepped out of the bathroom I nearly trampled Betsy Weston. She was standing directly in front of the door, wearing pink pajamas with kittens on them and gigantic pink slippers. Her long dark hair stuck out from her head, fuzzy with the static from the pillowcase. She stared at me with sleepy eyes, but she didn't look startled, so I assumed her mother had alerted her to my presence. I wondered what Julie had told her, though, or who I was supposed to be when the little girl was within earshot. Probably not the detective who was trying to find out who killed Daddy.

"Mommy says you're here to keep us company," she said, putting an end to that question. She stuck out her hand. "I'm Elizabeth. You can call me Betsy if you wanna."

I knelt down to put myself closer to her height and grasped her tiny hand in mine. She shook it gravely.

"Nice to meet you, Betsy," I said. "I'm Lincoln."

"Like the president?" She pronounced it "prezdent."

"Like that, yes." I'd been named after someone, but not Abraham Lincoln. It was Percy Lincoln, a soldier who'd saved my father's life in Vietnam. Seeking to honor the man but unable to force his son to go through life tagged Percy Perry, my father had picked the other name.

"I'm gonna go eat," Betsy announced, and then she walked around the corner and into the kitchen. I remained kneeling on the floor. A little girl. Interesting. Children weren't exactly my specialty. It wasn't that I disliked them; I just wasn't around them often enough to feel comfortable dealing with them. I found myself incapable of talking to them in the happy, high-pitched cartoon voices so many adults used for small children, so I generally talked to them as I would anyone else, only with less profanity. It seemed the best solution.

I walked into the kitchen, and Julie handed me a paper

plate with a raisin bagel on it. "It's all I had for breakfast food," she said. "There's a continental breakfast downstairs, but it ends at nine, so I'm afraid we missed it."

"Thank you."

"I'm making coffee, and there's apple juice in the refrigerator," she told me as she spread margarine on another bagel and handed it to Betsy. Today Julie was wearing olive shorts and a close-fitting white cotton shirt. She looked no less ravishing than she had in the swimsuit, but I tried to ignore that. Professional bodyguard Lincoln Perry at your service. No emotional attachment to his clients, and certainly no attraction for them. Can't have it.

"Coffee will be fine, thanks," I said. She handed me a ceramic mug with a palm tree and the resort's name emblazoned on the side. I left the coffee black and took a small sip, then looked at Julie, impressed.

"This can't be hotel coffee."

She laughed and shook her head. "No way. I can't drink that stuff. I found a deli down the street that sells gourmet coffee. I had them grind some for me."

Damn. It was going to be hard enough to ignore her physical beauty. Now she had to make good coffee, too. It got worse and worse.

I leaned against the counter and sipped the coffee, watching the mother and daughter. It was a hell of a situation I'd gotten myself into.

"What do we have planned for the day?" I asked. I wasn't sure if they felt safe leaving the hotel during the day, but I couldn't imagine spending twelve hours in the confined space, even if it was much nicer than your average hotel room.

"What do we have planned?" Julie echoed. "Well, I don't know. Do you think it's safe . . ." She looked down at her daughter and selected a new sentence. "Would it be all right if we went for a walk down the beach?"

"Have you done that before?"

She nodded, dropping her eyes to the floor and looking ashamed, afraid I might view this as a cataclysmic breach of safety protocol. "Yes, we have. We wear sunglasses and baseball caps and don't stay out very long." She glanced at her daughter again, but Betsy was oblivious, munching away on the bagel. "It's hard to spend the whole day in the room," she added.

"I understand. I just wasn't sure how you felt about it."

"So you think it's okay to go out, then?"

I nodded. "Why not? I'd stick to the hat-and-sunglasses routine, but this is a pretty busy place. There are thousands of unfamiliar faces around, and no one is paying attention to all of them." I wasn't sure how true that was, but I didn't like the idea of remaining in the hotel all day any more than she did.

"Great," she said, relieved. "Well, as soon as Betsy gets dressed we can go for a walk on the beach. Does that sound good, honey?"

The little girl smiled, crumbs stuck to her lips. "Grrrreat," she growled, à la Tony the Tiger.

"One other thing," I said, and Julie looked back at me. "I'd like to watch the video we talked about last night."

"The video."

"Yes. You told me you had it, correct?"

She dropped her eyes. "Yes, I do, but I haven't watched it. I'd prefer not to watch it, honestly."

"That's fine. I need to see it."

"I'll bring it out, and you can watch it while Betsy and I straighten up the bedroom."

She went into the bedroom, and the little girl tagged along. A minute later Julie returned with a VHS tape in hand. "Here it is," she said, offering the tape to me uneasily, extending it as far from her body as possible, the way you might hand someone a sleeping scorpion.

"Thank you." There was a VCR built into the television, of course—the Golden Breakers didn't rate five stars for nothing. Julie turned to go back to the bedroom, but I caught her arm gently.

"I thought of a few things I need to know."

"Okay."

"First of all, do you have any idea when this tape was made? What day, what week, what month?"

She bit her lower lip and shook her head. "I don't think so. No, I'm sure Wayne never told me. I assume it was fairly recently, though. It didn't seem like the type of situation that had weeks to develop."

"I see. And one other thing . . ." I dropped my voice a little lower and leaned down, putting my face close to hers. "Does your daughter know her father is dead?"

She met my eyes, and I saw a shimmer of moisture on hers. "No," she said in a hoarse whisper. "I can't tell her here. I *can't*. I don't know what's going to happen to us, and . . . and until I do, I have to keep her happy. It's hard enough to handle this when she's happy, but if she wasn't . . ." She shook her head again. "I just couldn't take it."

I nodded. "That's understandable. I'm not criticizing you or suggesting you sit her down on the bed and tell her immediately, but I wanted to know. Last question—what's your relationship with Aaron Kinkaid?"

She frowned, puzzled by the question. "Aaron? He was Wayne's partner."

"I know that. He's also helping us on this case, and he claims he was in love with you. Said their partnership ended because Wayne was mad about Aaron's feelings for you."

She rolled her eyes and laughed. "Aaron hit on me once at a Christmas party. He was drunk, and it was just a silly thing. Wayne wasn't happy, but it was no big deal. I can't believe it really meant anything to Aaron."

I looked at her, taking in her beauty, and I thought that what seemed like a silly, drunken advance to a woman like Julie could mean an awful lot more to a man like Aaron Kinkaid. She went back to the bedroom, and I looked at the tape in my hand. I was surprised to see it was an ordinary Sony VHS tape with eight hours of recording time. I'd expected Weston would use higher-grade stuff. I slipped the tape into the VCR, turned the television on, and pressed play.

For a minute there was nothing but a light blue screen,

and then a dimly lit room rolled into view. I leaned forward and squinted at the screen. There was a round card table and wood paneling, but nothing else was visible. I didn't recognize the room. A lone man was seated at the table. Only his upper body was visible, but there was a lot of it. He was an enormously fat man, balding, with bushy gray eyebrows. As I watched, he looked up at something out of view of the camera and nodded his head, then got to his feet and walked out of the room. Three new men stepped into view, and I recognized two of them—Alexei Krashakov and Ivan Malaknik. Krashakov was the tall, blond Russian who had given me the twenty. I'd never met Malaknik in person, but Cody had showed us pictures of him. The third man, who was shorter than Krashakov but muscular under a black shirt, I'd never seen before. He was clean-shaven and wore a silver chain around his neck. His dark hair was short and curly.

The three of them sat around the table and talked. I tried turning up the volume, but it was pointless, because there was no audio. Wayne Weston hadn't been as efficient as I'd expected. Somehow, I found that hard to believe. Probably there was an audiotape floating around, too.

Two minutes of talking passed. I'd been anticipating violence, but I was still surprised when it happened. All three men appeared to be laughing heartily when suddenly Krashakov slipped a gun out from under the table and shot the third man in the chest. I jerked when he did it. It seemed that out of place in the apparently jovial meeting. The third man slumped onto the table, and blood began to drip onto the floor. Krashakov and Malaknik got up and pushed the body out of the chair. Then Malaknik opened a rear door. The door appeared to open to the outdoors; a slight glow from streetlights on the pavement was visible. Malaknik disappeared outside, then came back a minute later with a blue plastic tarpaulin. Krashakov helped him roll the body onto the tarp. They folded the ends—to keep the blood from leaking onto their clothes, probably—and carried the body out the door. Several minutes passed, and then Malaknik returned with another man. I recognized him: Vladimir Rakic, who lived with Krashakov. Rakic had a bucket and a mop. The two of them set to work cleaning the floor. Krashakov never returned to the room. He was probably busy disposing of the body. Rakic and Malaknik worked on the floor for a while. I could hear Julie and Betsy Weston laughing in the bedroom, and I knew I might not have much more time. I hit the fast-forward button and advanced the film quickly. They continued cleaning the floor, and then they left, too. No one else came inside. Almost immediately afterward, the tape ended and the screen went blue again.

I rewound it and played the first five minutes again, staring closely at the first man in the room and the victim. I didn't recognize either of them, but I wanted to be able to offer a good description. I didn't know too much about camera surveillance, but my guess was Weston had been using a wireless camera system. He had told his wife a camera that was illegally installed captured the murder. That implied breaking and entering to install the camera, which meant it had to be small and well concealed. A closed-circuit camera seemed out of the question in that circumstance, because that meant the camera, recorder, and tape all had to be on the premises. That would be far more difficult to conceal than a wireless camera. Joe and I had equipment catalogs with some extremely small color video cameras that would broadcast a signal fifteen hundred feet or more. Some of them, the really expensive stuff, used satellite technology much like a cellular phone and could broadcast a signal as far as you needed it. Hubbard could certainly afford to pay for that, if he'd wanted such technology.

Betsy's laugh grew louder, and I realized they'd left the bedroom. I ejected the tape, put it back into its box, and slid it under the couch, then turned to them. Julie's eyes were searching me as if she could absorb what I had seen without asking. I kept my face impassive.

"Get the room cleaned up?"

"We made the bed real pretty," Betsy said. "Wanna see?"

Julie laughed. "I don't think Mr. Perry needs to see, hon."

"She can call me Lincoln," I said. "You guys ready for that walk now?"

"Yes!" Betsy said, clapping her hands. "I *love* the beach."

"Wonderful," I said. "To the beach we go, then. Hold on one second while I go brush my teeth."

I went into the bathroom, carrying my bag, and removed the Glock. I clipped my holster onto my belt near the small of my back. The holster fit inside the waistband of my shorts, helping to conceal it, and it clipped onto the belt with two snaps, meaning I didn't have to take the belt off each time I put the holster on or removed it. The gun was secure and hard to detect, but I could draw it quickly. I hadn't been expecting to need to wear the gun at all times, but that plan had changed. Death can come when least expected. The morning's video viewing had reminded me of that.

SEVENTEEN

It was an amazing day. The sun was out in full force, and the rays reflected off the sand and water, making the entire beach sparkle. There was a mild breeze off the water, and the temperature was in the mid-seventies. We walked along the tide line. Betsy walked very close to the water, jumping back when the waves came close and shrieking with laughter when the water touched her feet.

"It's cold," she said. "Too cold for swimming. That's not fair. I wanted to go swimming." Her skin looked dark enough that I was sure she'd spent plenty of time in the sun the past few days. Julie's was the same shade. I was trying not to pay too much attention to her skin, though. Once you started, it was damn hard to stop. Better never to get started.

"Don't whine too much," Julie said. "If you whine about the water being cold, Lincoln will probably get tired of you and throw you into the ocean."

"He would not!" Betsy regarded me with wide eyes.

I shrugged. "No promises."

"Mom!" she squealed. "Don't let him throw me in the ocean."

"He looks pretty strong," Julie said in mock seriousness. "I don't know if I could stop him."

There were dozens of people lying on the beach on blankets or in lawn chairs, soaking up the sun and relaxing, but I knew it was nothing compared to what you'd see in the summer, when tourist season was at its peak. We walked north along the beach for maybe a mile. We passed nothing but hotels and saw nothing but more hotels stretching on before us in either direction. It was amazing. How many hotels did this town have?

After about a mile we turned and headed back. Betsy was still playing her game of dancing away from the waves, and she held her mother's hand as they walked. They fit together so well, so naturally, mother and daughter, a little bit of one in the other. I wondered if Wayne Weston had fit in as well— if people sitting on the beach would have watched the three Westons stroll along and said, "Isn't that a perfect little family." Maybe I stood out to the people watching us as the puzzle piece that didn't fit. Perhaps I could combat that by walking hand in hand with Julie.

"Well, Lincoln?" Julie said.

"Huh?"

"Weren't you listening?"

"Sorry. Lost in thought."

She smiled. "Betsy was talking to you."

"I'm sorry," I repeated, and looked down at the girl. "What did you say?"

"I said I knew you wouldn't throw me in the water," she announced. "And I was right. We're back at the hotel and you didn't throw me in."

I snapped my fingers as if recalling a forgotten task. "I knew I had something to do before we went back inside."

She shook her head. "Nuh-uh. You aren't going to throw me in."

"Says who?"

"Says me," she said, and giggled.

I glanced at Julie, saw the smile on her face, and realized she was enjoying this silly exchange between her daughter and me. I stopped walking and slipped off my tennis shoes, the sunbaked sand warm against my bare feet.

"All right," I said. "You're going in now."

"No!" Betsy yelled, trying to duck behind her mother, but I reached down and scooped her up under her arms, then ran toward the surf, holding her high above my head. She was unbelievably light. I'd lifted cats that felt heavier. She was half screaming, half laughing as I stormed into the water. She'd been right, too—it *was* cold. I ran in up to my knees, and then a wave hit me, soaking the lower half of my shorts. I held Betsy over my head—making sure my T-shirt didn't ride up enough to expose my gun—and began counting.

"One . . . two . . . three . . ." I pretended to heave her toward the water, and she shrieked, but I didn't release her. "Okay," I said. "I'm feeling nicer than I thought. I guess I won't toss you in until this afternoon."

I carried her back out of the water, wondering if maybe my silly game had been a bad move, something that would irritate Julie. She was laughing as she waited for us, though, and seemed anything but irritated.

"You should have done it," she said when I dropped Betsy onto the sand beside her. "You would have had my blessing."

"I thought he *was* going to throw me in," Betsy said, gasping for breath but still giggling.

Julie glanced at my dripping legs with a small smile. "Cold?" she said.

"Little bit," I said, and she laughed again.

They wanted to go shopping, so we spent the next two hours wandering the strip. I saw more versions of T-shirts with the words MYRTLE BEACH than I'd thought possible, and some pretty bizarre creations made from seashells, but nothing that tempted me to take out my wallet. Julie and Betsy seemed to enjoy it, though. We ate lunch at a Subway and then walked back to the hotel. They went in the bedroom to relax, and I told Julie I was going to run back down to my room and make a phone call.

I called Joe.

"Seen the tape?" he asked as soon as I said hello.

"I've seen it. Someone definitely got whacked, but I don't have any idea who. I know the shooter, though."

"Who?"

"Krashakov."

"The big blond asshole?"

"You got it." I told him the details of the tape.

"You can't tell where it was taken?"

"Not really, but my guess is it's the back room at a bar somewhere—quite possibly The River Wild. That makes the most sense. You've already attached it to the Russians, and there's a logical reason for Weston to be shooting tape there."

"One thing's bothering me."

"Yeah?"

"Weston films this from a concealed camera, right? A wireless setup, you suggest. And, clearly, the Russians didn't know it was there. Yet when Weston talked to his wife he said the Russians were going to be coming after him."

"True."

"So how'd they figure out he had this tape?"

"Found the camera before he had a chance to remove it, maybe."

"And he'd taped a return address label to the thing? Carved his initials on the side? Those cameras are designed to be discreet. There aren't a lot of them in circulation, but it would still be difficult to trace one back to the owner in most circumstances."

"Good point." I didn't have an answer for that one, so I shifted gears. "You find out who the vic might be?"

"Not yet. I called a few of our old friends at homicide, and they said they'd get back to me."

"Okay. I was thinking of calling Amy, putting her on it."

"Be careful what you tell her."

"We can trust Amy, Joe."

"I know we can trust her, but I don't want us getting her in more trouble. Just because you're in love with her doesn't mean we have to call her at the first excuse."

"I'm not in love with her."

"Uh-huh." He grunted. "Speaking of love, how's the widow Weston look in person?"

"Homely," I said. "The camera does wonders for that woman. In person she looks much more like my great-aunt Nedra."

"I bet."

"Where's Kinkaid?"

"Sitting right in front of me."

"You two playing checkers?"

"Quiet, son. We're getting ready to break this case wide open."

"Hard to do that sitting on your ass."

"I know it is. That's why we're on our way out the door. I'd like to check on our Russian pals again, see where they are and what they're up to."

"Watch your back, Joseph."

"Always, son. Always. I'll give you a call on your cell phone tonight when I hear from homicide."

I hung up with Joe and called Amy's office number. She picked up on the first ring, which was a rarity, and she was in a shitty mood, which wasn't as rare.

"Do you miss me?" I said when she answered.

"No, I don't miss you. You're one of *them*."

"Them?"

"A male," she snapped. "You know, those folks with penises? You do have one of those, right?"

"What's your problem?"

"Men."

"Uh-oh," I said. "Surely it can't be a problem with Mr. Terry."

"Mr. Terry can kiss my beautiful ass," she said. "My friend Rochelle saw him in a restaurant holding hands with some bimbo and drinking wine last night. Rochelle said it was expensive wine, too. He only buys the cheap stuff for me. Bastard."

"I'm sorry, Amy," I said genuinely. I was no fan of Jacob Terry, but I liked Amy too much to enjoy seeing her hurt.

"Ah, screw him," she said. "I couldn't be with a man who used that much hair gel, anyhow. It was doomed from the start."

"I tried to tell you that."

"Yeah, yeah, you and your advice. I've never taken it before, and I'm not going to start. Just because you were right about Terry doesn't mean you're not an idiot. Now what the hell do you want?"

I hadn't planned on telling Amy all the details, but I realized she was going to pester me with questions, so I decided to go ahead and give her something to think about other than her hatred for my gender.

"I'm in South Carolina," I said.

"Really? What the hell are you doing down there? And, hey, didn't I hear about you being a witness to some guy who got shot near your building the other day? I called you, but you weren't home. Come to think of it, wasn't *he* from South Carolina?"

"Amy," I said, breaking in on her tangent, "do you want to hear my news or not?"

"Yes."

"I've got Julie and Betsy Weston."

For a long time, I could hear nothing but the faint murmur of background voices in the newsroom around her. When she spoke again, her voice was soft and serious. "You better not be playing with me, Lincoln. I'm not in the mood."

"I'm not playing with you," I said. "They're in South Carolina, and they have been since Weston was killed. But no one—and I mean *no one*—can know about this yet. There's too much uncertainty right now. Some big-league killers are looking for this woman, and they might have sources within the police."

"What are they doing there?" she whispered. "Do they not realize the FBI is looking for them?"

"Julie realizes," I said. "The little girl is blissfully ignorant. And they're here because Wayne Weston pissed off the Russian mob. He shot a videotape of a hit, and somehow they found out about it."

"So the Russians did kill him."

"Julie doesn't think so. She thinks Hubbard did it, or had someone do it."

"This is real big, isn't it, Lincoln?"

"Bigger than you can imagine," I said, thinking about Hubbard, Cody, and the Russians. It was big, all right. And deadly.

"I'm not going to breathe a word of this to anyone," Amy said, "but you've got to keep me updated."

"I will. Now, can you do me a favor?"

"Sure."

"Like I said, Weston videotaped some poor bastard getting killed by the Russians. We don't know who the guy is. I watched the tape and didn't recognize him. Some short, strong-looking guy with curly dark hair and a silver chain around his neck. I need you to check it out and see if you can figure out who some potential candidates might be. He's got to be connected to Belov and the rest of them somehow."

"I'm on it."

"Thanks. I'll call you later this afternoon and we can reconnoiter."

She laughed.

"What?" I said.

"Reconnoiter. That word just amuses me—it sounds so ridiculous. It seems strange, too, that you can only reconnoiter. Wouldn't it seem you should connoiter to begin with and *then* reconnoiter? Of course, that sounds kind of dirty. You know, like, 'The police caught the teens connoitering in the backseat of the car—'"

"Goodbye, Amy." I hung up and sighed. My friends. What can you say?

I went back upstairs and knocked on Julie's door. She answered a minute later with a bright smile. "Good news," she said. "Betsy has decided what she wants to do with the afternoon."

"What's that?"

"Play miniature golf," Betsy said. She was sitting on the couch with her feet sticking out in the air because they were too short to reach the floor. I suppose this is the type of thing parents never really pause to think about, but if you're not around children much, it looks pretty comical.

"Miniature golf," I said. The glamorous work of the private detective never ceases.

"That's right. I told her we'd need to relax for about an hour, though." She winked at me. "I figured you'd need at least that long to prepare yourself for a whole afternoon of us."

I sat on the couch next to Betsy and watched cartoons with her for the next twenty minutes. Then my cell phone rang, and I took it out on the balcony to talk.

"Hello?"

"You're in big trouble this time, pal." Amy.

"I thought I was going to call *you*," I said. "Couldn't wait to hear my sexy voice again, eh?"

"No, I just couldn't wait to tell you what kind of mess you've gotten yourself tangled up in."

I had a fair idea what kind of mess it was, but I waited for her to elaborate.

"I think I know who the murder victim was," she said. "You called him a short, muscular guy with curly dark hair, correct?"

"Yeah."

"Okay, that's a perfect description of the guy whose picture I'm looking at right now. In fact, he's even wearing a silver chain. He hasn't turned up dead yet, but he's been missing for three weeks, and he unquestionably has ties to the Russians."

"Who is it?"

"Yuri Belov," she said. "Dainius Belov's son."

EIGHTEEN

"His son," I said numbly. All the energy had drained from my body, and the small of my back felt very cold despite the sun beating against it. I was staring in the glass doors to the hotel room without really seeing anything, but eventually I noticed Betsy waving at me. I forced a smile and lifted a hand in response, then turned my back to the room and looked out at the sea.

"What are you going to do, Lincoln?" Amy asked.

"I don't know. This definitely explains some things, though. Maybe it makes things a little easier. Maybe it makes them harder."

"How would it make them easier?"

"If the Russians took out Yuri Belov, the hit surely wasn't authorized by his father. It was more likely the result of an internal problem, some feud or bad blood between Belov's soldiers and his son. That means Julie and Betsy may not need to fear the Russian mob as a whole, but only a select few."

"I guess," she said doubtfully, "but those select few seem pretty deadly."

Assuming they were responsible for the murder of not only Yuri Belov but also Wayne Weston and Randy Hartwick, yes, they were very deadly. And then there was

Jeremiah Hubbard to fear. Julie Weston's testimony could be tremendously damaging to him, as well. And, if Julie's guess that Hubbard was responsible for her husband's murder was correct, he had already proved he was willing to kill to protect himself.

"There are quite a few unsolved murders tied together with this," I said. "Nasty things are happening in the shadows, and this woman knows enough to make sense of it. Some powerful people are going to do whatever it takes to keep those things in the shadows. If that means adding a few more murders to the list, they won't lose sleep over it."

"You know the best way to bring something scary out of the shadows, Lincoln? Shine a light on it."

I frowned. "Clarify, Ace."

"I mean, let me write this story."

"Amy," I began, irritated that she was thinking of herself, but she cut me off.

"I'm serious, Lincoln, so listen to me. I'm not thinking just about the story, although I'll admit I'd love to write it. I'm thinking about the woman and her daughter. People are willing to kill them because Julie Weston has damaging knowledge and a damaging videotape, right? Well, if the knowledge and tape are made public, then killing Julie Weston and her daughter serves no purpose except revenge. And, if the case has been pushed into the public eye, any attempt for revenge is just going to make things much worse."

"The Russians don't care about that, Amy," I said. "They won't hesitate to kill for revenge, regardless of the consequences." But it was an interesting idea. It could possibly be the best way of keeping Hubbard at bay, if nothing else. "I'm not dismissing it entirely," I said, giving some ground. "I'll talk to Julie tonight and see what she thinks."

"Okay, Lincoln. But remember something—you have much of the same knowledge that led to Wayne Weston's murder and probably this Hartwick guy's. That makes you just as much of a threat to everyone involved as Julie Weston."

Encouraging. I hung up with Amy and walked back inside. Julie had taken my seat on the couch beside Betsy, and the cartoons were still on. She glanced up at me as I stepped into the room and frowned.

"What's the matter?"

"Nothing," I said, surprised she had read my face so easily. "My cell phone signal is bad on the balcony, that's all. Frustrating."

"Oh," she said, but I could tell she wasn't buying it. "Do you need to go downstairs to make another call?"

"No, I'm done with the phone for now." I put the cell phone back in my pocket and slid my hand up my spine, touching the butt of the gun under my shirt. It was still there, comforting if not comfortable.

"I thought we were going to play miniature golf," I said, trying to force some good humor into my voice. I could spend the rest of the afternoon dwelling on Amy's news, but that wouldn't accomplish anything, and it would probably stress Julie out. If I could make the afternoon fun for her and the kid, then I'd sit her down for a serious conversation after Betsy went to sleep.

"Let's go play!" Betsy said, leaping off the couch. "I'm gonna win."

"No, you're not," I said. "I'm going to win."

"I'll bet you an ice cream I win," the little girl said confidently. I accepted the bet with a laugh, and as I did so I saw a shadow of sadness pass over Julie's face. It was only momentary, and then the smile was back. I thought about the bet we'd made, and I realized it was probably something the girl had picked up from her father.

"I always beat Daddy and get ice cream when we play," Betsy said, confirming my suspicions as if on cue. "He says I'm short for good games."

"Short game," Julie said softly, looking away from us, out at the ocean. "He says you have a good short game."

Between my worries about Belov and Julie's recollections of her husband, I was afraid we were in for an awkward afternoon. I was wrong. By the time we reached the hotel lobby, Betsy had both of us laughing, and the more serious concerns were forgotten for a while. There were several miniature golf establishments within walking distance, but apparently Betsy had seen one with giant plastic alligators on a drive earlier in the week, and that was where she wanted to play.

Julie hadn't rented a car, so I had to drive. They'd taken a cab from the airport when they arrived in town, and Hartwick had driven them a few times. Other than those trips, they'd stayed in walking distance.

"It's too small for you," Betsy said of the Contour as she settled into the backseat. I closed the door of the little rental car and looked at her in the rearview mirror.

"I agree," I said. "It's way too small for me."

"It fits me, though," she said.

"Want to drive?" I asked, straight-faced.

"I'm not old enough to drive," she answered just as seriously.

"Oh. I guess I'll handle it, then."

We drove to the miniature golf course with the giant plastic alligators. It turned out to be just a few miles south, and the bizarre décor didn't stop with the alligators. They were there, all right, but so were a large plastic pirate ship, an octopus, and several pirate mannequins complete with eye patches and hooks. The course wrapped around a flowing creek and—like everything else in town—was lined with palm trees.

We played for nearly two hours. Betsy played first, and I tried to match whatever she had done on the hole to keep us close and make it more fun for her. It appeared to work, because on the last hole she was *focused*. She set the ball down on the plastic mat and backed away from it, then dropped into a crouch, balancing the putter against the ground, as if she were checking the break of the green.

"She's watched her dad," Julie said, but this time the memory brought a smile.

Betsy put the ball in the hole on her fourth putt, and I missed my fourth, making her squeal with a victor's delight.

"You owe me an ice cream," she taunted.

"It's not fair," I said, pointing my club at the plastic alligator that was watching over the hole. "He kept staring at me. It made me nervous."

She laughed some more at that, and then we returned our clubs and left. It was early, but Betsy said she was hungry. Neither Julie nor I wanted dinner yet, so I took us on a drive to kill some time and build our appetites. I drove south on Business 17 out of Myrtle Beach. There were signs for a place called Murrells Inlet, and Julie recognized it from the brochures.

"They have charter fishing boats there," she said. "Want to go to the docks and look at the boats, honey? Then we can go eat."

Betsy shrugged. "We can watch boats. I'll still be hungry, though." Agreeable to the idea but not impressed with it.

I drove to Murrells Inlet, and we walked the docks. I'd done a fair amount of sailing on Lake Erie, but I'd never taken a boat out on the ocean. Most of the boats at these docks were powerboats, and all of them were large. I thought back to the small sailboat I'd seen just off the beach the day before, and I wondered what it felt like to have something so tiny on an ocean so large.

"I love the water," Julie said, holding on to the railing of the dock and leaning backward, her eyes on the horizon line. "The ocean's so big. It's amazing. We could get on one of these boats, and if the weather was fine and there was enough gas, we could go all the way across it. Just go until we hit land again." She said it as if she wished we really could. I looked down at her but remained silent. She sighed. "Can't do that, though, can we? We have to stay here and face life. I didn't mind that before. But then it got all screwed up. Now I don't know what to do. Do we run, do we hide, do we go back?"

"It'll be okay, Julie," I said. "I'm going to help you get through this."

She smiled at me, but her sunglasses shielded her eyes, and I couldn't guess what she was thinking. She reached over and gave my hand a quick squeeze. "I know you're going to," she said. "And I hope you have some idea how much that means to me."

We ate dinner at a seafood restaurant in Murrells Inlet. It was the same type of food I'd eaten the night before, but it had been good then, and I saw no reason to seek variety. I ordered crab legs, and Betsy watched with interest while I cracked them and extracted the meat.

"They look scary," she said.

"Just from the outside," I said. "The good stuff is inside the shell."

"Can I try?" she asked. I was impressed. Most little kids tended to shy away from unfamiliar foods, certainly from anything that looked like crab legs. I looked at Julie, and she shrugged. I removed a small piece of meat and put it on Betsy's plate. She speared it with her fork and put it in her mouth without hesitation.

"It's *good!*" she exclaimed a moment later. "Let's get more crabs' legs!"

So we got more crab legs. And that girl could *eat.* I guess she hadn't been kidding about her appetite on the drive to the docks. We polished off two orders between us. Julie helped only slightly, content to stick with her shrimp for the most part.

"I think she ate her weight in crab," I said when we were done, and Julie laughed.

"She eats like a teenage boy, but somehow she stays tiny."

"Take her into a lab and ask them to find a way to distribute her metabolism in a pill or something," I suggested. "You could make a fortune."

We drove back to the hotel as the sun set behind us. The beach was nearly empty now, save for a few walkers and one group of kids playing with a Frisbee. The night air was still warm, though. We went up to the room, and Julie and Betsy played board games while I read the newspaper and tried calling Joe. I made several calls without receiving an answer. It was frustrating to know he had a cell phone and just didn't bother to take it with him or keep the battery charged. You can take an old cop to higher technology, but you can't make him remember it.

Around nine, Betsy went to bed. I was sitting out on the

balcony then, and I'd taken my gun out and tucked it against the wall behind me. Betsy stepped out, surprising me, and I moved my foot quickly, trying to hide the weapon from view. She held out her arms.

"Goodnight hug," she said. She hugged me, and I patted her little back, feeling very strange. I wasn't the type of guy who gave many goodnight hugs, but if she sensed that, she didn't care. I had to admit I was somewhat pleased she'd wanted one.

"Don't forget my ice cream," she said as she went inside. "I beat you."

"I won't forget," I said.

Twenty minutes later, Julie joined me. She noticed the gun, but she didn't comment on it.

"We need to talk," she said.

I nodded. "That would probably be a good idea."

She dropped into the plastic chair beside me. "What do you think I should do, Lincoln? I'm so scared, and so confused. But I know we can't keep this up. We need to take some sort of action instead of just delaying."

I told her about my conversations with Joe and Amy and about Yuri Belov.

"Amy thinks you should let her write the story," I said. "She thinks if everything was made public, it would eliminate the threat you pose to some people."

She leaned forward, interested. "What do you think of that?"

I shrugged. "I don't think it's a cure-all. To the Russians, it will probably just be added motivation. As far as Jeremiah Hubbard is concerned, it might be pretty powerful, though. He's a well-known public figure, and he cares about image." I drummed my fingers on the arm of the chair and sighed. None of the solutions looked too promising.

"I'd normally urge you to go straight to the police," I said. "But my partner feels Hubbard might have some pretty powerful sources there. If we rush into that, it could work out badly."

"So what do you suggest?"

"I still suggest the police, actually, but we need to approach them carefully. What we need to do is select a trustworthy, high-level police source and go there with your story. And we need to explain our concerns about Hubbard's influence and connections."

"I don't want to go into witness protection," she said softly.

I nodded. "I know that. And I can help you disappear on your own if that's the route you decide to take. I can probably find some people who know how to do that awfully well, in fact. But witness protection isn't the biggest issue here, Julie. Your husband was murdered, and so was Randy Hartwick. People need to be brought to justice for that. You can't leave everyone wondering about you and your daughter, either, and you sure as hell can't leave them suspecting you were murdered by your own husband. I can't allow that to happen to John Weston."

It was a stronger speech than I'd expected to give, but I meant every bit of it. Last night I'd been so startled by finding Julie Weston and so unnerved by Cody's apparent connection to Hubbard that I'd needed some time to think the situation out. But there was clearly only one solution, and that was using Julie's testimony and knowledge to bring about justice. Now it was my job to see that it was done, and that she and her daughter remained safe while it was done.

"I was hired by your father-in-law," I said. "My duty to him is to explain what happened to his family the night his son was murdered. I intend to fulfill that obligation. But I've given myself a second duty now, and that's keeping you and Betsy safe." I leaned forward and took her hand in mine. "I *will* keep you safe."

She smiled and squeezed my hand before I released hers. "I haven't felt truly safe for a while now, but somehow I believe you. And you're right. I have to talk to the police, or the FBI, or whoever. But shouldn't we go back to Cleveland for that? I don't really like the idea of going to police here in South Carolina who have no idea what's been going on."

"I was going to suggest returning to Cleveland. It's definitely the place to get started."

I expected her to say more about the interviews and testimony to come, but instead she looked up at the sky and sighed.

"The moon's still beautiful. Another beautiful night in general. Do you know what it must be like in Cleveland tonight?"

"About the same," I said. "There might be some frost on the palm trees by morning, though."

She laughed and looked down at the pool. "Oh, that whirlpool looks inviting. I'd love to sneak back down."

"Go for it. I'll stay here and watch Betsy."

"She doesn't need much watching. She's sound asleep. You could set fireworks off in there and she wouldn't budge." She stood, leaned back against the balcony railing, and studied me. "Let's go down for half an hour, at least."

I started to say I wasn't comfortable leaving the girl alone, but the thought died somewhere between my brain and my lips, smothered by the realization that I could see Julie in her swimsuit again if I went along with the suggestion.

"Why not?" I said. "Just half an hour."

Five minutes later we locked the room behind us and went downstairs. Julie was wearing the same black two-piece swimsuit she'd had on the night before, and she looked amazing.

I turned the jets on, and we shed our towels and settled into the warm water. The breeze was there just as it had been the night before, as was the moon, and from all sensory perspectives the experience felt identical to the previous night. From a mental perspective, though, it felt as if months had passed since then.

"Wow, that feels good," Julie said, putting her back against one of the jets. "I could never have one of these things in my home, though. I'd never be able to leave it."

"I think I could take one," I said. "A half hour a night in this would reduce my stress level by a factor of ten."

We made small talk for a while and then fell silent, each with our own thoughts. I'd brought the cell phone to the edge of the water with me, and I found myself glancing at it, wishing Joe would call. He and Kinkaid had been planning on pursuing more information about the Russians in the afternoon, and I hadn't heard from him since. I didn't like that. I also wanted to tell him about Yuri Belov.

While I was busy thinking about Joe, I suddenly became aware of a soft, gentle sobbing beside me. I looked down at Julie and realized she was crying.

"Julie," I said, reaching out to her without stopping to think about it and putting my arm around her shoulders. "It's going to be all right." She turned to me, wrapped her arms around me, and put her face against my bare chest, crying harder now. I was surprised initially, but then I realized I shouldn't be. The woman was running for her life, and her husband had been murdered. Just because she had done such a good job of holding up throughout the day didn't mean I should expect it to continue. That wasn't fair to her.

I didn't say anything, because I knew there weren't any words to comfort her for what she was feeling. Instead, I just held her while she cried. You do what you can. A few minutes passed, and then she got the tears under control and looked up at me, forcing a smile.

"I'm sorry," she whispered. "I didn't mean to make you endure that."

"Don't apologize," I said. She hadn't pulled away from me yet, and her arms were still around me. I didn't have any desire to move them.

"It's been hard," she said. "It's been really hard, but I have to put on the brave, happy face for Betsy. I can't let her see how scared I am. I can't afford to let that happen now."

"I understand," I said.

She exhaled heavily and put the side of her head against my chest. "I hope you understand how thankful I am to have you here. I hope you know how much you helped today, and how much better I feel knowing you're here with us." She lifted her head and looked into my eyes, our faces just inches apart, and I was very aware of the press of her breasts against my chest. "I've been so scared, and so lonely," she whispered, squeezing the back of my neck with her hand. "So lonely."

For one electric moment we remained in that position, staring into each other's eyes, and then she leaned forward and brushed her lips lightly against mine. It was probably intended to be little more than a peck—a gesture of appreciation in a moment of emotion. I went with it, though, returning the kiss. I couldn't help myself.

It was a long, good kiss. When she finally broke away, she was smiling, and I felt very small. I thought of John Weston, his dead son, and his granddaughter Betsy asleep upstairs, and I was ashamed.

"I shouldn't have done that," I began, but she leaned back in and kissed me again. And I meant to push her away, I really did, but I couldn't. I was too attracted to her. I went with the kiss again, and she shifted in the water, sliding her thighs over mine so she was sitting on my lap, still squeezing my neck and kissing me, her breasts rising and falling against my chest as my hands glided across her back, smoothing the beads of water against her skin.

If I'd ever been more aroused, I couldn't remember it. But even as our bodies pressed together and our lips met, other images were flashing through my mind. I saw the crime scene photographs of Wayne Weston's corpse, and I saw his father sitting on the deck of his son's house staring at the snowman with the world's loneliest eyes. This time, I broke the kiss.

"We can't," I said, breathing heavily.

"Ssshh," she said, putting her index finger to my lips.

"I have an obligation to John," I said. "It's not that I don't want to, but I can't . . ." I let my words trail off as she began kissing the side of my neck, and then I said the hell with it. I'd given her the chance to reconsider, and she'd passed. I wanted the woman, and I wanted her badly. I pulled her head toward me and kissed her again.

She ran her hands through my hair and over my shoulders

as we kissed, and I let my fingers wander up her back to the strings of her swimsuit top. I ran my fingertips over the knot, and she kissed me harder and squeezed me with her legs, encouraging me. I pulled at the knot, loosening the strings and letting her swimsuit top slide free, leaving her breasts bare and warm against my chest. We were alone in the whirlpool, but it was a hotel, and people could walk by at any minute. I wasn't even aware of the surroundings, though. Julie was all I could think about.

She slid farther up on my lap, lifting her chest slightly out of the water, the swimsuit top falling away completely, and she ran the palm of her hand up the inside of her thigh to my groin. And then my phone rang.

"Shit," I breathed between kisses. This couldn't be happening. Not now.

"Ignore it," she whispered, caressing my jawline with the tip of her tongue.

I twisted my head slightly and leaned back so I could see the cell phone's display. The caller ID was flashing the number, clearly illuminated against the green backlight. It was Joe.

"I've got to answer," I said, "it's my partner."

"No," she said, kissing my neck. "Call him back."

I pushed down the urge to take her advice, and I reached for the phone with my left arm. She groaned softly and nipped my earlobe with her teeth. I got my fingers around the phone and brought it to my mouth. She sighed and slid off my lap, feeling in the water for the top of her swimsuit. As I pressed a button to receive the call, I felt like screaming at Joe to leave me alone and call back in an hour. Or six.

"You've got amazingly bad timing," I said instead.

"I don't care," he said, and his voice was tense. "Lincoln, we've got major trouble."

"What is it?" Julie had found her swimsuit top, and she was retying it behind her back. Now she looked at me, catching the concern in my voice.

"Kinkaid and I couldn't find the Russians this afternoon," he said. "I had a bad feeling about it, so I drove out to the airport and showed the attendants some photographs. Krashakov and Rakic took a plane out of the city today, Lincoln. They're on their way to South Carolina. They're coming after you."

NINETEEN

I turned away from Julie, not trusting myself to keep my face from showing the chill that Joe's news sent through me.

"Are you sure?" I asked, but I knew he was. Joe was not a man prone to false assumptions.

"Positive," he said. "Kinkaid and I drove down to their house today, planning to keep an eye on them all night. The SUV was in the driveway, but it didn't look like anyone was home. I went for a walk around the block and talked to one of the neighbors, an old lady who was out feeding stray cats. She told me she'd seen the Russians leave in a cab an hour before we got there. I didn't like that at all—why leave in a cab when your own car is sitting in the drive, you know? So I went back and talked it over with Kinkaid. He thought maybe they were just trying to avoid using their own vehicle because they were going someplace where they didn't want to be noticed, but I disagreed. I was thinking about the airport right away. I made him go out there with me, and we showed pictures around until we found someone who recognized them."

"What time was their flight?" I asked. I had climbed out of the whirlpool now. The wind was cold against my wet body. My eyes were locked on the window of Julie's hotel room, where Betsy Weston slept alone.

"Four-thirty," he said. "There was a stopover, though, so the flight was expected to get into Myrtle Beach around nine tonight."

"What time is it?"

"Nine-thirty."

"Shit, Joe. Why the hell did you wait until now to call?"

"I've been trying to call, LP. It kept telling me your phone was either turned off or out of range."

Cell phones. You gotta love 'em.

"You need to get moving," Joe said. "Fast. According to the airport attendants I spoke with, Krashakov and Rakic were with two other men."

"Four of them," I said, my voice an unnatural monotone. "Great."

"Are you with Mrs. Weston and the girl?"

It seemed strange to think of Julie as Mrs. Weston now, although I wouldn't have thought twice about it a day earlier. "I'm with Julie," I said. "We're outside. Betsy is asleep in the room."

"Well, get the hell up there, get her, and get gone. When you're someplace safe and you have time to slow down, call me."

"All right." I hung up. My heart was still beating quickly, but it was no longer because of Julie. I turned back to her and saw she was standing at the edge of the swimming pool, clutching the towel to her body.

"I'm sorry," she said as I approached. She wouldn't look at me. "I can't believe I did that. I shouldn't have let that happen."

"It's my fault, so don't apologize. But right now we can't worry about it, and we don't have time to talk about it."

"What's wrong?"

I didn't want to tell her, but I had to. "My partner was at the Cleveland airport. He found out four of the Russians flew out this afternoon. They're coming here."

Her eyes went wide, and she raised a hand to her mouth. "Betsy," she said. "Oh, no." She pushed past me and ran for the hotel door. I followed, wishing I'd thought to bring my gun with me to the whirlpool. They'd been due in town at nine, Joe had said. It was nine-thirty. Plenty of time to have rented a car.

The elevator was on the ground floor, and it opened immediately when Julie pressed the button. We stepped in, and I took her by the shoulders and pushed her against the wall.

"I need you to keep being strong," I said. "I know you're scared, but we have to stay calm. I don't want Betsy getting hysterical, and neither do you. If she sees your fear, she'll respond to it. You need to get your things together and get her ready to leave, but you need to keep her calm while you do that."

"What do I tell her?"

"Tell her the hotel made a mistake and someone else needs our room. Tell her you're tired of the scenery. Tell her anything, I don't care what it is so long as she believes it and doesn't panic."

The elevator door opened again, and we stepped out into the seventh-floor hallway. I heard Julie exhale with relief when she saw the door was still closed and didn't appear to be damaged. I used her keycard to open it and stepped in before she did, just in case someone was waiting for us. I was unarmed, barefoot, and shirtless. Not ideal combat conditions. I turned the light on and looked around the room. It was empty, and the balcony door was closed and locked. Julie shoved past me and ran to the bedroom door, opened it, and looked inside.

"She's still asleep."

"Get her up, and get packed," I said. "We need to go very quickly."

She went in to wake the girl up, and I went into the bathroom for my own bag. I'd tucked the Glock back inside it when we'd gone down to the whirlpool. Now I withdrew it, checked the clip, and set it on the sink. Ten shots in the clip and one in the chamber. Eleven ways to make someone dead, and yet I found it comforting. I wondered what that said about my life. I pulled on a T-shirt and jeans, clipped the holster on, then slipped my feet into socks and tennis shoes. My body was still damp, but there wasn't any time to waste. I zipped the bag shut and returned to the living room.

Betsy was standing in the middle of the room, bleary-eyed. She was clutching a stuffed cat under her right arm, and her left thumb was in her mouth. She looked more asleep than awake, but she'd changed out of her pajamas and into shorts and a T-shirt. I smiled at her, trying to look at ease.

"Hey, kid. Too bad we had to wake you up, but we've got to switch hotels. You can go back to sleep as soon as we get in the car."

She nodded sleepily. "Don't forget my ice cream."

"'Course not." I walked into the bedroom and found Julie wildly throwing clothes into suitcases. She was still wearing the swimsuit. I stepped over and put my hand on her shoulder.

"Relax," I said. "Be quick; don't be panicked. Put some regular clothes on before we leave, or Betsy's going to know something's wrong and get scared."

She spun to me and grabbed my arms. "You have to keep her safe."

"I will."

"You *have* to."

"Julie," I said softly, "I will keep you safe. I will die for you if I have to, understand?"

"I'm not asking you to die for me," she said, and her eyes were wild and intense. "If they come after us, dying won't be any help at all. You'll need to kill for us. Can you kill for my daughter, Lincoln? Can you kill to save my daughter?"

Her fingers were digging into my biceps, and for some reason as I looked into her eyes I had the feeling she'd asked this question before and been disappointed with the answer. Probably she'd asked it of her husband, maybe even Hartwick. Both of them had succeeded only in dying for her and Betsy.

"I can kill to save you," I said, and she loosened her grip and nodded, believing something she saw in my eyes or heard in my voice, if not the words.

"All right," she said. "Now let's get out of here."

I went back into the living room and sat on the couch, watching the door. Both the deadbolt and the electronic lock were in place. No one was going to get in without making some noise, and if anyone made some noise I was going to shoot first and ask questions later.

"I'm tired," Betsy said, flopping onto the floor and sitting cross-legged at my feet. "I was having good dreams. I was riding a fish."

"I'm sorry. We'll let you lie down in the backseat of the car and get right back to that fish riding. I promise."

Julie stepped out of the bedroom with a small suitcase in each hand. At first I was surprised by how little she had, but then I remembered the undisrupted condition of her house in Brecksville. They'd been forced to leave as if their absence hadn't been planned, and that meant packing light.

"All set?" I asked.

"Yes."

I started to take the suitcases from her but then thought better of it. The hell with being a gentleman—if we ran into any trouble, I was going to need my hands free.

"You take them," I said, and she seemed to understand my reasoning. "Need anything else?"

"No."

"Let's go, then."

Julie had pulled shorts and a sweatshirt over her swimsuit, but her hair hung around her shoulders in damp coils. We took the elevator down to the lobby. Rebecca, the receptionist I'd flirted with the day before, looked up at us and smiled. Then she saw the little girl, and the smile turned a touch uncertain.

"Well, hi," she said. "I didn't see you this afternoon. I'm working the late shift today."

"Sorry I missed you," I said. I kept walking for the door, though. Offending a pretty receptionist was the least of my concerns right now.

"Wait," she said, and I glanced over my shoulder as I

pushed the door open. She was holding a manila envelope in her hand. "I have something for you."

Had something for me? What was this? I told Julie and Betsy to wait at the door, and I jogged back and took the envelope from her hand.

"It's from Lamar," she said, looking over my shoulder at Betsy and Julie as if she sensed something was very wrong about the situation. "He told me you'd be expecting it. He also said to tell you that you have the ugliest swing he's ever seen."

Hartwick's personnel file. After finding Julie in the whirlpool the night before, I'd forgotten all about it.

"Thanks," I said. "We've got to run right now, though. The little girl's not feeling so well, and we need to take her to a doctor." It was weak, but it was the best I had. We left.

I stepped into the street with all of my muscles tensed, as if preparing to be hit by a hail of gunfire. Instead, the street was nearly empty and as still as a rural lane. I hurried Betsy and Julie across and into the parking garage. The Contour was parked on the first level, close to the exit. I opened the trunk and tossed the bags in, then climbed inside after helping Betsy into the backseat. I started the engine, backed out of the parking spot, and pulled into the street. We'd made it.

I drove north slowly, trying to decide what the best course of action would be. We could go to the airport, but that would be a poor move. As soon as the Russians found we were missing, they'd immediately check the airport to see what flight we'd taken. And there was always the chance their flight had been delayed and we'd actually bump into them at the airport. That thought made me shudder. I could drive to Charleston or Columbia and try to catch a flight home from there, but I didn't want to do that, either. I decided the thing to do was keep driving through the night. I didn't have enough cash for three plane tickets, and I expected the Russians would probably have someone capable of tracing my credit card if I used it. That would allow them to know exactly when we'd return to Cleveland, which wasn't a pleasant idea.

"I think we'll drive for a while," I said. Julie nodded but didn't say anything.

"Where are we going?" Betsy asked.

"It's a surprise," I said, "but I promise you'll like it. Why don't you try to take a nap now?"

We pulled up to a red light. I glanced at the other cars around us, but their drivers weren't interested in us, just strangers in the night, like the old Sinatra song. The red light turned green, and I moved my foot to the accelerator but then paused, suddenly feeling as if I were forgetting something. It was a feeling I frequently had after leaving a hotel, and now wasn't the time to bother with it, but I couldn't ignore the sensation. I pressed on the accelerator when someone behind me honked, and we pulled away from the light slowly, but I still didn't feel right.

"What?" Julie said, sensing my unease.

"Nothing." I shook my head. There was nothing important to be forgotten, was there? I hadn't checked out, so I'd lose the deposit on my keycard, but that was hardly a concern. Julie had never officially checked in. I had my gun, and I had Julie and Betsy. That was all that mattered.

The tape.

"Aww, shit!" I slapped the steering wheel with my hand. I saw Betsy's eyes go wide in the rearview mirror, and Julie clutched my arm.

"What is it?"

"The tape," I whispered, trying to keep Betsy from hearing. "I left it in the room."

"Where was it?"

"I slid it under the couch when you and Betsy walked into the room this morning. We left in such a hurry I forgot about it." I felt stupid. It's always embarrassing to make a mental error such as forgetting something important, but this was worse. Returning to the hotel could be dangerous. Then again, this was the mother of all forgotten items.

"We've got to go back," I said. "That tape is too important."

I turned around at the next parking lot and started back.

We'd gone maybe twenty blocks from the hotel, but it seemed a much greater distance on the way back. I pulled into the parking lot of a hotel across the street and about a block down from the Golden Breakers. I left the keys in the ignition.

"I'm going to get it. Stay in the car, and stay out of sight. If I'm not back in ten minutes, then get the hell out of here. Drive to some crowded public place and call the police. They might not understand the details of your situation, but they can keep you safe." *Probably they'll do a better job of it than I am,* I thought. I climbed out of the car and started for the Golden Breakers at a jog.

Three cars were parked in the visitor spaces in the front circle; I didn't remember if they'd been there before. I pushed through the heavy glass doors and started for the elevator. Halfway there I stopped short.

The reception desk was empty. Rebecca was nowhere to be seen. How long had we been gone? Ten minutes, tops. She could have gone to the bathroom, or maybe out to smoke a cigarette. My gut told me she hadn't, though. I walked behind the desk.

She was lying on the floor, a bloody bruise swelling over the right side of her face. I dropped to my knees beside her and reached out to turn her over. When I touched her, her eyes opened and she jerked away from me as if I were the physical form of whatever evil had been dancing through her unconscious mind.

"It's okay," I said. Her eyes were foggy. They reminded me of the eyes of addicts and winos I'd seen in my days on the force, eyes that saw a world separate from reality. She started to drop her head back to the ground, but I caught it and forced her to look at me. "Where are they?"

She blinked hard, trying to come back to full consciousness. Blood was dripping from the cut on her cheekbone to my hand. I looked at it, felt its warmth on my skin, and was stirred by a seething, burning anger. She had nothing to do with this, but they'd hurt her anyhow. I removed my gun and slipped the safety off. Julie had asked if I could kill to protect her daughter. The Russians damn well better believe I could.

"Where are they?" I asked again, stroking Rebecca's cheek with my thumb, trying to keep her conscious.

"Sent 'em . . . your room," she stuttered, her eyes fluttering and rolling like pinballs. She was about to pass out again. I gave her a gentle shake, and her eyes rolled back into focus momentarily. "I sent them to your room. They took my master keycard." Each word was an effort. "I wasn't going to give it to them, but . . . they hit me," she said, and her tone changed, as if she wasn't telling this to me but was telling it to herself and was surprised by the news. *They hit me. A group of strangers walked into this hotel and hit me.*

I eased her back to the ground and looked around. She needed medical attention, but I needed that tape. The Russians were on the second floor now, though, and when they realized it was empty they'd be coming back down with more questions. And they'd be angry. I couldn't leave Rebecca here.

I set the gun aside and lifted her, holding her easily in both arms, and walked into the manager's office behind the reception desk. There was little more than a desk and two file cabinets inside. The door would lock, though. I set her on the ground, picked up the phone on the desk, and dialed 911. I dropped the receiver back to the desk, knowing they'd have to send an officer out to check on the call if no one spoke. I didn't have time to give them a rundown, either. I pushed the lock button on the inside of the door and pulled it shut behind me, then tried the knob. It was locked. The door wouldn't hold if the Russians tried to force it, but at least she was out of sight and help would be on the way. I ignored the elevator and went for the stairs.

I ran up the stairs with the type of desperate panic that would carry people *down* them if a fire broke out in the building. By the time I reached the seventh floor, my heart was pounding and my pores had opened up, releasing a fresh, cold sweat. I pushed the door open and pivoted into the hall, gun drawn. I was staring at a group of four middle-aged women. They saw the gun and started to scream hysterically. I froze for a moment, then ignored them and ran for Julie's room, fumbling in my pocket for the keycard. The women kept screaming as I opened the door and slammed it behind me.

The room was empty. I left the light off and crossed to the couch, then dropped to my knees and felt under the couch with my hands. Nothing was there. I slid my hand farther under the couch and drew it slowly from one end to the other. Nothing. My throat tightened. Where the hell could it be? I dropped the gun to the floor and hooked my fingers under the edge of the couch, dragged it away from the wall, then lifted it and tipped it over on its side. There was the tape, pushed to the far corner beyond my reach. I picked it up and slipped it under my shirt and into the waistband of my jeans.

Outside, the screaming reached a higher pitch. I turned to the door and switched the gun to my right hand, dropping into a crouch. The red light of the electronic lock glowed back at me, telling me the door was still locked.

When Randy Hartwick died in front of me, I'd watched a red dot appear and disappear on his chest. Now, as I watched this one, it disappeared as well, then turned green. Someone had slipped a keycard into the lock.

I went down on one knee and sighted the gun on the door as it swung open. The first thing I saw was not a person but the barrel of another gun, and then the room erupted into a clatter of automatic gunfire. I squeezed off two return shots, then threw myself on the floor, rolling behind the upturned couch as bullets splattered into the walls around me, showers of glass raining down when the balcony door shattered.

I slid my head past the edge of the couch and looked at the door, surprised to find it was closed again. The shots were being fired from the hallway, through the door and the walls. Maybe one of my bullets had found its mark on the man who'd pushed the door open. I put two more rounds through the door, and then the shots from the hall ceased.

I fired four more shots, taking my time with these, and

then got to my feet and stepped through the hole of jagged glass where the balcony door had been. The men in the hallway were regrouping, but they would undoubtedly open fire again soon. There was no time to hesitate; it was get out now or die later. I pushed the gun back into my waistband, next to the videotape, and put both hands on the railing. It was only seven stories up, but seven stories looks like a lot when you're about to swing your body over the edge of a railing. If I had any doubts, though, they ended when gunfire opened up again, punching into the walls behind me. I swung over the edge.

I slid my hands down the rails until I was hanging by the bottom bar. My body was suspended seven stories above the concrete surrounding the pool. Shots were being fired into the room again, and a few of the bullets banged off the railing above me, dangerously close. I kicked my feet backward, pulling my body away from the balcony, and then swung my body in an arc, releasing my hold on the rail as the momentum brought me back toward the building. I made it just over the railing of the balcony below me, landing awkwardly, my feet tangled with one of the plastic chairs.

In my landing the videotape had fallen free, but it was within reach, and thankfully the gun hadn't discharged into my ass. I gathered the tape up and looked inside the hotel room. It was dark. The glass door to this balcony was open, but the screen was closed. No one was home, but they'd still wanted the fresh air circulating while they were out. I appreciated the choice. I put my foot through the screen and then used my hand to tear it loose. Above me, I heard a door slam against the wall, then more shots. They'd entered the room. That meant in a few short seconds they would know I'd jumped off the balcony. When they didn't see my corpse on the pavement, it wouldn't be hard to guess what I'd done. I pulled the room door open and ran into the hallway.

I considered the stairs, but the elevator was right in front of me with the doors standing open, so I jumped inside. If they had men in the lobby, they'd be waiting for me whether I took the stairs or the elevator. I stood to the side of the elevator car, in a shooter's stance, and waited while the doors opened slowly. The lobby was empty. Behind the desk, the door to the manager's office was still closed. Rebecca was safe for now. I ran out of the building. As I went through the front doors, I heard another door bang open as someone stepped out of the stairwell. They would expect me to run toward the street. I ducked to the right and ran around the side of the building, toward the beach and away from the street. And right into two armed men.

One was Rakic, and the other was a fat, pasty-skinned blond man I'd never seen before. They had their backs to me, and they were looking intently at the balconies. When I came sprinting up, they heard me and turned.

Rakic shouted something unintelligible, and the pale fat man spun toward me, lifting a sawed-off shotgun. I shot him twice in the face, and he fell hard. A red mist sprayed onto Rakic. He dropped his own gun and fell to his knees, screaming and lifting his hands to his face, apparently convinced I'd shot him because of all the blood. I turned and ran back toward the street as someone fired at me from the balcony, the bullets kicking up bits of grass and dirt behind my feet.

I sprinted down the sidewalk, running faster than I'd moved since high school track, well aware there were three men still in pursuit and that I had only one round left in my gun.

I ran out into the street, and several cars honked at me and swerved to avoid a collision. I found the parking lot where I'd left Julie and Betsy. I'd told her to leave after ten minutes. How long had it been? They'd better still be there.

They were. I glanced over my shoulder and saw nothing but an empty sidewalk. I tucked the gun back under my shirt and wiped the sweat from my face, then knocked on the driver's door. Julie leaned over and unlocked it, and I slid behind the wheel.

"What happened?" she asked. I was covered in sweat and gasping for breath, and a few drops of the fat man's blood dotted my T-shirt. Betsy was sitting up in the backseat now, staring at me with eyes like dinner plates.

"Nothing happened," I said. "But we're leaving now. Betsy, honey, would you do me a huge favor and lie down in the backseat? We're going to be driving for a while, and I want you to take a nap. I'll get you an extra ice cream tomorrow if you lie down."

She went down obediently, but her eyes remained open, and she clutched the stuffed cat to her chest a little tighter. Scared. She was a little girl, not an idiot, and she knew something was wrong.

The parking lot had exits onto Business 17 and Ocean Avenue. I turned onto 17 and drove south, watching my rearview mirror carefully. A squad car passed us, lights flashing and siren wailing, and hung a left, heading toward the Golden Breakers. They'd be looking for me soon enough. Rebecca would tell them my name, and they'd put out an all-points bulletin. They would even have the license plate number on the rental car, since I'd been required to put it on the hotel registration form. I didn't fear the police at all compared to the Russians, but I also didn't want to be stopped. I wanted to get back to Cleveland, and Joe. Together, we'd work this out. Or die trying.

TWENTY

I drove south for an hour, even though it was the opposite direction from where I wanted to be heading. The less reasonable route, the harder it would be to follow, I figured. I probably had an hour or so before the APB on my license plate went out, and then every state trooper in South Carolina would be looking for me. And for good reason—I'd just killed a man. I thought about it in a detached way now, as if I hadn't actually pulled the trigger but watched someone else do it.

I'd pulled my gun several times in my police days, but I'd never fired to kill. I imagined tonight's incident would have more impact when the adrenaline died down, and I wasn't looking forward to that. It had been the definition of a self-defense killing, but it had been a killing nonetheless, and I'd never wanted to experience that, regardless of the circumstances or the victim. Julie had asked me if I could kill for her daughter, and I'd told her yes. I'd believed it when I said it, and she'd seemed to believe it, but I hadn't expected the statement to be put to the test.

I drove to Charleston and took the interstate north out of the city. Cleveland was probably a fourteen-hour drive from Charleston, which meant I had a long night—and morning—ahead of me. It was slightly after eleven when we left Charleston, but I couldn't even imagine sleeping. The adrenaline coursing through my veins was more intense than anything I'd felt before, and I thought I could probably abandon the car and run to Cleveland with Betsy on my back if necessary.

Julie and I did not speak. Betsy stayed awake until we hit Charleston. There the fatigue caught up with her and overpowered the fear, allowing her to sleep. Twenty minutes out of Charleston, Julie turned around and stroked her daughter's arm, making sure she was sound asleep. Satisfied, she pulled back into her seat and looked at me.

"Will you tell me what happened now?"

I kept my eyes on the highway. "I got the tape. The Russians were at the hotel, though. Your hotel room turned into the O.K. Corral for a few minutes, and I jumped off the balcony onto the one below it, then ran out of the hotel and right into two of them. One of the guys swung a shotgun at me, and I killed him." My voice was the same odd monotone it had been during my conversation with Joe. Detached. No emotion. Just routine talk from a cold, calculating, reflex killer.

Seven minutes passed before she spoke again. I watched the dashboard clock.

"I'm sorry" was what she said when she did break the silence.

"Why are you sorry? It's not your fault."

"Yes, it is. They weren't there for you. They were there for me."

"I might have led them to you, though. I used a credit card to pay for my flight and my hotel room. I assume they have someone who is capable of tracing that. I should have considered it to begin with, but I didn't. So it's just as much my fault as yours." I wasn't sure how the Russians had become aware of me in the first place, or concerned enough to try to trace me, but I figured that was how it had happened.

"No," she said, shaking her head in the darkness. "It's not your fault *or* my fault. We didn't do anything wrong, we're just paying the consequences. It's my husband's fault—his and Jeremiah Hubbard's." She said it sadly but firmly.

We drove on in silence.

"Are you going to drive all the way to Ohio?" she asked several minutes later.

"I'm going to try."

"That's not safe. You'll be exhausted."

"Julie, it would take a dozen tranquilizers to slow me down right now."

"Okay."

"Besides, the farther we get, the better. The police will be looking for the car."

"Is that a problem?"

I shrugged. "We agreed that we didn't want to deal with the local authorities, but I'm not too worried about it. If they pull me over, I'll go to jail and you can ask for the FBI. These hick cops will be happy to do it, because they won't have a clue what to do with you." Cody was with the FBI, but I didn't see how he could possibly have enough power to get to Julie and Betsy once they were under the control of authorities in a different state. Yet I continued to keep them out of police hands. A fool for a keeper, that's what they had.

"Why would you go to jail?" Julie asked.

"I killed a man, Julie. It was a justifiable homicide, but I'm going to have to prove that in court. All the cops know is that I shot up a hotel and killed a man. They aren't going to let me go home right away."

She reached out and gripped my arm. "I need you with us. If they arrest you, they'll separate us."

"I know. That's why I'm not going directly to the cops. But if they stop us, that's what's going to happen. We'll deal with that when we come to it."

Julie turned her head and stared out of the window. "I know it seems unimportant now, but we need to talk about what happened in the whirlpool tonight. I need to apologize for that."

"It's fine, Julie."

She shook her head. "No, it's not. I can't believe I did

that. My husband has been dead for ten days, Lincoln. Ten days. And I'm jumping on you in a hotel hot tub. Classy." She looked up at me and pushed her hair away from her face. "It was an emotional response to a lot of fear and confusion," she said. "That's all it was."

"Of course. I didn't think you might have actually found me attractive." It was a juvenile response, and I regretted it as soon as it left my mouth.

"That's not what I meant," she said.

"I know. I'm sorry."

She gave a short laugh and then sighed. "That was the problem, Lincoln—I do find you attractive. In so many ways. In *every* way. I've known you for one day, and yet I'm incredibly drawn to you. And I feel that's wrong. It *is* wrong, considering the circumstances. But I can't help it. You came to me when I needed someone, and you have all the qualities I'd always . . . I'd always thought my husband had," she finished softly.

We sat in an awkward silence after that. After a few minutes I realized she was crying. I didn't move toward her this time, though. I'd learned my lesson. Eventually, she reached out and took my hand in hers, brought it away from the steering wheel and to her face. She kissed my fingertips softly, her lips so warm they seemed to sear my flesh. A few of her tears fell to my skin as well. It was an appropriate mix. She placed my hand back on the steering wheel, took a deep breath, leaned back in the seat, and closed her eyes.

Then it was just me and the road. The traffic was sparse, and I stayed in the left lane with the cruise control set on seventy-five. Fast enough to make good time, but not fast enough on the interstate to attract attention from police. I watched carefully for them, and once I saw a state police car headed in the opposite direction, but it did not slow.

The dashboard clock rolled over to midnight, and a song lyric popped into my head: *lonely midnight drivers, drifting out to sea.* Who did the song? What was the song? I couldn't remember either answer, but there that line was, trapped in my mind. Funny.

We crossed over the state line early in the morning and then spent two hours driving through North Carolina before entering Virginia. The entire eastern seaboard in an exciting midnight tour. Police drove past and didn't slow. Julie and Betsy slept soundly. I stopped once to fill the car with gas, and I called Joe. He answered immediately, and I realized guiltily that he probably hadn't slept at all, waiting for my call. I told him what had happened, and I told him I hoped to be in Cleveland later that morning. We wished each other well, and then I drove on, a lonely midnight driver drifting out to . . . to what? A quick, simple solution, I thought optimistically. I didn't believe it, though. Not even for a second.

Dawn broke as I pushed us through the mountains in West Virginia. The hills came up out of a gray mist, becoming more defined with each passing minute, the fog and shadows fading as the sun rose and burned them away. My mind was still alert, but my body had begun to ache—the hours of sitting in the cramped Contour combining with the lack of sleep to make me long for a bed and some hours to enjoy it. Julie woke around six, stretched, and smiled sleepily at me.

"I can't believe I slept that long," she said. "I'm sorry. I should have stayed awake to help you pass the time."

"I wouldn't have been much for conversation anyhow," I said. "My brain was pretty much dead to everything but the highway in front of me. I was surprised that you didn't wake up when I stopped for gas, though."

"You stopped for gas?" she said, and then laughed. "Has my daughter stirred?"

"Not once."

"Good."

We drove on for a while, and then I noticed the needle on the gas gauge was creeping toward empty once again. This was the longest stretch of driving I'd done in years, and the thing that most surprised me was how quickly the gas seemed to disappear. I stopped at an exit that boasted several gas stations and a Cracker Barrel restaurant. The Cracker Barrel meant coffee. Coffee would be very nice after ten hours on the road.

Betsy stumbled out of the car groggily after Julie woke her. She stood in the parking lot and rubbed her eyes with her tiny fists, then gave a great yawn, opening her mouth so wide I thought I could drop a basketball into it.

"Where is we?" she asked with all the energy of a sloth.

"Where *are* we," Julie corrected, and I wanted to laugh. We were driving through the mountains, hiding from gun-wielding thugs and even the police, and Julie was still correcting her daughter's grammar. Priorities.

"We're in West Virginia," I said. "Do you know where that is?"

"Of course," Betsy said as if I'd asked her if she knew her own name. Oops. Never underestimate the children.

"Are we going home?" she asked, and Julie and I exchanged a glance.

"We're not going home, exactly," Julie said, and I was relieved that she'd decided to field the question. "But we're going to be close."

"Do I get to see Daddy?"

Julie's smile stayed in place. "Let's go eat, honey. You're wearing me out with all these questions. It's too early for them."

Betsy shrugged and started for the restaurant, then stopped and stared at me. I followed her eyes and saw she was looking at my shirt, where a cluster of tiny dried drops of blood remained.

"What happened?" she said.

"I had a nosebleed while you were asleep. Nothing to worry about." I looked away from her. If there's anything that feels worse than lying, it's lying to a little girl. We went inside the Cracker Barrel, my legs wooden and awkward as they propelled me across the parking lot. Yeah, I'd been in that damned Contour for too long.

I had scrambled eggs, toast, bacon, and six cups of coffee. The coffee was strong and rich, and it rejuvenated me, giving a sharper edge to my mind and making the morning feel more like the start of a new day instead of the continuation of a long, strange night. Julie had an omelet, and

Betsy ate silver-dollar pancakes drenched in an obscene amount of syrup. Kids. I'd chosen the wrong profession, all right. If I'd wanted to make money, I should have been a dentist. She didn't ask about her father again, which surprised me. Most of the young children I'd known weren't prone to giving up on a question like that until they'd received a satisfactory answer. Maybe she'd sensed some note of warning in her mother's voice, or maybe she'd asked the question so many times in the past few days she was giving up on the satisfactory answer. Or maybe she was just distracted by the pancakes.

"Honey, why don't you go to the bathroom?" Julie said when her daughter was done eating. "We're going to be in the car for quite a while again."

"Okay." Betsy left her plateful of syrup and went to the bathroom, and Julie turned to me.

"So what's the plan for the day?"

"We're meeting my partner outside the city," I said. "Then the three of us will sit down and talk."

"What about your reporter friend?"

I was surprised she'd brought up Amy. "I can ask her to join us," I said. "Is that something you want?"

"Yes." She nodded. "Yes, I think that is definitely something I want."

I sipped my coffee. "I see. Would you mind telling me why?"

"Why I want the reporter involved?" When I nodded, she said, "Insurance, I guess."

"Insurance?"

"Yes. For example, if anything were to happen to me—if, heaven forbid, the police screwed up, or Hubbard paid them off—my story would still be told. I'd like to know that."

"You're more scared of Hubbard than of the Russians, aren't you?"

She held my eyes for a second and then nodded. "Yes," she said, "I am. He killed my husband, Lincoln. You don't have to believe that, but I know it's true. And I know my husband was scared of him, too. My cocky, brave husband, who always thought he was invincible, was scared of Jeremiah Hubbard. So scared that he preferred to throw his life away—throw *our* life away—rather than upset the man. You think Wayne avoided the police because he was afraid of the Russians?" She shook her head emphatically. "No way. He was concerned about them, obviously, but the only person who *scared* him was Jeremiah Hubbard."

I thought about Cody and his FBI badge, and I thought about Richard Douglass, the top attorney in town, and maybe I was a little bit scared of Jeremiah Hubbard, too. At least the Russians used methods I understood, methods I was familiar with. Hubbard worked through different channels entirely, controlling situations with a checkbook instead of a gun. And there was no doubt his checkbook was far more powerful than any number of guns.

Betsy returned from the bathroom, bringing an abrupt end to my conversation with her mother. I paid the bill, relieved myself of some of the coffee, and then went back to the car. I was approaching twenty-four hours without sleep, but I wasn't feeling it yet.

We drove out of West Virginia and into Ohio. As we headed north, Julie occupied Betsy by playing silly games like racing to see who could find all the letters of the alphabet on road signs. They were both stuck on *X* for quite a while, until Betsy spotted a hotel sign boasting of expanded cable. She wrapped the game up by finding a *Z* in a sign for a radio station called "Rock 93, WZPL." The victory seemed to take something out of her, though, because she fell asleep again around eleven, as we neared Akron.

"Home sweet home," Julie said as we drove through Akron and continued north on I-77 toward Cleveland. "Somehow I feel safer now."

I pulled off the interstate at a rest stop a few minutes later. Julie went to the bathroom, but we let Betsy continue sleeping. I leaned against the trunk of the car and called Joe.

"Where are you?" he asked.

"Just south of the city. Where are you?"

"Don Gellino's lake cottage. You remember it?" Don

Gellino was a retired cop who owned a small cottage in Medina County. He called it a lake cottage, but the body of water it stood beside wasn't much more than a large pond. Good fishing, though, if Don was to be believed.

"I remember it. How the hell did you end up there?"

"Don's in New Mexico for the winter staying with his kids. He left the key with me and asked me to check in on it from time to time. I thought it was as good a spot as any for our purposes."

"Can't argue with that. Is Kinkaid with you?"

"Not yet. I'm supposed to call him soon, though. I just didn't think it would be a real good idea to drop him on Mrs. Weston on top of everything else she's got to deal with."

"Good choice," I said. I didn't want Julie to see Kinkaid, either. Whether my reasoning for that decision was based on Julie's welfare or my own feelings for her was another question, and not one I felt like dealing with at the moment. "Julie wants Amy there, too."

"Why?"

I explained her reasoning as best I could. "It makes some sense, Joe. If there's anything usable as leverage with Hubbard, it's going to be the threat of going public."

"I don't see why we need leverage with Hubbard. We're not negotiating a business deal, you know. This woman needs to talk to the police."

"Let's do it her way, Joe."

"Fine."

I hung up with him and called Amy at her office. I got the voice mail, so I tried her cell phone, and this time she answered.

"Lincoln, I've been waiting to hear from you all day. You have no idea how close I've come to going to the police with this."

"With what?"

"With *everything*, jackass. When I saw the story come over the wire this morning, I about died."

"Story?"

"Yeah, the story about the shootout at the Golden Breakers hotel. Don't tell me you weren't involved with it. I'm not that clueless."

"I was involved with it," I said. "Did the story give my name?"

"No, it didn't give any names except the cop they interviewed and the hotel owner, some guy named Burks."

"Lamar Burks, yeah. So what *did* the story say?"

"Just that there was an exchange of gunfire in and around this resort hotel early last night, and no arrests have been made. Apparently a desk clerk was beaten up, but she's in stable condition."

"There wasn't anything about someone being killed in this shootout?"

"No. Should there have been?"

I frowned. "Yeah, there should have been. If there was a body at the scene, would the reporters know about it by now, or could the cops be holding out?"

"Press would have it by now," she said confidently. "All we got on it was a little brief on the national news wire. I called the South Carolina bureau of the Associated Press for more details, and they told me they didn't have anything else. No one was injured, and no arrests had been made, they said."

No one was injured. Had I imagined shooting a man in the face? No, that didn't seem like the type of thing that was easy to misinterpret. I'd killed him. If his body hadn't been there, the Russians had taken it with them. Once I thought about it, that move made some sense. Leaving the body behind would have tied them to the shootings, and they were probably even more eager to avoid that than I was.

"What happened?" Amy asked.

"I can't tell you about it now."

"Dammit, Lincoln—"

"Look, I've got much bigger news for you," I interrupted. "After I tell you this, you're going to love me."

"What?"

"I'm back in Ohio, I've got Julie Weston with me, and you've got an exclusive interview with her if you want it. If you don't, I can call your buddy Jacob Terry and see if he's interested."

"Shut up."

"Okay."

"When and where can I talk to her?"

I gave her directions to Gellino's cottage. She told me she'd be there in an hour, and I suggested she bring a video camera and an inkpad with her. For Julie's interview to carry any significance, her identity would need to be verifiable, and I figured video and fingerprints should take care of that.

"I'll see you soon," she said. "After the night you had, I bet you're relieved to be getting closer to home and some support."

Closer to some support, all right. For me and the Russians. I hung up the phone and gazed down the highway, watching the innocuous stream of cars and wondering how long we had until the illusion of safety would be shattered again.

TWENTY-ONE

Don Gellino's cottage was near Hinckley, a tiny rural town south of Cleveland. I'd been there twice several years earlier, when Gellino had cookouts in the summer. It was a beautiful place. The pond was nestled in tall, thick pines and surrounded on one side by a jagged cliff, and the cottage was small but pleasant. Gellino had spent one June building a massive redwood deck looking out on the water. I'd forgotten just how nice a spot it was until I pulled off the state highway and onto the narrow, rutted gravel drive that led down to the pond and the cottage.

"Who owns this?" Julie asked as we passed through the rows of tall pines.

"A cop who retired four or five years ago and now spends the winters out in New Mexico with his kids. Joe has a key. It seemed like a good spot for us to use today."

Betsy was awake now, sitting up in the backseat and humming softly to herself. I was impressed with her. In the past ten days she'd been taken from her home to hide in a hotel room, then taken in the middle of the night from the hotel to drive for fourteen hours in a car with a man who was basically a stranger to her. Now she still didn't have any idea where we were going, but she wasn't complaining. Agreeable kid.

The gravel drive followed a gentle slope down through the trees, and then the water and the cottage came into view. Joe's Taurus was parked in front of the little house, but Amy hadn't arrived yet. There were patches of snow here and there under the trees, and the warm breezes of the South Carolina coast seemed a distant memory.

"It's pretty," Betsy said, pressing her face up against the window. "Are we staying here now?" There was something about the question that implied she was growing used to expecting another temporary home. I glanced at Julie and saw her grimace slightly. She didn't answer.

"You might stay here for a little while," I said. "Not long, though."

I pulled the Contour to a stop, and we got out. Joe was standing on the deck, watching us. He'd been inside, but he still had his jacket on, which meant he was wearing a gun. He looked tired.

"Good to see you," he told me when I led the way up the steps and onto the deck. "If I cared about your sorry ass, I would have been worried for the past few days."

"Uh-huh." I introduced him to Julie and Betsy. Betsy hid behind her mother's leg, acting shy for the first time since I'd known her. Joe could do that to you.

"Nice to meet you, ma'am," he said to Julie. "It's real nice to meet you, actually. For a while there I didn't think I was ever going to have the chance." He looked up the drive. "Lois Lane is running late, which is no surprise. I suppose we'd better go inside and have a little talk."

"Sounds good."

We went inside and sat in the living room. The walls were covered with the faux-wood paneling often seen in vacation homes. There was one large rack of antlers on the wall, several mounted fish, and a lamp made out of what appeared to be the skull of a buffalo. Charming. Old Don Gellino knew how to decorate. The carpet was a mixture of dull shades that reminded me of a calico cat's fur. It was a shrewd choice; most stains blended in pretty well. The furniture was old and well worn but comfortable enough.

It was cold inside the cottage, and Betsy was shivering as she sat down. The three of us would have to do something about our summer clothes. I asked Julie if she had sweatshirts or jackets in the car, and she said she did. I went outside and brought their bags in, and they went into one of the bedrooms to change. When they were gone, Joe turned to me and shook his head.

"I don't believe it. They're still the top story on every newscast in town, and yet I'm sitting here with them." He was staring at my shirt, examining the blood near the collar. "Rough night, eh?"

"It wasn't the best night, that's for sure."

"Think the Cleveland cops have heard about it yet?"

"Possibly. I talked to Amy, and she said Myrtle Beach police are looking into an exchange of gunfire at the hotel last night."

"No surprise."

"But there is a surprise. They don't seem to have turned up any bodies."

He frowned. "Are you sure you killed the guy?"

I saw the fat blond man's face disappearing in that red mist again. "Yeah, Joe. I'm sure."

"Well, I guess they must have taken the body and run. Regardless, it's good news for you. You're only wanted for a few small-time felonies now."

Tires crunched on the gravel outside, and we got up and crossed to the window. Amy's Acura had pulled to a stop beside our cars. She'd had the body damage repaired and the car repainted. She got out of the car and started up the steps to the deck, carrying a bag in each hand. One looked like a video camera carrying case.

We went out on the deck to meet her, and she surprised me by setting the bags down and hugging me fiercely.

"You're not dead," she said when she stepped back, and

then she looked a little embarrassed when she saw Joe watching us with a smile.

"No such luck," I said.

"Good. That means I still have the chance to kill you myself. As soon as I get Jacob Terry out of the way, you're next on my list." She leaned forward, looking past me and into the cottage. "As nice as it is to see you again, Lincoln, weren't you supposed to bring a few others along?"

"Oops," I said. "I knew I forgot something at that gas station in West Virginia."

"Seriously, where are they?" she said, and at that moment the bedroom door opened and Betsy stepped out, wearing jeans and a sweatshirt now. Her mother was right behind. Amy whispered, "Well, son of a bitch. It *is* them," and then walked inside.

"Mrs. Weston?" she said, offering her hand. "I'm Amy Ambrose." She shook hands with Julie, then knelt on the floor beside Betsy and shook the girl's hand as well. "You must be Betsy."

Betsy looked at her shyly, but she didn't duck behind Julie's legs as she had with Joe. "Amy Ambrose," the girl said, pronouncing it carefully. "You have a pretty name."

"Love the alliteration, don't ya, kid?" Amy said.

Betsy looked at me, confused. "Alitternation?"

"A litter nation," I said. "It's the dream of cat owners everywhere."

"What?"

"Ignore him, honey," Amy said. "He rarely makes any sense."

"You have pretty hair, too," Betsy said. "Can I . . ." She stopped talking, embarrassed to ask the question.

"Can you touch it?" Amy asked, and Betsy nodded and giggled. "Sure," Amy said, lowering her head and letting the girl run her fingers through the soft blond curls.

Julie laughed. "A pretty name *and* pretty hair," she said. "You've been met with approval, Miss Ambrose."

Amy got back to her feet. "That's reassuring. I spent a little extra time on the hair this morning to be sure it would stand up to heavy scrutiny."

Joe cleared his throat. "I hate to interrupt, ladies, but before we start working on our pigtails or putting on toenail polish, there are a few other things we have to attend to."

Ah, Joe. Always on the blunt side.

"Yes," Julie said, not offended by his remark, "there certainly are. But Betsy doesn't need to be here while we attend to them."

I was afraid Joe might suggest we lock the girl in a closet, but apparently he was in a tenderhearted mood, because he just shrugged, leaving the decision up to Julie.

"Speaking of nail polish," Amy said, "I've got some in my purse." She looked at Betsy. "Would you like to paint your nails, honey? You can pick the color." Betsy nodded, and Amy took her into the bedroom and left her with enough nail polish to coat her entire body. It would keep the kid occupied for a while, though. Joe looked at me and sighed.

Amy came back out of the bedroom, and Julie pulled the door shut and sat on the couch. A little cloud of dust rose up from the old cushion. She took a deep breath, rubbed her temples lightly with her fingers, and then looked up and forced a smile.

"All right," she said. "Where do we start?"

"We start by planning a course of action," Joe said. "I understand you're afraid, Mrs. Weston, and I understand the reasons you had for not contacting the police, but that has to stop now. You have testimony and a tape that can put several people in jail. Several people who *need* to be put in jail."

She nodded. "I understand that. But I also understand what will happen to me if I go to the police, Mr. Pritchard. There will be trials, won't there? There will be trials for the Russian murderers, and there will be a trial for Jeremiah Hubbard, and probably a trial for whoever killed Randy Hartwick. Trials that will likely last for months. And I'll be expected to testify at them, right? At all of them. What happens to my daughter during that time? She won't be allowed to go to school, because people may try to abduct her or kill her. We won't be allowed to live in our home, for the same reasons. So she's going to spend the next six months—the next year, maybe—hidden away someplace with body-guards? In the summer, when she should be at the swimming pool or playing with her friends, she's going to be tucked away out of sight? Oh, and of course I won't be able to allow her to turn on the television or pick up a newspaper, because she's going to see Daddy's face staring back at her or hear the television newscasters talking about the trials. I will not let that happen to my daughter, Mr. Pritchard."

"With all due respect, Mrs. Weston, I don't care," Joe said. "You have information about several serious crimes. You need to come forward with that information."

"What information?" she said, spreading her hands. "I have a tape of a murder. I've never even seen it. So give them the tape. The only testimony I could provide would be about my husband's work with Jeremiah Hubbard. I don't know anything about these Russian men. He didn't tell me anything, and I did not ask. But I have that tape, and if I give that to the police, people are going to want to kill me. If I *don't* give it to the police, they're going to want to kill me." She smiled bitterly. "I'm not very well liked."

"So what *do* you want to do?" Joe said, and I could tell he was fighting to keep the exasperation out of his voice.

"I want to tell people the truth," she said, and there was something in her voice that made me think of the night in the whirlpool, of the press of her body against mine. "I want to make it clear that my daughter and I are alive and that my husband was not a killer, and then I want to leave. I can't stay here, obviously. Wayne understood that, and that's why he tried to run. He can't leave anymore, but I can. And I can take my daughter with me."

"Where are you going to go?" Joe asked.

She smiled. "Please don't think I lack trust in any of you, but I'll keep that information to myself."

Joe shrugged. "Fine. But I have to say that might be the stupidest idea I've ever heard."

"Why's that?"

"You're afraid people are going to come after you for re-venge, right? Well, if that's true, why not go into witness protection and let the professionals help you disappear? It's a much safer bet than running on your own."

"He has a point," I said.

She shook her head. "If we go into witness protection, there will be people who know where we are. Someone, somewhere, will have the paperwork. Do you think Jeremiah Hubbard can't buy that information? Do you think some clerk is going to turn down five, ten, fifteen million dollars just to give him an address?"

Joe frowned. "I thought we were worried about the Russians coming after you. Now it's Hubbard?"

"It's *everyone,* Mr. Pritchard. My husband was very good at what he did. He made plans for our . . . our disappearance, I guess you'd say. I trust my husband's ability much more than I trust any government agency."

"She may not have to testify," I said, and they all looked at me. "She could sit down and give an interview to the pros-ecutor's office or the district attorney, sign an affidavit, and go on her way. They'll want her to testify, but it's better to give them something instead of nothing. This could be taken care of much quicker, and she and Betsy can be gone much quicker."

Joe shot me a look that said if he wanted any of my input he'd beat it out of me, and then he turned back to Julie.

"Ignore my dim-witted partner," he said. "I'm not inter-ested in issues of testimony or affidavits anymore. I'm just telling you that this idea you have of disappearing on your own is not a good one. People can be found, Mrs. Weston. We already found you once, and that was basically an acci-dent. Do you really think you can hide from people deter-mined to locate you?"

She leaned forward, gazing directly into his unhappy face, meeting him head-on in a clash of will and determina-tion, and it seemed as if there were only the two of them in the room.

"Either way, we're going to have to leave this place behind," she said. "The life we knew is gone now. My husband is dead. Betsy is the only thing I have left, and I am going to take care of her on my terms. End of story." She pointed at Amy. "I will do an interview with her, and she will see that the truth is told. If you insist that I provide the police with an affidavit, I will do that. But then I will leave, and I will take my daughter with me. I have broken no laws, and no one can force me to stay here."

For a long time, Joe held her stare. Then he sighed and leaned back in his seat. "All right, Mrs. Weston. If you want to disappear again, we can't stop you. But we can see that you do it right."

She smiled at him, and this time there was warmth behind it. "Thank you."

Joe waved his hand at Amy. "Go ahead and do your thing, Lois Lane. Is that a video camera I see?"

"Yes. Lincoln told me to bring it and an inkpad for fingerprints."

"He's not always dumb," Joe said, "just most of the time. Get to work, then. We'll leave you alone." He looked at me and cocked his head in the direction of the deck. "LP, I'd like to see you outside for a minute."

We went outside as Amy got to work setting up the video camera. I could tell she was excited, and I didn't blame her; this was going to be the story of her career. I'd be sure to remind her of that in the future anytime I needed a favor.

Joe and I stood together on the deck, leaning against the railing and watching through the window as Amy and Julie talked.

"You don't like it, do you?" I said.

He leaned over the railing and spit onto the grass. "No, LP, I don't like it one damn bit. This isn't a group of teenage punks she's dealing with; it's the most sophisticated organized crime outfit in the world. And one of the wealthiest—and apparently most devious—men in the state. Hiding from them isn't going to be easy."

"When Amy runs this story, Hubbard's going to be under

fire. He's going to have bigger things on his mind than finding Julie and Betsy."

"You think so?" He shrugged. "It may piss him off enough to make finding them his priority. But I'm more concerned with the Russians, at least for the immediate future. That tape is going to put a few of them in jail, and it's also going to stir up some serious internal trouble when Belov finds out who killed his son. That adds up to some major motivation for them to find this woman and eliminate her. Even after we've turned the tape in, they'll want her dead. You know how these mob guys are; revenge is the highest priority to them. And whacking Belov's son wasn't a one-man decision. For every guy that tape puts in jail, there will be three more on the streets who had a hand in it and will want Julie Weston dead."

"How much power does Belov have?"

"Everything I've learned in the past two days suggests he has a *lot* of power. He's big time."

"Perfect. We can utilize that power. I'm thinking Belov would be awfully interested in seeing that tape. Could be, he's even so interested in seeing it he'd be willing to make it clear to anyone involved that Julie and Betsy are not to be harmed. After all, they're not producing a tape that will hurt *him*. They're producing something he wants to see."

Joe stared at me, considering the idea. "True. But the people the Westons need to fear clearly aren't doing a good job of following through on Belov's wishes. They killed his son, LP."

"I figure once he has that tape he'll go about handling the situation in his own way. A serious housecleaning is what I'm picturing."

Joe nodded thoughtfully, understanding. "Some people are probably going to die."

"Hell," I said, "they're going to die anyhow. When we turn that tape over to the police, it's a matter of time until the contents leak back to Belov. But if we wait until then, we'll have nothing to use for leverage."

"So we're going to *use* the Russian mob to protect Julie and Betsy *from* the Russian mob?"

"Complex," I said, "but probably efficient."

Joe sighed and ran a hand through his hair. "This means we've got to talk to Belov, doesn't it?"

"Into the belly of the beast," I said.

"You know, LP, things are much calmer around here when you're out of town."

"I missed you, too."

TWENTY-TWO

Amy interviewed Julie for an hour and a half. Betsy came out of the bedroom midway through the interview and joined Joe and me on the deck. Her fingernails were painted in half a dozen different colors; Amy packed plenty of nail polish in that enormous purse. Joe found an old Frisbee in the cottage, and we tossed it around with Betsy while Amy and Julie finished up inside. The air was cool—frigid compared to South Carolina—but not as bad as it had been when I left the city. Maybe winter was going to lose this battle after all. Around one that afternoon, Amy came out and motioned for me to join her on the deck. I tossed the Frisbee to Joe and jogged up the steps.

"Huge, Lincoln," Amy said when I reached her. "Absolutely huge. This is the story of my dreams." She was smiling widely.

"Glad I could help, Ace. Only problem is, you can't write it for tomorrow."

She frowned. "How long do I have to sit on it?"

"At least another day. Joe and I have to sort out a few things before you can run it. Before you even can mention it to your editors."

"What things?"

"We're going to see Dainius Belov."

She raised her eyebrows and folded her arms across her chest. "You're kidding, right? Or are you just suicidal?"

"I don't think we've got much to fear from Belov. Remember, it was his son they killed. Joe and I are guessing old Dainius is awfully interested in finding out who murdered his kid. We're counting on a little cooperation in exchange for a copy of the tape."

"You're giving him a copy of the tape?"

I nodded. "That's where you come in. Do you guys have equipment for that sort of thing?"

"Yes."

"Good. We're going to need a copy of the murder tape, and you probably should make a copy of your interview tape as well. Leave copies of both tucked away someplace safe, and then bring me back one copy of the murder tape and the original."

"Sure thing, boss. The technology guys won't want to leave me alone while I'm copying the tapes, but that's nothing I can't get past using my feminine wiles."

"Feminine wiles," I said. "Uh-huh."

She winked at me. "There's nothing more fun than being a tease."

Julie stepped out on the deck behind us and smiled at me. "Is my daughter driving Mr. Pritchard crazy yet?"

"He's been crazy for years, Julie. She can't do any more harm to him."

Amy poked my chest with her finger. "All right, I'm outta here. But I need that tape if you want me to make a copy of it."

I went down to the Contour and took the tape out from under the driver's seat where I'd stashed it. I didn't like handing it over to Amy; the thing attracted danger and death like a James Bond car. But I needed a copy.

"Keep this damn thing out of sight," I said. "Can you bring the copies back out tonight, or is that a problem?"

"It's a long drive, but I'll do it." She opened her car door but didn't get in. "How long has it been since you slept, Lincoln?"

"A few hours, at least."

"Go to bed, stud. You'll need some energy when you're arrested."

She left, and I walked back up the steps and onto the deck. Joe was still playing with Betsy in the yard. I sat down at the picnic table beside Julie and shook my head.

"He looks like a doting grandpa out there. Amazing."

She laughed. "He seems more taken with my daughter than he is with me, that's for sure."

"Don't let his attitude bother you. He just wants to handle the situation in the way he thinks best."

She looked at me. "Do you think I'm a fool, Lincoln?"

"For trying to run on your own?" I shrugged. "I don't know, Julie. I'd like to work things out so you didn't have to run at all. But I don't see that happening. If you stay in town, you're taking a huge risk. In general, I'd advise you to let the professionals help you hide, but Wayne *was* a professional, and you seem to think he had things pretty well planned."

"He did."

"Do you have enough money?"

She smiled. "We've got plenty of money. Wayne put all our money into an offshore account, and then he put some of Hubbard's money into it as well. It was Hubbard's payoff for Wayne keeping his mouth shut."

I didn't ask how much money it was. It was probably quite a lot. I yawned, and Julie frowned.

"You still haven't slept, have you?"

I shook my head.

"Go inside and lie down," she ordered. "Your partner is here to keep us safe. You need to sleep."

I started to object but then thought better of it. I did need sleep, and as long as Joe was here there was no point in continuing to exhaust myself. I told Julie I'd take a nap, and then I went down to talk to Joe.

"I'm going to grab a few hours of sleep," I said. "Think you can keep them safe while I do?"

"Can't do a much worse job than you have," he said. "Go

sleep. When you wake up, I'll drive back into the city and see if I can arrange a meeting with Belov."

I went inside and lay down on a narrow, musty bed. The door was closed, but the sounds of Julie's voice and Betsy's laugh were with me as I fell asleep.

When I woke again the room was dark. I rolled onto my side and looked at the window, saw nothing but shadows outside. I looked at my watch. Almost seven. I'd slept for nearly six hours. I climbed out of the bed, pulled my pants and T-shirt back on, and went into the living room. Joe, Julie, and Betsy were sitting at the small square table in the kitchen with a pile of playing cards in front of them.

"Hi, Lincoln!" Betsy waved at me. "We're playing Go Fish. Wanna play?"

I looked at Joe. "Go Fish?"

He grunted. "It's more intense than I expected."

"I keep beating him," Betsy said, and Joe shot her a sour look that made her laugh. I caught Julie's eye and grinned. Joe Pritchard and his new best friend Betsy. How adorable.

I sat in the living room while they finished their game, and then Joe came out to join me.

"About time you got up, Sleeping Beauty. I was running out of games to play with the kid. If you'd slept any longer, I was going to teach her how to clean a handgun."

"Lovely."

"I'm going to head back to the city now," he said. "It's going to take some time to get in touch with Belov. When I do reach him, he may want to meet with us immediately, or he may want to do it tomorrow."

"Try for tomorrow," I said. "I don't want to leave Julie and Betsy alone."

"Okay. But with a guy like Belov, there's no dictating the schedule. If he says to meet him at midnight at home plate in Jacobs Field, we're going to meet him at midnight at home plate in Jacobs Field. Understand?"

"Yeah. Hey, did Gellino leave any food in this dump?" My brain might have taken six hours off, but my stomach hadn't forgotten that my last meal had been nearly ten hours earlier.

"Not much, but Lois Lane is bringing food with her."

"She is?"

"Yeah, she called while you were asleep, and I answered your phone. She said she made copies of the tapes, and she'll be out here in about twenty minutes. I told her to be sure no one's following her. I'm not expecting anyone will be, but it doesn't hurt to watch your back."

Joe left, and Amy arrived shortly after. She brought a pizza with her, which made Betsy's day. I carried wood in from the pile under the deck and started a fire, and the four of us sat beside it, eating the pizza and playing silly card games. The night before, I'd been exchanging gunfire with professional killers and dangling from a seventh-floor balcony; now I was chaperoning a Girl Scout slumber party. The varied experiences of a professional detective. And to think, some men are car salesmen or accountants. What a bore.

Amy left around nine, and I promised to call her the next morning with more information on our plans and when she could run the story. At ten, Joe called.

"If you've got a copy of the tape, I've got Belov," he said.

"Amy brought them by. When and where do we meet Belov?"

"Tomorrow morning. And you'll love the place."

"Where?"

"Inside Tower City Mall, next to the fountain."

"You're kidding me. The city's most dangerous gangster wants to meet us in the mall?"

"Uh-huh. My guess is we won't stay there long, though. He probably wants to start in a public place so he can be sure we aren't setting him up. Once we show, I imagine his thugs will send us elsewhere to meet him."

"Great. You know our last meeting like this didn't go so well." I closed my eyes and saw that red dot on Hartwick's chest again.

"Yeah. But in this case, if anyone dies, it'll probably be us."

"A comfort," I said, "that's what you are."

"Speaking of comfort, I just got a call from Tim Eggers.

You're wanted for questioning by police in South Carolina, and now our old friends at CPD would love to chat with you, as well."

"They can wait."

"Uh-huh. The good news is, the Russians must have taken the body with them, because the South Carolina cops have no idea anyone was killed."

"That is good news."

"Thought you'd like it. We're supposed to meet Belov at nine. You want to leave the woman and girl alone, or should I call Kinkaid?"

I thought about it. "I've got a better idea," I said. "Why don't you bring John Weston out?"

"Weston? Why the hell would I do that?"

"We *are* still working for him," I said, "although in all the chaos, that's been kind of easy to forget. Julie wants to see him again before she pulls her vanishing act, so tomorrow morning will be as good a time as any."

"Okay, I'll call Weston tomorrow morning and drive him out. The old man's going to be beside himself. Once we've met with Belov, we need to get Julie to some sort of police presence. Any ideas on who that should be?"

"Yes," I said. "James Sellers told me there was a prosecutor who had handled quite a few cases with the Russians. I think she'd probably be the best bet. Once we've met with Belov, I'll get in touch with her."

"Okay. I'll be out to the cottage tomorrow around eight, hopefully with Old Man Weston riding beside me."

"Was that your partner?" Julie asked, stepping out onto the deck after I'd hung up with Joe.

"Yes." I told her about our meeting with Belov and what we hoped it would accomplish. "He's a dangerous, powerful man," I said. "If he doesn't want you to be harmed, it could mean a lot."

"I plan to be far, far away from all of them anyhow."

"I know, Julie, but it can't hurt to have Belov on our side. He's the man in charge."

She sat down on the picnic table and motioned for me to

join her. She was wearing an oversized sweatshirt that said MYRTLE BEACH, and she had the sleeves pulled down over her hands, trying to keep warm. I'd finally pulled a jacket on over my T-shirt. The night air was cool and fresh, laden with the scent of pine needles.

"Will I talk to the police tomorrow?" she asked after I'd sat down beside her.

"Yes. After Joe and I meet with Belov, I'm going to get in touch with a prosecutor who has some experience with this sort of case. I'm expecting she'll be a little more understanding of your fears and safety concerns than others might be."

"All right."

"I told my partner to bring your father-in-law out tomorrow morning," I said. "Is that okay?"

"John? Wow." She exhaled loudly and closed her eyes. "Yes, it's okay. I need to see him before we leave." She opened her eyes again, and there was surprise and recognition in them. "He doesn't even know we're alive, does he?"

It's amazing how some people can lose sight of the things that matter most to others. I shook my head. "No, Julie, he doesn't."

For a while we sat in silence, and then she had another question. "You're very close to Amy, aren't you?"

I shrugged. "Why do you ask?"

"There's just something in the way you interact with her, that's all. Both her and your partner . . . you just seem to let your guard down with them. It's the first time I've seen you do that. I figure you must be close with your partner if you were willing to go into business with him, and if you act similarly around Amy, you must be pretty close to her, too."

I looked out at the dark pond. The water was still covered by a thin layer of ice, and it looked as black and smooth as a freshly paved stretch of asphalt.

"I'm probably closer to Amy than she realizes," I said. "Last summer, when I was just drifting along without any purpose, and pretty content to remain miserable, she forced me out of it."

Julie tilted her head to the side, her face half obscured by the shadows. "Explain."

I told her about my dismissal from the police department. I hadn't shared the story with her yet, and she listened with interest.

"After that, I was a little lost," I said. "Hell, I was very lost. My life had been made up of two parts: work and my fiancée, Karen. Then they were both gone. I used what little money I had to buy a rundown gym on the west side, and I just faded out of my old life. I didn't keep in contact with anyone from the department except for Joe, who wouldn't let me avoid him. I worked at the gym during the day, worked out in the evenings, and sat home alone and brooded with the rest of my time. I was listless. Then a guy who went to my gym was murdered, and Amy showed up on my doorstep asking questions and insisting I help her look into it. She was a real pain in the ass, but she was relentless. Eventually, I gave in. Somewhere along the line, I found my way again. Joe saw the change in me, saw how revitalized I was by having a case again, and asked me to go into business with him. I agreed, he retired, and here we are," I concluded. "Amy played a pretty big part in getting me back on my feet, which is sort of funny, considering I was a stranger to her. And, I have to admit, a bit of an asshole to her at first."

"I see," Julie said. Then, after a pause, "I'm glad I asked that question, Lincoln. I found out a lot more about you."

"Scary stuff, isn't it?"

"No, it's not. And I'm sorry about what happened, about how you lost your job. It sounds like this Karen woman really let you down." The corner of her mouth twitched in a cold smile. "I know what that feels like."

"No," I said, and shook my head. "What happened to me happens to a thousand guys every day. Most of them handle it better, that's all. What happened to you is an entirely different circumstance. Don't compare the two."

"All right."

I turned to her and moved slightly closer on the wooden

bench. "You amaze me," I said. "You know that? The way you're facing all of this, it's incredible. You must be terrified at the idea of leaving your old life behind, but you're determined to do it because it's the best thing for Betsy."

"I am terrified, though," she said, her voice almost a whisper. "I'm scared to death, Lincoln. And I've never been more lonely."

I put my hand on her arm. "You're not alone, Julie. As long as I can help you, I'm going to be here trying to do it."

"Promise?"

"I promise."

She leaned forward and looked into my eyes. Her face was so beautiful that I was almost nervous when she put it that close to mine.

"Then come with us, Lincoln."

I stared at her. "Come with you?"

She laughed, and her cheeks flushed slightly. "This is an absurd request. There's no way you can accept it, and I know that, but I'm going to ask anyhow, so you can decline it, and we can move on. Come with us, Lincoln. I've got a beautiful, safe place to raise my daughter, and I have plenty of money. I don't want to have to raise her alone, though. I don't want to *be* alone."

"Julie, you've known me for less than three days."

She nodded. "And yet I'm asking you. Shouldn't that tell you something?"

Yes, I thought, it should. But what?

I sat stupidly on the hard wooden bench of the picnic table, fumbling for a response. I had to tell her she was crazy, of course. But I didn't.

"I'm sorry," she said. "I should never have asked such a thing. It's absurd, and it's certainly not fair to you."

"Don't worry about it."

"Remember when I told you in the car that what happened in the whirlpool last night was a mistake?"

"Yes."

"Well," she said, "this is not a mistake." She leaned in and kissed me softly on the mouth, holding the kiss for a while, and then pulled away. As attracted as I had been to her the previous night, it couldn't touch what I felt for her then.

After a while we left the picnic table and moved to one of the wooden lounge chairs. It wasn't the most comfortable thing in the world, but at least we could lean back in it. Julie curled against me, and I held her as we sat there and let the night pass. It grew later, and the air grew colder, but we didn't leave the deck, not wanting to give up the night any quicker than we had to.

TWENTY-THREE

I woke shortly before eight, lunging off the couch and reaching for my gun. I had my hand around the butt of the Glock when I stopped and realized where I was. The little cottage was still and quiet, and there was no cause for alarm. I didn't remember any violent or frightening dream left behind in the world of sleep, but there I was, reaching for my gun. Dream or no dream, it wasn't a positive start to the day.

I put the gun away and went into the bathroom, hoping to get a shower in before Julie and Betsy woke. The water heater didn't approve of my rousing it into action at such an early hour, a point it made clear by refusing to offer more than a tepid stream. I left the shower quickly, dressed in the previous day's clothes, and returned to the living room. Julie was awake now, sitting at the kitchen table.

"You find some coffee?" I said.

She made a face. "There's a jar of instant coffee. It's going to be pretty bad, but it beats no coffee at all."

"Barely."

"When is your partner going to be here?"

"Eight."

She looked at her watch. "Not much time. I'd better wake Betsy so she's ready to see John."

When she returned to the kitchen, she busied herself with the coffee. There was no mention of the night before, or of her request. A few minutes after Betsy joined us in the kitchen, I heard tires on the gravel drive and looked at my watch. Eight o'clock exactly. Joe is nothing if not prompt. I watched from the kitchen window as John Weston pulled in behind Joe, climbed out of his Buick, and walked up the deck steps, using a wooden cane with a brass head to support his balance. He was wearing an olive parka and light blue pants and moving at as fast a clip as he could, although the steps were causing him some difficulty.

He entered the cottage in front of Joe and stared at Julie and Betsy as if they were greeters at the gates of heaven.

"Grandpa!" Betsy squealed, jumping out of her chair and running to him. She wrapped her arms around his legs and hugged him tightly. The cane fell to the floor as he picked her up and lifted her, and then the tears came. Julie joined them then, and I noticed belatedly that Joe had never actually stepped inside. I went out on the deck and found him sitting on the picnic table.

"Morning," I said.

He nodded. "I figured I'd sit out here for a while. It's their family, and their reunion. Got nothing to do with me."

"Old John seems pretty happy. How'd he react when you told him?"

"Called me a lying son of a bitch and said he'd break my legs."

I stared at him. "You're joking."

He shook his head and grinned. "Nope, that's what the old bastard said. I called him this morning and said I needed to come out to the house. Said I had some news for him. I go out there, he meets me at the door, and I told him he could see his granddaughter today if he was so inclined. He told me if I was lying he'd break my legs."

"Oh," I said, "*if* you were lying. Well, that's different. The old-timer was simply expressing his gratitude."

"I guess."

The door opened, and John stepped out. He had the cane

again, and he was wiping at his eyes with the back of his mangled hand. He walked to stand in front of us, but Julie and Betsy stayed inside.

"Whatever you want to be paid," he said, "it's yours. And whatever it is, it's not enough."

"We'll bill the standard rate," I said. "Unlike you, Mr. Weston, we expected us to succeed."

He smiled at that. "Yeah," he said. "I guess you did." He offered his hand to me and I shook it. "Remember when you told me why you were in this business?"

"Yes, sir."

"So do I." He cleared his throat loudly. "And, son? I guess you two are pretty damn good, after all."

"Yes," I said, "we are."

"Your partner here wouldn't explain anything to me, though."

Joe shrugged. "I figure it's Mrs. Weston's tale to tell. We found her. She can explain it."

I nodded. "We've got some things to take care of, John. Your daughter-in-law is still in danger, and we need you to stay here and watch them while we're gone. No one should know where they are, and it needs to stay that way for a few hours. It should give you plenty of time to talk with Julie."

"All right. But I'm going to want to sit down with you, too. I want to know how you found them, and what the hell's been going on."

"We'll get to that," I said. "For now, we've got a few things left to settle."

His eyes went from Joe to me, and he seemed to understand the nature of those things. "Okay. Well, good luck. And thanks."

Betsy began calling for him from inside, and he turned and limped back to her. Joe and I got off the deck and left. Julie called after me once, but I pretended not to hear her. I didn't want to talk right now.

"We're going to be cutting it close," I said, looking at my watch.

"We'll make it," Joe said. "I suggest we take two cars,

though." I had been standing with my hand on the passenger-door handle of his Taurus. I nodded and went back to the Contour.

"Let's go," I said. "I hate to keep the mafia waiting."

"You got the tape?"

I patted my hip pocket. "Got it."

We took I-71 back into the city, across the Cuyahoga and into the heart of downtown. Joe pulled off the highway and onto Ontario Street with me right behind him. A red light brought us to a stop facing the Terminal Tower. Jacobs Field was on the right, empty now, waiting for warmer weather and baseball before it turned into one of the centerpieces of evening activity downtown. The light changed, and we made a left turn and followed the road as it wound down the hill, closer to the river, then back up to the bridge. A group of seagulls sat along the edge of the bridge, watching the river. We crossed the river and drove past the Northern Ohio Lumber and Timber Company building, an ancient brick structure with red wooden doors. The Contour rumbled across a short section of brick road, approaching the lift bridge, and I saw the skyscrapers looming above me. I've always enjoyed this stretch of the drive, where the old commercial section of the river district and the new high-rise office buildings converge. We curved back to the right, following the signs for Tower City parking. Joe pulled into the lower level of the garage and found a spot easily, and I parked a few cars down. It hadn't been so long since we'd parked in this same garage on our visit to Jeremiah Hubbard.

"Well," Joe said as I locked the car and joined him, "this is certainly the dumbest idea we've ever embarked on."

"Should be fun."

"Yeah, right."

I did not ask Joe how he'd managed to contact Belov, and I would not ask him. Some things you just don't need to know. Maybe Joe had vast underworld contacts.

We took the escalator up to the mall entrance. Usually at the top of the escalator you're met with the conversational din of the food court, but this early in the morning the food court was closed and quiet. Out in the atrium a tall fountain cascaded down in front of us, and store employees moved about, readying for the crowds that would soon arrive. I'm not a shopping mall fan, but I enjoy walking through Tower City when I'm downtown. It's a beautiful facility, with wide banks of windows looking down on the old commercial buildings along the river. I didn't take much time to appreciate the scenery today, though. I was too busy looking for Belov or his soldiers. The mall wasn't busy, but there were enough people around to make me feel somewhat safe. That feeling vanished when someone stepped up behind me and pressed the barrel of a gun into my back.

Beside me, Joe said, "Morning, gentlemen." I didn't risk turning my head, but it seemed safe to assume Joe had a gun in his back as well.

"Morning," a male voice with a faint European accent said behind me. "We're going to be walking back down to the parking garage now, and then we're going to see Mr. Belov. That is what you want, no?"

"Yeah, that's what we want."

"Excellent." A hand slipped under my shirt and removed the Glock swiftly and smoothly. The videotape was left in my pocket. "You may turn around now."

I turned and looked into the face of a man with the palest blue eyes I had ever seen. They were like chips of glacier ice. He was tall, several inches taller than me, and had fine, straw-colored hair and a broad-shouldered, muscular build. When I faced him, he gave me a wide smile of straight white teeth.

"We are old friends, yes?" he said. "Or at least we shall act like it."

I got the message. The blue-eyed man had a partner who was much shorter and rounder, with dark, shaggy hair and several days' worth of stubble. Both of them were wearing ski jackets and jeans. The jackets were open, exposing the guns they'd tucked back into their pants.

I looked at Joe. "Do you think we get our guns back?"

He shrugged. "We'll see."

We followed the Russians back down the escalator and into the parking garage. The blue-eyed man led us to a black Lincoln Town Car and climbed behind the wheel. Joe and I got in the back, and the bearded man climbed in with us.

"A Town Car," I said. "Nice choice. Very in keeping with the organized crime tendencies." No one laughed. Tough crowd, in a couple of ways.

We drove out of the parking garage and back down toward the river. I kept my breathing even and steady and drummed my fingers on the edge of the door. Relaxed. No need to be concerned, right? Would've felt a little better if they'd let us keep our guns, though.

The blue-eyed man drove us back across the river on the Cleveland Memorial Shoreway and then turned onto Lake Avenue. A few decades earlier, some of the city's most expensive homes stood on Lake Avenue. Now the rich were moving to the suburbs, but there were still some beautiful houses on the street. We turned into the driveway of one of them, a massive Victorian structure.

"One of Mr. Belov's homes," the blue-eyed man said. One of them. The place probably cost more than I'd make in ten years, and it was a lakeside retreat for Belov.

We got out of the car, and now the bearded man had his gun out again. He waved it at the side door of the home.

"Go inside."

I opened the door and stepped inside with Joe and the Russians right behind me. We were on a small landing. A set of four steps led up to the kitchen, and another set of steps led down to a closed door.

"Down," the bearded man said.

I went down and opened that door, too. This room had been remodeled into a basement office. There was a black desk with a glass top, a glass coffee table, a small bar with a bottle of Scotch, a big-screen television, and several black office chairs. The bearded man pushed me down into one of the chairs. A small man with a gray mustache sat behind the desk. He wore a white shirt with a maroon tie, and his face was lined with deep creases and dark circles under his brown eyes. It gave him a weary expression. If you passed him on the street you might have guessed he was a bookkeeper for some small-time company, a guy who had been commuting to work in the same office for forty years and was hoping to retire to a two-bedroom house in Parma.

"Here they are, Mr. Belov," the bearded man said. He stepped behind the desk and set our guns on the floor near Belov's feet. The blue-eyed man leaned against the wall, his hand maybe six inches from the butt of his gun.

"Which one of you is Mr. Pritchard?" Belov said. His voice was soft, but it had a hard edge, as if it might easily turn into a bellow.

"That's me," Joe said.

Belov nodded slightly. "You have interesting ways of trying to reach me, sir."

"I didn't know the best way to go about it. I hope you weren't offended."

"Not at all. And my maid appreciated the fifty dollars."

I looked at Joe. "You gave the maid fifty dollars?"

"And a note," he said. "She promised she'd see that it reached Mr. Belov. He called me shortly thereafter."

So much for Joe's vast underworld contacts.

"And who are you?" Belov said, turning his flat brown eyes to me.

"Lincoln Perry," I said. "I'm his partner."

He held the stare for a moment, then lifted his hand and pointed at the bearded man. "This is Alexander." The point switched to the blue-eyed man. "And this is Thor. Thor is quite a volatile, dangerous man. You would be well advised not to upset him."

I looked over my shoulder at Thor, and his glacier-ice eyes stared at the wall in front of him, appearing not to see me. I was sure he wouldn't miss any movement in the room, though. I believed Belov when he said Thor was dangerous.

"Now that we have all been introduced, we can begin," Belov said, as if he were preparing to open a seminar on the opportunities of purchasing a time-share condominium. His hands lay on the surface of the desk, fingertips pressed against the glass but palms arched slightly, as if he were playing a piano. Now he tapped his hands softly on the glass and stared at us.

"You said you had a tape I would be interested in seeing."

"That's right," Joe said. "I'm sure you'll be interested."

"And you want something in exchange for this tape," Belov said, still tapping on the glass. It was not a question.

"Yes," Joe said.

"What is that?"

Joe nodded at me.

"There's a woman and a little girl who have information that could be damaging to people in your organization," I said.

"My organization," he echoed.

"Yes. These people have tried to kill them already, and I'm afraid they will probably try again. We would like your help in seeing that does not happen."

His eyes never left mine. "I do not know anything of a woman and a little girl."

"No," I said, "you probably don't. But some of your associates do. It is your associates that we're concerned about, sir."

"And what has the woman done to cause these problems?"

"She hasn't done anything," I said. "Her husband was a private investigator, like us. He caught something on videotape that people didn't want to be seen. Your associates discovered this, and now they want the tape. They also want to kill the woman, because they think she's seen the tape. She hasn't seen it."

"And her husband? This investigator?"

"He's dead."

He stopped tapping his hands on the glass, and the abrupt lack of movement seemed to suggest an impending eruption, like the brief pause when a fuse has stopped burning but the charge hasn't exploded.

"What is on the tape?"

I looked at Joe, then back at Belov. "Information about your son's death."

"What information?"

"Will you see that the woman and girl are not harmed?"

"What information?" he repeated as if I had not spoken. He was more intense now, though, and behind me Thor had come off the wall and was standing upright. The comment about Belov's son had gotten their attention, all right.

"There's a man named Jeremiah Hubbard," I said. "I'm sure you've heard of him. This woman's husband was working for Hubbard, trying to come up with blackmail material to use in a property acquisition. The property they were interested in was The River Wild, a strip bar that I understand belongs to you."

He didn't say anything but motioned with his hand for me to continue.

"Your son was murdered. Probably inside of The River Wild, because we believe that was where this investigator was using surveillance cameras. We have the tape of your son's murder."

He leaned back in the chair and looked at Thor, then at me. His expression hadn't changed, but his breathing was quicker.

"You have the tape."

"Yes." I took it from my pocket and set it on the desk.

Belov handed it to Alexander, and he slipped the tape inside a VCR that was mounted above the television. Belov turned his chair so he was facing the screen, and Alexander pressed play. We all watched as the blue screen came up, and then it disappeared as the room came into view. Beside me, Joe was leaning forward, watching intently. I'd forgotten he hadn't seen the tape before.

We watched the entire thing in silence: the laughter at the table, the shooting, the body removal, and the cleanup work. Belov never said a word, and neither did anyone else. He never turned, just sat where he was, staring directly at the screen, never reacting to what he saw there. When the tape returned to the blue screen, Alexander reached over and shut the television off. He moved cautiously, as if afraid any action might enrage Belov.

For a long time, Belov remained staring at the blank television screen. When he finally spoke, his back was still to us.

"The woman and the girl. What are their names?"

"Julie and Betsy Weston," I said. "The father was Wayne Weston. You've probably heard a lot about them on the news recently."

"And Mr. Weston is dead?"

"Yes."

"Do you know who killed him?"

"No. It might have been the men on that tape; it might have been someone working for Jeremiah Hubbard. We're not sure."

"And some of these men have pursued the woman and girl?" All this with his back still to us.

"Yes. They followed them to South Carolina. Followed me, maybe. I killed one of them two days ago." There was no need to tell him that, but I also didn't see any reason to keep the information from him.

Belov was silent again. After a while I said, "The woman will be leaving soon. She's afraid to stay here, and she's not going to. We don't want anyone to pursue her, whether they come from your people or from Hubbard's people. We were hoping you could help us with that. I thought seeing the tape might be worth that to you."

"Have the police seen this tape?"

"No." I hesitated for a minute and then decided not to lie to him. "But they will. They'll probably see it today."

Alexander muttered something under his breath, not pleased by the news, but Belov didn't react. We sat there for another five minutes without speaking. I had nothing left to say, and Dainius Belov didn't seem like the type of man you rushed. When he did break the silence, it was with two short sentences.

"The woman and the girl will not be harmed. You may go now."

Thor pulled open the door and stood beside it, and Alexander picked our guns off the floor and followed us out.

Joe and I didn't say anything to Belov as we left. He never turned from the blank television screen.

We walked back up the steps and outside to the car. Thor drove us back to the Tower City parking garage, and when we pulled inside, Alexander handed us our guns. I opened the door and stepped out, then turned and motioned for Thor to put the window down.

"Can we trust him?" I said.

A slight smile played on his lips. Amused by my question. "They are more safe now than ever before." The window slid back up, and he pulled the Town Car away.

Joe and I stood in the parking lot and watched them drive off. I leaned against the trunk of a car beside me and said, "Wow."

"Belov doesn't look like the most dangerous man in the city, does he?" Joe said.

"No, he doesn't. But I'm still pretty sure he is."

"Uh-huh."

"Do you believe Thor?"

"When he said Mrs. Weston and the girl are more safe now than ever before?" Joe nodded. "I do. Guy like that? Who's to doubt him?"

We walked back to our cars. Before he got inside the Taurus, Joe said, "You know, I'd pictured more yelling, more profanity, more threats. At least two or three references to how our bodies could be dumped in the Cuyahoga. Instead he acted like we were discussing stock quotes."

"Uh-huh."

"Somehow," he said, "that scared me more than anything."

"Yeah," I said, "me, too."

TWENTY-FOUR

We drove to my apartment. As soon as I turned onto the avenue I felt good. I was home now, and things were wrapping up nicely. Julie was still going to run, though. That thought spoiled my mood.

I didn't go inside the apartment but transferred my things out of the Contour and into the truck. I was damn sick of that little car. Once I'd made the vehicle switch, we went to the office. I found Sellers's phone number, then gave him a call. He remembered me, and when I told him what I had to offer I thought he was going to have a stroke. He promised to have Laura Winters call me back immediately. She was the prosecutor who'd handled several other cases with the Russian mob in town, and Sellers said she'd probably be salivating at the thought of taking on Jeremiah Hubbard as well. True to Sellers's word, Winters called within minutes. I ran through things again with her, and I was impressed by the way she kept silent and let me get through the story without shouting at me for failing to contact authorities sooner, as Sellers had done.

"Well, Mr. Perry, this is real big," she said. "How soon can you have Mrs. Weston here?"

"This afternoon."

"All right. I want to see her here at one, and I want you and your partner here, too. From what I've heard, the police are trying to locate you, but I'm not going to bring that into play yet, because I don't want this place turning into a circus before I have a chance to sit down with Mrs. Weston." Her voice had a nice hard edge to it. She sounded like a woman who probably did some serious ass-kicking in court.

"Thanks," I said. I knew she wasn't going to like what I had to say next, but it was probably better to prepare her over the phone, before I was within slapping range. "One other thing, Ms. Winters—a reporter for the *Journal* already has this story. She's probably going to want to run it tomorrow."

For a while there was just static in my ear. "Mr. Perry," she said eventually, "you're going to be a colossal pain in my ass, aren't you?"

I was smiling, but only because she couldn't see me. "I hope not, ma'am. But I know this isn't a real good start. Just remember that I *am* bringing you Julie Weston and the tape. That should help a little, shouldn't it?"

"It *should,* but that's no guarantee it will. I'll see you at one." She hung up on me.

Joe looked at me. "Good to go?"

"She wants us there at one."

I drove us back to the cottage. Amy had joined Julie, Betsy, and John now. I told them about our visit to Belov, and I told Amy that she couldn't consider including such information in the article. She said she understood, and I believed her. I trusted Amy as I trusted few others, which was what Julie had noticed the night before.

The mood at the cottage was light, but I didn't share it. I was tense, as I had been when I woke up in the morning reaching for my gun. Belov hadn't provided me with enough comfort. Krashakov and the rest of them were still out there, and they'd found us once before.

While the rest of us passed time inside, Joe took Betsy outside to play. I was amazed by how taken he was with the girl. As long as I'd known Joe, he'd never had a particular affinity for children.

"Are you ready to meet with Winters?" I asked Julie while we ate.

She finished chewing and frowned, then nodded. "Yes. I think I am. I guess I'll have to be."

John reached over and patted her hand. "You'll be fine."

I was about to say more when Joe stepped through the door, grim faced.

"Mrs. Weston, come here, please."

Julie saw something in his face that scared her, and she dropped her sandwich back onto her plate and said, "What is it? What's wrong?" A mother's instinct telling her something Joe's words hadn't.

"We've been playing hide-and-seek," Joe said. "I can't find her, and she won't answer my calls."

I was out of my chair even before Julie moved, my hand reflexively creeping toward my gun. This was it, I thought. That bad feeling I hadn't been able to shake was well founded, after all. The Russians had come, and they had Betsy.

Joe put his hand on my shoulder and pushed me back as I moved for the door.

"Relax, LP. The kid's just hiding. I've been outside the whole time, and nobody's here."

"Let's find her, then."

We all went out on the deck, with me leading the way. Julie shouted Betsy's name while I scanned the woods, looking for a trace of movement, my hand still hugging my hip, ready to reach for the gun.

"Elizabeth Ann Weston, you come here this minute!" Julie shouted, and her voice went up in pitch at the end, a note of panic there.

We stood clustered together on the deck, listening for a response. A cold silence mocked us.

"Shit," I said, starting down the steps. "They're here."

"Wait," Amy said, grabbing my arm. "Listen."

We all froze again and listened, and this time I heard it, too. A faint voice coming from one end of the cottage.

We hurried around the corner of the cottage, John Weston

limping along behind, swearing profusely about his failing legs. At the far end of the cottage Betsy's voice was louder.

"I'm stuck," she was yelling.

"She's in here," Joe said, dropping to one knee beside the wall. "It's some sort of crawl space." He pulled on a short, square wooden panel at the base of the wall. It didn't move. He grunted and wrapped his fingers around the edge, then gave it a mighty heave. The panel came loose, exposing a dark, dank crawl space beneath the cottage—and the cute little girl with the frightened face inside.

"I'm sorry," she said, her eyes beginning to well with tears as she saw the concern in our faces. "I got stuck. I pulled the door back so he couldn't see me, and it stuck." The tears began to flow freely then, and Joe took her under the arms and lifted her out gently, handing her to Julie. Julie stroked the girl's hair and whispered softly in her ear, but she held her in an unusually tight grip, the way you might hold something dear to you that had been salvaged from the ruins of a fire.

I took a deep breath and leaned against the wall. Amy caught my eye and grinned, and I shook my head and laughed at myself. The adrenaline rush I'd just felt had matched anything I'd experienced in South Carolina.

"It's a hell of a hiding spot, I've got to give her that," Joe said, peering into the crawl space. "And I'm stunned she went inside. Most girls her age wouldn't go in there without a flashlight for all the candy in the world."

There was no more hide-and-seek. We stayed inside the cottage and made small talk or sat in silence. Betsy gave up her crying spell quickly, and we adults tried to downplay the scare she'd given us. Without giving it conscious thought, I found myself rising every few minutes to stand at the window and scan the tree line. During the few minutes Betsy had been missing, I'd been sure the Russians had arrived. Now she was back, but I still hadn't lost the feeling. After a while, Joe tapped me on the shoulder and motioned for me to join him on the deck.

"What's up?" I said when he'd slid the door closed behind us.

"We're going to see Winters in a couple hours. The girl doesn't need to be dragged along for that, and neither does John. Winters asked for us and Julie, and that's who should show up. The more people we bring, the more chaotic things get, and I don't want that."

"So?"

"So I'm not real comfortable leaving John and the girl here alone again." Betsy's brief disappearance had rattled him, too.

I nodded. "Me neither. I've had a bad feeling ever since she got stuck in that crawl space. Julie isn't going to want cops here yet, though."

"I know. That's why I think we should call Kinkaid."

I frowned. "Julie's got enough on her mind today as it is, Joe."

"Julie won't deal with him, then," he said. "You can take her out ahead of time, and I'll wait for Kinkaid to show. We need somebody here, LP, and he's the guy for the job. But if you don't want him here, we can leave the girl with a seventy-year-old man for protection." He shrugged. "It's your call."

I gazed in the window at Betsy and John Weston, thought about Krashakov and Rakic, and nodded again. "Call him."

Joe used his cell phone and called from the deck. I listened while he gave Kinkaid directions, and I remembered Julie's explanation of their history to me. A silly drunken advance that was quickly forgotten, she'd said. Not so quickly forgotten for Aaron Kinkaid. I knew how badly he wanted to see her again, and I almost felt guilty for sneaking her out before he arrived. Not *too* guilty, though.

"You didn't tell him Betsy will be here," I said when Joe hung up.

He shook his head. "I'll tell him when he gets here. I didn't want to have to explain how Julie's here now but going to be gone when he arrives. It seems a little shitty."

"He'll deal with it."

"Yeah."

Julie and I left not long after that. John Weston gave her a hug and a kiss on the cheek, then sat back down on the couch, his eyes never leaving his granddaughter. Joe lingered, waiting on Kinkaid, and Amy left to get started on her story. While I drove, I told Julie that Kinkaid was coming to keep an eye on things at the cottage.

"He hasn't really convinced himself that he's in love with me, has he?" she said.

"He's doing a fine job of pretending, if nothing else."

"Ugh. How awful. Will he be there when we come back?"

"Yes. Is that bad?"

"It doesn't matter."

I drove downtown slowly to give Joe time to catch up with us. I didn't like the idea of leaving my gun behind, but I couldn't get it past the metal detectors at the prosecutor's office, so I locked it in the truck's center console, and we walked inside the building and waited on Joe. We waited for fifteen minutes, but he didn't show. Maybe Kinkaid had been slowed up. Maybe something had happened. I was starting to grow worried when Joe finally came jogging up the steps and into the building.

"Sorry," he said as we walked to Winters's office. "Kinkaid wanted more of an explanation than I had time to give. He'll want still more when we get back."

The door to the office opened before I could respond, and a woman stepped into the hall. She was nearing fifty but still an attractive woman, with strong, firm features and auburn hair. She looked at us, her gaze lingering on Julie a bit longer than Joe or me, and then forced a tight smile.

"What a treat," she said. "And I was planning on going home early today. Which one of you is Lincoln Perry?"

"I am." I shook hands with her.

"Here's how we're going to do this," she said. "I'm not going to talk to all of you at once. We'll go one at a time, and because you called me, you'll go first, Mr. Perry. Mrs. Weston and Mr. Pritchard can wait." She held the door open, and

Joe and Julie sat in chairs in the outer office while I followed Winters into a small conference room. She closed the door, sat behind the desk, and clasped her hands together.

"I need to have some idea of what I can expect to hear from this woman," she said. "And I've picked you to give me that idea, because you picked me to dump this shit storm on."

I gave her the rough summary. While I talked, she listened and kept her mouth shut, which impressed me. Rare is the attorney who can handle listening and keeping her mouth shut.

"What a mess," she said when I was done. "Mrs. Weston has this tape with her?"

"Yeah," I said, "but it may be too late to get any convictions with it."

"Why is that?"

"If Dainius Belov found out who killed his son, they might have been dealt with in less formal proceedings."

She looked at me carefully. "Is there any reason to believe he has found out who killed his son?"

I shrugged. "It's the mob, Ms. Winters. They turn on each other easily."

"Uh-huh." She tapped her foot on the floor and stared at me. "You know what I wish when I look at you?"

"That you were twenty years younger and single?"

A slight smile crossed her face, and she sighed and shook her head. "I wish that I could believe you're going to tell me even half of what you really know. Now, let's ask Mrs. Weston to join us. I'll leave your partner waiting in the wings for now. There are some others who are also anxious to speak with you and Mrs. Weston."

"You want me to go?"

"No, I've changed my mind. You'll stay for now, because I'm far from finished with you. I'm afraid you have no idea what you're in for, Mr. Perry," she said, opening the door to get Julie.

"No?" I said.

"I'm one of the last tough, old-fashioned broads," she said.

"I see."

She turned on her heel. "Or maybe I should say, a hard-core bitch."

I had to laugh. "It's going to be a long afternoon, isn't it?"

"With this mess?" she said. "You're dreaming if you think we're going to wrap it up in an afternoon."

Swanders arrived, along with another prosecutor and one of the higher-ups from the FBI. He was a small, quiet man who didn't say much, but his face darkened considerably when I told him what I suspected of Agent Thaddeus Cody. Swanders avoided eye contact with me for most of the meeting. I couldn't tell if he was mad at me or embarrassed that he'd been so clueless about so much. Probably those two emotions went hand in hand.

When they were done with Julie and me, Winters opened the door to call in Joe. I felt bad for him; it had to have been a long, tedious wait. Once Joe was inside, Winters stepped back into the lobby and asked Julie where Betsy was.

"She's with her grandfather," Julie said. "Someplace safe."

"Mrs. Weston, I simply cannot have that. I cannot have either of you in an undisclosed location, and I'm afraid I must provide you with police security for the time being. I'm going to have to request that you stay in a hotel here in the city where we can see you have adequate protection."

"That's fine," Julie said, as if she had absolutely no problem trusting her safety to the police. I tried not to stare at her.

"Now, if you'll tell me where your daughter is, I'll have an officer dispatched to pick her up and bring her here."

Julie frowned. "With all due respect, ma'am, I don't like that idea. The upcoming days are going to be very hard on my daughter, and I don't need them to begin with a police officer taking her away from her grandfather. If you want us to stay at a hotel, let Lincoln drive me back to get my daughter and bring her in myself."

Winters didn't like it, but she didn't fight it. "I want her brought to the Marriott by the airport as soon as possible," she told me. "We'll have officers waiting there, and they'll have a room ready for you. When you're settled in, we'll talk again."

"Should we wait on Joe?" I asked.

Winters rolled her eyes. "I know he's your partner, Perry, but I think you can handle playing taxi without him. Go get the girl and bring them both to the Marriott. I'll keep your partner safe."

"If it's just going to be the two of you in there, at the very least, let me leave him an extra gun."

"Go get the girl, Mr. Perry." She stepped back into the conference room and closed the door.

I drove Julie back to the cottage. On the way, she asked for more details about our meeting with Belov. I told her only that he'd promised to see that she and Betsy weren't harmed. I did not discuss the methods Belov would likely use to ensure their safety.

"Did you get a chance to talk to John without Betsy around?" I asked.

"Yes."

"And does he know you're planning to leave?"

"Yes."

I glanced away from the highway and looked at her. "And when are you planning to leave, Julie?"

"Tomorrow."

I put my eyes back on the road. "I see."

We were silent then until we returned to the cottage. I parked behind Kinkaid's car, and as I shut the truck off he stepped onto the deck and waved. I turned to Julie.

"He's going to want to talk to you," I said. "And I'm going to give him space to do it. Make it quick, though, because we need to get you and Betsy back into the city before Winters sends out a search party."

"All right."

"Lincoln, good to see you, man," Kinkaid said when we walked into the cottage. He gave me a hearty handshake, but his eyes were locked on Julie. "I was pissed with you and Pritchard at first, because you guys were cutting me out of the loop, but now that I understand what's been going on, I don't give a damn about any of that."

"Hello, Aaron," Julie said. Betsy jumped off the couch and ran to give her mother a hug. She made a wide circle around Kinkaid.

"Hi, Julie. I'm sure glad to see you," Kinkaid said, sounding like an awkward teenager on a first date. His freckled face was flushed.

I cleared my throat and looked at John Weston, who was sitting on the couch. "John, can I see you outside for a minute?"

He followed me out. I didn't want to leave Julie alone with Kinkaid, but I was even less interested in hanging around to listen to him gush about his feelings for her, which would surely begin soon enough. I told John about our interview with Winters and her request that Julie and Betsy stay at a hotel under police watch.

"That's probably a good choice," he said, averting his eyes. He didn't say anything about Julie's planned departure, and I didn't, either.

"Well, son, I'm old and I'm tired," he said. "If you're going to take them back into the city, I'm going to go home. Have Julie call me from the hotel, would you? I'll see them again tomorrow."

I told him I would, and he shook my hand and limped off to his Buick. I didn't want to go back in the house and deal with Kinkaid and Julie yet, so I climbed in my truck and began sorting aimlessly through the things I'd taken from the Contour and dumped into the back of the cab.

A manila folder was lying on the floor where I'd tossed it. Hartwick's personnel file. I still hadn't looked at it. I picked it up and flipped through the pages. There was no real need to research his background now, but I had it, and I was trying to kill time. I got to the page of references from his employee application and stopped, my eyes locked on the third name.

"I knew there was a reason not to trust you, asshole," I said aloud. The third name on Randy Hartwick's list of references was Aaron Kinkaid. Even more interesting was

Kinkaid's job title at the time of the nearly decade-old application: chief of security, Richard Douglass and Associates. Kinkaid had worked for Jeremiah Hubbard's attorney.

I walked up on the deck and looked inside. Kinkaid was standing in the kitchen, talking to Julie, while Betsy sat at the table. I stood there for a while, watching them, wondering about what he knew and how long he'd known it. It was time for—as Randy Hartwick had suggested with his last breath—a little answer-sharing. I didn't realize until I reached for the door that my hands were clenched into fists.

"Hey, Aaron," I said as I stepped inside, "I hate to interrupt, but I've got a few things I need to explain to you. You mind?"

"Hell, no, man. You're the boss." He followed me into one of the little bedrooms. When we were alone, his face opened in a wide smile and he slapped me on the shoulder.

"Good to see you again, Perry. Pritchard and I were a little concerned about you while you were down south."

I smiled back at him and hit him once in the jaw with a stiff left jab. It backed him up and jarred him, but he got his hands up to protect his face. I kicked him in the groin, then caught him behind the ear with a hard right as he dropped. He landed on all fours, then went down on the floor and curled up, gasping for breath. I pulled Hartwick's personnel file from my jacket and threw it on the floor beside his face.

"Chief of security for Richard Douglass and Associates, eh? That's real nice, Kinkaid. You told us you never met Jeremiah Hubbard. I find that a little harder to believe now."

"I don't know what you're talking about," he wheezed. He was sliding his left hand under his shirt. I kicked him in the stomach, then reached inside his shirt and removed the snubnose .32 he had in a shoulder holster. Apparently he'd left the Colt Python home for something a little more discreet today. I threw the gun across the room, pulled him into a sitting position, and slapped him hard in the face. I didn't want to make enough noise to alarm Julie and Betsy, but I was going to get some answers from Kinkaid.

"Tell me the truth, you son of a bitch," I said, jamming

my thumb into a pressure point near his collarbone and making him writhe in pain. "You told the Russians I was in South Carolina, didn't you?"

"No," he said, trying to shake his head while twisting out of my grasp.

"Aaron," I said, "the game is over. Tell me the truth."

"All right," he said, sagging back against the wall. "All right."

TWENTY-FIVE

When Wayne Weston and Aaron Kinkaid went into business together, Hubbard came to them through a referral from Richard Douglass. The job description was simple and open-ended—perform the most thorough background investigations possible, whenever and on whomever Hubbard requested. He offered big money, and they took it. There was never a case for the rich man's wife, Kinkaid explained; that was just bullshit offered to Joe to establish an initial connection between Weston and Hubbard.

There had also never been a legitimate problem between the two partners over Julie Weston. "There was nothing between Julie and me," Kinkaid said. "I got drunk and hit on her once, but we both laughed that off."

So the pair had worked for Hubbard for a while, but it quickly became evident that Weston was better at the type of assignments Hubbard had to offer, and soon he was working almost exclusively for the multimillionaire. Kinkaid and Weston talked things over and decided a separation was the logical solution. Hubbard agreed to fund Kinkaid's security company in Sandusky as a silent partner. He left the city, and Wayne Weston stuck around, doing some legitimate cases but basically working as a professional blackmailer. He was good at it, and Hubbard was making him rich.

Then came the past winter and Hubbard's vision of a building project in the Flats. Weston went to work collecting background information on Beckley and the owner of The River Wild. It was then that he ran into the Russians.

"Wayne found out the owner was in bed with the mob, and he wanted to back off," Kinkaid said. "But Hubbard thought it was a great opportunity, you know? He wanted to be able to threaten this guy with criminal charges if they could get any sort of real evidence. So Wayne broke into the bar and set up a wireless camera to get an idea of what was going on in the place."

Most people wouldn't be foolish enough to try to threaten men connected to Belov, but Hubbard had been so big for so long that he could no longer even comprehend the idea of being afraid of someone, even someone like Belov. So when Weston got the tape, his rich, arrogant boss decided to use it, Kinkaid said. He sent the tape to the strip club owner, but he didn't tell Wayne Weston. The next day, Krashakov came looking for Hubbard. Apparently, he had intercepted the tape before Dainius Belov received it.

"He made them a deal—he'd keep his mouth shut if the Russians would sell the property to him," Kinkaid said.

"And they took that?" When he nodded I was stunned. "The Russians made a *deal* with him? Why the hell didn't they kill him?"

He shrugged. "I guess because they wanted to use him. They saw the potential there; I mean, Hubbard's about the richest guy in town. Why would they want to kill him when they could use him in the future?"

Good point. "So where did you come in?"

"I called Hubbard to warn him about you guys when Pritchard came out to interview me. A day later, he calls me back and says you two showed up in his office asking questions. He explained everything that had gone down with Wayne and the Russians, and he offered me big money if I could get involved with you and keep him informed. I told him I wasn't going anywhere near it unless I could talk to the Russians and be sure they weren't going to consider me a threat. I met with Krashakov and explained how it would be beneficial for all of us if I hung around. He never liked having me involved, but he wanted to find Julie and that tape, so he went with it." He looked at me as if he were about to let me in on a secret. "Krashakov's one scary son of a bitch."

I wanted to hit him again, but I didn't. "Who set up Belov's son?"

"All I know is Krashakov wanted to make a power play, and Belov's son was the first obstacle in his path. There's been some tension between those two for a while, I think." He wiped at the blood on his chin. "I'm in a bad spot, too, Perry. Wayne thought the Russians were going to kill him, and now I'm playing the same role. You think I want to be part of this? Shit, no."

"So why *are* you part of it, Kinkaid?"

He snorted. "You think I got a choice? Hubbard owns my business. Hubbard owns *me*. You don't just walk away from a guy like that."

I moved away from him, pacing the little room. He watched me warily.

"Does Hubbard own Cody, too?" I asked.

He looked at the floor. "I don't know."

I reached down for him, and he threw an awkward punch that I avoided easily as I got my hands under his arms and lifted him. I slammed him back against the wall, twice, hard enough to make the door rattle in its frame. Julie and Betsy had to hear it, but I was too mad to care.

"Yes," he said, "yes, dammit, he's paying Cody. Now get the hell off me, Perry. I'm telling you the truth."

I dropped him and stepped back. "So what's Cody's game, exactly?"

"He's almost legitimate. He was working on the FBI task force that's trying to take down Belov, and he knew Weston was involved with them from the wiretaps. Hubbard paid him to keep his name out of it. He wasn't supposed to derail the investigation, he was just supposed to steer it away from Hubbard."

"Which means he was derailing the investigation," I said. "So let me get this straight—Krashakov was making a power play by eliminating Belov's son. But who was selling Hubbard the club?"

"Krashakov. He was the muscle in charge of it, even if he wasn't the owner on paper."

"Dainius didn't know about the River Wild deal?"

"No. That was Krashakov's move. He had the authority to sell the club as long as Belov got a cut."

"You sent the Russians down to South Carolina after me, didn't you?" I said.

He pushed himself back against the wall as if he were trying to burrow into it for protection, but this time he was smart enough not to lie. "Yes."

I thought about Rakic and the fat, pale man, about that shotgun swinging toward me, and gritted my teeth. "What about Hartwick?"

"He wasn't a weapons smuggler."

"No kidding. I mean what about his murder, Kinkaid. Did you set that up, too?"

"No."

"Kinkaid, it's over now. Understand that, you cowardly son of a bitch?" I drove my foot into the wall just beside his head, and he jumped as if I'd struck him. "Now tell me what happened with Hartwick."

"I only lied a little about Hartwick," he said. "I wasn't lying when I said he was the most dangerous person I'd ever known. He was a loose cannon up here, Perry. Hubbard couldn't afford to have him here, and neither could Krashakov. As soon as I heard Hartwick was in town, I knew he was here for blood. That's how it worked with Randy. He wasn't here to investigate, he was here to kill."

"Bullshit," I said. "He was trying to figure out a way to buy some safety for Julie and her daughter, just like Joe and I have been. If he'd wanted to kill Krashakov, he'd have done it and gone back to South Carolina."

"I don't know."

"I'm sure you don't, Kinkaid. So Hartwick showed up in town, and you told Krashakov where he could be found, didn't you?"

He was looking at the floor, where drops of his blood were gathering in a small pool. "They were in the cemetery with me. When I left you and Pritchard and went out to smoke a cigarette, I called them, and they parked near your office and waited. They took the shot from the hill in the cemetery and left. I killed a few minutes and then went over the fence when I heard you shouting for me."

"Who made the shot?"

"Krashakov. He's had sniper training."

"Why'd he only take Hartwick out?" I asked. "Why leave Joe and me alive?"

"I told them about the progress you were making, and I said if they gave me a few days to work with you, I might be able to find the Westons and the tape. Hartwick was too dangerous to . . ." His voice trailed off, but I knew how that sentence was going to end. Too dangerous to leave alive.

"And when I *did* find Julie, then you called Krashakov and told him where to find us?" I thought of Betsy Weston alone in the hotel room just minutes before Krashakov and his thugs had arrived, and I was filled with a surge of anger unlike any I'd felt before. Kinkaid had called them and told them where to find us, then let them fly down to finish the killing.

I took three steps back toward him, ready to grab him and slam him against the wall until I put him all the way through it, but before I could get my hands on him the door opened and Julie Weston stepped inside.

"Lincoln," she said, staring at Kinkaid's bloody face, "what's going on?"

"Get out," I said. "I'm not through here."

She started to object, then looked at the blood on the floor and turned quickly, closing the door behind her. I turned back to Kinkaid. He was staring at the door.

"There's something I need to tell you," he said.

"No shit, Aaron. There were a lot of things you needed to tell me."

"It's more important. Krashakov knows where we are."

"What?"

"I called him when I found out you'd gone to the prosecutor's office. He went crazy about it, and he made me tell him where the girl was staying."

"You son of a bitch. How long ago was this?"

"Maybe an hour. I tried to calm him down, but he was threatening to kill me. I didn't want him to refocus that anger on me, but now that I've seen the little girl . . ." He looked up at me. "You've got to get her out of here, Perry. Krashakov will kill her. He'll kill all of you."

I stepped away from him, hearing Thad Cody's voice in my head when he'd told Joe and me about the Russian mob's thirst for revenge. "We Italians will kill you," he'd quoted from the wiretap, "but the Russians are crazy—they'll kill your whole family." If Krashakov knew that we'd gone to the prosecutor, it meant he'd be coming to kill, and only to kill.

"Shit, we don't have much time," I said.

I threw open the door and stepped out of the bedroom, holding Kinkaid's gun in my hand. Betsy saw it and ducked behind her mother. "Put Betsy in my truck," I said. "We're leaving."

Even as I spoke, I heard the crunch of tires on the gravel drive. I ran back into the bedroom, ignoring Kinkaid, who was cowering on the floor, expecting me to strike him again, and went to the window that looked out up the drive. At the top of the drive a shiny black SUV had come into view through the pines.

There was no time to think, only time to react. We could not drive away, and the little cottage would not offer protection for the firepower the Russians would bring. We could flee into the woods, but they'd see us, and eventually they would catch us.

I stepped into the living room and pressed Kinkaid's gun into Julie's palm. "They're here. Take Betsy and go down the back steps and into the crawl space where she hid before.

Keep Betsy absolutely quiet. If anyone tries to come inside, use the gun, but don't waste bullets."

She stared at me, her mouth open, jaw slack, but I spun her and shoved her forward, out the door and onto the deck. She grabbed Betsy and ran down the steps and around the corner of the cottage. The cottage would screen them from view from the drive, but if they ran away from it they'd be seen. Now I was left alone inside with Kinkaid and no weapon. My gun was still locked in the center console of the truck, and I'd never make it there.

"What should we do?" Kinkaid said, stepping out of the bedroom, looking as scared as Julie. I knew he *was* scared, and because of that, I also knew he'd tell Krashakov exactly where I'd sent Julie and Betsy. I took one quick step toward him and threw an uppercut at his jaw, dropping my shoulder and using my legs as a source of power for the punch, the way it's supposed to be done. I hit him flush on the chin. His head snapped back and he sagged to the ground. I clubbed him once on the back of the skull for good measure as he dropped. At least he'd be quiet now.

I stepped away from Kinkaid and into the kitchen, pulling open drawers in search of a knife. Before I found anything more useful than a corkscrew, Alexei Krashakov stepped inside from the deck and pointed a 9-millimeter Beretta pistol at my chest.

TWENTY-SIX

I stood where I was and watched as Krashakov walked into the room, followed by Rakic and Malaknik. Great. The whole gang was here.

Krashakov kept the gun pointed at my chest. It was the first time I'd seen him face-to-face since we'd stood on the porch of his house.

He smiled. "You owe me twenty dollars."

"I'll give you fifty and send you on your way."

He shook his head slowly. "I'm afraid it will not be so easy."

"One hundred, then."

He slapped me on the side of the head with the Beretta, and a band of bright light like heat lightning passed over my eyes. When I could see clearly again, I was on my hands and knees on the cheap linoleum floor. The man was strong. There weren't too many people who could bring me to my knees with a single blow. I'd hardly seen his hand move.

He laid the barrel of the gun against the back of my head as Rakic went from room to room in the cottage. He came back out and shook his head.

"No one is here except for him." He gestured at Kinkaid's inert form.

"You are pretty good," Krashakov said to me. "That was very nice work at the hotel."

"Glad you approve."

"No. I do not approve. You killed a friend of mine." He slammed the butt of the gun into my upper back, sending a spasm of pain through my back and shoulders.

"Where are they?" Krashakov said.

I didn't answer, and Rakic said, "It will be best to tell us quickly. The longer you wait, the more pain you will feel." He had a thick, wet voice, like someone suffering from chronic bronchitis. "Where is Mrs. Weston?"

"Mrs. who?"

Bad idea. Krashakov slapped my head with the Beretta again, setting off a few more flashes of heat lightning. This time it took longer for my eyes to refocus. My field of vision was beginning to seem like a Texas sky during a nighttime thunderstorm.

"Where is the woman?" Krashakov said.

"It's over, boys," I said. "The prosecutor knows what happened, and the media knows what happened. It's time for you to run. Killing me will only make it worse." I didn't tell them that Belov knew what had happened. They'd kill me for sure then.

"He's lying," Rakic said.

"Where is she?" Krashakov repeated.

"With the police. She's at the prosecutor's office telling them the whole damn story. You can go down there and ask for her, if you'd like."

"You lie," Krashakov said. He jabbed the barrel of his gun at Kinkaid. "Not long ago, the woman and girl were here, and they were with him. Now he is unconscious, and you are alone. Your truck is still outside."

"I told you, they're not here."

Krashakov lifted me and threw me forward, into the counter. My head connected with the edge of the sink, and then he grabbed my shoulder, spun me around to face him, and hit me three times in the stomach with savage uppercuts. I fell back to my knees and gagged, choking back a rise of vomit in my throat. He kicked me in the head and pointed the Beretta at my chest as he stood over me.

"We do not have time to play games," he said. "You will tell us where to find her, because I wish to kill you last."

"I'm your favorite, eh?"

"Hold him," Krashakov snapped, and Rakic and Malaknik stepped over, grabbed my arms, and moved me out of the kitchen and into the living room. Behind me, the door to the deck was still open, and cold air rushed in past my face as the wind picked up outside. Krashakov knelt beside me in the doorway, using his left hand to pin my right ankle to the ground. He pressed the muzzle of the Beretta against my kneecap.

"One chance," he said. "Then this knee goes. You will get another chance, and then the other knee goes. After that, I will have to be more creative." His voice was calm and uninterested, speaking in careful, stilted English.

I looked at the gun pressed to my knee. So much for my evening runs. I closed my eyes and saw Julie's face and heard Betsy's laugh. I would not give them up to these bastards. Not for one knee, or two knees. Not for one life.

I opened my eyes again, ready to tell Krashakov to hurry up and go to work, but he was jerked away from me as if someone had tossed a lasso around him and yanked him backward. He shouted and tried to bring the gun up, but it was knocked from his hand as Thor stepped inside the cottage from the deck and drove a Buck hunting knife deep into the front of Krashakov's thigh. Krashakov started to scream, but Thor's gloved hand was wrapped tightly around his throat. His other hand was pointing a gun at Rakic. Behind him, Alexander stood calmly, pointing a Soviet-made AK-47 assault rifle at Rakic and Malaknik.

Kinkaid lurched up on his hands and knees behind us, still groggy. He looked at the hunting knife protruding from Krashakov's thigh, said, "Oh, holy shit," and fell back to the floor, covering his head with his hands.

"Let him go," Alexander said. Rakic and Malaknik released me and stepped away slowly. Krashakov had been fighting against Thor's grip but without success. Thor stood calmly, oblivious to the power of the man struggling against him. His handhold on Krashakov's throat cut off the man's air supply, and after a few seconds Krashakov went limp and slid to the ground, unconscious. Thor let him drop.

"Dainius would like to see you, gentlemen," Thor said to Rakic and Malaknik. "We will take your car."

Rakic started to mumble something, but Alexander stepped over to him and struck him repeatedly with the butt of the AK-47, driving him to the ground. Then he took the weapons from both Rakic and Malaknik and ordered them outside. I slid onto the deck and watched as Thor walked down the steps, dragging Krashakov behind him with one arm casually wrapped around the other man's throat. When he reached the drive, he opened the rear door of the Navigator and shoved Krashakov's bloody body inside. He reached inside, withdrew his hunting knife, and carefully used Krashakov's pants to wipe the blood from the blade. Then he stepped over to the cowering Malaknik, who was waiting at the base of the steps, and hit him once in the jaw. Malaknik crumpled as if someone had dropped a Honda on him. Thor picked him up as if he were a small child and tossed him into the car on top of Krashakov. Alexander hit Rakic in the back of the head with the assault rifle and dumped him in beside them, then dug a set of car keys from one of their pockets and closed the doors.

Thor turned to me and fixed his glacier-ice eyes on mine. I was still sitting on the steps of the deck.

"You were looking for them, and they were looking for me," I said.

He nodded once.

"Good timing," I said.

He nodded again, then walked past me and back into the cottage. I followed. He gazed around the living room and pointed at Kinkaid, who was still lying on the floor with his hands over his head. A wet stain had spread across the back of his pants.

"Do you want him?" he said.

"Yes."

"Fine. Understand that you never saw this. You never saw us."

I nodded. "I understand."

He looked at Kinkaid. "Make sure he understands it as well."

"He won't be hard to convince."

"No, it does not appear that he will be."

He turned on his heel and walked back out onto the deck and down the steps. Rakic was already inside the Navigator. Thor opened the driver's door but didn't get inside. I thought about asking where they had come from, but that was only going to be answered with a cold, empty smile, so I let it go. They must have left their car at the top of the drive so as not to tip Krashakov off to his followers.

Thor was still standing with the driver's door open. "Dainius sends his thanks for your help in resolving this matter. If someday you should need his help, he hopes you will not hesitate to seek it."

"All right."

He started to get in the car, then leaned back and looked at me again. "Dainius is a good man to find favor with."

I thought of the hunting knife sinking into Krashakov's thigh. "I believe it," I said.

They were gone then. I stood and watched the Navigator pull up the drive and out of sight, and I tried not to wonder where it might be headed. Kinkaid was sitting on the deck now, and he looked ill. I walked up and knelt down beside him. Ten minutes earlier, I'd wanted to beat the shit out of him. Now I didn't think I could lift a fist to anyone if I had to. I felt weary.

"Kinkaid," I said, "those men would have killed you. They still may. You have worked against them, and they are not men to work against."

He was breathing in ragged gasps. I stared at him and thought about Hartwick, about the fat, pale man, and about the gun that had been pressed to my kneecap. I thought about all of it, and I tried to come up with some more rage. I couldn't.

"Go back to Sandusky, Kinkaid."

I stood on the deck and waited until he had started his car with trembling hands and driven away. Then I went to get Julie and Betsy.

I went down to the crawl space and started to pull the panel away, then thought better of it and yelled out my name before I took a bullet in the chest.

They crawled out and into my arms, and they were both crying. I sat on the ground and held them as Betsy buried her face in my chest and Julie wiped at her eyes and tried to compose herself.

"What happened?" she said. "Oh, Lincoln. I was so scared. Where'd they go?"

"They left," I said. "And they won't be back. That's all that matters." I stroked Betsy's soft hair with my hand and then gently tugged her face away from my shirt. "Hey, pal, relax. Everything's fine. You're fine."

We sat there for a while, sharing a hug that meant more than any embrace I could remember, and then Betsy said she was cold, so I picked her up and carried her inside.

"You're taller than my daddy," she said as we went up the steps, and I closed my eyes and didn't respond.

They got what things they had left in the cottage, and I put them in the back of the truck. Then I stopped Julie in the drive.

"Put Betsy in the truck, and then I'd like a moment alone with you."

She stared at me for a few seconds, then nodded and went up the steps. I watched her hips move as she went. Tomorrow. She was going to leave tomorrow.

I walked down to the pond and tossed rocks out onto the ice. They bounced across the surface without breaking the ice near the shore, but when I started lobbing them out into deeper water, they found pockets of broken ice and sank. The effort made the aches Krashakov had left behind flare up anew, but I ignored them.

A few minutes later, Julie walked out and joined me. She stood next to me and watched me throw the rocks. I didn't stop throwing them until she spoke.

"Betsy's in the backseat of your truck," she said. "We're ready whenever you are."

"Okay." I tossed a few more rocks out at the pond.

"I don't want to leave you," Julie said.

I dropped the rock that was in my hand. "I know."

"You can't come with us."

I shook my head. "No. I can't."

She sighed. "But I can't stay here anymore, Lincoln. I can't raise my daughter here."

"No. You can't."

She moved to stand in front of me, then slipped her arms under mine and wrapped them around my back. She stepped in close and pressed her body against me, and I looked down into her beautiful face and beautiful eyes and for a moment I think I forgot to breathe. She squeezed me tightly, then leaned back, still holding me, and looked up at my face and smiled.

"Were you standing this close to your husband when you shot him?" I asked.

Originally it had been one of many possibilities in an unknown situation. Then it had been an idea dismissed as absurd. It had crawled back as a nagging doubt, developed into an always-present question, and then swelled into a strong suspicion. Now, as I looked down into her face, it became the truth.

"No," she said, and her voice was a hoarse whisper. "I wasn't quite this close."

She let go of me and stepped away. At least she hadn't tried to deny it. It shouldn't have meant much to me, but it was something.

"When did you decide that was what happened?" she asked.

"I'd wondered about it for a while. Wayne was a professional, and I had trouble believing he would have let someone get in a position to kill him with his own gun and make it look like suicide. Certainly he wouldn't have let any of the Russians pull it off. And for a while I bought your story about Hubbard, probably because I wanted to. But that one was weak, too, because you told me you had plenty of Hubbard's money to fund your disappearance. And if there's one thing near and dear to Jeremiah Hubbard's heart, it's his money. If he was planning to kill Wayne or have him killed, he wouldn't have paid him off first. Then when I stopped to think about how determined you are to take Betsy and leave the country, it made me even more curious."

"I see."

"I saw another side of you the night in the hot tub, and it didn't make sense," I said. "It wasn't easy for me to put my ego away, but when I did, I began to question whether I was really attractive enough to make a grieving widow shed her clothes in the middle of a hotel courtyard."

She gave me cold eyes. "You think that was an act? Some attempt to distract you, keep your mind away from Wayne?"

I shrugged.

"Believe what you want," she said. "But that wasn't the case."

"You settled it last night," I said.

"I did? How?"

"When you asked me about Amy. You told me I let my guard down when I was with her and Joe, and that it was the first time you'd seen me do that. I got to thinking about it, and I realized that was probably true. You'd never seen me let my guard down before, and I wondered why not. I wondered why I kept it up when I was with you. That's when I started coming up with the reasons. There was a pretty long list of them, things that you said that didn't quite make sense, and . . ." I sighed and shook my head, then looked back out at the frozen pond.

"And what?" she asked. Her arms were folded across her chest, her eyes focused on the ground.

"And I saw it in your eyes the night we left South Carolina," I said. "When you stopped me in the hotel and asked me if I could kill to protect your daughter. There was something about the way you said it." I shook my head again. "I tried to tell myself you'd asked Wayne the same question and you'd been disappointed, because he'd only died for her. But that wasn't it. *You'd* been willing to kill for her, and you were trying to tell me that without saying it. You were testing me to see if I could match that dedication."

She stepped closer to me and put her hands on my arms. "And you *did* kill to protect her," she said. "Just like I did."

"No," I said, pulling away from her, "I didn't. I'd like to say that I did, because it's a hell of a lot more noble. But truthfully, when that man swung the gun in my direction, I pulled the trigger to save myself. Neither you nor your daughter passed through my mind, Julie. It was a self-preservation instinct."

She walked away and stood near the shore with her back to me. I followed her down and stood beside her again.

"Tell me how it happened."

She kept staring out at the water. "I hadn't planned on it. You don't have to believe that, but it's the truth. I was so scared, Lincoln. We were running, fleeing our own home in the middle of the night because people were going to try to kill us. Betsy was in the rental car, and I walked back inside with Wayne. He gestured around the living room and told me to take a good look because I was never going to see it again. When he said that, I stopped being scared and started being angry. I was never going to see it again. My own home." She shuddered, recoiling against the memory as if it were a frightening, physical thing.

"Then he put the gun in my hand. He told me he wanted me to take it with us in the car, in case anything happened. I might need it to protect Betsy, he said. That's what my life had come to, Lincoln—a life where my husband gave me a gun to protect my daughter as we fled in the night. Why? Because the bastard was so damn greedy. And he'd never even told me, Lincoln. He'd never told me what he did. We lived our happy, ignorant life, and he put us in danger. He put my baby in danger."

She looked up at me. "He showed me how to take the safety off, and then he put the gun in my hand. And I put it to his temple and shot him."

For a long time there was nothing but the sound of the wind in the pines and the ice in the pond creaking and groaning as it melted and shifted. The sun was hidden behind the clouds, but the temperature was in the low forties, warm enough to melt the ice. I stared out at it without seeing anything. Minutes passed, and then I turned and walked back to the truck.

Julie followed. "You're going to tell the police, aren't you?"

I stopped and looked at her. "I don't work for the police, Julie. I was hired by your father-in-law to find out what happened to his son. I have done that now. I will go to him, and I will tell him what I have found."

I got in the truck and started the engine. Betsy was in the backseat. She gave me a bright smile.

"Your car is tall," she said. "Mommy had to lift me inside."

"I like them tall," I said. "You wanna drive?" When I asked her, my voice broke, and then I didn't say anything else. Julie climbed into the passenger seat and fastened her seat belt. On the drive back into the city, I did not speak. Not a word. Betsy and Julie talked. I drove.

I brought them to the Marriott. I parked the truck and helped Betsy down out of the cab. She squeezed my neck with her arms as I set her to the pavement, and she told me she would see me in the morning. I told her I'd look forward to it.

"You still owe me an ice cream," she said as she bounced toward the hotel. I leaned against the truck and looked away.

Julie stepped up next to me. We both watched Betsy. "I'll keep her safe and happy," she said. "I will tell her Wayne is dead, but when I tell her we will be far away, and we will be safe. I will see that she is raised well, and raised happily, and not raised in danger or in the shadow of all the publicity."

"Will you ever tell her the truth?" I asked. "Will you tell her what you did?"

She swallowed hard and didn't look at me. "I don't know."

"Mommy, come on," Betsy called. She was standing at the door to the lobby.

Julie turned to me. "Are you going to the police?"

"I'm going to see John, like I told you."

She looked into my eyes, searching for another answer I would not offer, and then she nodded. "Okay, Lincoln." She leaned up and kissed me softly on the cheek, letting her face linger near mine for a few extra seconds. "I owe my life to you, and my daughter's life. You may hate me now. You have that right. Just know that I have nothing but gratitude for you."

She turned and walked away, carrying a suitcase in each hand. Betsy tugged open the door, straining her little body against the heavy glass, and then they went inside. I got in the truck and drove to John Weston's.

TWENTY-SEVEN

The windows of Weston's house were dark, but he answered the door when I knocked. He was wearing pajamas and a robe, and he looked exhausted.

"Come in," he said, stepping aside to let me pass.

"I'm sorry to bother you so late."

"Son, don't you ever apologize to me for anything. You want to come here at two in the morning every day, I won't complain. I owe you more than I can ever repay."

We went into the living room and sat down. The haze of cigarette smoke was thicker than I'd ever seen it before. He fired another one up and took a few puffs while I waited.

"Something's on your mind," he said. "You came here to let it out. So let it out."

"You know they're leaving," I said.

He nodded. "Yes, son, I do. And as much as I hate to see them go, I will respect my daughter-in-law's decision. She has the best interests of the little girl at heart. I firmly believe that."

I nodded. "So do I."

He'd turned on one lamp, but the room was still quite dark. The cigarette smoke hung heavily in the air, and it was warm enough to make me sweat. He ground the cigarette out in an ashtray and waited for me to speak.

"You hired me to find out what had happened to your family," I said.

"Yes. And you've done that."

I shook my head. "I've told you what happened to your granddaughter and her mother. I haven't told you what happened to your son."

He waited, but I didn't say anything. Sometimes it's hard to find a place to start.

"Son, I'm old and tired. Tell me what you have to say."

So I told him. I told him my reasons for the initial suspicion, and I told him of my conversation with Julie. I told him I had not talked to the police about her yet. When I finished, it was quiet for a while.

"I hate to hear it," he said eventually. "But I can't say that I blame her. And I *know* that Wayne doesn't blame her, wherever he is. Wayne lost sight of his family. He lost sight of his loyalty, and of his honor." His voice was wet and gravelly.

"We need to call the police," I said. "That's what we need to do."

The tip of his cigarette glowed a bright red as he inhaled. "Who you working for, Mr. Perry?"

I looked at him. "I'm working for you."

He nodded. "Seems like I should get to make this call, then, doesn't it?"

I shook my head. "It's a felony, sir. She killed a man. I can't let that go."

He blew a cloud of smoke at me. "You've spent some time with my granddaughter, haven't you?"

"Yes, sir."

"What do you think of her?"

I looked at the floor. "She's an amazing little girl. She's bright and fun and polite. She's a very special kid."

"You're damn right she is." He cleared his throat and put this cigarette out, too. "I'm a sick old man. I don't have much time left. Other than Julie, I'm the only family that kid's got. You want to tell me who's going to raise her if her mother goes to jail?"

I shrugged. "Foster care, I guess. She'd be a ward of the state."

"That's right. Now look at me, son."

I looked up and met his eyes.

"You are my employee. I am going to give you a request, and I expect and demand that you will follow through on it."

"All right."

"You take the night off," he said. "Go home, go to bed. In the morning, you do what your heart and your head tell you to do."

I told him I would, and then I stood up and said I'd see myself to the door. I made it halfway there before he spoke again.

"Mr. Perry?"

I turned. "Yes, sir?"

His face was hidden by the shadows and the smoke. "I hired you to bring me the truth. I didn't ask you to bring me any sugarcoated bullshit. I asked for the truth, and you brought it to me. I thank you for that."

"You're welcome," I said. I wanted to ask him if he felt more or less lonely now than he had before, but I didn't. I stepped out into the night and closed the door softly behind me. I'd brought him the truth. It sounded like a noble task, and I felt I should probably be proud to have done it. I wasn't, though. Sometimes providing the truth isn't any fun.

I stopped at a restaurant in North Olmsted and picked at a plate of food until I grew tired of pretending the night was normal and I had an appetite, and then I drove back to the apartment, changed clothes, and went down to my gym. Grace was long gone, of course. That was good. I didn't want to make any lighthearted small talk.

My head was pounding and throbbing from the beating Krashakov had given me, but I didn't take any medication. I welcomed the pain tonight. The gym was nearly empty, and I worked out furiously. It had been a few days since my last workout, and my muscles needed the exercise. The headache intensified, and so did my effort as I tried to cleanse myself through the exertion, the sweat, and the pain. It wasn't working. I went at it for almost two hours, until my body gave up on outlasting my need for the exercise. I went back up to the apartment.

I had just stepped out of the shower when the phone rang. I picked the cordless phone off its handset and said hello.

"Where is she, Mr. Perry?" Laura Winters.

"Where's who?"

"Julie Weston. Please tell me she's with you."

"No. I dropped her off at the Marriott hours ago."

"Shit."

"What happened?"

"She disappeared, that's what happened. We had officers watching them, but she got away. She took the girl down to swim in the indoor pool, and they were watched the whole time. When they got on the elevator to go back up, the cops waited for another one so they wouldn't scare the girl. That was the last time they saw them."

Slick. Wayne Weston would have been proud.

"Try John Weston's house," I said.

"We sent officers over there. It looks like he's gone, too. Neighbors saw him put two suitcases in his car and drive away earlier this evening."

That was more of a surprise.

"She did this on purpose, didn't she?" Winters said. "Your reporter friend told me Julie Weston was planning to leave. She said she didn't want to trust the police to keep her safe."

"I heard her say that, but I never knew any of her specific plans to leave," I said honestly.

"You knew she was going to run, you asshole. Well, we'd better find them."

"You have her story," I said. "That's enough."

"I'll decide what's enough, Perry. And, whether we find them or not, you'd better have your ass in my office tomorrow morning. I've got a long line of cops wanting to talk to you about an even longer list of crimes."

"I'll be there."

I sat on the floor of my living room with the lights off. Julie was gone. It would have been easier for her to get away when she'd been with me, but she'd waited until the police had her. Probably she'd wanted to cut me a break and make things at least somewhat easier for me with the police. Thoughtful. Now it was their fault she'd disappeared, not mine. I could have stopped her if I'd called the cops soon enough. John Weston had told me not to, though. Didn't mention he was going with them.

I called Joe and told him the news. He wasn't surprised, not by Julie's vanishing act, or John's decision not to call the cops, or even that John had gone with them. He was a little more surprised that Julie had killed her husband, but it's hard to throw a total shocker at a thirty-year police veteran.

"You all right?" he asked.

"Fine."

"Sure." He paused, then said, "Get some sleep, LP. You've earned it."

"See you tomorrow, Joe."

At one in the morning, Amy came over. She didn't call, but that was fine. I wasn't asleep, and she knew I wouldn't be. I let her in, and we sat on the couch, and I told her what I knew. I told her all of it, from Thor and Krashakov to my conversation with Julie at the pond to John Weston's request that I take the night off to think things over.

"Wow. She killed his son, and he let her go. Went with her, even."

"He let Betsy keep her mother," I said. "They might seem like the same decision to anyone else, but I don't know if they were to John."

"And it's not like he's got long to spend with them. Six months to a year, right?"

"What are you talking about?"

"John Weston's dying, Lincoln. Didn't you know that?" When my face told her that I didn't, she shook her head. "Wow, I thought you knew. Julie told me in the interview. He's in the late stages of terminal lung cancer."

I didn't know what to say to that. I didn't know what to say to a lot of things anymore.

"What'll happen to Hubbard and Cody?" Amy asked.

"They'll prosecute Hubbard. My guess is the FBI will handle Cody internally. It will be difficult to prove exactly how much he knew and how much he hurt the investigation, and they'll break their backs to keep something like that out of the media spotlight. He'll probably end up filing papers in the Des Moines office by June."

She shook her head. "It's been a hell of a day for you, Lincoln."

"Yes, it has. I was thanked for my cooperation by one of the city's deadliest criminals and cursed by a prosecutor. Sounds like I handled everything pretty well, right?"

"You're alive, and so are they," she said. "You didn't handle it that badly."

"They are alive. Alive, and long gone. Good thing we made Weston give us the retainer check."

"My story runs tomorrow," she said. "There are quite a few quotes in it indicating that Julie was still scared and that she wanted to disappear to protect her daughter. There's nothing in it indicating she killed her husband, though."

"And there shouldn't be. Let the police deal with it now, Ace."

She looked at me. "It bothers you, doesn't it? You could have taken her to the police instead of dropping her off at the hotel. You could have told someone what you knew. But you didn't."

"Yeah, it bothers me. It bothers me because I'm not sad about it. I know she killed her husband, and I know she's gone now, and I'm not at all disappointed. I want her to be gone. I don't want her to be in jail."

"But she killed a man. She murdered her own husband."

"Well, sure," I said. "There's that."

Amy nodded. "And you can rationalize it a little, can't you? You can look at the situation and justify her actions, or at least justify her freedom."

"Yes," I said. "But I shouldn't be able to. Killing is

killing. It's not my job to justify it. She took a life, Amy. And John's okay with letting her go, because he wants the best for his granddaughter. But it probably would have been best for her to have both parents alive, don't you think?"

Amy pulled her legs up on the couch and tucked them underneath her. "You almost died for her, you know."

"Yes."

"Twice."

"Yes."

"Any bitterness about that?"

"No."

We sat on the couch and stared at the wall. All the lights were off, and that was how I wanted it to remain. I was content to stay in the dark again.

"You loved her, didn't you?" Amy asked softly.

I shook my head. "No, I didn't love her. I'd known her for three days, Amy."

"Okay, so you didn't love her. But maybe you wanted the chance."

I shrugged. "Screw it."

She smiled at me. "Too tough to care, eh, Lincoln?"

I shook my head again. "Not too tough. Too smart."

She touched the back of my head lightly, her fingers caressing the swollen knots left by Krashakov's gun. "People come and go in our lives. We don't get to pick when and how they come, and we don't get to pick when and how they go. We just learn from it, deal with it, and move on. That's how it goes. And that's what you have to do now."

"Deep," I said. "You should be a writer."

She flicked her finger against one of the knots hard enough to cause a little pain. "And you should be an ass. Oh, wait—you've already got that covered."

I laughed, then sighed and put my head back against the couch. "I do what I can."

"Yes," she said, "you do. And that's all you can ask of yourself, Lincoln. Now I'm going to let you get some sleep. You're going to need it for a day under the interrogation lamps."

"It'll be a blast," I said. "The cops are probably selling tickets if you want to be there for the show."

I walked her down to her car. She gave me a long, hard hug, then climbed into the Acura and drove away.

I went upstairs and dug Betsy Weston's diary out of the drawer where I had stashed it. I read through a few of the entries again, smiling at her spelling mistakes, able now to put a voice and an attitude with the thoughts. Then I snapped it shut and threw it in the garbage can. The heart-shaped prism I had taken from her bedroom that same afternoon was in the drawer with the diary. I started to toss it in the trash, too, but I didn't. I took it down to the gym and used the fishing line to hang it in the little window next to the desk. The sun would emerge from behind the clouds again one of these days, and when it did, the prism would sparkle, and maybe it would make Grace smile. You do what you can.

I locked the office and walked out to the parking lot. A jet roared overhead, flying quite low as it came in for a landing at the airport just a few miles away. The sound was tremendous, a blast that seemed to shake me until it was all I was aware of. I looked up at the sky and watched the trail of smoke and the lights as the plane roared in. I wondered where it had been and where it would go next. I wondered if it had carried Julie and Betsy Weston someplace. Eventually, the plane descended so low the buildings obscured it from sight. The cloud of vapor it had left behind faded slowly into the night sky, and then there was nothing left but the memory of the sound.

I went upstairs and went to bed.

Keep reading for an excerpt from

Michael Koryta's next mystery

SORROW'S ANTHEM

Coming soon in hardcover from
St. Martin's Minotaur

I watched Ed walk toward us, and when Draper saw my face
he turned and swore under his breath.

Ed was wearing jeans and a white T-shirt. There was
blood on the shirt and a nasty gash over his right eye. His
dirty blond hair was tousled and long, and beneath it his face
was tan and smooth. Not yet thirty, and facing life in prison,
if the jury went easy.

"A friend in need," he shouted as he approached, and it
took only those four slurred words to let me know he was
hammered. "Where does that put me, Lincoln? I'm in need,
my man, that's for damn sure. But you a friend? Shit."

Draper put his hand out and caught Ed's shoulder, trying
to turn him and send him back up the steps, but Ed shrugged
it off. His movements and his speech showed he was drunk,
but his blue eyes were sharp and piercing. When we were
kids, people used to take us for brothers, with the same dark
blond hair and bright blue eyes.

"What are you doing here?" he said.

"I heard you were in some trouble."

"Some trouble? You jerking me off, man? Some *trouble*?" He looked at Draper and laughed wildly, but Scott
didn't crack a smile. He was glancing at the door, probably

thinking that a cop could step inside at any minute, that there was probably one watching the bar from the street.

"He's taking a few hours to get himself together," Draper said to me, eyes still on the door. "Had to get his mind in order, sober up, cool off. Maybe call an attorney, maybe get his hands on a car and bail." He snapped his eyes back to me and now they were hard and unfriendly. "I'm not going to make the call, Perry. Wasn't when he showed up, and I won't now."

"Nobody's making any calls just yet," I said. Ed was watching me with a leering grin, swaying like a sailor on-board a pitching ship.

"The hell you doing here?" he said, and his voice was filled with wonder and not anger. "I mean, *damn*, Lincoln. You just gotta be there when I go down, huh? Gotta soak it up, savor it?"

I met his eyes, and I waited for my own response, waited for the words to form themselves into something that would get through to him, tell him how it had been for me, tell him why I'd had to do it. The words didn't come, though. After eight years of waiting for them, I shouldn't have been surprised.

"Good luck, Ed," I told him, and then I turned and walked for the door.

He started after me, and when Draper tried to pull him back, Ed told him to stay the hell inside. I pushed the door open and stepped out into the cooling air, stood on the sidewalk with my hands at my sides and my eyes on the ground while Ed joined me. He took out a cigarette and lit it, and we stood there together in silence. The smell of the alcohol was heavy on him, but somehow I had the sense his mind was sober right now.

"They execute a guy for murder in Ohio, don't they?" he said.

"Sometimes."

He nodded and smoked some more.

"Sometimes they don't," I said. "Depends on the circumstances. What are yours?"

He laughed, and it was a menacing sound, so empty it chilled me to the core.

"What are my circumstances?" He laughed again. "Oh, man. You don't even want to hear about it, Lincoln. They are not clean. I can tell you that. They are not clean."

He began to walk down the sidewalk then, swaying and weaving but moving fast enough, and he motioned for me to follow with a jerk of his hand. I shot a glance down the street, looking, as Draper had, for a police presence. When I saw none, I followed.

"My circumstances," he said around the cigarette, "are a little difficult to explain. I hear there's a videotape of it, though, and that's all the jury needs to see. If a picture is worth a thousand words, then what's a video? And words from an ex-con? Probably worth a million of those. A guy like me could run the world dry of words, still not have enough."

The breeze picked up, rustling the trash and gravel on the sidewalk and sending dust and bits of fine dirt into our eyes. I blinked against it, ducked my shoulders, and put my head down.

"What happened, Ed?"

He worked on the cigarette for a while, and when I glanced at him the gash above his eye was brighter than it had been, the wound opening up again and spilling more blood.

"In the beginning," Ed Gradduk told me, "it was all about money. The revenue stream, as my old man would have called it. I found one, buddy. It was already there, but I got my piece of the action, played my role and took my cut. All you can ask, right?"

I didn't answer, and we walked on in silence for maybe a block, Ed sorting out his thoughts.

"So it was money," he said. "A lot of money to some people, less to others."

"And to you?"

"Enough to me," he said. "It was enough. But then . . ."

The menacing laugh came again, and with it the temperature seemed to drop ten degrees. "Then it stopped being about money. Got personal."

"Why?"

He stopped walking and looked at me, tilting his head to the side.

"A man told me a story."

I raised my eyebrows. "What story?"

"The one he didn't want to tell," Ed answered. "And I do feel bad about that. It was hard on him, because he knew it'd be hard on me. Stuff like that, well, it doesn't tell easy, Lincoln. But I guess that's how it goes. The stories that matter most are the hardest to tell."

"Did you kill the woman?" I said.

He blew smoke wearily. "I did not kill the woman. And I don't give a damn if they have a video or a picture or a thousand eyewitnesses to whatever it is they say happened, Lincoln—that's not how it went down."

"I can help you, Ed," I said, and he raised his eyebrows and snorted. "I can help you, but you've got to tell me the whole score. Give me the names, give me the facts, lay it out there."

His eyes had drifted past me, over my shoulder and into the houses behind me. He pointed at them with his cigarette.

"Andy Butcher used to live in a house up that street. 'Member him? Crazy little shit. We were standing out in his front lawn that day the bus from the Catholic school went by." He laughed and smiled, seemingly carefree, just another guy out for an evening stroll. What murder charge? Nope, not me.

"The bus from the Catholic school goes by, and one of those shirt-and-tie boys tosses a Pepsi bottle at us? You remember it; I know you do. Little prick throws a Pepsi bottle at us, and it hits the grass instead of the sidewalk, doesn't bust. And Andy, shit, he picks it up and takes off running. Bus must be doing twenty miles an hour, but he catches up to it."

I remembered it, the scene playing through my head

now like a movie clip: Andy Butcher sprinting after the bus
with the bottle in his hand; the bus slowing because a car
had just swung out of a driveway in front of it. Andy makes
a jump right at the side of the bus. Ed and I stand back in
the yard with our mouths hanging open, staring in amazement, as Butcher hooks his left arm through the half-
opened bus window and hangs there, clinging to the side of
the moving bus while he brings the bottle in with his right
hand and smashes it against the stunned Catholic school
kid's face.

"Man, we ran like hell," Ed said.

I nodded, and somehow I wanted to smile, even though
this was no time to reminisce. "We did," I said. "The bus
driver got out, started chasing us, screaming about getting
the police."

We'd gone probably twenty blocks that day before any of
us had the sense to cut in one direction or the other, get out
of the driver's line of sight. Ran through a few yards until we
collapsed in a heap, laughing our asses off and exchanging
high-fives.

"Butcher, he was one hell of an athlete," Ed said. "Never
played an organized sport in his life, but he could catch a
moving bus and hang in the window. Amazing."

"Ed, you've got to tell me what happened," I began, not
wanting to talk about Andy Butcher anymore, but he held up
his hand and interrupted again.

"People talk about memories like they're the best things
in the world, Lincoln. They love the word, love the feel of it,
say it with this breathlessness, all nostalgic and shit. *Memories*, they say. Oh, how I love those memories."

He tossed his cigarette to the pavement and ground it out
under a well-worn Nike. "Sometimes, they hurt." He looked
up at me. "Memories, I mean. I know there are good ones,
but bad ones? Man, that's the worst. You'd do whatever you
could to put them away, drive them out of your mind, lock
them out for good. But you can't do that. They'll keep coming back, and, Lincoln, those suckers can *hurt*. It's like your
memory's bleeding, you know? And you can't do anything

but give it some time, wait for it to clot. Can't stitch it up. Just got to wait it out."

"Ed," I said, and I tried to fill my voice with some of the commanding tone I'd used on the bartender, "give that talking-in-riddles shit a rest, all right? Maybe you didn't want to see me down here, but I came, anyhow. And if you want my help, I'll do the best I can. But you got to tell it to me."

He kept walking, and while his steps seemed a little surer now than they had when we'd left the bar, it still wasn't difficult to tell he was drunk. His eyes looked sober, though, and there was a serious cast to his face that told me his mind was—finally—very much in the moment.

"You don't need to be a part of this, Lincoln," he said. He still moved with shuffling steps, his feet almost seeming not to come off the ground at all. It was the way he'd walked when he was twelve.

"I know that."

"I went to the prosecutor," he said. "You know what he told me?"

"I don't know, Ed."

"Told me to go home and keep myself out of trouble. Told me he had enough problems without a con like me coming to him with wild schemes and rumors. You believe that? The man's paid with taxpayers' cash, Lincoln, and he sent me out of his office. Told me to stay out of trouble."

"Why'd you go to the prosecutor?"

"I'll tell you something else—I tried to do it the right way. The *legitimate* way, you know?" His eyes had a milky cast to them again, wandering, fading back into the recesses of his booze-addled brain. "I tried. And they sent me home and told me to stay out of trouble. And I said the hell with it. I'll get them to take a look at him one way or the other, right? Because, Lincoln, the man needed somebody to bring it back to him. One way or the other."

A car was drifting up the street behind us. I was looking at Ed's face, but he turned to glance at the car, and when he did his eyes went flat.

"Shit."

I turned and looked myself, and when I did I echoed him. It was the Crown Vic that had been parked outside his mother's house. The cops realized we'd seen them, and the driver punched the accelerator, closing the gap with a squeal of rubber. A flashing bubble light came on at the top of the windshield, and Ed Gradduk ran.

"Don't run! Let them take you in, and we'll go from there," I yelled, but he ignored me. I ran after him and tried to grab him, hating the cops for showing up just when Ed was beginning to explain things. My hand caught a piece of his shirt and when I tugged it he spun off balance before twisting away from me. The loss of balance sent his right foot off the sidewalk and into the street. I saw him glance up at the minivan that was traveling in his direction, then back at the Crown Vic coming from the opposite side. He looked at them both, then tried to run across the street as I lunged after him again. He made it a couple of steps, but there was too much alcohol in his bloodstream for such rapid movements, and halfway across Clark Avenue his feet tangled beneath him and he went down.

The Crown Victoria driver had been pushing it, trying to get in front of Ed and block his path across the avenue. When Ed fell, the driver didn't slow immediately, his reaction time poor. When he finally did register what had happened, he locked up the brakes. The car rode the skid maybe thirty feet, into and over Ed Gradduk.

I stood on the curb and screamed something that was supposed to make sense but came out like the howl of a wounded animal, and then I ran into the street, too. Ed's body lay under the car, and the stupid son of a bitch in the driver's seat put it in reverse and backed up, rolling the front wheels over Ed once more. I screamed again, and then the car was in park and the cops were clambering out of it, shouting at me to keep back. I ignored them and ran toward Ed, reached under the car for him.

I had my hands on Ed's shoulders when the cop who'd been driving grabbed me and tried to pull me back, shouting at me to get out of the way. I spun and put my right fist into his stomach without thinking about it, then crawled back under the car while he doubled over and dropped to the pavement. Ed's body was only partially covered by the front end of the Crown Vic, and as I tugged him free I knew he was dead—blood was flowing from his nose, mouth, and even his ears, the flesh ripped and scraped, bits of the skull stark and white against the blood and torn skin. It's odd how something as inherently natural to the human body as bone can look so horribly out of place when you see it exposed. I got only a glance before the second cop wrapped his arm around my throat and pulled me back, pushing the barrel of his gun in my ear.

There was more shouting then, but I don't remember what was said. Some of it was directed at me, some of it was from me. The cops were shoving me away, and I was screaming in their faces, calling them every name in the book. The middle-aged woman who'd been driving the van from the opposite direction got out of her vehicle, took one look at Ed, dropped to her knees, and vomited in the street. More cars had gathered now, and people were standing on the curb, watching the scene. One of them was moving forward, and I turned away from the cops in time to see Scott Draper just before he threw a punch at my head.

"You cocksucker," he screamed. "You shoved him! You shoved him!"

"He ran," I shouted back, and he swung at me again as the cops tried to get in our way. "I tried to *stop* him, you stupid bastard."

He was still trying to get at me. I realized that he must have been following Ed and me the whole time to arrive this quickly, that knowledge making me as angry as he appeared to be, and then I was trying to get at him, too. I was aware of the cops only as objects in my way, and I sidestepped and shoved past them. I grabbed Draper by the shoulders and knocked him backward onto the pavement. I would have gotten a punch in if the fat cop who'd been driving the Crown Vic hadn't succeeded in catching my wrist. He slammed me onto the ground next to Draper. That's where I remained while they put the handcuffs on—facedown on the pavement, my right cheek against the road, my left eye watching a trickle of Ed Gradduk's blood work its way toward me, cutting a determined path over the gravel as if its last mission were to touch my flesh.

· · ·

They let me go home around midnight. Charges of interference and obstruction had been threatened but I had not been booked. The fat cop who had been driving, a guy named Larry Rabold, lightened up once he learned who I was, but his partner, the one who had stopped me on the sidewalk, was not so fraternal. His name was Jack Padgett, and he didn't show any desire to let bygones be bygones once he'd found out I had been a cop. They talked to me for about an hour, asking all about Ed, particularly what information might have been exchanged in our brief conversation. They seemed unconvinced by my claim that I hadn't spoken to him in years.

"Why the hell did you come running down to his house as soon as you heard the news, then?" Padgett had asked. It was a good question, one I'd already failed to answer earlier in the night, and I still hadn't come up with anything satisfactory. They'd both been intrigued by my description of how things had gone down with Ed and me a few years back, and I knew they'd check it out and see if they could find anything to indicate I'd had contact with the man since then. They would come up empty, though.

Once I was kicked loose I called a cab to take me back to my truck. Clark Avenue was dark and quiet save for a few stragglers on the sidewalk and one woman waiting for a bus. I stood at the curb and stared up the street to where my oldest friend had died a few hours earlier. They'd hosed the blood off the pavement and the night heat had already baked it dry.

I climbed inside the truck and started the engine, sat there listening to the traffic noise and wondering if I'd be able to drive without seeing visions of Ed running into the street. I took a look at the clock. It was time to go home and go to bed.

I drove to my partner's house.

Joe Pritchard lives on Chatfield, maybe three minutes from the office. He was in the neighborhood long before I arrived, and it was through him that I learned of the gym I own when it went up for sale. Recently dismissed from the police force and with no real career plans, I'd purchased the gym and moved into the building. Joe's retirement a few years later had led me into the PI trade.

His house is a brick A-frame that is common in the neighborhood, two blended triangles with a chimney rising along the front wall. I once heard that the houses were all products of Sears and Roebuck kits that became popular as the neighborhood expanded following World War II, but I don't know if there's any truth to that. The neighborhood around Chatfield has been maintained better than most, although the majority of parents send their children to private schools rather than enrolling them in the public system. That was the case when I was growing up, too, but my father couldn't afford it—and had no desire to send me to one of the private schools even if he could. If I couldn't make it in a public high school, he often said, how the hell was I going to make it as a cop? Even then, it was what I told everyone I was going to do, and my father was right—four years at West Tech were invaluable to that career acclimation.

Joe's house is the shining star of a nice block, with a perfectly manicured lawn, gleaming windows and cobblestone path between the house and the sidewalk. Quite the homemaker, our Joe. Most of the backyard and a stretch between the driveway and the house are filled with beautiful flower gardens, heavy on the impatiens. There's a garage behind the house, stocked with rakes and hoes and potting soil and fertilizer, and if you want to find Joe on a Saturday or Sunday afternoon you need only look in the yard or in the garage. When we'd worked the narcotics beat together, it hadn't been that way. Joe's wife, Ruth, tended to the flowers and yard like they were her reason for living, but Joe never did much more than shovel the driveway, and then only in the heaviest snows. It was winter when Ruth died, and when spring broke the next year Joe hated the idea of seeing her flower gardens fail to appear in the fashion to which the neighbors had become accustomed. Now I think he spends more time on them than Ruth ever did.

He met me at the door with a wary look, but it was clear he'd still been awake, which I'd expected. Joe is late to bed and early to rise and always alert despite that. There are some qualities you don't leave behind after thirty years of police work. Poor sleeping patterns are among them.

"It's almost midnight," he said, closing the front door and following me into the living room, "and you wouldn't show up here at that time just for small talk. So that makes me think this is case-related, and that troubles me. Why? Because the only cases on our plate are small-time, and you wouldn't need to discuss them at this hour. So I'm guessing you've decided to involve yourself in whatever shit went down with your convict buddy."

Took him maybe ten seconds to reason that out.

We sat in the living room and I asked him if he'd seen the news, if he'd seen the footage of Ed Gradduk on his way to do murder. He told me that he had.

"You remember anything about the guy?" I asked.

His eyes flicked off mine momentarily. "You kidding me? It was the first case we ever worked together, LP. And in all the cases we've worked since, I've never seen you so locked in. You were robotic about it. I liked working with you, could tell you had ability, but at the same time I was a little concerned about your emotional stamina. You seemed burned out already, like an old cop who's hung on five years too long."

I nodded.

"I remember it didn't go the way you'd expected it to go," Joe continued. "And the kid took a fall. But that wasn't your fault. He had options. Not your fault he decided against co-operating."

I was silent.

"There's more to it than you ever told me," Joe said. "And it involves the girl."

I looked at him, surprised. He was waiting for a response.

"There's more to it," I said. "And it involves the girl. But not in the way you're thinking."

He shrugged. "Whatever. That's not the issue of the night, though. Tell me what happened."

I took him from Amy's phone call to the scene in the street to my interview with Rabold and Padgett. I realized halfway through the story that I was rubbing my temples, trying to drive away a headache that I didn't consciously feel.

"I'd ask you why you ended up going down to Clark Avenue," he said when I was through, "but I expect you don't really have an answer for that."

"Accurate expectation," I said.

Joe stared at the muted television. It was tuned to ESPN Classic, as it always seems to be, and the network was airing a basketball game between the Bulls and the Jazz from sometime in the late nineties.

"Rough seeing a guy die like that," he said. "Especially when it was a guy you used to be close to."

"Uh-huh."

"I'm taking it this abbreviated conversation with Grad-duk meant something to you. Makes you, what, curious? Skeptical?"

"Makes me think the guy could have been set up."

"But he told you it was all on tape."

"Well, it is all on tape. Amy, Ed, and the cops all agree on that point. You just said you saw it on the news."

"So he murdered the girl."

"He said he didn't."

"But the police have a tape of him setting this house on fire. The same house from which a body was recovered."

"Yeah," I said.

"Cut and dried," he said, but I knew he was too good of a detective to buy that for even a minute.

"Who was the woman?" I asked. "I don't even know her name."

"Anita Sentalar. They had a long feature about her on the news tonight. She's a thirty-seven-year-old attorney, good-looking, intelligent, single."

"And the connection to Gradduk?"

"Undisclosed, as of yet."

"Maybe she was already in the house, dead."

He snorted. "Oh, yeah, I like this idea. Someone else kills her, leaves her in the house, and Gradduk just happens to come by and set fire to it, concealing the body? What, he's trying to do someone a favor by torching the place? Insurance on that dump wasn't worth a thing, from what I've heard."

"What's the tape show?"

"Shows him going into the house and coming back out. Shows his face pretty clear. Shows his car and apparently they could zoom in enough to get a plate number off it."

"And the fire?"

"House went up about twenty minutes after he left it. There was a small explosion of sorts before the flames, I guess. Fire investigators think he used a timer and an incendiary device."

"Twenty minutes? Damn, Joseph, that's a hell of a lot of time."

"Camera didn't show anyone else going into the house after him, though."

"Camera had a panoramic angle on the house? Covered every side at once?"

He sighed. "Just the front."

"So a dozen people could have waltzed in and out the backdoor during those twenty minutes?"

"Maybe," he said. "But what's Gradduk doing in a vacant house in the first place if he's not the guy who set it on fire?"

"That," I said, "is what I'd like to look into."

He sighed again and leaned back in his recliner, rolling the footrest out and up. I was sitting forward on the couch, elbows on my knees, watching him. Joe was the best cop I'd ever worked with, and he was my business partner. If I was going to get started with this thing, I wanted his support, for both reasons.

"He told me he went to the prosecutor, Joe. Said he went there, and was sent home. At the very least, I want to talk to the prosecutor. See what Gradduk went in there with."

"If he sent Gradduk home," Joe said, "it was probably with good reason."

We sat together in the dark living room and watched the soundless old basketball game, Michael Jordan slicing his way through the lane, tossing in off-balance shots and drawing fouls.

"This guy Gradduk," Joe said, "was not the kid you remember growing up with. He'd done time, and it looks like he should have been doing some more. Shitty brakes on a Crown Vic saved him the agony of years in a cell, and saved the taxpayers the cost of putting him where he belonged."

I didn't answer.

"Regardless of what he said to you, the man appears to have murdered someone, Lincoln."

"Appears."

"Why does it matter?" he said, and he grabbed the remote and snapped the television off. "If he did kill her, or didn't? He was never convicted of the crime, just suspected of it. The man is dead, LP, and dead he is going to stay, with or without your involvement. And, whether you choose to believe it or not, you did him no wrong. Not last night, and not the time before that."

I sat and thought about everything I wanted to say to that, how I wanted to tell him that it went back to walking the same sidewalks and fighting the same guys and chasing the same girls, that it went back to twelve years of a bond that you simply can't match upon reaching adulthood, not even with your partner.

"Ed never caught a break in his life," I said. "From the

cradle to the grave, the guy was taking it on the chin. Did he earn it sometimes? Sure. Every time? Hell no."

"And he's gone now. Can't help him anymore."

"It's not about helping him. It's about making sure someone else isn't getting away with something far more heinous than any of Ed's sins."

He sighed and shook his head, looked past me out the dark window toward the rows of flowers his wife had planted and he still tended. You do things for the dead, even if you don't have to. Maybe because you don't have to. Joe knew that as well as anyone.

He stared at the window for quite a while, then turned back around and picked up the remote. He turned the television back on, settled into his chair, and put his attention on the game.

"We'll go see the prosecutor," he said, and that was all he said until I got to my feet and let myself out of the house.